FLESH WOU

Also available in the 'Echoes of War' series:

Echoes of War

FLESH WOUNDS

DAVID HOLBROOK

I shall be mad if you get smashed about;
we've had good times together, you and I;
although you groused a bit when luck was out,
and a girl turned us down, or we went dry...

Yet there's a world of things we haven't done,
countries not seen, where people do strange things;
eat fish alive, and mimic in the sun
the solemn gestures of their stone-grey kings.

Vodka and kvass, and bitter mountain wines
we've never drunk, nor snatched at bursting grapes
to pelt slim girls among Sicilian vines,
who'd flicker through the leaves, faint frolic shapes...

The Soldier Addresses His Body
EDGELL RICKWORD

BUCHAN & ENRIGHT, PUBLISHERS
LONDON

First published in 1966 by Methuen & Co. Ltd
This edition published in 1987 by
Buchan & Enright, Publishers, Limited
53 Fleet Street, London EC4Y 1BE

British Library Cataloguing in Publication Data

Holbrook, David
Flesh wounds.—(Echoes of war).
I. Title   II. Series
823'.914 [F]   PR6058.04
ISBN 0-907675-76-X

For Jonathan, my son

Printed in Great Britain by
Redwood Burn Limited, Trowbridge, Wiltshire and
bound by Pegasus Bookbinding, Melksham, Wiltshire
Cover printed by The Furnival Press, London

1942

FIERCE BLUE GAS-FLAMES roared in rings under two large aluminium saucepans full of water. The drab basement of the church hall, made into a canteen room with two large cookers at one end, was lit by four naked, fly-spotted bulbs. Their yellowish glow merged with the pale azure of the rings of jets. Outside it was still dark.

There were orange speckles in the grey-green irises of Lucy Selby's eyes, and the incandescence shone in them. She had a habit of wrinkling the crowsfeet at the corners, and narrowing her lids slightly, to make her eyes sparkle. She did this now as she chatted to Paul Grimmer, and the young man felt himself dissolve. His lips moved, and a noise came out, but he had no idea what he said. His vision swam in the faint blue image of her face, flashed rose-pink as it was from time to time, as water fell into the gasflames, and his lips trembled.

'At least you've had a year,' she was urging.

'I've done nothing. I've wasted it, really.'

He sighed. He stood awkwardly over the cooker, looming rather above the dark girl, waiting to help her make porridge. They were preparing breakfast for a student work party. He was a dark thin boy of nineteen: Lucy was small, quick and alert.

'I feel as much a nobody as I always did at school,' he went on, recovering his voice. 'There hasn't been one experience that Cambridge has given me, that's really mattered . . .'

He tried to add 'except you', but nothing came out, except an incoherent noise, tailing off into an odd little groan. His vision swam again. He meant it, and he must say it. He was desperate, for he had fallen in love with Lucy, just as his 'year'

7

was over – how much time had he left to tell her? He had worked hard to get Lucy's name next to his on the rota: they were alone, but only for a few minutes, he knew, till the others came. The dark Sunday morning had closed them in, and here they were, face to face, so startlingly, in the raw dark, yet entranced by the glowing domesticity of the flames. Their two young faces bent solemnly, reflectively, over the gas stoves. Lucy shook her dark hair back from her face. She seemed a little pale, translucent in the gaslight.

'Sorry?'

She knew, he could see, that he wanted to say something. The boy had the sense of leaping as if from a tower or cliff. Sudden pain shot through his body and his knees quailed. He fought with his voice and ground out the insignificant phrase, croakingly.

'Ex-cept . . . you . . .'

There was no reply, only the exchange of looks, in the pale blue light of the flames. There was no need for anything to be said. Both had talked with other friends about their feelings for one another: there was an accumulation of uncertainties and pondered evidences behind them. But there was no doubt, now, after this awkward and painful moment, before the oats were measured into the turbulent water, that they were in love. Stunned, they began to move, setting the tables for breakfast, for the others.

From time to time one or the other would stop work and stand leaning on the back of a folding chair, fidgetting a little with embarrassment, or poised against the wall with a pile of gleaming plates.

'I wonder what good it all does?' Lucy asked, as the last of thirty thick white china dishes was out on the tables. 'Helen's bringing the milk: it's our ration for the whole week.'

She had a small active body and regular white teeth. Paul had seen her about Cambridge all his first year. He had completed it, and this was all he was allowed to do, before National

8

Service. So he had to go down from the university, but stayed working in a factory in the town, helping to make radio sets for the services, while awaiting call-up. While he was there the plating shops and some of the assembly lines had fallen behind schedule. So he had invented a voluntary work-scheme for students, and it was for this he and Lucy were preparing breakfast now. A party of undergraduates went into the factory on Sundays, to help with deficiencies in the supply lines. They were only paid apprentice rates and it came to no more than pocket-money – but it was not the money they wanted. Most of them were active in left-wing student politics, and they wanted to feel they were 'contributing' to the war. They enjoyed the contact with 'real' things – with making and doing, in the acrid fumes of the plating shop, or among the heaps of condensors and resistances, smelling of synthetic resin and solder. They felt they were producing something to aid the buzzing planes that continually crossed the sky, among the searchlights and balloons at night, and to help the distant guns overhead from time to time.

College breakfasts did not begin until eight-thirty on Sundays. The student working party had to be in the factory by eight. So, some of the women students volunteered to climb out of their colleges at six, to cook breakfasts of reconstituted egg in the hired hall in Round Church Street, before the party cycled off across the river to the factory in the dim autumn morning, each Sunday of the Michaelmas Term. Today it was Lucy's turn.

Paul put down the pile of plates he had been carrying and came over to her.

He had an untidy head of hair, a long face, and green eyes. He was full of energy, working with angular speed, but ungainly and a little brash in his manner, really little more than a schoolboy. He was dressed in corduroy trousers and a blue tweed sports jacket, with a hairy pink tie and a maroon check shirt. Now he and Lucy were acting a little to one another. The

A*

pale lights in the darkness suddenly seemed theatrical, their shadows sharpened by gold or pink flares, as the drops of condensation fell into the roaring flames.

'I don't know. They seem to think so, the management, I mean: though I know a lot of the student work gets chucked out on inspection.

'John Black – you know him: the tall Irishman?'

'I think so,' said Lucy, puzzling, 'He's older than most of us, isn't he?'

'Yes. I sleep with him, you know.'

Lucy grimaced. Paul laughed, the exaggerated laugh of the adolescent wanting to appear sophisticated.

'Not by choice. I mean, it's a cheap way to share a room.'

'He does marvellous work on that press, making radio chassis. I know they're pleased with him. But poor Marion was in tears last week at the dinner-break, when they found she'd been soldering one wire to the wrong tab all morning.'

'Well, I've got a kick out of it. It seems to me one of my enthusiasms that worked: a lot of them don't. Doesn't it help us feel we're . . . "making a contribution"?'

' "*Your* courage, *your* endurance, *your* cheerfulness will bring *us* victory"?'

Lucy quoted sarcastically from the unfortunate government poster, and darted back to the gas-stoves. As she drifted some salt into the whirling water she moved lithely in her woollen frock, and the young man was aware of her breasts stirring under the blue stuff.

'But I suppose I really don't know – "at bottom", as Matthew Arnold says.'

'And "bottom" is a long way down, as Old Possum re-plieth.'

Lucy laughed gaily, showing her teeth again and wrinkling her nose, and turning her body to him. Paul was dropping spoons carelessly into the gleaming cups, along the brown linoleum surface of the tables, chink by chink. Before he could finish the tables he had to struggle to put away four black-out screens, made of tarred felt tacked to lath frames. These had been lowered, and lay awkwardly against the linoleum-covered tables on the street side of the room. Paul overcame their tendency to break up and got them more or less conveniently stowed away at the back. Every now and then, outside, a pair of legs would saunter past, the heels click along the pavement, in the dimness. The windows were filthy with the mud that bouncing rain had thrown across the area from the pavement.

It was seven o'clock, on the fourth of October, 1942. The basement belonged to the Saxon Round Church in the alley opposite St John's College. A newsvendor was already busy on the corner, with news of the campaign in North Africa, setting his papers out on the low wall, from which the iron railings had been removed to make guns. Soon, now, the others would arrive, untidy young men and women of eighteen to twenty, to clatter down the concrete steps into the canteen room. The hall was opposite the end of a row of tenements, comically tilted, in grey brick. Beneath the parapet, the end wall bore a board inscribed, in closely painted tall letters, 'Prziborski'. The name suggested sinister and significant things: but it was only a barber shop serving the town streets behind.

The basement was extremely ugly. The walls had once been painted a coarse cream, but they had gone patchy and grubby with that neglect which, in war-time, was another, indirect, "contribution to the war-effort". The light was obscured above its windows, by Prziborski's tall narrow tenement, and by the greater bulk of the University Union building behind, rambling and ill-shapen, and covered with Virginia Creeper, at this time turning a glorious red that glowed in the morning dusk. The autumn mist of the night was coagulating into drizzle as the sun rose upon it, and the heavy dampness fell darkly on to the pavements.

The room was warm now with the heat that billowed from

the stoves. Lucy was dredging porridge oats into the boiling water between her fingers. Paul's inward self went out to touch and caress the girl, who seemed to him so much alive, and yet so deliciously domestic, though he resented her ebullience a little too, so early in the morning. He himself was a little depressive and morose early in the mornings. He really preferred to be alone before eleven. At the thought he grimaced at his own egocentricity. What had they been saying? Silences unnerved them a little now.

'Oh well, it fills in the time, before I go away.'

'What are you going *into*?'

'I thought I'd go in tanks.'

'Tanks? Oh lor'. What, *you*?'

'What do you mean – "me"?'

'Well, you're so . . .'

'I'm what?'

He came up and she looked up from the pan into his face. He gloated on the freckles on her pretty nose, with its freckles and sensitive nostrils.

'So . . . well you're not . . . practical . . . and yet, I suppose you must be – to lay on all this, for instance.'

'Do you think about what sort of person I am, then?'

'Oh yes!'

'Why?'

'We all do. The women I mean. We think about the men, and talk about them.'

'About me?'

'Oh yes!'

'What do they say about me?'

'Will you mind?'

'Of course not.'

'That you're an "only".'

'Oh my God. They sound like old Mums!'

He grinned, but he was really hurt and annoyed. Lucy laughed. He looked glumly at her under his dark untidy hair.

12

He wanted to know more of what the girl students said about him.

'We'd have thought you the last person to go into tanks.'

'I've been training, here, already – in armoured cars.'

'What, that place out at Grange Road?'

'Yes. The S.T.C. – Public Schoolboy's back door. You go straight to pre-O.C.T.U.'

She pulled a face.

'Well, why not?' Paul protested defiantly.

'Rather a back door way in, isn't it, to become an officer?'

'And become the Class Enemy? Well, I'm supposed to get into the Second Front, aren't I? I don't think they let you through all that easily. Perhaps I'll not stay the course,' he concluded, happily muddled.

'A year ago you'd have gone to jail as a pacifist. Now the Left has all swung round.'

'Well, there you are – since Russia. We've done it now. So, if I'm to be in for the thing I might as well get in the thick of it.'

Lucy sighed. Paul looked sheepish.

'Now it's the John Cornford image you all follow, Cambridge man who died in Spain. There's his last photograph in the Socialist club-room, smoking a cigarette in Barcelona or somewhere.'

She held her arm up mimicking a casual gesture.

'You all want to go like that. Before Russia came in all the left-wingers wanted to lie down in the tramlines like Ghandi. Let's hope to God you don't get signed up and then everything switches round again. I suppose you get shot then, for desertion?'

'Lucy, you're being a bit scathing. I've done what I thought best. . . . Honestly, I think the Left has been a bit bloody naive so far . . . about the Nazis . . .'

Lucy nodded to the porridge, chastened a little by his ardour.

'I'm sorry to talk to you like a political meeting . . .' Paul added quietly.

13

Then he gulped, and admitted: 'I don't really want to go at all.'

She glanced at him uneasily, aware that he was suddenly trusting her, by confiding so, in a sincere voice – pleading for them to come to a closer touch, though it panicked him. If she accepted, his troubled green eyes told her, she mustn't abuse the confidence. Again there was a pause, in which the water in the other pan could be heard beginning to turn over, softly boiling. Lucy began to measure out porridge oats in a conical aluminium measure while Paul tipped a small spoonful of salt into the seething saucepan.

The war compelled, and they had learned not to drop the defences which sustained an indifference in the face of so much compulsion. One's life wasn't one's own: the future was never certain. Promises in relationships could only be snatched at. No-one could look forward to a slow peaceful unfolding of life, of home. Men left new wives and never saw them again: others were to come back after years of absence to find their children strangers. Each young man or woman clung inwardly to some deluding gleam. But they mostly put aside discussion, both of the future, and of their deepest inward preoccupations. Except in such moments of closeness, when the defences came down, as they came down now between Paul and Lucy, in the strange basement lights.

'You mean, you're afraid?'

Lucy wanted to know, sincerely. Her eyes were very bright, near the blue flames as they curled round the saucepan bottoms.

'It isn't so much the fear – though I know the sort of thing I'm in for, from reading Graves and Barbusse. I have a horror of that, yes. But it's rather that what I've got to do is as remote as it could be, from what I *want* to do. And what I want to do would be hard enough – because I know nothing about it . . . I know nothing about anything!'

His voice was suddenly loud and poignant in the empty basement room.

'Nothing! And yet I've got to go and learn to fight, and then actually fight . . . I don't even have a vote! . . . oh yes, I don't doubt that it's *right*, to fight Hitler. It's just that I'm bitter, down inside, because all my natural inclinations are to get down to peaceful things . . . the harder things to get going . . .'

'What sort of things?'

'Oh, I want to marry and have children, and do some work . . . do something for people . . . for the community. . . . We seem . . . so . . . dished, before we've even begun. I know nothing,' he said loudly again, to conclude a stammering speech.

'After the war, perhaps,' urged Lucy, 'things will be better . . . people will be more determined not to let things slip, in the old ghastly way, perhaps. We shan't lose what we've gained in war-time itself, surely?'

'For the duration, maybe. But after? Don't you think it won't all slip back to the same old aimlessness? Oh yes: it'll be the same old thing, you see! There were a million unemployed in *1940*, you know. Even in the thick of that! It's better now. But it'll come back.'

Lucy sighed, and solemnly stirred a saucepan. The porridge was glutinous, and formed now, ready.

'Well, we can only see. I can't believe things will be allowed to slide. Quick, turn the gas down, or this will burn!'

'But look how we talk.' Paul went on, warmly, seizing a large wooden spoon to help her. 'We talk as if there was a future, but we can't even be sure of that.'

They stirred thoughtfully together.

'I suppose one is hoping for that, in going out, and fighting.'

'One couldn't dare think of there being no future at all.'

'Perhaps people like us – students – are always doubtful about the future? We have time to think about it, while later – in one's work, that takes up one's time. It seems to be enough answer, in itself. The war seems to answer a lot: it seems a meaning in itself sometimes, yet's it's not.'

'There was a master died at school just before I came up in

15

1941: we carried him to be cremated. Then afterwards, we saw the casket – a box, no bigger than . . . what? . . . that teapot. When I saw it, I wondered what meaning there was at all, in anything.'

'Oh, that's a big teapot. They can send you smaller than that. A little parcel that goes through the post: like a box of chocolates, or cigars – no bigger. A whole woman's ashes.'

Lucy's eyebrows went up in astonishment. One of them was jauntily crooked and gave something of an ironic air to everything she said. Paul went on:

'There was writing on the blackboard, his writing, for a day or two. That was all that was left. And a pain in my shoulder, where the coffin had rested. It was too heavy for us, really, but that was all water, and went off, I suppose. That's all one is: flames! And a little impulse – like those lamps.'

'Well, what *can* be left?'

'One's work. . . . That is, if one does any lasting work.'

Suddenly Lucy's face brightened.

'Oh, and one's *children*.'

He loved her for her face brightening with anticipation of her fertility. But then he remembered how in school the children were taught to dive under the desks, when the teacher called out, 'Screaming bomb!' One wouldn't want one's children going through all that. And you away.

'If you had children, everything that's just painful would become an agony – left at home with their mother all alone . . . it would be unbearable.'

'What does one do, then? Simply shrug one's shoulders, suspend living and wait . . . then just to die sometime?'

She looked across at him with the dark earnestness of a Jewish girl of nineteen.

'Or live in spite?'

'I try to live in spite. But I don't feel we – our generation – can ever know joy – not the true relaxed joy. I don't mean we shall miss the May Balls, and holidays abroad. I mean the in-

16

ward thing. We've got that feeling now that will never leave us – that any time there may be an air-raid: any day may bring news of a defeat, a new invasion, a new and terrible weapon, the end, personal or social. Of course, one gets used to it. But I don't think any of us will ever get that discomfort out of our systems. Even the children must feel it, sitting there waiting for the sirens.'

'No. Nor the feeling that the bottom may drop out of life, at any time. Never.'

'It's so hard, in all this, trying to discover who one *is*.'

They gave each other a wry smile. Paul felt so glad of Lucy: her very vitality was a balm to his fear, of the war, and of its outcome.

The blue dramatic light had gone, when they turned the gas down. A grim and ordinary daylight came in now, blatantly, instead. Lucy's eyes were darker, and her face was full of trouble, at the thoughts they had evoked of the loss-filled future. They stirred the porridge again for a time silently, and talked on in an abstracted, trance-like way.

'So, I'm afraid in so many ways.'

'. . . just have to live for the moment.'

Lucy lifted her face to his.

'But – *isn't* this a good moment?'

She moved her whole body towards him, in such a way as to express with the whole of herself she liked him, and felt for him. Suddenly, in something of a swoon, Paul put his hand behind her shoulder, and, pulling her towards him a little, kissed her on the lips. The touch was so unexpected, and so little was his body prepared for it, that a quick feeling like a pain shot through him. Inward voices began to clamour, where they had lain dormant, or had never yet stirred. Then he and Lucy grew solemn and quiet again. They were relieved when the others began to appear at last, clattering down the stairs and bumping into the tables and chairs clumsily in the poor light, to fetch bowls of porridge.

17

As he and Lucy ladled it out together, Paul began to doubt whether anything had happened at all. The gas-lit episode was gone. Yet he could not doubt the feeling of the responsive pressure from her lips against his mouth, and the smell of her flesh was still captured in his nose.

*

After breakfast, Lucy went off to the factory, and Paul stayed behind to wash up. To his discomfiture he was left alone with Lucy's college acquaintance, Helen Pyke. He was dazed and thrilled by Lucy. He knew Helen was one of Lucy's closest friends, but this increased his resentment. He wanted to know Lucy as well as Helen knew her, out at Newnham. To make matters worse, he had himself once made love to Helen, but he wasn't proud of that. Helen was a tall mannish blonde. Paul was cagey with her now: she knew how callow he was, only too well. He had once startled her by fumbling impetuously at her breasts against the girls' college wall, after a club social, a little fuddled and aggressive.

She wore her hair long, but had a man's way of moving her body, and a deep voice. She was one of those emancipated girls from a progressive public school, who seem to have freed themselves too much from feminine things. She wore her green slacks with a long pullover pulled over them, and sandals. Her teeth stuck out a little, but in an attractive way. Yet this feature made her look crushed and submissive, though she was anything but that, as he knew. He recalled with discomfort the feel of her mouth on his. Helen had cheeks of definite roundness, and they were shiny, like apples. Paul could not now imagine how he could ever feel passion for her. She seemed so comfortably friendly. He was far from wanting to touch Helen now. Yet she reminded him that he had boldness within him somewhere with a woman. Then he saw an opportunity and jumped at it – for, he realized, what he wanted urgently was more time with Lucy. Surely Helen could wangle it somehow, so that they could have the next Sunday off together? But he wondered if she'd play. She mightn't want Lucy to be treated as crudely as he'd treated her – 'like some kind of object', as she'd furiously said, 'for your petty little ends.' He quailed, fetching up the dirty plates.

'Who came to do the porridge this morning?'

Paul carefully turned his face away, bending over a table.

'Lucy Selby.'

How thin the name sounded! Yet she was already everything to him.

'Oh good.'

'Good for what?' asked Paul, emboldened.

'Oh for her. She's been working too hard. And I think some bloke gave her up a month or so ago. You know, one of the selfish sort, who said she wouldn't give him what he wanted.'

Helen shook a mop, out, angrily. Paul blushed, coming up with a pile of plates. He couldn't hide it. Helen looked him full in the face, and her face went soft. Paul felt she was not holding anything against him: his embarrassment at being alone with Helen gave way to pleasure at a woman's company.

'She was glad to have you, I bet.'

'That's the nicest thing you've said for a long time, Paul.'

'I mean, you're great friends.'

'Yes.'

'She's . . . I . . . I've seen her at English lectures,' Paul concluded lamely.

Helen had a woman's perception, despite her free school air of healthy freedom. She suddenly saw that Paul was more human than the youth who had pinned her against the wall in Sidgewick Avenue – because he was beginning to suffer over her friend. She found she liked him, and became confiding.

'Yes, she's done one year reading English. Now she's just hanging about like you. Then she's going into Rep. You can do your National Service in Rep – a girl can.'

'Good idea,' said Paul.

'Do you like her?' Helen drew back her long hair with a

19

damp hand, and looked at him penetratingly, yet shyly. She was wondering whether she could have wanted more of his attention as lover. But then she remembered how she had divined a latent cruelty in him and his instability, and had decided not. Yet she shrank from exposing her friend much further to him. She no longer trusted him.

'She's lively, isn't she?' Paul countered. He took a tray of cups into the store-room. Helen noticed that he was blushing again, as he fumbled with the cups, clanking them together sharply by mistake in his awkwardness. At the sink she thought to herself with inward indignation of the kind of surprises she felt Lucy was sure to get, from this raw youth. But by the time Paul came back Helen had accepted that whatever happened wouldn't be her fault, and then with a sigh she found she wasn't even jealous. She tossed her long blonde hair, and found she could even suppose that Lucy might be good for Paul Grimmer.

'Be kind to her, won't you?' she said, with a meaningful smile.

At first Paul's mouth fell with resentment and his face became taut and glum. He was angry that Helen had so quickly divined his feelings. He was confused because the way he had gone for Helen had been so without meaning, and he was discomfited that anyone should divine how uncouth he could be. Gradually his anger faded, however, as he came to see the goodwill in her remark, and saw how generous it was. It reassured him, too, for he could not find it easy to accept that women wanted love and could tolerate a degree of insincerity and even unpleasantness in the search for someone to love them. Helen, he could see, did not consider it repulsive that he had made a 'pass' at her, even in that fumbling way: nor did she disapprove of him for finding her friend attractive. She was even glad that he would now want to make love to Lucy. He suddenly realized for the first time that there was a community of women – out there at Newnham – who needed men, who actually wanted them, fumbling and all. He had never seen it

20

like that before. So, he spoke more freely, glad of Helen's womanly understanding. Brighter light was coming in now through the dirty windows at pavement level, into the basement canteen room. He took Helen's arm and confessed, his face urgent and happy.

'I think she's lovely. You can tell her if you like. I'm glad she's a friend of yours. Look, Helen – do make sure she comes next week.'

'I tell you what,' said Helen, with a sigh and a wry smile, 'I'll go to the factory in her place. I'll tell her to come very early, to help you. And you can take the day off and take her out. I'll fix that up with her. How about that?'

'Will she? Do you think she really would?'

'Oh, yes. I'm sure she would.'

'Do you mean . . .'

'Oh, Paul, surely you've noticed: she's crazy about you.'

Paul choked rather than laughed, and a pain shot through him. He couldn't believe what she said: it seemed he had waited so long, to hear of such a thing. Light-headed now, he put his arm round Helen's shoulders, only to feel her brace herself and shake him off, as she shook the last water out of a dish-mop.

'But please, Paul, don't hurt her, will you? She was really in a bad way this summer.'

'Do you think I would?'

She gave him a dignified look, rather like the one he had glimpsed under the lamplight once.

'I don't know much about you, do I?'

*

Paul Grimmer shared a room and a double bed with a tall Irish student who was exempt from call-up, as a subject of Eire. They each paid half of the rent of a cheaply-furnished bedsitter on the first floor of a ramshackle ancient building, above a shop that sold fishing tackle opposite Magdalene College. This was by Magdalene Bridge, next to the Pike and

Pickerel Inn. At night and early in the morning the room shook to buses and lorries thundering across the rickety cast-iron structure over the River Cam, in the darkness of suppressed headlights, and extinguished street lighting. At night only a few torches flickered as passers-by groped their way home in the blackout. But still each morning Paul awoke to feel relief that no bomber had stolen in at dawn. At home, in Norwich, while he had been at school still, and in the vacations, aerial attacks in the small hours had been frequent. Cambridge rarely saw enemy aircraft.

Paul spent his day in the radio factory out across the river examining plastic washers tucked in the connecting ends of thousands of aluminium elbow joints. These small components were about the size of an acorn, but turned from bright grey metal. If the washers were cracked, damp could accumulate and spoil the insulation. The connectors were used for leads in tank and aircraft radio sets. He sat at a bench to which women in overalls brought metal trays of elbow joints from the assembly lines. Paul set these out in ranks, on a tray covered with brown linoleum, examined each end and then tried them out on a test plug for accurate perforation and alignment. He invented a method of setting the elbow joints out before his hands so he could step up his speed, and check two thousand a day: before long the shop-steward came and told him to slow down. Six hundred was about right.

'There's a war on, isn't there?' Paul bridled.

'Yes, but we've got our relationships with the employer to think about, mate.'

Paul took in that he was an intruder in a whole world of complex relationships between working people and their employers. It was their life. But in his rawness and idealism he became resentful and tactless: his schoolboy politics became petulantly aggressive.

'This is how the trades unions hold up the second front, I suppose.'

'If you want a second front, mate, you'd better go and bloodywell do it. All I'm concerned about is that you shouldn't affect the rate for this job to the disadvantage of my members.'

The unions had resisted Paul's student part-time work scheme, too, but the management had persisted. So every Sunday the young men and women bicycled out of Cambridge in groups, chattering, along the towpath in the morning mist. They rumbled over the rickety pedestrian bridges and wove laughing and chatting through the sleepy streets to the radio factory, disturbing the cool autumn mist among the pollarded willows, now going grey and beginning to bare. They wore the informal and dowdy clothes of wartime utility – the men in corduroys and jerseys, the girls in slacks and leather jerkins.

It was a relief from academic work – from lectures, memorising, and books. These abstract activities, the dons' lectures and the paper examinations, seemed irrelevant to the bustle and urgency of war. Once a week they could make a material 'contribution' – and yet gain a touch of home, too, with the gas-stoves and big porridge saucepans. The young men felt a satisfying touch of home care, as they ate the porridge and scrambled eggs which the girls cooked for them, on their way to work. It was out of this that sudden relationships, like that of Paul and Lucy, sprang.

Paul Grimmer had little more to him than the experience of having perched for three brief terms as an English student, between school and army. His uncertainty about himself was in that he felt so much no more than that, an unfledged undergraduate. What could he say of himself, in terms of 'belonging' to class and region? He was what the complacent dons' wives of Cambridge call, 'rather a rough boy, you know – come up from the grammar school' – a half-educated urchin of the unformed new suburbs of the capital of remote Norfolk.

Inwardly he had sought to make something of himself, with

a passionate energy of mind, scraping together what he could of intellectual conviction and identity of person, between sixth-form discussions, and the 'recent additions' shelves of the grubby old Central Library down by the timber wharves on the River Wensum.

Paul's father had been brought up in a railway village, Melton Constable, near Holt, in a grim grey house, one of a row, built on the plans for workers' dwellings derived from the industrial north. In the new works, about the turn of the century, his grandfather had built coal trucks for the new branch of the Midland and Great Northern Railway to the North Norfolk coast. Paul's father Frank left the crowded family back-to-back at fifteen and went to work as a clerk to the railway at Thorpe station, in Norwich. When he married, at twenty, he took a better job as despatch clerk with a firm of motor wholesalers, supplying spare parts to garages, for the new flood of cars and cycles. There he was still, at forty-one, now manager of a department, and much of his life's striving had been given to send his only son to grammar school and university.

The family lived in a semi-detached house, on an unfinished road, in a gridiron of new streets, among allotments. It was an area of new development, as the City spread away farther into the surrounding fields.

The life of the raw streets of a new meagre housing development was vacant and cold. There was little feeling of neighbourliness, and a chill, pinched respectability settled on the inhabitants of the new houses, as the fabric of their semies dried out. A boy in those mean tidy streets was Mr Black's boy or Mr Green's boy, the hairdresser's or the insurance accountant's. All degrees of status and identity had to be won, not from known and respected service to the community, but in terms of petty differences and small superiorities; and grammar school places counted a great deal. So, Paul was Mr Grimmer's clever boy, who played the piano. Piano playing, like progress at school, was one of the scarce expressions of anything beyond material existence, in those dull streets. The thin metallic noise of it fluttered out from behind the net curtains into the somnolent street, between the staked rowans. The rest of the culture of Smithson Avenue was summed up by the *Daily Express*, the wireless, and the twopenny library at the off-licence stores.

But the scholarship ambition had consequences, too, beyond prestige and material things. So, Paul Grimmer became restless, driven to discover a world beyond the cheap raw brick residences, the aubretia clumps in the crazy-cracked concrete, and the rickety swagged double gate. He began to discover politics, and poetry, and pored over reproductions of Impressionist paintings and the Surrealists. He went off to act at the Maddermarket Theatre, and joined a discussion group on philosophical and social topics, run by a large enlightened clergyman who wore a purple pullover with large holes, and had a loosely connected family of ten children. Paul awoke to the buildings of his city, its innumerable ancient churches, the severe Octagon Chapel, the great aspiring stretch and point of the medieval Cathedral, and the Elizabethan inns. He stood in fascinated awe before the dramatic lights of the Cotman seascapes in the Castle Museum.

But the awakening split rather than enriched him. There were so few – the director of the amateur theatre, and his headmaster, who painted – who felt as he did that the most marvellous thing about man was the beauty of his artefacts – sonatas, poems, spires, canvases. Most people he met, like his parents' friends, simply saw no farther than the end of the day's work, a good meal, and the newspaper. Paul's father was excited by the football results, and would make things out of wood for the house, and even sometimes draw buildings of historical interest from photographs. But Paul knew the man actually did not hear music; and he seldom read a book. To their neighbours in the semi-detached houses around, the important things – those which awed them – were the Norwich

Union insurance business, the chocolate, boot, and mustard factories, and the dynamo works by the railway station. They weren't interested in 'Life' at all, Paul complained to himself.

But then he discovered the city, which, even in the thirties, still had Elizabethan slums, and some areas of rough vitality that frightened but fascinated him – Ber Strete, and the back streets down the hill slopes between St Giles' and Dereham Road. It was gloriously teeming, with rich unhygienic character, violence and filth. He would come home at night through the narrow streets above the Maddermarket Theatre, and there a raucous crowd would burst out of the noisy public houses, clinging to one another, with a slapping and thrusting of limbs, bottles flying, and fat women with men hanging to them. One night one of the bulging women from the pub, with florid blonde hair, turned off the pavement into an entrance, stood with her legs planted apart, and pissed, splashing, like a cow. The boy, to his embarrassment, had to step gingerly in the lamplight, over the flood, as it ran down the hill. A caped policeman passing shone his lamp on the woman, and shouted at her angrily, 'Bloody women!', then stamped away growling. The stench from some of the houses in the back alleys was overpowering: the doorways gave off shouts and cries, of pain, laughter, rage and passion. But the City enchanted and terrified the suburban boy. Those experiences of walking home between pub fights and figures grunting in the alley shadows went well with Baudelaire and Rimbaud, whom Paul had begun to read avidly, if haltingly, and with a dictionary.

Yet he continued to feel nobody: even the culture he took in, from Van Gogh's life-story to Louis MacNeice's translation of *The Agamemnon of Aeschylus*, somehow failed to touch the inward callowness of the despatch manager's boy in the semi-detached house named 'St Olaves', with its tall sewer stench-pipe ascending bang in front of the drawing-room window. The inward Paul had so little character, so little identity, and this was racked by the torments of adolescence – the gawkiness,

26

the sullen rituals of adolescent masturbation, the facial spots and the guilt, the failure of religious belief after confirmation and the social uncertainties after the outbreak of war. Even the culture he loved seemed not for him, and he could never overcome the feeling. He could not achieve the easy assurance that such things 'mattered', of the cultured people he met, doctors, clergymen and musicians. In their presence he would break out into a tepid sweat of discomfort, in case he was forced to admit he had never read Spengler or Marx, and had to listen to Music Hall with his family on Saturday night. He felt he was nothing: a worm, a nonentity, in a shabby and rather old-fashioned boy's tweed suit. Yet he loved to be where the talkative arguers, enlightened men who questioned the existence of God openly, spoke out clearly. He liked conversation, even though he seldom dared take part in it: at home one did not have conversations. Mother and Father talked at one another or to you; but more often than not neither of them listened to the other, except over such questions as whether there was a clean shirt, or a pair of socks.

Even after his first year at the university Paul did not feel yet sufficiently purged of this neutral background, of 'St Olaves' in Smithson Avenue. So now Paul felt he must find himself – if possible before he was absorbed into the featureless swarm of the Army, and sank into another loss of identity. So he worked furiously, to make a real contribution through his radio factory work – the first work to go out from him into a real world. And then to maintain touch with the university, with socialist politics, with matters of the mind and of the arts, and with the intelligent talk of young men and women of his own age. He could see it must slip away, the bright touch with the University: already he clung to the contact, with passion, although there was much of Cambridge he loathed – the air of cushioned and sherried privilege for public-school men for instance. Yet to him now the university had become the focus of his identity, and what, at best, the university stood for – a

27

concern for meaning in human life. And now the point of the focus was Lucy.

He spent the next week in delirium, for he was quick in engaging his affection. Already he was bowled over by the dark vivacious Newnham girl. At nights he could hardly bear the proximity of his Irish bedfellow with his endless pillow-talk of his unpaid bills and his sexual conquests.

'Do you think Heffer's would sue me first, or Bodger's,' he would wheedle in a soft Cork voice, 'or shall I give the buggers half each?'

But Paul would be already asleep, dreaming of Lucy Selby.

*

It was now the middle of October and the autumn touches of yellow and orange in the trees began to glow against the white buildings. The flame-coloured margins of leaves on the horsechestnuts began to spread inwards. The weather was blue and fine, and the buildings stood out in bright clarity under pale autumn skies and waning sunlight, and limbs and boles began to shine nakedly and blue. Under the chestnut tree in front of the massive East end of King's College Chapel, on the thick emerald grass, a discard of russet and brown began to touch in vivid patches beneath the rising faces of magnesite stone. The willows on the Backs had gone grey and were shedding their leaves in an untidy strewing. The grass in the mornings by the river was white with heavy dews. Mists rolled under the towers at times, so that only their pinnacles remained above, bathed in wan sunlight. The lights were low and slanting, saddening: the bells sounded sweet and thoughtful in the mists and autumnal chills.

Paul had never seen Cambridge so beautiful. It was delicious to leave his lodgings in the mornings, where the buses rumbled between the tall old buildings hanging so closely together over the street, and bicycle over the bridges with the white morning mist over the water on either side. And lovely to come home

28

after a day's work in the humming and stuffy factory, breathing the smell of the trees, their yellowness showing in the moonlight. The mists were frost-thickened and brought a penetrating smell of river rot as they crept down between the stone masses of the college buildings. The college precincts seemed a world apart. Every morning he glided in a light-headed joy over the wild scarlet and amber splashes of fallen colour on the wet grey stones.

Lucy appeared on the next Sunday in a bright pink frock, with stockings and a necklace of small green glass beads. She had put on for him her one cherished pair of silk stockings, rare as they were in the war years. She was in her best for him, he could see, with a nervous thrill. She wanted to be boldly courted. He was a little alarmed, even afraid, of her. If only he had had a sister! He knew so little about women! This time, he knew, things would be crucial, for Lucy was boldly inviting his courtship. Electric impulses moved across the nerves of his belly, like small fish cavorting in a pool. He was afraid most of offending her, by being insistent or rough. But their long earnest talk in the blue flames last week had reassured him.

After breakfast, Helen, in honey-coloured corduroys and a hairy green pullover, waved them goodbye with what was almost a motherly smile, as she bicycled off to the factory down Prziborsky's alley, her blonde hair hanging down her back. Small, freckled and dark, Lucy went back into the Church Hall to laugh in peals with Paul over the washing up. They had lost their solemnity in badinage over breakfast. She tossed her head in joy, showing her white teeth, small and even. Paul tried to laugh with her, but was miserable with the gripe in his inside, the strange inward sense of hunger, that went with an absence of appetite. He couldn't swallow. He was in love. A knot of pain grew in the pit of his abdomen and his hands trembled wildly. He didn't know what he was eating or saying; he couldn't eat. He could only drink cup after cup of scalding coffee as if to soften an inward pain. Under the stimulus of the coffee his heart beat faster and seemed to fill the room with sound. His throat was closed by a contracting tension, and now as the others left he relapsed into becoming over-solemn and dull.

The washing-up party began to clear away the breakfast things. Paul passed Lucy and repassed her. He was going blind with passion, but was terribly aware he had said nothing for ten minutes, but had merely been tense and silent. Perhaps Lucy thought him a bore? But then she sparkled at him, smiling at him with her crowsfeet and her mouth, her dark eyebrows expressive. There was nothing in her face but open delight at his presence.

Paul's embarrassment broke. He bubbled over suddenly with ebullience, and acted for her again. He imitated the foreman at the factory, and guyed the factory workers and shopsteward, over the elbow-inspecting incident.

'Well, 'ow many helbows 'as you done, then?'

Lucy doubled up over his repetition of 'hexcessive helbows', and there were tears in her eyes.

Then they both began to grow thoughtful once more and exhausted with excitement. Brooding, they cleared away automatically. Both of them went to fetch two cups from the dead crockery left higgeldy-piggeldy on the tea-slopped tables. They both came round a corner of the tables and Lucy's body touched him. He stood in front of her, barring her way. He must let her know again how he felt: it was decisive. But dare he? Still holding two cups each, she looking up at him with a young and open look, as though beseeching him to be kind, his face troubled with the momentousness of the moment, they kissed again, their eyes closed. They stayed with their lips together for a long time, the world dropping round them, both gliding down the dark river of mutual acceptance. The cups went out of balance, drooped and dripped, but they clung to them, swaying. A spoon slid and fell, ringing.

A few of the remaining students, a few, struggling into

scarves and duffel-coats, noticed, and there were gasps and cries of surprise. Then, in envy or gladness, they talked and laughed more loudly, like children, excited by the presence of the new assignation, but nervous, too, because there was such a seriousness about the lovers, almost grim.

They began to finish the washing up, feeling suspended. Paul and Lucy wiped the crocks together, exchanging polite conversation now, a little ashamed of their lapse. So they talked about English at Cambridge and the books and poetry they had enjoyed 'in spite of' the Tripos. One by one those helping them, not quite knowing what to say, put on their outdoor things and left. Paul and Lucy stayed in the dreary basement with its stale smell of food, taking a long time to lock up. Between every cupboard and switch they kissed, holding one another close now, lost in amazement, stroking one another's backs. Lucy's mouth had an electric quality, Paul found, as he explored it with his tongue: it thrilled his nerves, but tautened the misery of his desire. They washed their faces, laughing gaily together in the gent's lavatory before they left, while Lucy made up again and put on fresh lipstick. In the intimacy, and under the strength of his aroused blood, Paul lost his power to speak again; so they locked up the dull little redbrick hall silently, almost glumly.

Then they wandered painfully through the Cambridge streets, mostly empty so early on the Sunday morning except for men reading fresh papers in shirtsleeves. They wandered along the gravel paths through King's College grounds down to the bridge. There Paul sat Lucy up on the parapet and stood with his face pressed against her body as she swung her legs under the tall yellowing trees, the ducks flying down from time to time among them, alighting on the water with curling bow waves, and spreading arrows of wake behind them, on which the dead leaves drifted.

All the morning they walked about Cambridge, mooning, lost in one another, and then, tired with love, ate salad and

French bread at the Peacock Restaurant, opposite St John's. The small sooty triangle of graveyard garden there, with dark ever-greens under the tall chestnut trees, was splashed with fallen colour. In the arty little café students could buy a bright, generous salad, cheaply. Customers were allowed to spoon their own platefuls from gaily patterned pottery bowls of grated carrot, green salad, purple beetroot, and tomatoes. This display was the more colourful and bright among all the drearinesses of wartime food. The lovers were totally absorbed in one another, pale and withdrawn from the world as if in a state of shock. What was happening to them seemed so huge: they could hardly believe such overwhelming feelings were theirs. Paul could only partially notice people he knew, figures whom he recognized who tended to wrangle demonstratively at club meetings, like Gabriel Gatz with his bushy black beard, and Clifford Colon. The pretentious exhibitionism of the general mob of students, the bright and empty chatter, so divided from the life of deep feeling, no longer had any meaning for him. He lived only in the delicious background of ancient stone and October-touched foliage, in the reflection of his face in Lucy's grey-green eyes with their flecks of orange, and his whole world was made gay by her crowsfeet when she smiled.

In the afternoon they went to Lucy's room in college and made love. It was cool, as the October darkness closed in, and they lit the gas-fire. They undressed and lay on cushions on the rug and sofa, both rich striped wool coverings, rich reds set off with black. The painful feeling of being throttled by desire returned to Paul's body again, to see her body quite naked. He felt a strange fear as she took off her last things, a strange denial, as she drew off her petticoat and last undergarments, that this could be happening, as in shock: he almost cried: Don't! Still virgin, he had dreamed so much of the moment it was difficult to accept the real nakedness when it came. She was pale and her face was lost in a shadowed happiness, but went over to him, to softly reassure him with her caresses from time

32

to time. She moved about naked, nimbly, like some pastoral creature from The Song of Songs. Her body had freckles, like her face, here and there: the waist and groin which seldom saw the sun were ivory, and her thighs had a white translucent pallor. Her small breasts were firm and upright, one a little smaller than the other: Paul kissed them and called them Gemini, the unidentical twins. The nipples were brown and stiff with cold and excitement. The girl's body strained in its young ripeness towards him. He gazed astonished at the difference between Lucy's body and his own, the secret gates of her only dimly apparent in the roots of her black body hair. He burned as he undressed himself, and stood, too, for the first time completely uncovered before a woman. He expected her to be alarmed. But she was not alarmed: she only adored, and gave off a bloom from her pale body for him, like a flower.

They drank some red wine and ate an orange together, and lay for a long time before the gas-fire. In passion Lucy passed some pulp of orange from her mouth to his in a kiss. Overwhelmed, Paul was disturbed by an inward fear, and a shadow passed between them.

In his fear he spoke destructively, and Lucy had to resist him.

'Is this the first time you've been naked with a man?'

'Yes, of course,' Lucy replied.

Though he watched her closely he couldn't detect a lie. But secretly he felt it was one. And then grew angry with himself for doubting, and asking. At last in the warmth of her arms, he grew peaceful.

'This is the first time for me,' he said simply.

For a time, chilled by the mechanics of contraception, they lay together unmoving, clasping one another as if stunned. The cold of the stuff chilled desire for a while: then the disturbance passed slowly away. And as it passed they became warmly aware in one another's arms of the gravity of the moment, the meaning in both lives. An aeroplane throbbed across the afternoon, and the threatening sound drove them into an activity of joy, anxious to press the most out of their moment, before it was taken from them.

Paul was surprised at the awkwardness. For the first moment the act of love seemed ridiculous. They smiled at one another, Lucy with tears in her eyes and Paul perplexed but tender. But their faces had gone expressionless with desire. Lost in physical heat, he thrust his mouth down on hers, and, driven by the compulsion of the flesh, he found his way. Almost at once, the great wave of his desire broke as soon as he felt his flesh between the gates of her soft hot body. Overwhelmed, they sank breathlessly together into a trance which became sleep, for a short while, under a rug they had dragged over them.

Afterwards they bathed together in a large Victorian bathroom, with white paint and dark green walls, up the wide corridor of the women's college. There were faded brown portraits of former principals, watching them dimly with rigid disapproval. They laughed happily but silently now at the devilment, in the splash and suds of the bathing. It was, Lucy told him, still an hour at which no men should be in the building: she pointed mischievously to a framed printed notice to this effect. But Lucy didn't care: she had 'gone down' officially, and only occupied a room until the new term began. So, they recklessly splashed and dried themselves, and padded in coat and dressing-gown along the corridors back to her room.

After a while they dressed and made tea, drowsily. Then they slipped out of the gate. Clinging they walked to the end of the road and parted where scarlet and orange leaves lay clung to the mist-wet paving stones. The drab flagstones shone dismally, but the fallen leaves made a pattern which, recalled each autumn as October came, never left the memory of either. Whenever he saw red leaves in the Cambridge streets in October lying so, Paul recalled the perfume Lucy wore that day, of which he never knew the name, but which stayed with him young and strong, and returned whenever he caught the evocative scent of a field of beans in flower.

34

Her perfume, and the rich smell of a woman's flesh in love, were still about him next morning, as they had been all night, when he opened the envelope containing his call-up papers.

*

'Can't stand much more of this.'
'You'll get plenty, brother!'
'Christ, how long do we have to stick this bastard?'
'Bloke hit him last week.'
'Fucking good job.'
'R.T.U-ed, mate.'
'One bloody way out.'
'Squ-a-a-a'...'
'Shut up, cunt.'
A ventriloquist voice came suddenly from close behind the recruits, wheedling in a monstrous falsetto.

'Was some lard talkin' in the rarnks just then awoile? Was some little lard complainin' to his deer old mother about the narsty dreel staff sarn't?'

The voice shrieked, the N.C.O.'s eyes rolling as if they had come undone, under the flattened peak of his Guards hat.

'By Chroist I'll break you in, if I have to keel harf of ye t' do't!'

He gave a curt order:
'*Squaaa! Dees . . . m'ss!*'

They broke away in relief, gladly relaxed, a muddle of khaki-wrapped young men.

Staff-sergeant MacAllcane squinted madly, rolling his eyes again, large and writhing, like scallops in a death agony.

'S'YE WEER!!'

Amazed at his power over them, already electric and paralysing, the squaddies formed up again, quickly, humiliated, scurrying. The man tapped his feet and clenched and unclenched his fists as he mumbled his patter vindictively.

'At the words-a-commarnd turn smartly t' the roight (salut-

35

in'-if-a-nofficer-is-on-pareed) and then pausin' . . . countin' soilently t'y'self, by numbahs –

Hup! Twoop! Threep!'

The drill sergeant gave a demonstration, banging his great legs on the ground, his coarsely prominent buttocks snapping taut as he waved a great hand in front of his egg-like eyes squinting under the peak, saluting with an affected oscillation.

'Then brerk away, rememb'rin' to starnd and march always like a soldier and not . . . *loike a shower of swate violats!'*

He piped high:

'Or there'll be *THROUB-BEL!'*

'*Dees . . . m'ss!'*

But the fatigued youths were forced to perform the movement three times before the staff sergeant was satisfied. The extra drill ate into their 'break', so they lost their cocoa and biscuits. Hobbling, they form up in three lines, to march off to gunnery instruction in a black roofing felt and plywood hut, smelling of sweat and gun-oil.

Here they were introduced to the Army classification of trees, into three categories: bushy-topped, fir and poplar. Also to the antique coarse jests on which the instructors relied to enliven their memorized rigmarole – about the 'body-locking' pin, 'commonly known as the Ladies' Delight', and about God being the first to invent a double-purpose weapon. The hideous blunt-nosed Bren machine-gun lay unlaughing at the young men's feet, on the concrete floor, splashed with dark stains.

Later, after a lunch of Spam, wet boiled potatoes, beetroot, cheese and bread, they spent an hour rattling the bolts of heavy teak and blued steel rifles. Then they carried them for a cross-country run in full kit through the scrubby Surrey countryside, over the gravel hills, scratching their legs on the gorse and swilling their feet through streams yellow with sandy clay, among the birch-trees. Before tea, of bread, beetroot and cheese, with thick brown stewed issue Indian tea, they had another half an hour with MacAllcane. At the end of it he told them how to blanco their webbing, how to polish their buttons, pleat their battledress, and clean their boots.

Several of the men in the barrack rooms of the pre-OCTU at Blackmoor were N.C.O.'s from established units. Some of them had been in the Army for several years. The other students who came with Paul Grimmer were from university training corps, boys of eighteen or nineteen who had done a few days' training each week for a year in armoured cars about the fields near Cambridge, during their first year's studies. Paul arrived, on the day stated on the buff forms, in casual student's garb, blue-grey slacks, his maroon check shirt and a blue herringbone tweed jacket. Like the other arrivals, he displayed the students' ease of manner – a tendency to drawl and lounge, and to affect a disparagement of effort, in the relaxed college way, always rather on the defensive and unsure of themselves. The raw and hesitant party was shown into a long barrack room, bare and gritty. There were rows of black iron beds and coarse blankets. Each recruit was allocated a space. Four bare electric bulbs burned without shades between the dismal green walls of olive drab Service paint. A few days before, the floor had been polished like a mirror and the stove black-leaded by the previous squad. Now, in the spirit of Blackmoor, it had been deliberately spoiled for the new squad – the floor scratched and dirtied, and the stoves stained with water.

That first evening Paul and the other students stared in amazement as the long-service sergeants dashed into a feverish activity of housewifery. They covered their webbing with the watery yellow blanco, smoothed the surface of their new boots with hot spoons, tucked their khaki serge trousers under their mattresses to keep the creases sharp, and polished their hollow brass buttons. They even polished the backs of buttons, and some went so far as to burnish the nails in the soles of their boots. Paul shrugged – he had no stuff, and no idea where to begin. So, depressed by the prison-like atmosphere, of bare black boards and discomfort, pre-cadet Grimmer was soon in bed between the coarse issue blankets, trying to exclude from his mind the noise of tramping and voices in the bare echoing room. The equipment he had been given was lying in a heap by his locker: mess-tins, boots, and a tangle of raw webbing belts. Bored by the train, and shaken up by the journey in the back of a three-ton truck from Farnborough Station to Blackmoor, he was tired: he was going to have an early night. No orders had been given. No-one had explained anything. He was utterly at sea in the bare barrack atmosphere. It was like being flung into prison. He couldn't fathom why the sergeants were in a frenzy of grooming, spitting and rubbing and filling the room with a disgusting smell of hot bootblack and pungent yellow blanco. Surely they would be given time for all that! What kind of race were they in for? The watery cleaning compound gave off an odour like sweet glue, with a peppery tang, that mingled with the coarse smell of rough shoddy blankets.

In the next space was a plump short sergeant, about ten years older than Paul, with shining false teeth. He was chuckling, active in his khaki shirt with bare arms, bright on his wrist a large wrist watch. He flashed his teeth at Paul, and threw his head back, shouting. 'Cor! Look at 'em!'

'What's matter?' asked Paul, sleepily.

'Cor! You'll find out tomorrow!'

Sergeant Miffin shook his head and grinned with a gesture of pain and punishment, throwing his head back again.

'Ogh! Cor! Huh! You'll see!'

He shouted across to another sergeant, bent over a smoking boot.

'Hasn't even started on his bloody boots yet. You'll look lovely tomorrow,' he said to Paul.

'I read in the paper the Army was going to use dubbin for its boots,' said Paul sleepily, trying to keep his end up, and turning over under the hairy blanket.

Sergeant Miffin rocked, putting his head down almost be-

38

tween his legs, hissing with indrawn breath, and laughing chestily.

'Cor! At Blackmoor. Very, very likely. Ogh! Cor, Christ! Wouldn't like to be in yours tomorrow, mate!'

It was late October and the nights were becoming deep and long. It was still dark next morning when from the warmth of his coarse bed Paul heard *Reveille* blow. The bugle call was sad and wistful. The antique evocative beauty of the faint horn music touched off a dream of castles, and Lucy gliding to his side on a stairway. As she touched his shoulder a stinging pain shot through it, and he woke sharply to find his neighbour, Miffin with the pearly set of false teeth, walloping and shoving his sleeping body.

'Wakey, wakey old mate. You want to get smartly outa that wanking pit!'

His first morning in the Army! Paul groaned drowsily and sat up snorting on the hard iron bedstead. All round the room men writhed in humped postures, glum and sleepy, some folding their blankets, some struggling with unfamiliar clothes. Half-clothed in their drab khaki shirts, coarse and collarless, they looked pathetic, wiping the shreds of residual lather from their ears, padding back from the 'ablutions' on the rough concrete floors, or tidying their strewn belongings away in lockers. Soon, as the nondescript mass of men dressed a sharp division became visible between the trained and the untrained. The N.C.O.'s were quickly shaved, soon standing erect, spruce in shining black boots, pale painted khaki gaiters, their trousers creased, each button shining, cap badge – a silver mailed fist encircled by arrows – bright in a black beret pulled down to the regulation level, one inch above the left eyebrow. They tugged at each other's blouse pleats and heaved their belt-buckles, fussing, like women dressing.

The others – students and raw recruits – still struggled with tangles of webbing and buckles, and wriggled into ill-fitting boots and blouses, unkempt.

39

Paul was one of the last to join the parade. Like the other students, crammed into unfamiliar stiff garments in the violent haste of the early morning, he looked a wreck. His harness was too loosely buckled, and his battledress sagged like a scarecrow's clothing. He shuffled into the ranks among the ranks of shining rigid N.C.O.'s, and held himself more or less erect. Nothing would meet – Paul's blouse did not seem to belong to his trousers, one gaiter was on upside down, his belt was loose, his beret awry, his boots were gaping, the laces knotted wildly like strands of liquorice in a village sweetshop. All the student recruits looked as unlike soldiers as it is possible to look. The sergeants could not bear to look at them. They could not bear to be on parade with such shambling novices, even in the same squad.

The moon was still shining. Paul had not even had time to shave. He had no breakfast, and couldn't imagine when the rest of his toilet was to be completed. He was used to taking time over everything, reading, and sipping his tea. Now he took his place somewhere in the three uneven ranks, and stood in his relaxed way with his hands behind him. The sergeants and corporals from the ranks were exploding *sotto voce* with scorn at the students, and making fierce breathing noises of disdain and contempt.

'Pshaw!' breathed Miffin between clenched false teeth. 'My Christ, look at 'em! Ogh! God! To think. . . . It's a bloody disgrace to *associate* with 'em!'

He stood gleaming from top to toe, like a mint stuffed pouter pigeon fresh from the taxidermist, his chest rounded out artificially under the neat pressed pocket-pleats, his two shining black boot toes standing up like proud iron doorstops. Beside Miffin and the other sergeants the students looked like straw-filled dummies to be used for bayonet practice. But now they were all 'pre-cadets': all had to merge into the testing experience of being 'bashed' by Blackmoor, to see who could stand it.

Paul stood sleepily on his feet in the hard new boots, feeling at crutch and armpits the stiff unwieldly coarseness of new khaki serge, and with the unfamiliar constriction of webbing strapped round his chest. The parade ground was a huge four-acre square of pale grey asphalt, dusty and depressing. At one end bulked four blunt utilitarian red-brick barrack blocks, like the wings of a prison. Among these were temporary black huts, some bulging elephant huts, some of creosoted wood, some covered with black roofing felt. The huts were decorated pathetically in the bizarre Army way with fire buckets painted red, lines picked out meaninglessly in white, and white-splashed stones of variegated shapes arranged round the corners of verandahs like surrealist sculpture – *objets trouvés* – or archaeological specimens in a museum. In places there were white flagpoles, and polished brass shell-cases hung on chains for fire-alarms. The camp, ugly among the Surrey woods, had that air of a colonial trading station, planted somewhere in a clearing hacked from the savage jungle, that characterises British military establishments everywhere. The verandahs, rockeries, brass gongs, flagpoles, the white stones and the touches of garish red paint made one feel that the Indian Mutiny was only just over, and the compound was only just recovering its morale, displaying a few fetishes made from household refuse, and the products of useless effort. In the main block there were even one or two cutlasses and cuirasses in glass cases, from the good old days of the cavalry charge, when unruly Sepoys could be lashed to gun muzzles and blown to pieces as punishment. Unfortunately the brave totemism of helmets in glass cases and the gleaming brass ware was a little tarnished by the horror of the Great War, one could feel that. The inventions of Gatling, Maxim and Vickers had spoiled everything.

Over this insubstantial camp of black dwellings, bolted together from sheets of corrugated iron and matchwood section, above the dusty and mournful expanses of hard asphalt, rose the moon like a bright cheese. Those grim cold days at

Blackmoor found Paul Grimmer standing out on the bleak drill ground day after day in the early morning in the icy darkness, while the booted shadows of men went by with clanking mess-tins from breakfast, as he watched the clear-edged moon. Bright and tangible, often in what seemed to him incredible distortions, it changed shape day by day, and shone unnaturally in the greenish dawns. He had never so often seen the moon in the morning. He could even see it moving in the sky as he stood at parade, against the tops of the black few scrubby trees lining the great windy square.

In this moon-tormented vacancy there first came upon them the monstrous Staff Sergeant MacAllcane.

'Squadrrgh! Squa'– SHOR'!'

A high gutteral animal noise came out of the darkness. Sergeant Miffin and the other N.C.O.'s, as if their nerves were in an electric circuit, like frogs' legs in a galvanic experiment, braced their pleated chests, threw back their chins, glazed their eyes, and, lifting their knees unnaturally, banged their polished boots with unnecessary noise on the asphalt. They stood rigid, trembling a little as if in fear. The students relinquished their relaxed student lounges with some resentment. They did not look alarmed, nor did they tremble in obedient rigidity. Their indolent presence alongside filled the sergeants with anxious apprehension. Miffin looked quite paralysed, his eyes clicking from side to side, like a rabbit in fear.

'Sy'weer!'

Miffin and Co. stood at ease – but such an ease as was tense and rigid in dread. The students went amiably relaxed. A second or two later a slow high-pitched hysterical enquiry came out of the figure before them.

'Suffering Chroist, whaat have they sent us this toime?'

Under MacAllcane's flattened cap was a bull-neck with large muscles, while the head seemed set back into the shoulders in a way that was almost deformed, because of the blinding peak. The head was so close cropped as to seem shaven. The

42

face was contorted in affected incredulity. The eyes were popping with assumed amazement, and squinting. Between them was a large and bulbous nose, burnt by the parade ground sun. This organ was flattened under the black japanned peak, and the tip of it nearly met the chin, over a mouth which gaped with mimicked dismay, like a stage mask. As he moved, MacAllcane had to contort his neck, even to see ahead: one had the impression of a savage wild animal, half-blinded with rage or pain.

The voice wheedled.

'What in Hell's blessed name do they call the craytures we've got here. What are ye?'

'Squad One, sern't,' Miffin barked quietly between his clenched set.

'Some of us . . .'

Miffin was trying to express an apology for being classed with the students who came so short of being soldiers around him. He was ashamed of the company he, spruce and alert, stood among. But he was cut short.

'*Quy–at!*'

MacAllcane's eyes seemed to go red in the veins like blood-spotted eggs and he squinted more narrowly under his hat. He began to bawl in his parade voice, an incredible utterance. Paul suddenly realized how much it sounded like the noise of a Punch showman, and had to suppress the thought hard, in case he smiled.

'What's y'name that marn?'

They all jumped.

'Sergeant Miffin,' Miffin miserably protested.

'Oh dear no. Oh deerie me, *noe, noe, noe.*'

MacAllcane wheedled, insultingly, in a high flute.

'Yes,' protested Miffin, bridling, with an angry little quiver of his buttocks.

He had expected *entente*. But he got none. The rebuff brought two colour spots to the small plump ex-sergeant's cheeks.

43

'D'ye know what y'are? Ye're all Pre-cadets. Oi'll tell ye' what y'are. Ye're Pre-cad*et* Miffin.' He pronounced it mincingly, insultingly. The pink spots flamed in Miffin's cheeks. 'Ju-u-ust thart! Whatever ye' were before, ye're not now. *D'ye see, thaht marn?*'

His voice rose again to a hysterical squeak, with a spasm of the taut buttocks.

Miffin made a hurt, frightened sound with his lips, unwillingly. He felt as if he were being stripped of his rank, humiliated. Paul was revolted by the cunning technique of the staff sergeant, crushing those men with most self-respect first. The moon began to wane, and they lost it, wheeling and turning with stiff necks. The growing light of the early autumn morning illuminated the instructor's figure a little more each minute: it grew more and more incredible. The leggy giant carried a pair of huge wooden compasses to measure a pace with. He played with it in his histrionic performance on the square: as he walked along he walked the dividers along beside his own legs, like an extra pair. Paul felt his aim was to reduce all men to mere pairs of wooden dividers too, pacing the depressing flat square, the asphalt surface with its dusty shingle of grey stones blowing round their feet.

'A-a-arnd . . .'

MacAllcane screwed his voice up to a scream.

'Oi'll tell ye' what ye' are, all of ye'. Look at ye'! Look at ye'! Who said ye' were soldiers? What crayzy man ever sent ye' to thees camp. What crayzy man ever supposed I could make soldiers of ye'?'

'*Ye're a bahd oidle show-er!*'

The man would wheedle in a soft voice, then scream like an animal in a fit, as he prowled round them. He had no consistent accent: he spoke neither Irish nor Scots, but a mongrel admixture of his own parade-ground noises, Aldershottish. And between volleys of sound he would lick his large cruel lips with a wide tongue.

44

'Deed ye' muthers love ye'? Ye're no gud t'me.'

'Starnd up that marn whoile I'm haddressin' ye'!'

'Oi'll send ye' back t'ye muthers afore I've dun with ye' crying, cry-IN', I weel.'

MacAllcane then suddenly dropped the tension of his performance, supposing he had made his mark. He fell them out by one of the huts, and introduced himself, in a quick guttural patter. Paul supposed this was his notion of bonhomie.

'M'name's MacAllcane. I'm the staff sergeant in charge of yer dreel. Ye'll be bashin' that square two or three times a day. You work wi' me, we'll get the starndard up well enough. If we get wrong wi't one another, then ye'll have throubble . . . throubble . . . d'ye heer me? That's all I can seyr. THROUB-BEL! Roight, now we'll prarctise fallin' in.'

MacAllcane left them in a huddle by the hut and walked out into the square, his folded dividers under his arm. Holding his head up he hollered what he had explained as the *wordsacommarnd.*

'R-oi-oi-oight mahr-kha-a-ahr!'

Miffin marched stiffly out to a place in front of the instructor, and halted.

'*Ohn . . . p'ae'd!*'

They shuffled out, and pushed their outstretched fists against one another's shoulders.

'Dress b'th'roight, dress b'th'roight': MacAllcane was as incantatory as if he were conducting Mass.

'*Dress b'th'ROIGHT, thart dozey marn there.*'

Paul had looked to his left.

'Squaa-a' . . . !'

MacAllcane went on with a patter, as if in parenthesis to the major commands, jiggling about on his pattering boots, his buttocks quivering:

'Hon the wordsacommand brace y'self ready for the followin' or subsequent wordsacommarnd . . .

'*Squaa-a* . . . SHUN!

45

'. . . bringing the right leg firmly-and-sharply-together-with-the-left at the same toime bringin' the arms to the soides . . .'

'*No dayloight between th'harms and the buddy!*'

Gradually the Blackmoor sound came to mean something.

Having set about breaking them in, in general, MacAllcane now turned with dogged cunning on the N.C.O.'s among them, to bring them down. In his crude way, MacAllcane could see that this group were still taking refuge from humiliation, in the sense of their own superiority, fortified by their assurance that they, at least, were dressed correctly. But there was to be no *rapport*, and Paul could see that, defeated in trying to establish it, Miffin was in despair. MacAllcane picked on him. They were being allowed a pause for more instruction on how to dress.

'Here's a marn that's done the thing, but he's not done ut Blackmoor way.'

'The Blarnco's tew dark: we use a pale Blarnco. So he'll have to dew it all over again.'

'He's done his bewts wi' a spoon and thart's against ordthers. Ye'll dubbin ye'bewts . . .'

Paul felt triumphant: he had been right about shiny boots; and Miffin was wrong!

'. . . but ye'll *shoine* the bleeders, tew – d'ye *onthastarnd?*'

They shrugged. If the Army officially required one thing, and the unit another – their boots made dull and plastic with dubbin, and hard and polished, at the same time – they would do it.

So the evening was spent again in the filthy acrid smell of Blanco, pressing, smearing and polishing. Miffin and Co., softened now, relaxed their air of superiority to the new squaddies. They were all in the same cart. The plump little sergeant grinned at Paul who was busy too, now, with the filthy yellow 'bullshit'. Miffin showed his neat false teeth and admitted.

46

'I thought I'd learnt every bloody trick the Army had to play. But, Christ, they got a few new 'uns in this fucking place!'

So they all struck up a comradeship, being thrown together by resentment, and brutality. Miffin showed Paul how to fold his bed, how to lay out a kit for kit inspection, how to adjust straps and roll the extra ends neatly on the webbing.

'Bloody bull, old mate, that's all that counts in the bleeding Army.'

'Or there'll be *throub-bel!*' mimicked Paul, squealing in MacAllcane's voice.

Miffin grinned. 'Christ,' he said, 'I'd just like to see him catching you taking the piss.'

The squad came together under Miffin's influence, to organize a plan for what he called 'beezing' the squad's barrack room: 'beezing' was Army for beeswaxing. The large room had thirty iron black enamelled beds in it, each with a wooden locker, and two metal stoves with hearths each side of a central chimney. The soldiers were told that they were responsible for the room, and that standards of cleanliness in the squad would count in the final decision about each of them – as to whether they went forward to OCTU, to be trained as officers, or were sent back to their units.

The thirty young men looked dismally round their room, at the deliberately dirtied floor, dull and now well trodden, the rusty stoves and the black and grubby hearths. Miffin, who was a neat housewifely little man, couldn't bear it. He wanted to get his own back on the place, by proving his worth, his soldierliness. In one Guards' barracks, Miffin said, they made the squaddies beeze the corridor with black boot polish, using small shoe brushes. Then, when it was glassy, someone slipped on it and broke his thigh. So, they were made to unpolish it, using similar methods.

'That's how they make you bloody stupid. You get stupid after a bit. You'd do *anything*, mate.'

Miffin showed his teeth, in a cruel, crushed gesture.

So, with Paul as an aide, they organized the squad to 'beeze up' the room.

There was little to do, after tea, when they were not on guard duty, except lie about in ungainly postures and doze, in a vegetable state of fatigued despair. There was stale tea and rock cakes that tasted of baking soda in the NAAFI canteen, and a few copies of *Reveille*, *Blighty* or the *Daily Mirror*, on the spill-ringed tables. To walk about outside the barrack room was a danger, for if your hat wasn't straight, or you put your hands in your pockets there might suddenly come the distant flute of one of the drill sergeants, high and penetrating.

'Oidle, that marn!'

Unless the cadet responded abruptly, the call would come again.

'*Oidle!* Come here that marn . . . *Doub-bel!*'

Then the unfortunate soldier would have to run over at the double, and give his name. Later he would be put on a charge for being 'idle on parade', when in fact he had really been off duty. It was never possible to relax, except in a NAAFI coma, or on your own hard bed.

'If they haven't got a bloody rule they invent one,' said Miffin. 'And if they can't do that they get you under Section 40 of the Army Act, about "any action to the prejudice of good order and military discipline . . ." Get in a dump like this and you've had your fucking chips. You might as well be in prison. You're not you any more. It's *throub-bel*, *throub-bel*, *throub-bel*, all the bleeding time.'

So they stayed in their room and 'beezed'. Miffin found a 'bumper' – a large brush on a hinged pole with an iron weight pressing it to the floor. Using this, teams of men scrubbed the floor until it began to shine. They rode on the brush, like fanatics of some strange sport, to bite its bristles deep into the floor, and bring up the surface. They bought floor polish,

48

Zebo, Bluebell, Windowlene, hearth-stones, and dusters, out of their own pay, and 'beezed' the floor until it was as brilliant as glass. This glassy rink became sacred, Miffin's floor, and they walked on it gingerly, like cats on wet grass. A student squaddy carelessly slid in his boots one day, and looked ruefully at a long scrape.

'What the Christ did you do that for, *cunt*?' Miffin gnashed, hardly able to restrain his little fists, which he clenched tightly by his plump sides. A misty sweat broke out on his shiny forehead, in rage.

Then they black-leaded the two stoves and whitened the hearth with whitening stones. Others cleaned the windows.

The room was sweet and brilliant, and they 'beezed' their personal kit up to go with it. Miffin got round the quartermaster sergeant to provide them all with the same colour blankets and even the same colour holdalls and hussifs and the same shape of messtins.

'Miffin,' someone shouted at kit inspection in mock despair, 'look at this bloody nailhead in my left boot-sole, mate: it ain't regular.'

'Chuck him out! Spoils the whole room Miff!'

But the moment of Miffin's triumph came. One Friday the grotesque MacAllcane opened the door for the inspecting officer, slammed his boots with affected clatter on Miffin's brilliant black wooden floor, and saluted.

'Squahd one, sahrr!'

The officer under his breath asked:

'Mostly university men, what?'

'Mostly *oidle*, sahrr,' MacAllcane fawned in squeaky gutturals.

But it was the wrong note. The officer was impressed. He found it hard to find anything wrong. The squaddies had learned to stand rigid, their faces impassive and anonymous, allowing no lapse of personal relaxation which might be taken advantage of, to humiliate one of them. But, standing so, they

49

had heard the officer in the room opposite, which had been inspected before theirs, MacAllcane happily fluting.

'Take 'is nime, sahrr? . . . Take 'is nime? . . . *oidle*, Pre-cadet Rahbinson. . . . You'll find ye'self on a charge . . . right, sahrr . . . *oidle*, that man!'

Then the officer walked through their room, silent. He stopped at one young student's locker.

'Is that your book?'

'Yessir.'

'Put it away. You should put all personal belongings away.'

The student had left out a copy of *The Strategy of Modern Warfare* by Major General Lockheed, a paper-back. The officer had seen the title and was trying not to smile.

'Take 'is nime, sahrr?' yelled the monstrous drill instructor.

'No, I don't think so, Sern't MacAllcane. Look, I think these chaps have done awfully well. Can't they have a forty-eight?'

MacAllcane swayed for a moment and readjusted his great cap over the bumps behind his ears. He even went a little green and pale with anger and panic: the grip of his tyranny was for a moment loosened. Then he recovered, saw inwardly how he could both obey and disobey the suggestion, saluted, and said,

'I'll report to the Ahd-jew-tahnt, *sahrr*.'

Miffin gave him a malevolent glance of triumph.

When they had gone the plump Miffin sat on his bed hugging himself.

'Christ,' he said, 'if I don't get pissed tonight.'

Paul was already writing to Lucy, asking her to meet him for forty-eight hours leave, on blue NAAFI paper. In his heavy boots, with his stiff hands and tired limbs, he felt he was on another planet from that on which was to be found the elegant beauty of Cambridge, and the sweet softness of Lucy somewhere between her sheets.

*

But it was another month before they got their forty-eight hours leave. MacAllcane saw to that. He had to get his grip on

50

the squaddies, and they weren't to be allowed out until Black-moor had subdued them. So the days passed, from the moonlit or pitch-dark early mornings, to the dismal evenings under the weak bulbs of blacked-out huts. After tea they were so crushed, worn and humiliated that they could do nothing but sleepily arrange their kit for the morning, keep the room 'beezed up' and lounge for an hour over a tepid pint of indifferent NAAFI beer with a rag of a magazine.

Of course, the young men were being made bodily fit and strong, swinging down trees on ropes, scaling cliffs, leaping over plank runways high above-ground, running through woods and leaping ditches. But the strain of the harsh testing discipline was tremendous – the crushed inward tumult, of feelings of impotent vengeance and resentment, at being 'bashed' on the square, twice daily, exhausted them. None of them felt he was himself any longer. Personality was subdued to the driven life of body: even the body could barely keep up – all else that was human in them was relinquished.

One or two men cracked. Some failed to turn up on parade: these went straight back to their units. Others got drunk in defiance and became disorderly. One Irishman came in drunk and urinated on another cadet asleep in his bed. He was put on a charge and given a punishment parade. This meant drilling for an hour in the hot sun under MacAllcane. When he came back in from the ordeal the man was pale and inert with weari-ness and suppressed rage, covered in sweat. Next day he threatened to strike the staff sergeant on morning parade, and was marched off. He was 'Returned To Unit' that day.

So when Paul was put on punishment parade for being 'dirty' on parade – the inspecting officer had found a spot of gun oil on his pocket flap – he knew he had to bear it, or lose his chance of taking part as an officer in the invasion of Europe. How humiliating a path he must take, to follow the intentions to which his political beliefs had brought him! But he could no longer think of meanings and connections at all. He told him-

51

self what MacAllcane said: 'Ye're not in the Army to think.' He must endure all the lunacies.

When the day to be charged came, he thought he had been blessed by a stroke of luck. His name did not appear on the list of those due to report at 4 p.m. before the Orderly Officer. The office orderly typing the list must have made a slip and left his name out. So Paul lay low, and went off to take a bath in the bath house, in the steamy mist of hot carbolic over the cold concrete floors. He sudded himself gleefully with the tarry red soap, his limbs relaxed and warm. Suddenly in the distance he heard the high flute of MacAllcane.

'Pre-cadet Grim-marr!'

With fear in his stomach he leapt from the bath, cursorily wiped the wet from his body, and rammed himself into his battledress. His limbs in the serge were steamy and damp. He struggled with his boots and gaiters, his head swelled and bursting with heat and steam, his fingers all thumbs, his warm wet feet too big for his boots. He ran to the Orderly Office where all was shouting and confusion. He had to be marched in, on the dusty bouncing wooden floor.

'Where the bloody hell have ye' been, me lard? This'll be bard for yew! Pre-cadet Grim-mahr, pre-cadet Grim-mahr, SHOO', leftroightleftroight . . . hallet . . . lefttoin! Pre-cadet Grim-mar, sahrr!'

The great hand oscillated under the blinkering peak.

'What's the charge, Staff Sern't?'

'Dorrty on p'rae'd, sahrr! Also tried to slip the charge, sahrr!'

All the stamping and shouting in the flimsy wooden office seemed ridiculous. The air was full of dust from under their boots.

'Punishment parade. Dismiss.'

When he got outside Paul found his flies were still undone and gaping.

'Got a bloody medal?' a grinning orderly asked, as he passed Paul doing them up.

The young man suddenly felt humiliated, unmanned, sick of it all. MacAllcane was obviously thirsty for blood: he fixed the punishment parade at five that evening, for Paul and one other student pre-cadet, the one who had failed to tidy away his book on strategy.

Nothing could have been more meaningless and destructive than the sordid affair that followed, thought Paul. The two young men were dressed in steel helmet and pack, and the braces and belts of full kit. They carried rifles with slings, while the leggy staff sergeant, almost as exhausted afterwards as they were, marched them round and round some few square yards of asphalt at the quickest possible pace for sixty minutes, in the gathering dusk.

For the first five minutes Paul felt that he could stand it. But after a while the futility of the deliberately repeated orders, left turn, right turn, left turn, right turn, and the deliberately provocative way the men were made to feel that they were being given futile orders to punish them, made his blood boil. For the next twenty minutes, his feet sore, his neck in agony, his sweat running in cold rivulets down his back, Paul considered attacking MacAllcane with his unloaded rifle. His vision was beginning to go red with the blood of exhaustion, and he moved his legs automatically to the voice; they felt limp, lifeless and trembling. Meanwhile his mind hallucinated a whole series of attacks on the hideous drill instructor. The man kept licking his lips with a big tongue: the corners of his mouth were scabby with dried saliva. Paul's most satisfying fantasy was a heavy clean swipe with the butt on the lumpy back of MacAllcane's head, driving in pieces of skull like crab shell, into the man's brain. Then he hallucinated a butt blow into the staff sergeant's testicles, and, while the man groaned on the ground in torment, crushing his popping eyes under the heels of his boots. As the visions came he tightened his grip on his rifle, and cold sweats ran over his face. Then he found his body gone over simply to automatism, and he looked compassion-

53

ately at the other young victim. The boy looked terrible, grey, with rivulets of sweat in his hair, and wild eyes, his mouth loose and panting. Up and down they marched, in stupid stiff quick drill movements on the great asphalt space. The evening was dark and cold, but they were seething with sweat. Mac-Allcane kept it up, panting for breath himself now. He simply kept to orders: he uttered no abuse. The warrant officer had learnt not to issue insults on punishment parades: he still bore a scar where an incensed soldier once split his face open under punishment. Unable to prove provocation, the man was still in the glasshouse: but he had taught the staff sergeant cunning at punishment. The man relied now on a cunningly monotonous regular sequence of maddening orders. They could feel his delight at making them step and step round the depressing open square, to no purpose but their own humiliation.

Paul never imagined it could be as bad as it was, to do an hour's punishment parade. The time seemed interminable. MacAllcane even had to give them two rests near the end while he recaptured his own breath. When they were dismissed they could not move: they stood, cramped, their feet aching, their clothes clinging in sweat, their vision red, their mouths dry and their tongues swollen. From the other young man came sob-like gasps, and Paul's own humiliated emotions rose in his throat like a lump of burst heart striving to burst out. Gradually some feeling returned to their limbs and they hobbled slowly to their barrack room. There was no shrugging the effects away. It would take the whole evening, he knew, to recover the least faculty. It took him an age to remove his kit, he was so stiff and sweat-soaked. He meant to get back into his interrupted bath: but instead fell into stupid reveries about killing MacAllcane, lying in his chill sweat as it dried. Then he lapsed into dreams of becoming an officer at Blackmoor, taking some terrible revenge on the man, and sending him away to the front to certain doom. At last he fell asleep on his bed, still clothed. Miffin tucked him in.

'Poor old sod,' said the sergeant. 'Now the poor bastard's no longer a squaddie.'

But Paul did not wake up.

The next day he could hardly walk, and his ankles were swollen.

'I'm going to report sick.'

'Oh Christ, you amateur!' said Miffin.

'Well, I can't go on parade like this. Why shouldn't I go sick?'

'You'll see,' said Miffin darkly.

To go sick one had to be out of bed and dressed at 7 a.m., an hour before the fit men were to be on parade. This was to prevent malingering. An orderly came in in the raw darkness at a quarter past to take a list, calling, 'Anyone sick?' A man who had ruptured himself came hobbling painfully across the dark square in rain supported by another who had a boil on his leg. Paul followed. In the medical hut sat one other customer, a cadet with a terrible cough, and a temperature, said the orderly, of 104.

'Who wants to see the quack?' asked the orderly.

The others seemed worse than he was, so Paul gave them the chance to go first.

'We all do,' said Paul.

'No we fucking don't,' groaned the man with the temperature.

'Nor me,' said the man with a boil. 'You want to keep away from him mate. He's bloody crazy. Jack, you'll do my carbuncle, won't you?'

'Righto, chum,' said the orderly. 'Only you'll have to see him if it's the first time. And you will, old mate, to get to hospital.'

'Oh, bollocks,' said the man with a rupture, who was breathing in groans with pain.

The four men sat on the slatted benches in the cold wooden waiting room, until after nine o'clock. The boil was dressed,

but the soldier had to wait for a chit to get off duty, from the
M.O. The infectious case coughed and gurgled. Paul felt that
if he sat there long enough his swellings would go down, and
he would be put on another charge, for malingering. He
gingerly felt his ankles: they were still puffy and hurt. Ah, well.

There was a fussing inside at nine o'clock, and he could hear
the old doctor's wheezy oiled voice. He sounded drunk, slurred
and fuddled. The orderly, he could see, was steering the officer
into his chair, saying,

'Yes, sir, yes, sir.'

'I want t'shee 'em all, Jenkins. Shee?'

'Yes, sir.'

'You don't let me shee 'em all. Open the bloody door.'

Jenkins opened the door. The doctor, squinting with one
eye, counted the men.

'Are there four of the buggers thish morning? Or five?
Buggered if I can shee.'

'Four, sir.'

'Firsht, pleashe.'

'First one is just a chit, sir.'

'Chit be buggered. I want to shee the sholdier.'

'Fucking Christ,' murmured the man with the boil. 'He's
screwed already.'

The M.O. had the boil in, stripped off the new dressing, and
poked at the thing clumsily with trembling fingers. Paul
noticed he hadn't washed his hands: nor did he close the door.

'Thish hurt?' he asked.

'Ow, fuck,' shouted the soldier.

'Naughty, naughty,' said the M.O. 'Take your troushers
off.'

'But I . . .'

'Never mind, my boy! Take your troushers off.'

So the man stood there, while the M.O. examined his buttocks and felt his groin and his testicles, in full view of the
others.

56

'No pain there?' said the M.O. holding the man's private parts.

'No, sir.'

'Righto. Put a dresshing on and give him a ticket, off duty. Nexsht, pleashe.'

The rupture went in next. He took his trousers off straight away, and the M.O. went through much the same procedure. At one point the man let out such a terrible yell that everyone jumped.

'Naughty boy,' said the M.O. 'Yesh, hoshpital.'

He wrote a chit. Paul could see he could hardly write. His pen kept coming down nowhere near the place.

'Nexsht.'

In staggered the man with a high temperature.

'Wash a matter?'

'I've got a sore throat, sir . . . and a temperature.'

'How do you know?'

'I took it, sir.'

'Where'd you get shermometer?'

'I had one, sir.'

'Oh I shee: one of them that fanshies being ill. Keepsh a shermometer in his knapsack, eh? Swinging the lead, eh. Naughty, naughty.'

He laughed, wheezily, gurgling.

'Take your troushers off.'

'But, sir, I . . .'

'Orderly!' shouted the mad doctor. *'Take thish man's troushers off!'*

But the man had them off. The doctor felt his genitals.

'Cough!' he said.

The man coughed. He was bewildered and exasperated and was obviously wondering whether the episode wasn't a delusion of sickness.

'Nasty cough you've got there. Go to bed.'

The M.O. wrote out a chit. No duties for a week. No more:

the man went out doing up his buttons, carrying his piece of paper. This was not for drugs, but permission to stay in bed.

'Nexsht.'

'Old cunt,' he muttered under his breath.

Paul staggered in and saluted. He thought that might bring the man round. But it had the wrong effect.

'Nothing wrong with you,' said the M.O. challengingly, 'Another lead shwinger.'

'Orderly!' he roared.

'My ankles are shw . . . swollen, sir,' said Paul quickly. He had taken off his boots, gaiters and socks, painfully.

'Take your troushers off,' snapped the M.O.

There was nothing to do but to obey. The fat old man, with hanging jowls and grey hair, felt Paul's body – and then Paul realized this was no drunken automatism, but an act of strange sexual amusement. The drunken doctor fumbled in Paul's groin for what seemed ages. Then he seemed to doze off. Paul seized the chance to pull his trousers up, and went out hobbling to show the orderly his ankles.

'They got like that after a punishment parade yesterday.'

'O.K. mate, I'll give ye' some ointment. Then I'll get a chit off of 'im. 't'll be O.K.'

Paul sat in the waiting room again. He could see now why no-one at Blackmoor ever went sick.

He heard the orderly wake the M.O.

'Form to sign, sir. Bad legs. Off duty a week. Just 'ere, sir.'

'What? Oh yeah. Get me a whishkey, Jenkins, will you.'

The old man belched.

'Just a minute, sir.'

Jenkins appeared at the door, in a white apron, with ointment and a paper.

'I saw you last night with that sod MacAllcane drilling you.' he whispered to Paul. 'The sooner anyone's out of this bloody madhouse the better, old mate. Here, I've got him to give you a week off duty. He don't know no better.'

'Thanks,' said Paul, staggering back to his beret, 'You'll lose nothing by that.'

The orderly closed one eye slowly and then opened it.

'You don't want to go up front with tanks, mate. You want to get a cushy job like this here.'

'What, and deal with him? No bloody fear. Rather face Jerry any time.'

Turning away, Paul found himself startled to discover such bravado cliché on his own tongue. He hobbled off to enjoy the luxury of being off duty, hanging around Blackmoor, without having to go on the square. He continued to go to the lectures on field strategy, and found that, unburdened by the weight of drill fatigue, he was even able to follow well and ask intelligent questions. But he found it depressing and dull in the ugly camp, sitting about in the damp huts by himself. He became too miserably aware of his condition. Their 'forty-eight' came that week-end.

*

'Ring the fucking bell.'

'For Jesus Christ's sake, mate, pull the plug.'

'Here goes our bloody forty-eight!'

'Driver advance!'

'I'm on, Charley!'

'Want to make yourself bleeding scarce when that bastard's around.'

The driver of the ramshackle country bus, a man of fifty-five, a veteran of the 1914–18 war, knew the MacAllcane type. He watched the staff sergeant vindictively while he doubled grotesquely across the dusty square, swagger-stick under his arm, knees coming up like cranks, ridiculously.

'Starp! Starp the ve-hi-cuhl! There's a marn I must have . . . *Hallet!*'

Then, as the drill instructor's popping eyes stared unbelievingly under the flattened peak, the driver let in the clutch, and

the bus, after a spasm of grunts, whined away. The staff sergeant's authority did not extend beyond the bleak Blackmoor
square. There was a mutinous cheer from within. The voice
rose to a scream:

'Oi want thart MARN!'

But the bus plunged down the dusty camp road between
scrub and gorse, towards Farnborough. A happy babble broke
out among the released tank men. It was their first 'forty-eight'
recommended by the inspecting officer. MacAllcane had held
it up for a month, until the pre-cadets' spirits were broken to
his satisfaction. At the turning into the main road there was
another mutinous cheer.

'Fucking roll on,' someone near Paul Grimmer muttered.

'We shall pay for that!'

'Who cares?'

'Not for forty-eight fucking hours I shan't.'

'See yer Monday, Mac.'

'Don't think about it, mate.'

Paul, sitting next to Miffin in the hard red-leather bus seat,
found his forehead was bathed in sweat. He pulled off his beret
and mopped himself.

'Who did he want?' he asked Miffin.

'Smethers. That twat from Eton.'

Smethers was a general's son, wangled into the pre-OCTU,
they all said. The poor bony lad was stupid and constitutionally
untidy, yet had to be 'carried': no-one dare tell his father he had
so far failed on every count. But in revenge the N.C.O.'s picked
on him mercilessly while the squaddies felt he was letting them
down. In dismay he would wail, in an affected county accent:

'I c'd never do anyfing wight. I was kicked by a horse in my
yoof, thet's why! Heh! Heh!'

He was really mentally deficient, and strangely unbalanced,
a shambling ruffian, but childlike, too. MacAllcane had spotted
him from half a mile away, shoddily dressed, with his webbing
all undone, as he sidled towards the Friday evening leave bus.

'*Oidle*, that man! Come heyre!'

Smethers, whimpering, had crushed into the bus. The others were trying to push him out again, while he gave a toothy wail.

'Don't be so croo-wel! I want to get to the waces!'

He squealed as they pushed him back.

'Don't! He's *coming!*'

So they had dragged him in and urged the driver away. The men were twisting round in their seats, stamping and muttering in anxiety. It appalled Grimmer to see them, men older than himself, some middle-aged, reduced to the nervous anxiety of tyrannized children.

There was never any certainty they would get out of the gate, for their leaves, brief as these were. If the man could, MacAllcane would fault them on dress, even on the way to freedom – boots not clean, belt stained, beret not adjusted to the regulation angle, one inch above the right eyebrow. Paul had seen married men almost weeping with fury and frustration, because they had been stopped from going on leave, for being 'improperly dressed'. Some even had their passes cancelled. Whether they were or not depended entirely on Mac-Allcane's whim: his victims would go on guard duty instead. The warrant officer had no interests in the world outside the scrubby perimeter of Blackdoor camp: he hated the rest.

Miffin blew out a sigh of relief and lit up a Woodbine. He even allowed himself a chortle, rounding his plump pink cheeks.

'No stopping us now, Paul old mate. Two nights away. I suppose you'll be poking some poor little college girl, you randy sod.'

Paul grunted, and half-smirked at Miffin, so as not to lose face, or offend the little sergeant. But inwardly he felt dismay – it seemed such an impossible distance, between the 'beezed' barrack-room and Lucy's effervescent femininity, between the Army sneer and his true youthful feelings. He settled down on the red Rexine seat, his hand clutching the chromium-plated strip along the rim of the back in front, as the bus swung about the country road. He felt the crackle of paper in the thigh pocket of his battledress trousers, where he kept Lucy's letters.

Lucy was at Amersham now, where she was acting in repertory theatre. They were going to spend the week-end there, at the Crown Hotel. She had bought herself a wedding ring, and they were going to pretend to be married, signing themselves Mr and Mrs in the hotel register. All this was arranged by letter. As he read her letter in the dark winter morning after parade, Paul could hardly believe that there was a world in which such things could exist – a girl who loved you, and wanted to conspire to sleep with you in a hotel, and who wrote 'I love you Lucy' at the bottom of her letters. Surreptitiously every night in the NAAFI he had studied her handwriting lovingly: it seemed to him beautiful that a girl's hand should take up a pen and write 'I love you', for him, deliberately, meaning it.

The thought of this, and the crackle of her letters in his pocket, had sustained him through these first uncomfortable weeks. Last week Lucy had written:

I wonder what it will be like, again, when we meet? Helen Pyke, who came down to see me in The Seagull *last week (we had lunch together: she's gone into a factory in London, in 'personnel' work, whatever that is) said her brother's just come home and sleeps all day. (Will you?) She said men in the services get hard, as if they don't have proper feelings. No being – they're all boots, and snores, and swearing. I'm beginning to wonder if I shall like you any more . . . darling, I mean that as a joke: I hope it isn't a bad one . . .*

The letter had worried Paul. He read it again and again, trying to read between the lines. He feared Lucy would find him dull and stupid, in the moments of fatigue which would be bound to come, as a reaction, on leave. He felt his body had become hard, unyielding, and his spirit blunt and cruel. Whatever would they talk about?

So he had been glad when the medical pass had enabled him to avoid drill periods, guard duties and physical training the week before. He could soften up, for her.

He had a good deal of anxiety in preparation for getting away: he borrowed a flat-iron for his battledress, and polished his badge and boots with special thoroughness. Then, looking in the barrack room mirror, he saw the image of everybody's wartime sweetheart, the raw healthy youth with closely-cut hair, a black beret, big black shiny boots, a blousy battledress, coarse and yellow, and his webbing powdery with yellow Blanco, its brass clips bright.

But how boring it seemed, too: all the finicking dress regulations. My God, he thought, what will Lucy think she has got? The easy-going student she knew has been turned into something like a convict. He felt the coarse-cut pepper-coloured uniform reduced him to the animal man. Look! His buttocks even stuck out now like MacAllcane's.

The feeling came back to him in the bus. It was true what Miffin said: now he was a licentious soldier. He feared that Lucy would feel all he wanted from her was her body. He did want her body; but he wanted more to be loved, and he wanted gentleness. Yet he had avoided drinking tea all the week, because the troops maintained a legend that it was dosed with bromide, to lessen sexual desire. It certainly seemed to make you dull. But that might be the fatigue. Paul was taking no chances: yet his abstention seemed cold-bloodedly calculating, and caused him much inward debate. It seemed impossible to keep oneself adequate for the relationship of young love. Did giving oneself to the Army mean that all one's inward life must die?

*

In the train, Paul's resentment returned – at having to give himself up so wholly to the service life. He had had no premonition of how much the Army could take one over, body and soul. The train seat, which was no better than the usual stiff upholstery of a third class compartment, seemed so soft; and so delicious the ride on gentle springs, through the Surrey woods, towards London. No-one shouted at him: he could wander up and down the train corridor as he liked. It was raining, and the passing woods were blurred by raindrops, framed by the band of blackout paint round the edge of the carriage windows. The rain and the woods seemed so beautiful, after all the ugliness of the barracks and the square: yet he feared the softness, too, in case his feelings should give way. He travelled on with an increasing sense of loss: the train's movement reminded him that he belonged to neither world – neither the harsh drilled routine of the Army, nor what already seemed the strange relaxation of civilian life. Half in one, and half in the other, he knew nothing and was nothing: yet he was being drilled into an automaton, in that lunatic place – for what?

Miffin sat with him, as far as Guildford: the former sergeant was going to Chichester, where his home was. Strangely, as they relaxed, so, too the camaraderie, formed in self-defence against Blackmoor, evaporated. Wanting to indulge in his thoughts of Cambridge and Lucy, Paul found Miffin a bore now, and found he resented the way he patronized him. 'Damn his service experience', he thought. Paul's distaste fastened itself on Miffin's impossibly even set of false teeth, as he sat opposite, and they talked, in the aimless way, in Army badinage.

'You'd better be back by twenty-three forty-five hours, too, mate, on Sunday night.'

Paul yawned and stretched.

'Actually, I was thinking of getting in about six on Monday morning.'

'Ogh! Christ, you half-and-half! They'd have you for that. Cyor!'

Miffin made his mouth cruel, twisting his lips round his shiny teeth.

'Who's to know?'

'Well, you see. Midnight's the latest. Nought, nought, nought, one a.m. and you'll be up before the Orderly Officer, right in it, chum.'

'Why do they make such a hell of it? They make you feel

64

you've done something *wrong*, Miffin. I haven't done anything wrong: I just joined the Army.'

'Silly bugger!'

'But why do they?'

'It's a tradition, that's what it is.'

'Well, they ought to change it.'

'Ogh! Huh!'

Miffin clicked his teeth, shook his head back and gave a choking laugh, snorting.

'Bloody squaddies wanting to reform the whole bloody army. Cor! Ogh! Beats me!'

Paul, Miffin's barrack room lieutenant, looked at the plump little man with suddenly opened eyes. He had been glad of Miffin's spruce comradeship. But, outside the barracks, he was just a sergeant. Just a common sergeant, Paul thought angrily. ' "It's a tradition," ' Paul said inwardly, mockingly, to himself, 'that's all he can say. He'd do anything. He's just a little sergeant.' But then he felt an ungrateful prig: he had been glad enough of Miffin in the barrack room.

'Well, all that lunatic cleaning: what use is it all? It's a madhouse.'

'Get's you there, that's what it does.'

Miffin held his thumb down on his plump khaki thigh.

'I don't want to be "there",' protested Paul.

'You bloody got to be, mate. Look here. Suppose you got to be sent out on a night patrol – or to burn a village, Boers, or Fuzzies. You're there. Got to do it. Ogh! Yes!'

Miffin pressed on his thumb, fiercely.

'I only want to do . . . what I *want* to do.'

'Ha! Ha! Ogh!'

Miffin gasped with ridicule, throwing his head back, and writhing about in his seat. After MacAllcane: to say 'I only want to do what I want to do!'

'Ho! Ho! Roight mark-er! Oidle!'

Miffin shouted in MacAllcane's falsetto. The other cadets in the corridor heard the familiar sound. One pulled the compartment door glass down.

'Pack it up bloody Miffin.'

'Yeah! Forget him for Christ's sake.'

Miffin thrust the window up again with threatening gestures from his fat little fists.

'I mean,' Paul said, a little flustered, 'I want to fight against Hitler. And the Japs, if it comes to that. And Musso . . . Fascism. But not against anyone else.'

'You're a soldier of the King, chum: know what that means? You've taken the Queen's shilling, mate. You'll do what you're told. As a person you don't exist no more. Not while you got that on.'

Miffin flipped Paul's lapel, and held his thumb down, symbolically, again.

Paul looked out of the window, glumly, taking in the flavour of his submission to the war machine. He'd never thought of it: now he could feel the full force of his enlistment. It was true! He had taken the Judas shilling! He could be sent – against strikers, nationalists, Russians, left-wing progressives with sympathies like his own, by the MacAllcanes! He had often wondered how men had put up with the mud and horror of the 1914–18 war, the stench and degradation. Now he knew: he could see a never-ending surge of phantom soldiers scrambling over the embankments along the railway, to certain death, for no purpose. Heaps of bodies, the legs and boots sticking out of the mud. At the *wordsacommarnd!* That was what Miffin's thumb meant: the capacity of one man to gain submission from another, and employ him destructively, for the ends of class or political power.

'Never thought of it that way, eh?'

Miffin spoke more kindly. He could see that the young man was feeling depressed, away from the manic camaraderie by which they sustained their morale in camp.

'Never as bad as it looks. After all, you're getting where you wanted. Might be out there in the Desert, diggin' 'oles, in the bloody pioneers, like my brother. No choice mate. We're all right. It'll get better after the first six weeks. Sandhurst is smashing: forty-eight every week, fortnight in Wales, off in trucks on TEWTS and camps all week. Right out of the sods' way. Christ, we don't get operational for another eight months. You'll survive till then. Unless you work a sticky-bomb up your arse or something.'

'Or get R.T.U-ed.'

'Ah, well, then you've had your lot. P.B.I., pioneers, f'sst! Ogh! Stiff and cold the week after. S'only a matter of time. But I shouldn't bloody moan if I was you.'

The passing Surrey woods had grown bleak under Miffin's perspectives of Army life, and his sardonic view of the odds of survival. For a time Paul tried to lift him out of it.

'What're you going to do after the war?'

Miffin clicked his teeth.

'Women.'

'No, I mean seriously.'

'Never thought about it, chum.'

The plump little man's whole allegiance was to the Army.

'What about you?'

'I want to get back and work.'

'Work?'

'Get my degree.'

The sergeant made a jeering noise.

'Geer! You students never did a bloody day's work in your life!'

Paul gave up. Miffin's so very artificial teeth seemed to him offensive now, expressing stupid prejudice, and a kind of pig-headed contempt for everything he valued. Yet, he could not forget how much Miffin was a boon in the next bed, even for his brusque and waspish camaraderie, even for his irritating chaff. But he was glad when Miffin got out and marched away with his shiny-capped boots and his white kit bag with the long number stencilled on it. Yet after the man was gone, and he was alone among a carriageful of strange damp Air Force men and strange soldiers from other units, he felt worse, without even the Blackmoor chaff to support him. To his dismay he realized how much it now meant to him already, the banter of the squad, the backchat and mythology of the Blackmoor squad, squad 14B – even their mutual hatred of the monstrous MacAllcane. It was his life! Yet how much of it could he relate to Lucy or anyone else in the world outside without boring them? He shrank to think that his life had become this, a few blunt catchphrases of repartee, and squad anecdotes, to relieve a drab version of prison existence. Yet he was already, he knew, deeply attached to the Army itself, even to all its authoritarian and cruel paternalism, even to the most senseless aspects of its routine.

After a while, reflecting on what he had been through, he began to feel proud of himself. Then, at last, glad to dull his mind to the turmoil of the upheaval of his young life, and in the stale air of a compartment exhausted by the breath of packed servicemen, he fell into that comatose sleep of a million soldiers, in a thousand trains, of any day in the war.

*

Paul walked to the theatre from Amersham station to freshen himself up, in the rain, his heart beating. He hoped the show was over, and Lucy was free. The little town, even in the black-out, seemed homely and friendly to him, the shops and buildings hugging one another in the darkness along the main street, showing here and there a warm chink of light through the window screens. So different from the grim bare wastes of Blackmoor! Yet something disturbed him, about the untidiness, the friendly muddle of the little old town. Already a soldier, out in Civvy Street he felt insecure and clumsy. He got lost, couldn't find the theatre and became irritated. He began to feel ridiculous in his heavy boots, clattering on the invisible wet pavements.

At last he found the theatre, the foyer entrance painted white and black, with large photographs of the actors and actresses, framed on the walls. There was one of 'Lucy Selby', but he hardly recognized her: the rather bad studio portrait emphasized a crease-line along her neck, and the crimped effect of her dark Jewish hair. Besides, the pose was so artificial, so calculatedly languishing, with a ham halo effect in the shadows behind. He stood there hating it, and was a little frightened by its publicity gambit. He took in that Lucy was an actress, and wanted to be a successful actress: she had this other life, on which he would impinge less and less. He had half a mind to turn away, and take himself off, out of her way. He looked round, the rain falling softly about him – soft curtains of gentle rain-mist. The town was silent, except for one unseen car, following the dim light from its headlight suppressors, going down the hill. He was tired, and wanted to go to bed. Yet he could only go to bed with Lucy. He shrank from the effort he would have to make between now and then, to find her again. He could feel in his thigh pocket the stiff paper of her letters on which he had lavished so much love: it would have been easier to go to bed with the letters. But Lucy was a real woman, living her own creature life, and, though he had come so far, he was afraid to meet her, let alone spend his first night with her, only an hour or so away now. Paul quailed. He felt sadly unprepared.

He was disturbed in his reverie by sounds of applause within: the first half of the show had ended. A door opened, and the applause grew loud: then it banged shut again, and a man's voice said, 'Jolly *good!*' A curly-haired young man leaned in at the door of the ticket office, talking to the girl inside.

'Never have thought they could do it.'

'It's all home-made, you know, the whole panto. Cheers you up, don't it?'

'No doubt about it. I died, mostly.'

The man guffawed. The show was a kind of revue-panto-mime written by the company themselves, called *Why Do*

Women Leave Home? They had put it on before Christmas so that the theatre could be closed for the holiday. The posters were cheerful amateur daubs: Paul found them embarrassing. After Christmas, said a notice, they were going to do *Thunder Rock*, *Johnson Over Jordan*, *Ten Little Nigger Boys*, an evening with *Rope* and other thrillers, and *The Seagull* again, 'by special request'. It was all very much provincial rep. Paul inwardly felt it was untidy and ill-organized, tatty, really, in a way he inwardly despised.

Paul asked nervously for Miss Selby. The girl in the ticket-office was a thin girl with glasses, just out of sixth form, the kind who is chosen in provincial towns to sit in ticket offices to lure customers, by smiling at the world going by, as if on the threshold of some great life-adventure. She beamed at Paul, in a somewhat studied way, but warmly.

'She's backstage, I expect. Would you like to go round? It's down the passage to the left – a door half-way down. Mind the dustbins – and I think there's a plaster saint, rather going to pieces, I'm afraid.'

'Like me, dear.'

The curly youth took up his flirtation with the ticket girl, and Paul stumbled round to the passage in the rain. He found himself smiling, beginning to unwind a little, to soften into the old feelings, of student relaxation. Yes, that was *him*, not the taut and disagreeable soldier. As he did relax, he felt strangely unfamiliar at once, with the rough collar of his battledress blouse, the thick issue socks, and the clattering boots. But the girl and the wavy young man had smiled at him happily, melting his raw feelings of disparagement of 'civvies'. Up to that moment, he had seemed to have forgotten, in only a few weeks in the Army, how people in the outside world could be gay and kind to one another, without great effort. He already found it unfamiliar, to be among a life in which there was no destructiveness to maintain, by the malice and anxiety of 'good discipline'.

He found the stage door, and climbed up concrete steps through a blanket black-out curtain. On the back of the stage he could see Lucy, dressed to go out, in a white raincoat, laughing and gesticulating with two of the other actors. He felt faint with joy as he saw her small active body moving, and her shapely legs, in stockings for him. She really existed. And she loved him. He clumped forward in his clumsy boots, still carrying the holdall.

'Or you could do that,' said Lucy, twisting her hand round and round in an elaborate gesture of courtesy.

'Bit stagey, don't you think?' said a dark clownish little man.

'Oh, Solly, yew are *awful*,' said Lucy, in peals of laughter, skipping about, and gripping her lapels, pretending to hide her face in them. She seemed so full of vitality: he caught the zest of the young woman he loved. After the long painful period of barbarity and the abrupt change to barrack life he began to recollect the atmosphere they shared, and his heart began to swell.

Solly noticed Paul, and nodded.

Paul went rigid with embarrassment in his new squaddie uniform: he couldn't think how to look. He looked ashamed, then pleased.

'There's a soldier,' Solly added.

Lucy looked, didn't recognize him. It was a painful second. Paul thought, it's not true she loves this man, in this dress, not me. Uncertain what to do, he took his beret off. Lucy recognized him and laughed, with astonishment, and gladness. She had expected him: but not so changed.

'It's *my* soldier. It's Paul. They've made him a soldier. Oh, darling, *darling*, what *have* they done to you?'

She ran and put her head on Paul's battledress blouse and hugged him. She wanted to be a little theatrical in front of her theatre friends. But it didn't turn out like that: she burst into real tears of joy. Paul softened and held her. It was all right: it

71

was 'them' again. Forgetting the others were watching he held her head tenderly with his hands, and said brokenly,

'Hello.'

Then she held up her face with a wet tear on each cheek and he kissed her. The woman's soft warm lips were a benediction. He felt his body, taut and bruised, relax in a delicious calm. His stiffness and his raw arrogance melted. The other two men were silent with envy, and with some anxious curiosity. Young men not yet called up were both fascinated and afraid of the service life, its regimentation, and its alien ways.

The lovers broke away and sniffed, and grinned. The others were all a little embarrassed, and quiet, fascinated. Then a little party began. They clubbed together and sent a call boy out for beer. Lucy called everyone in the theatre, 'Darling!' and they darlinged back: but though they were all devastatingly bright and theatrical, they had the artist's respect for emotion. The moment between Paul and Lucy was a life drama for them. They wanted to celebrate, even in stout, that in the middle of war, the lovers were alive and their love beautiful.

Lucy and Paul watched the second half of the Christmassy show from the gallery. Some of it was very amateur, in the writing, the music, the acting and the production. But Paul had never felt such total enjoyment since he was a child, as they sat side by side on the shabby red plush-covered seats of the little rep, with its rather gimcrack stage fittings, all patched curtains with untidy wires protruding. He was so glad to be with Lucy that he wanted to find everything in her life radiant and good. So he watched the show without further impulse to be critical. He laughed uproariously, especially at some of the gags the young actors had invented for themselves. Solly had a scene with a large stove very obviously painted on a back-cloth: he was a kind of comic palace steward. Every time he put his hand on a painting of a stove he would make a sizzling noise with his mouth and shake his hand as if he had burnt it. At this Lucy's eyes shone and she went off into peals of laughter, and Paul joined her, turning to watch her profile in laughter with the pretty crowsfeet at her eyes. From time to time he drew her to him and kissed her behind the ear, in her nape, loving the quality of translucence in her flesh.

She told him about everyone and how funny they were, and how some of them must have a great future. Then the audience sang songs with the cast, old Victorian songs:

When she left the village she was pure:
But when she came back
Alas! and Alack!
Her . . . golden hair was hanging down her back . . .

Afterwards Lucy and Paul went backstage to say how much they'd enjoyed it. The actors, half in pantomime coats and half in underclothes, were excited and ebullient. There was much warm chatter in the light of the rows of bare bulbs round the mirrors, and much more darling-ing in the stale smell of grease-paint and blending powder, the stale theatre odours that always excited him, with their suggestion of a world of rich sophistica-tion, somewhere. At last, all the bottles of stout were empty, and Lucy and Paul went off. The cast bowed and waved them away, with great warmth and a joy in the love of lovers, un-poisoned by envy. It was rather like a wedding.

Paul and Lucy walked secretly in the mists of unseen rain down to the Crown, as if in a dream. They were so entirely 'us' now that there was no problem about falsifying their names in the Visitors' Book. The anguish of being strangers had all vanished.

It was wonderful to bath in the ample hot water of a good hotel, and to sink between the sheets of the large soft sprung bed. It was good to feel the long hours of seclusion before them, the first night either had slept all night with a lover. It was a marvel to be in love, and in bed together, and to be young, and free, even if it was only for forty-eight hours. As he stretched in the bed, waiting for Lucy to come back from the bath, Paul felt as if he had awakened from some long and deathly illness, some interminable coma of dullness in body and mind. He flexed his naked body like a young animal, voluptuously, and felt almost overwhelmed with the creature life in himself. Paul dived to Lucy's small soft breasts in the ample bed: he was enthralled by the exquisite suppleness of her small naked body in the deep warm spaces of the bed. The first time their love was quickly over. But, after a sleep, waking again, he found for the first time the true country of love, the dark deep forest of unknowing where love rides on and on, far, far beyond awareness or thought, beyond what can be called delight or even ecstasy. He found himself in the country of experience which one knows only in great pain, perhaps in birth, perhaps approaching death, in which the mind, suspended, can only survey in amazement the mindless depths of life in the flesh. As he rode Lucy's body on and on towards fulfilment he felt his soul wandering in the grey halls of love, gazing wonderingly around at the soft cliffs and chasms of the total loss of self.

In the sunny morning he woke to study the bold and vigorous wall-paintings from Tudor times, heraldic and magnificent above the head of the bed. A maid in a brown uniform and with a sidelong look brought tea, and Paul woke Lucy to drink it. She yawned and smiled, and then began to bubble with happiness, and act for him.

'I must pour, I must pour. . . . Do you take saccharine? Oh, I mustn't say that downstairs. They'd think I 'ardly knew you dear!'

She gave a long bubble of laughter, and put her thigh across Paul's. They sat naked, his shoulder to her breast, sipping their tea. Then they bathed, and dressed. Paul put on the civilian clothes he had brought in a holdall. They felt weak, slight and insubstantial, walking on air. Then, a little awkward, they went down to breakfast. Bafflingly tongue-tied, among the strangers at the other tables, they smiled at one another, a little sadly, as they had once, so long ago it seemed, in her

74

college room, when they had first made love. But after the first
cup of coffee from the white-metal pot, on whose bright surface the mist of steam came and went, all Lucy's theatre-
trained self-possession came back. She bubbled again with
cheeky vivacity, and was expressive with her hazel eyes and
her curled black lashes. She allured Paul by wrinkling her
freckled nose. She enjoyed being wicked. She was young and
lovely, and she revelled in it.

They spent their two days in a world of their own, enclosed
and apart in their love spell. Without speaking much, they
walked about in mackintoshes in the showery weather, following paths into fields and woods where the trees were now bare,
softly clinging to one another, sleepy and entranced.

Paul sucked every vestige of joy out of each hour of this
first freedom. The fine fans of the forms of bare trees spread
and spread above them live veins against the sky as they walked
arm in arm in the soft rain. The feathering growth spoke of
the meaning of existence, of the continuing shoots of living
things searching out towards the atmosphere of the sun, expressing, in their tentative irregularity, each a unique pattern of
significance. Each tree had its finely searching life. Paul recaptured what he had felt as a small boy, a sense of at-oneness
with the natural world, a cosmic song of which he was one
burden, a great joy in all creation, from the grass-roots to the
topmost fans of the elms. And from time to time he kissed
Lucy's rainsweet face, and her orange-flecked eyes, brooding
solemnly, as they were, on the secrets of their night.

*

When he reached the barrack room on the Sunday night
after a tedious journey in a dim train, Paul looked round,
astonished. There was the bare floor, as bright as a beetle's
back, and the bare ugly room, cold and prison-like. There was
his hard iron bed, with the coarse rough blankets, brown and
hairy, one among thirty others, ranged against the olive drab
walls. Men farted and belched down the stairs in the noisy

75

concrete lavatories. In the beds some snored, others joked loudly and vulgarly. Even the warm-hearted Miffin galled him.

'You don't want to just stand there looking shagged, old mate: you want to kip down in that wanking pit and get ready for tomorrow. We shall cop out, by Christ.'

It seemed impossible that the sweet bed of his love, and this coarse prison where men shouted their continual obscenities, should be part of the same life. How could one bear to go from one to the other?

*

By the early summer of 1943 Paul Grimmer changed his green shoulder lanyard for a red one, to indicate that he was in the last stage of his training to be a tank officer. Gunnery, wireless, tank maintenance – all these had occupied a month's instruction each, in the early part of the year. He had spent days on the Norfolk coast, his face stung and scorched by cordite flames, firing the 75 mm. tank gun at targets along the cliffs, the dust whipped up in clouds in front of the tank, the tracer-lit projectiles bouncing faintly away on the grey sea. He had hummed about the woods in Surrey in the back of a fifteen-hundredweight truck, practising call-signals and 'netting' frequencies with a penny, slotted in the screws of the No. 19 short-wave radio set. He had struggled with the great crow-bars used to tighten the caterpillar tracks of tanks, on bitter winter mornings when the icy steel stuck to the hands. He learned to drive four kinds of tanks – the English Covenanter, Valentine, and Churchill, and the American Sherman. Often they drove through scrubwood, the small trees falling away under the thirty-ton armoured vehicle, smashed by its advance, looking like dividing waves through the periscopes. He was wiry and fit – could run five miles at a good pace through the scrublands, and could wield a sledge-hammer, axe and shovel with efficiency.

In Army language, he 'took a pride in his appearance', and

found a satisfaction even in his marching. He even found exciting the monthly Passing-out Parade, on which the whole OCTU went on parade as a Battalion, marching and countermarching, and coming to a halt with a startling bang on the big drum to the fifteenth beat of *Lillibullero*, when 'advancing in review order'. Then, the emerging subalterns would slow-march up the steps of the classical façade to the old building at Sandhurst, as if they were going to their own funeral, which, in truth, they often were. At the end, the Adjutant would ride his white horse up the steps and into the building after them, dropping turds behind him. The horseman could just squeeze into the corridor by the Fancy Goods Shop, which sold hot sausages to the hungry cadets at break times. It was all something of a circus, the Royal Armoured Corps OCTU.

Paul felt, in his body, tremendously alive. No other experience in his youth had made him feel so full of animal energy, except the wilder days of his boyhood, at ten or twelve, when he had roamed the woods and fields from morning to night. But, in his mind and feelings in himself, he grew increasingly dead. Insidiously, the tank training replaced every interest in life with its own preoccupations and excitements. At first, it had seemed foolish to care which troop won the cross-country, or which instructor's group made the best show at target-practice. Sullenly, Paul's independent student spirit refused to embrace Sandhurst, its obsession with trifles of 'smartness', its worked-up morale commanding specious loyalties: but in the end he acceded. Competitive impulses that would have seemed childish to the student won the soldier over, and he put in extra work, cheered, strained and exulted with the rest. Gradually he submitted his independent self to the Royal Military College, and his scruples sank low within him. A crude animal energy took the place of his more tender feelings, and he came to despise the soft life of those outside the barrack walls, those whose trousers were uncreased, who did not 'belong' to the khaki squads, and who did not carry a pistol at the belt.

It was finally at Battle School that he discovered with a shock that his contempt for the tender life extended even to his relationship with Lucy. The drag of emotional ties: the way the woman would drain your strength, and soften you! He disliked the way love could wound you, by the lapse into softness, the painful flow of deep feelings in the body. It brought back those fears for the future which harsh training had suppressed, and which the excitement of exercises on beaches and in woods seemed to assuage.

The R.A.C. OCTU Battle School was at Capel Curig, among the Snowdon hills in North Wales. The cadets lived in a youth hostel which the army had taken over, crammed with beds in the bare rooms, the lodging deliberately plain and the rations hard. Before this last fortnight of field training the cadets were given a forty-eight hour leave. Paul had spent this with Lucy, staying with friends in Cambridge, in a ramshackle house out at Chesterton. But nothing had gone right; he was tense and hard, braced for the last ordeal of his training, impatient even with the hours of his leave.

Lucy could not understand his restlessness. On each leave together they had yearned for the furlough hours to linger, and lay awake through the night, unhappy to hear the chimes marking away the time of each 'thirty-six' or 'forty-eight'. But this time Paul was on edge, and seemed to come to her unwillingly. He seemed to caress her resentfully, and merely out of habit. Her body seemed to him a weak and childish thing. When she turned to him questioningly in bed, puzzled by his abstraction, he rejected her. He was repelled by her mood of beseeching. Her body seemed to him to have an unwholesome pallor, while his was all warm, active and tense. She found it hard to arouse his desire, and when she tried to wake him in the dawn, he would not, but turned over and clung to his sleep. So it was, all the week-end. He was keeping his strength for the mountains. They parted, shattered and puzzled: all the meaning and joy had gone from their being together. The friends with whom they were staying, a bearded young chemist and his genial wife, unwittingly made things worse. They never left them alone, but chatted away chirpily all the time, in pleasantries. But the lovers sat glum and miserable.

Lucy came to the station, as usual, to see him off. At the last moment, in her white raincoat, she became a woman, in all the fullness of her young femininity, as a girl can, in misery, drawing on all her powers to deal with her life, suddenly aware that she is alone, and must make her own life alone. Paul had climbed into the train and was leaning out of the window. This time they were not clinging, sleepily, as they used to do. Paul was already – and gladly – hundreds of miles away.

'Paul . . . I'm sorry it has been so . . . bad.'

'Bad? I didn't think it was bad. What do you mean?'

His voice was ill-tempered and clipped, and he looked away.

He bridled, wanting to deny the difference between what was between them now, and what had gone before. In doing so, she saw, he wanted to deny their love altogether. The train was only pausing: how much dare she say? After all, he was going away, to war, or something very like it: her eyes came up to him in a last soft plea, the speckles in her irises very vivid.

'I hope you enjoy the Battle School. I'm sorry . . . that's not quite what I meant . . . I suppose I meant . . . I hope you . . . survive it.'

'Oh, I'll survive it!'

'Don't be so cold to me, Paul.'

To his irritation, that she should express tender fears for his safety, and thereby 'undermine' him (as he put it to himself) there, under the red and green signal lights glowing on the steam, this remark only provoked deeper resentment. Survive! One didn't allow such gravity of feeling. He looked at his watch, wishing the train would go. Suddenly there was a scream in his ears, a high piercing note that seemed to him to come from the depths of Lucy's misery, and pierce his, clearing the hard, pent-up rejection that hid his tenderest depths and

79

fears. The inward needs that he was seeking to strangle met hers, for an instant; at the same instant it was too late – the scream was the guard's first whistle. Paul passed his hand over his face, and gave a miserable smile. Lucy's heart leapt: it was the first soft look he had given her since he had arrived in Cambridge on the Saturday.

'I'm sorry,' Paul brought out, hoarsely.

The girl put her hands tenderly on each side of his face, and kissed his eyes. Her cheeks against his were slithery with tears. His voice broke and he murmured softly and quickly in her ear, among her hair.

'It had to be like this. Perhaps one day . . . a longer time . . . we could . . .'

The whistle blew again. They spoke no more, but gave up the rest of the time to a long parting kiss, salt with tears, and the bitterness of realization, that this was the beginning of the end between them. Oh, the softness of her hands, and the lovely familiarity of the movements of her arms as she waved to him, as the train drew out, leaving the small white figure weeping under the coloured signals!

But that was not life now. This was life, thought Paul Grimmer, as he topped a crest in the Glydyrs, the sweat running into his eyes. Strapped to his back was the blunt barrel tube of a two-inch mortar, and a cartridge parcel of three bombs. He wore his steel helmet and pouches, and carried a light Sten sub-machine-gun. His feet were wet through, and sore with broken blisters. The valley up which they had come had been walking ground, but there had been long steep banks, tiring and often boggy, and a good deal of slippery rock. At the most precarious places hidden instructors had exploded small charges, or fired over their heads with machine-guns, the concussions echoing prodigiously round the mountain valleys.

But they hardly noticed these impingements: every effort of attention went into finding the next foothold, and urging the body upwards, clutching at tufts of wiry grass here to help over a rock edge, or crawling up tilted rock, where there was no other passage. Sweat ran from under the rim of the lining of their steel helmets, and under the rough collar of the battle-dress blouse, where it chilled under the rub of serge. A mass of sweat chilled in the small of the back, while other warm slithery patches made the cloth drag, at shoulders and thighs. Flies from the mountain sheep hovered maddeningly before their eyes and nostrils.

Yet every ridge brought a fresh vista, the cloud shadows lying over the green and blue patterns of the valleys. The clouds came like soft curtains, dragging over the sharper top-peaks, bare and sometimes foreboding as the vapour darkened them. At last, they could see the sea, with the great smoothed hills undulating down to it, a great metallic path to the horizon shining beneath the afternoon sun.

On another exercise they set out across the lakes by Capel Curig, Llynnau Mymbyr, in an assault boat, rowing towards the wooded slopes on the flanks of Moel Siabod. They had instructions to assault the hill. As they rowed a range officer fired a Bren gun at them from the road. This was to give them their first experience of coming under close fire. The day was bright and breezy, and the lake cheerful with ripples: it was good to be out among the hills and alive. Paul was in a platoon with Miffin, who had been with him all the way through Sand-hurst, and a young man called Dowsett, a large fair boy.

'Keep your head down, chum,' shouted Dowsett, who was rowing.

'They get an allowance for casualties,' shouted Miffin. 'Five per cent. We're expendable, see, so you want to watch out.'

'Anything that's got your name written on it . . .'

'He looked a nervous sort of bloke,' said Paul, 'the one with the gun.'

'Brewed up in Africa,' said Miffin, trying to rattle them, 'like this here.'

Showing his teeth in a grin, clicking, Miffin shook his hand as if in palsy. They laughed, out in the boat in the middle of the lake now.

'Quy-at!' hissed Miffin. 'We're supposed to be surprising the bloody enemy.'

It all seemed a joke. But tension mounted, as they crouched in the green boat, of folding wood and canvas, not knowing what to expect, the paddles plashing quietly on the lake. Paul remembered what happened when he first fired a Bren gun himself, in the STC at Cambridge, at the Barton Road Range. He had fired from the hip, and the heaving and pulsing gun had forced itself back on him, driven by its own gas blasts, heeling him over. He had fallen on his knees, and had been bowled over backwards. Red lights had shot away over the hill at the back of the range, into Madingley Village. And yet, in his panic, he couldn't let go of the trigger, until the magazine was empty, and the frightened instructor could wrest the smoking gun from his grasp. That was at the beginning: it was just before the time he had first made love to Lucy. He began to daydream, of the red leaves on the wet pavements outside her college, as he parted from her, the first time, after . . .

His dreaming vision was sliced by lines of red light, only an inch or two off the end of the boat where he crouched. At the same time someone seemed to be boxing his ears, and a series of painful blows went through his head. Afterwards there was a pumping noise, afar off, as of a distant gun, and then echoes, and soaring whines, as the bullets ricocheted off the surface of the water. There was a stunned silence, then a mutter of expletives and oaths. The oars worked faster: with frightened faces the cadets crouched lower. So ruthless, the noise of the projectiles – so destructive the power in the air, tearing towards them. Their eardrums were bruised. Their faces bristled with the savage brutality of the noise of the close racing steel. Then it came again, with further bursts. Do something! Do something, their inward field trained voices urged them: but there was nothing they could do, except curse and crouch in fear.

And now, as the boat approached to within a hundred yards of land, the shore banks broke into plumes of flame and smoke, as charges were exploded. Again, the pain in the ears, the bristling skin, the stunning fear and the cursing resentment.

But then, afterwards, as they panted up the hill, it became fun. All good clean sport, even assaulting the sheer slopes on the other side. They formed up at a crest, and began to march across the main road, up a valley, towards the Glydyrs, where they were to spend the night in a ruined farmhouse, using their own resources to make them comfortable. It was all a holiday, really: good fun. Yet for the first moment under fire in the boat they had heard, in the ruthlessness, the voice of death, and had a little bitter taste in the mouth, now, of what, soon, they were in for. There was something a little too grim about the actual hurtling steel.

Next, however, came the waterfalls with their glistening rocks and spume: the ferns in the gullies as they made their way up the bed of the stream: the empty vales, echoing with bleating sheep-calls, vastly indifferent as the night came down. Then an early wash in a stream, and on again, in dew-soaked battledress, drying as the sun came over the mountain shoulders. Finally another triumphant vision of the sea, and hills — mountains all round, brown and clean, with a dozen blue lakes on their laps, or in the woody crevices between them. They sang on the mountain tops, calling to the echoes.

Paul exulted in the clean vigorous life, the effort, the danger, even the long route tramp back, along the bleak Llanberis Pass road, checking the long procession of telegraph posts off, one by one. He felt alive more than ever before, and with his lungs bursting with mountain air, he found himself in contempt of the soft life of home, and of Lucy and Cambridge. Untidy, lazy, slack students and such people! Whenever he remembered Lucy, turning pleadingly to him in bed or at Cambridge station, he felt resentment at the mess, of all those tender feelings, and the life of man and woman. The woman, meeting you from her inward needs for love and security! Hopeless! She would sap your energy! The woman's body, with its slow slow need to be aroused, and its odours, clinging round you! He thought of that other life suddenly even with distaste, as he counted the telephone poles along the interminable mountain road, his feet, throbbing with pain, going pace to pace like unthinking and insentient creatures with an automaton volition of their own.

*

Later, in September, Paul joined a tank regiment, the East Northshire Yeomanry, training up in Forres, near Inverness, in the north of Scotland. Soon, the regiment would run its Sherman tanks on to the flats of a train, and shift to the assembly areas near the ports of southern England, for the invasion of France, Operation Overlord. He was a one-pipper now, a second lieutenant, absorbed in his work. He had been trained as a mines and explosive expert, and had to train all the three hundred tankmen in the Regiment to use explosive, and to detect mines and booby-traps. The nervous strain of seeing that no soldier dropped a grenade, or handled sensitive explosives roughly, told on him. He feared the troopers' clumsinesses, and their indifference. He feared most that a man might blow his jaw off by crimping a detonator with his teeth: it had been done elsewhere, he knew. He invented night exercises in which men crawled through woods, de-fusing dummy mines as they went. If the tankmen blundered at the tricky fuses, big charges would go off in the banks alongside, covering them with a rain of earth and stones.

He became enclosed in his devotion to the exacting tasks of preparation for the invasion. He became absorbed, too, in the stag pack of young officers. He had become careless about writing to Lucy long ago, and she wrote back as carelessly, often only telling him a little of the parts she played, and people she had met. She gradually dropped 'I love you' and wrote 'love, Lucy'. They had sunk to a level of friends, hardly with the air of being even former lovers. Paul seldom thought of her at all.

Then one day she wrote only, 'Yours, Lucy'. It had been inevitable: but he gazed at the letter suddenly thunderstruck. The concept of 'us' had been so much with him that he had never asked himself whether 'we' was still a living concept. The fact was that he had done nothing to court or claim Lucy for six months: he had simply taken her for granted, writing only a few desultory letters. He gazed out with shocked distaste at the wild Scottish landscape with its lines of dark conifers and dun multicoloured heath, and hated it for absorbing him so.

Lucy was in Cambridge that week-end. He asked for a 'compassionate' forty-eight, and found it could just be fitted in. He managed to get a sleeper on the train to London, and set off from King's Cross early next day, to face what inwardly he knew must be the inevitable last pain. She had sent a postcard in reply to his letter announcing his arrival. She said she 'might' be able to meet him 'for a while'. 'Might' – he suddenly saw the reality: he was alone. He had no woman. 'Us' was over. Their love was ended. He had lost her. He tossed in the hard train bunk all night to London in a chill fear of what he would find. Yet he knew.

He found a stranger. They met outside the Copper Kettle Restaurant in King's Parade for tea, and sat awkwardly in an upstairs room at one of the dark polished oak tables. Lucy wore her white raincoat over a brown suit. The familiar surfaces of white stone still rose across the street. Lucy was a little agitated and looked at her watch frequently. He saw a tenderness in her still, but it was no longer for him. They were reserved with one another, and inwardly Paul hated her. Lucy divined this, by her acute perception: something in her still responded to him, as happens between old lovers, and it frightened her. Paul looked a her familiar throat line in anguish, at the pale flesh of her body, with a hopeless sense that it would never again be given to him.

'I'm coming to work here in Cambridge,' she said, flatly.

'I'm sorry to have been so bad at writing.'

'It didn't matter.'

'We've been so busy. I've been training the whole regiment in explosives.'

'Was it dangerous?'

She said it without caring: there was no soft look of concern.

'I fell down a well once, that's all. And when I blew up an old armoured car the turret flew over the heads of the troops watching. Some of it went into the village. The kirk took it up and in the Sunday sermon the pastor said Forres had become like Sodom and Gomorrah, what with me and the regimental dances.'

Once Lucy would take such an incident up, and they would make delicious fun of it. Now she looked bored, and looked at her watch again. She wrinkled her crowsfeet at him: but it was no real smile. There was no sparkle. On her wrist was a bangle of Indian filigree work in silver.

'That's lovely,' Paul said, taking her wrist.

She drew her wrist away, coldly.

'Who gave you that?'

Despite himself his voice brought from the depths a dead undertone of hate. He knew, she divined.

She rose.

'Let's go. I have to meet . . . someone at his rooms.'

'Oh, really? Someone?'

Paul's voice was grim now.

Suddenly the real, living Lucy came through, and her face spoke to him for one moment as his Lucy, with sincerity in her eyes and on her tongue between the bright white teeth.

'It's no good, Paul. It's all over, between us. A long time ago.'

Her voice broke with the press of old emotions, the old love which could not be denied, even if it were dead.

Paul's head swam, to meet the truth at last, face to face with

86

his woman in the flesh, the pale translucent flesh. Their togetherness from the gold-touched autumn days with the dead leaves, flame-coloured, wet on the greasy pavements in Newnham, to the long warm Amersham nights, flashed past him like a rush of visions, precipitate. Could that be denied? Yet here was Lucy, as a stranger to him, denying it. She still wore the same white raincoat over her brown suit. He realized with a cold spasm of grief that she meant she had had another lover for some time.

They walked miserably down towards Trumpington Street. The end was to come sooner than he expected. Opposite the Gothic tower of the Pitt Press the door of a house opened and there stood Gabriel Gatz, the bearded gad-fly of the varsity *avant-garde*. Gabriel wrote portentously on modern writing, on Rilke and Kierkegaard. But he was already showing a nose for commercial entertainment: after the war he would promote 'pop' and write scripts for war films. Paul had heard that somehow Gatz had managed – perhaps because he was really unfit – to stay out of the Services. So – Lucy would have a man at home now, for every day. How fortunate, Paul bitterly sneered to himself. Gatz came out full of possessiveness, and took Lucy's arm with demonstrative affection.

'Gemini, darling, we must hurry – for the rehearsal.'

He gave a look of theatrical disdain at Paul.

'Hullo,' he said with venomous antipathy in his face.

'Gemini' was the little name Paul had used only in bed with Lucy, because of her uneven breasts, the unidentical twins. His jaw fell. To hear it in another's mouth revealed the terrible betrayal, of all that 'we' had been, when they had lived enclosed and apart in their own world as lovers. His head swam, as his body began to learn what had happened, in shock, with a wounding bitterness he had never felt before. He acted that he did not care: but yet he staggered, visibly, even in his uniform.

Lucy saw it and gave him one final poignant look, from her true self, of compassion, and saw the pity of it all, and of the betrayal. Not that she showed any doubt about Gabriel Gatz; she accepted the fat litterateur's embrace and showed herself glad to be with him. Paul's heart sank to be confronted so with the treachery of the emotions in the flesh, that can reduce a love so to ashes, as though it had never been. He felt a disgust at the way a woman's flesh can turn its polarity, like a magnetic field, and curl round a new lover, offering the cast-off man only cold negative repulsions – yet betraying to the new relationship even the secret little names.

Lucy saw what he felt, and suddenly broke for a moment from her new man's forceful possession, to run out to Paul. Her face again beautifully his, she kissed him tenderly, holding his hand tightly, and cried out loudly in the street, stamping her foot.

'Paul Paul! I'm terribly, terribly sorry. It was . . . all the time . . . I can't . . . you were . . . Paul, I'm *terribly* sorry.'

She went back with a woman's high animal cry of misery in a flood of tears to where Gatz bit at strands of his black beard and snorted angrily to himself.

'Oh Christ! The bright lieutenant!'

*

But it was not until he changed trains at Newcastle that Paul felt the final shock of separation: the truth took that long to sink in, bodily. He made the mistake of going out into the streets in the rain between trains, and there felt the raw truth of his predicament, a young man of twenty-one, done with home and girl, on the way to his first battle.

It was pouring, and the empty trams ground relentlessly along the wide wet cobbled streets. Huge lorries of coal or pig-iron growled and bellowed splashing through the streets. The buildings were dark, wet, black and unprepossessing. Ship superstructures could be glimpsed behind the great steel bridges over the broad Tyne. Steam and smoke blew across the dull wet view from time to time. The industrial north laboured on at the effort to make war: and Paul felt at one with it, even with

88

the rain dripping from the peak of his service cap, even with the wind driving the damp under his British warm. At least he confronted the war as a trained combatant, and a saucy young officer. The steps he took now, back to the station, were his first steps to the battlefield. He knew that. He was off.

But inside he was all stony with the deadness of loss. His body felt torn away from all the tender comforts of life, of home, an exile. The long brutalizing training, from nights on the bare slopes of Snowdon to the sweltering cruelty of the parade ground, these had dulled the flux of his feelings. They had made him thick-skinned, and able to withdraw his feelings at will, into an inner resistance. But yet at the soft centre there remained a youthful impulse to live, to love, to strike roots, create, and grow. Lucy and Gabriel had everything that he yearned for. They could begin life. That fat swine! Angry tears started to his eyes and a tram swam. A tram swam, he thought, and grinned miserably. Am I going crazy? But a soaked soldier passed, scowling, and gave him an insolently limp salute. Shall I pull him up? Oh Christ, no: I wish I could give up the whole thing to lie, disarmed, in peace, demobilized, free, in a field of warm meadow grass, as I did as a child.

He wept freely now, biting his lips. If someone sees! Well, God, even tank subalterns are human. The voices in his own heart made him sniff with laughter, the noise came like a sob. He went into a telephone box to recover, breathing in the damp and choking staleness of tobacco. Someone had been sick in the box long ago and the acid sweetness of vomit lingered. He thought he saw someone come to wait to use the phone, so he lifted the receiver to his ear and heard the mechanical burr with comfort. Now, let us pull ourselves together.

'Us' and 'me' and 'we'. He lingered on the words, a burning lump in his throat. His thoughts went back to Lucy's last letter, a chill over all the words. The terms, the 'we' and 'us', no longer there. Someone else had entered. Put all such tender thoughts from your mind, one voice within him had said to the other. This is the soldier's lot: the fellows at home keep the girls amused. But Lucy couldn't – not his Lucy? Not the woman of the 'we'?

This won't do, he said to himself as a too loud sob broke from him, like an animal sound in the stale air of the telephone box. The windows steamed up inside, and the rain rolled down the outside. He wanted his mother. He wanted comfort – the comforting hand, the soothing voice, the ease of bed, the happy laughter of togetherness. He wanted Lucy, the Lucy of 'we', that 'we' that walked in the rain in the woods near Amersham.

'O God, make it come back.'

But it never would. Perhaps never again would he know the comfortable ease of lying in gentle bed with a loved woman. Never again the clasp of arms and her legs ecstatically round your body! Never again the sweet morning eyes, a little ashamed, or the tentative shared breakfast. He had to swallow an absolute loss.

'That bastard has the lot.'

His own voice startled him, ringing a little between the concrete floor of the box and the steel frame of the telephone kiosk. Am I going mad? he thought. Is this what they call a mental breakdown?

Don't be a damn fool, he told himself. The girl will get married. She'll go through the whole gamut of Jewish betrothal and marriage, top-hats and all. All the mumbo-jumbo. It's different. Be realistic: be happy for her. Be creative about it. She's chosen. You offered her nothing.

And in any case you didn't like her hair.

He grabbed at this. It was true. Even at the sweetest moments, he had disliked Lucy's crimpy Jewish hair. It never became loose and fine and languid. It was always crimped in tight bushy dark wodges, like horsehair in a mattress. One could never run one's fingers through it.

Thank God. Here was an element of rejection he could

cling to: he strove at the image, and brought himself round to a little self-possession. He had after all made his choice months ago, in a café after the Passing Out ceremony. It was then he had been presented with the possibility of marrying her. He had shown he didn't want that. It was not the actual girl, he told himself but the whole ease and intimacy of civilian life for which he wept. Damn the woman for dragging me down to this soft weakness of body and mind.

Paul mopped his eyes, and his face, and looked in the small kiosk mirror, disgusted with himself. What did he come here for? A good snivel?

He looked at his watch. He felt sick now, and in pain.

His train was due to leave in ten minutes. A tram was slowing round the long bend in the dull rain. He ran out of the phone box and boarded it hazardously, slipping on the wooden step.

'Ye shud not due that,' said the conductor, half sternly, half concernedly, in the Northern way, grim and yet humane. And he hauled Paul up into the interior where cloth-capped workers and damp soldiers sat in rows on the dark varnished seats.

'Blam! Blam!' The tram slewed and gathered speed up the long cobbled track to the station, the granite setts bright with rain.

The dull metallic gong was like a signal. Seconds out of the ring! Paul felt himself dedicated to the world of clangorous metal, of combat. The next round! The rhythmic swaying of the tramcar, its acceleration, its purring grinding onwardness soothed him. He was ashamed now of his clinging: his skirt-clinging. He completely rejected his yearning for the tender softness of a woman's company. Now he wanted only the other directed purpose – to be a servant of the large destructive machines with men in war. He wanted it to begin – the work for which he had been trained. If he wanted a woman – well, he could have one in some French brothel. The release of passion: that was nothing. The personal involvement, the caring about

91

real relationship – it was that that was too painful, too cloying. That bright young time of boyhood was gone for ever. He rejected it. If he survived . . . well: one way or the other, that was not to be thought of. The likelihood was that he would not. He hoped not, he swore. So there was only death to be served, and the clinging weakness of relationship would only be a hindrance.

'Blam! Blam!'

He was glad it was all over. The tram ground shuddering to a halt. He ran into the station.

He found companionship in the warmth of the railway compartment and the purposiveness of his journey on to Forres. Through the rain-streaked misted window, criss-crossed with anti-blast lace, he watched the subdued northern spring swing past. The last leave was over. He was on his way to 'Overlord'. He looked at the middle-aged man opposite in a grey pin-stripe suit reading *The Scotsman* – did he know about 'Overlord'? Probably not: Paul only knew himself because he had been called in to advise on a scale model of a section of coast at a 'top secret' conference. But the soldiers crowding into the corridor outside the first-class compartments, squatting on their kitbags, knew what was coming: everyone had been for embarkation leave that spring.

By the time he reached his regiment, in his excitement about Overlord, he had forgotten Lucy again.

D–I

THEY HAD PLENTY of time to reflect on the hugeness of the undertaking: the first few days of that June were cold and rough, a disastrous gale. At times Overlord seemed doomed with all its 180,000 men. Whatever would happen if the thing failed! There'd be no chance of mounting the Second Front again that year, surely?

Paul's Squadron embarked on its Landing Ship Tank late on the 3rd June. They were scheduled to sail on the 4th, but the whole enterprise, as the world knows, was put back for twenty-four hours.

This delay at the last moment in the wintry weather, off the Isle of Wight, made them all glum and depressed. There seemed no break in the sequence of depressions coming in from the Atlantic. As they embarked there had been something like jubilation. But now spirits fell as they had nothing to do but study the heaving grey sea, and feel their precariousness, anchored out in deep water with all their tanks and crews down in the great hold, swinging below the ocean surface. For hours Paul watched the bubbling crests of waves rolling along the steel plates of the ship, from bows to stern, hissing and curling. Out in the vastness of the offshore water, the ship's metal sides seemed so thin, and the dark stormy sea so deep and unpredictable.

The South Downs inland were patched with dark cloud shadows and sea fog, as the grey scud moved brokenly across the sky. Here and there lurked battleships, grey-blue shapes in the haze, riding their anchor chains. Smaller hulks rested on leaden or glittering sea, along the shore round the mass of the Isle of Wight, their grim outlines broken by the cubist crazes of camouflage paint. The ships lay out, uncannily still, after so much bustle during the days before. On the Monday, the last blusters of the dismal summer gale waned a little. There were a few gleams, and the wind dropped. Would they go now? All was tense and still in the ships, as the wind murmured in corners of steel plate, in ventilators, and in cables of the rigging.

Paul looked along the shore to the west, fading away into the grey-blue gloom. He knew that something like three thousand landing craft were ready to move out of all the ports all along the coast, from Falmouth to Harwich. Five hundred warships

93

stood by them, ready to sweep channels free of mines, and to guard the flanks. All over England all aircraft, paratroops, and radar services waited, alerted, listening for code signals.

The Solent and the offing were familiar enough. They'd been out once before, in good weather, in April. They had loaded the tanks aboard ship and sailed over towards France, on a feint, 'Exercise Fabius', turning back in mid-Channel. Some had been convinced at the time that the sailing was the real thing, but they came back next day, to disembark at the Gosport hards. Then for weeks they had been enclosed behind fences, in security camps, in a great park at Petworth in Sussex. There, King George VI had come to inspect them, hundreds of men lined up in the park meadows. It was hot, and they had been badly bitten by midges on a sweltering May day. The small sad figure of the King, in general's uniform propped up in a tracked carrier, looked like a waxwork image. His face seemed brightened with cosmetics as he was propelled round with a posse of attendant brass-hats in red-ribboned caps behind. The midges seemed more real. Even Paul's colonel, a handsome county gentleman, was sceptical: 'The King came swanning in, lookin' as if he'd been to Lizzy Arden's. What?' he exclaimed, going off in incredulous guffaws.

But they knew now that Overlord was imminent, because all contact with the rest of England was suddenly cut off, and the regiment was shut behind guards and barbed wire fences. The assault was mounted; there was no going back. All the contents of the loading tables had moved in convoys and by train, hundreds of regiments, to assembly areas near the South Coast ports, in the rich countryside of Sussex and Hampshire. Stretches of meadows, of the downs, of woods, and of the back streets of towns were lined with shifting and buzzing troops and vehicles. Yet they had seen no bombing. The troops made their final preparations, welding, packing, tightening, greasing, loading, undisturbed, in the open air, in the spring sunshine.

Paul's regiment was due to land early on D Day. He had

94

joined them because they were experimenting with floating tanks – 'DD' amphibians – but in the course of the planning the East Northshire Yeomanry had changed to waterproofed tanks which were to be landed in shallow water direct from ships, at about five hours after H Hour, or H + 5 – as it appeared in the tables. The tanks were waterproofed by their crews, who were trained in sealing the steel underplates of the hulls with sticky cements and adhesive black rubber compounds. In hidden garages and hangars they lay under the machines working this caulking into the cracks between the steel plates with knives and screwdrivers. Then they tested their vehicles on the shores of Pembrokeshire, and in lakes concealed in wooded parks. The waterproofed tanks, designed to wade ashore from a hundred yards or so from the beach, had metal chimneys over their air intakes and exhausts. They could drive through six feet of rough water. When they had been driven out of the sea up on to the beach a charge was exploded from within, and the intake chimneys and sealing tapes round the guns were blown away by lashings of an explosive cable called Cordtex. The huge steel turret with its long 75 mm. gun, coaxially mounted with a machine-gun, could then be traversed and fired. All the waterproofing could be blown off in this way, while all the hatches were still down.

The Sherman tank was American. It weighed thirty tons, and was driven by a diesel engine of four hundred horsepower. It was a tall domed tank, with long flanks of steel plate, containing a crew of five. There was the crew commander who rode in the skull-like turret, standing with his head out between the flaps of the top hatch. The gunner sat inside on one side of the gun with his eye pressed to the rubber end of a telescope. Next to him in the fighting compartment was the loader who kept the gun supplied with ammunition from the racks inside. The gun fired large brass rounds, the projectile composite with the propellant casing, called fixed ammunition. These were stored in clips round the base of the turret and in the hull. Each was about as big as a man's arm, and had to be thrust by hand into the open breech. The feed-belts for the machine-guns were in boxes. The loader was also the wireless operator. Below, in the boat-like hull of the machine, were the driver and the co-driver beside him, the latter maintaining and firing a Browning .300 machine-gun, by himself, in the bows. The tank was driven along on two tracks of large steel plates, pulled over bogies by a sprocket. Besides all the private belongings and weapons of the men each tank carried about a hundred rounds of gun ammunition – armour-piercing shot, high explosive and smoke shells, and some bursting phosphorous shells. Then there were cans of water and diesel, cases of tins of food, boxes containing machine-gun belts, Verey pistols, tarpaulins, hand grenades, Primus cookers, a set of digging tools, drivers' tools, 'Homelite' battery charging motors, crowbars, spare bogies, short-wave radio sets and inter-communication telephones, and much else, stored away in bulkheads or lockers within, or lashed to the outside of the grey steel elephants. The tank commander spoke to his crew through a microphone: they all wore headpieces. The huge engines thundered so much and the tracks clattered and squealed so loudly, that it was useless to rely on the unaided voice for commands to the crew, even without the noise of battle. The same microphone connected the subaltern commanding each troop of three tanks by radio to his sergeant's and corporal's tanks, and also to squadron headquarters, by the turn of switches on the No. 19 set. This was a grey-painted short wave set, about as big as two biscuit tins. The fighting crew was protected by steel, nearly four inches thick on the turret front, two inches on the flanks – by no means enough, however, by the standards of German ballistics. In fact, the Shermans were very vulnerable, and the enemy called them 'Tommy-cookers'.

Each tank was an elaborate organization, and a stored hive of belongings. For this reason it was important that each man should be thoroughly trained and efficient in handling every machine and skilled in every routine. Thus the radio operator could always load the gun if need be, or the gunner could drive, if the driver was killed or hurt. And it was vital that everyone should be neat to the point of obsession for in such a tight organization, often with the lids closed down under shell-fire, or in a moment of panic, lives could be lost, if, say, a trooper's mess tin fell down and jammed the turret mechanism, so that the gun could not be turned on an enemy. Carelessness could even cause a blow-back from the gun or an internal explosion, and this might set off all the ammunition in the racks round the enclosed space of the fighting turret.

So the tank men were drilled in tidiness, and in meticulous routines. Everything must be instantly ready, and men in efficient regiments came to despise those in others who let their armour go filthy. A good regiment cherished its men above all. Paul knew his commanding officer's great quality was his unwillingness to take any risk so long as saving the lives of his men was compatible with the objectives he was given.

For Paul's regiment alone some seventy of these elephantine machines, each weighing thirty tons, had been loaded at the Gosport hards on to landing craft. Two squadrons embarked on 'landing craft tank'; Paul's on 'landing ships tank'. The former were smaller ships and were to run right up the beach. The bigger ships (LSTs) had doors which opened at the front, and from the space between the doors a drawbridge let down on chains. Both LCTs and LSTs rode forward on to the hards – the loading slopes – for embarkation, and the tanks tracked in backwards. But only the LCTs would run up on to the enemy beaches. The LSTs were to open their doors half a mile off-shore, and unload their vehicles on to large naval 'Rhino' ferries which would run in to the beaches. These ferries were to be towed over by the Navy.

At embarkation the great hall of each ship's hull filled with some sixteen tanks, the doors were closed, and in the semi-darkness men swarmed over the grey-green metal hulls, attend-

D

ing to wireless sets, to odd bogies or picks and shovels strapped on here and there to brackets on the hulls. Some of the tank-men had bunks in other compartments in the ships, while others slept in the narrow spaces between the vehicles packed in the hull. The tanks were carefully shackled by chains to big U-bolts on the decks, in case the crossing was rough, and the cargo was inclined to shift.

Waiting in the long queues of vehicles on their way down to the 'hards' had given the troops an elated holiday feeling. The process had gone on for a week, endless convoys of vehicles, decorated with green and yellow hessian nets, and aerial masts, flagged with unit insignia, had waited along the roads at all the southern ports of England, their engines ticking over, or silent, waiting. Out in the Solent small infantry assault craft, LCTs and LSTs, awaited them, some sporting barrage balloons against dive bombing. The marriage of the ships with their cargoes was the culmination of years of planning. There was little im-patience, but much expectancy. Fortunately, though the Ger-man radio spoke of troop concentrations, there was still no bombing: calculated deception had drawn enemy attention to Kent and Sussex. The serious-faced troops gathered along miles of suburban streets had been given cups of tea or news-papers by women in the semi-detached or terrace houses. They could say nothing: but there was no need. The crowded con-voys and the nervous excitement of the men were sufficient evidence. Everyone knew, and behaved in such a way as to convey, by their tense and solemn manner, that Overlord was imminent.

With much throbbing and halting of engines, bursts of the noise of bells and clatter of chains, Paul's LST had at last drawn away and anchored a mile or so offshore. On board the weary and excited troops ate a series of dull stews with plain bread in the mess decks with their plain deal shelves, suspended on chains, swinging as the ship rocked at anchor in the roads.

Then the grey cold gale had blown up, causing dismay and

perplexity. But there was nothing more the men could do. They felt a depressing sense of flop. They tried to rest, but were anxious and downcast. For the first time for weeks they could put their feet up, over tea and cigarettes, and knock off packing and loading. But they could not relax. Some luxuriated in washing and shaving thoroughly for the first time for days. Others were writing home busily. But these had to write 'APO Europe' on their letters, although they were just off the English shore, but this only emphasized the strange, tense state of limbo they were in.

Paul was phased with that portion of 'A' squadron riding in the LST as a spare officer, attached to number two troop, but riding in the troop leader's tank, as a co-driver with a radio connection to brigade HQ. He was also assisting with Unit Intelligence and had a special function in mine detection. At Gosport he had checked the stowage of the three tanks of the troop for the lieutenant in charge of them, Peter Dowsett. Dowsett had come to the East Northshire Yeomanry with Paul from Sandhurst. He was Paul's age, a hefty young man with a bony rugby-playing physique, and pale hairs growing out of his nostrils. He was one of those fit, amiable, efficient young men who have little or nothing to say, but communicate simply by giving off animal energy. Paul liked him, but could not suppose how it was possible to live, outside soldiering, with so little articulate identity.

At four o'clock on the afternoon of June 5th Paul went up on deck for a breather, and to see whether there was any break in the weather. He was glad to get above the blue diesel fumes of shifting tanks in the hold, away from the minutiae of loading tables and kit checks, and emerge into the clean damp sea air. The offing was still cold and grey. He surveyed the clean grey sweep of sea, mottled with broken shadows and a dull gleam of afternoon light. The ship was moored far enough away from the shore for the mainland to merge into a great natural form.

The haze of distance dissolved the rashes of nondescript development that spoils the landscape of the South Coast. There were thin blankets of smoke over the roofs of Gosport. The Downs loomed behind the shore. Here and there out at sea the water was running with light, sliding and sparkling beneath broken clouds. The fine definite straight blue edge of the horizon was clean and vast. Still hulks of anchored ships lay everywhere about the blue and grey of the moving water, with the breeze shadows gliding across it, among sporadic gleams.

How beautiful the world seemed at that moment! In a suspended trance Paul found himself looking at the features of sea and land as if outside time – not at 'Gosport' or 'the Solent', but masses of the earth's surface, the thin green skin over chalk, figured with straggling marks of human accretion, rising out of the eternity of the globe's formation. Around it the dark wrinkled face of the ocean was drawn out across the spherical surface of the globe. Above flew the gathered shreds of air and vapour, veined by thin gleams of sun. Everywhere lay the outlines of man-made moving forms, against the primaeval earth. This was existence! How lovely it was!

It was then that he suddenly saw the first small ships heading the long procession of the 'Overlord' flotilla, setting forth.

At once Paul looked at his watch. It was just after four o'clock. There was no doubt now – the line of little boats was moving. It was just a line of drab, small landing craft, with silver barrage balloons aloft, coming out in a long queue, at a snail's pace, into the heaving sea. At first he wondered what they could be doing. Were they shifting place for the night? Surely they weren't setting out to sea? Gradually the snaking progress turned towards the perfect ring of the horizon, under a still dark and lowering sky. No doubt about it now: they were making for the open sea, and for France.

The first files to move out looked pathetically small against the great stretch of sea, and the wide prospects of offing and shore. They were infantry landing craft, low in the water, olive drab in colour and shaped like open shoe-boxes with ramps at the bows to let down on the beaches. Each small vessel flew its own balloon and the open holds were covered with nets, knotted with coloured hessian, green, yellow and brown. Some seemed little bigger than life-boats. Aboard them men could be seen with steel helmets, also tufted with camouflage, crawling round to secure and trim the machines on board – armoured cars, field guns, cartons of explosive charges and gun ammunition. In some of the LCTs rode the DD swimming tanks and engineer tanks of the 79th Armoured Division to be landed to clear the first obstacles. The ships came out from Gosport in a long string, as regularly spaced as target ducks at a shooting booth, moving out into the open sea steadily, with slow audacity. More and more came on behind, towing their comic little silver fish above, like an uncanny water carnival.

The procession moved steadily away, and faded into the uncertain water of the Channel. The great historic moment was silent, a silent way of small boats. Everyone on the ship, it seemed, had now come up on board, but they did not cheer or wave. They stood stockstill, their faces solemn, fervent with wishfulness. The fingers of the assault looked so sparse and vulnerable – a procession of frail ducks, to be thrown against the Atlantic Wall. Nothing could stop the immense movement of 'Overlord' now. Out in the grey sea the awkward little craft endlessly bobbed, in long lines over the hissing and restless deep water.

After watching for an hour, Paul Grimmer felt still and numb. In another hour or so, they would go too. A nervous shiver went over his body, and he found he was clenching his teeth. This anchor-raising moment, he knew, whatever the outcome, was a dreadful moment in the war. It would always be known, recorded and written about, for those who had never known war, and even when war itself was no longer known.

Paul went down to the lower deck where sailors were dishing

out another tepid brown stew with chunks of bread on the mess tables, hung on chains. He went down the clattering steel companionway with Dowsett. He was nervous, Paul could see, and was glancing round with anxious curiosity. There was something like a charge of electricity in his pale bushy eyebrows. Yet his nervousness did not show itself in chatter, but rather in an animal excitement. In this mood, in games, Dowsett could be aggressive, and he would hurt people without meaning to do so. He would smash them over by a shoulder barge, out of sheer puppyish energy. Then, kindly as well as clumsy, he would be much concerned afterwards, nervously patting back his floppy straw-coloured hair, and pouting his large mouth. When he was drunk he made clumsy horse-play, and Paul hated him then, as he would squash you painfully against the wall, or throw furniture about. He hoped Dowsett wouldn't drown him tomorrow, by shying or bolting like a raw colt on the ferry.

Paul watched Dowsett's large hands, covered with pale hairs, break some bread into his stew and cover it with salt. Tomorrow this great puppy of a youth would have his life in his hands! The next twelve hours, he said to himself, are going to be the worst in my life – and then, just as we land perhaps Dowsett blundering outside a taped lane, and – oblivion. Or any time now, if we hit a sea mine. Mentally, he drew an imaginary line across the open Channel, and pinned the end in Normandy. Here are Dowsett and me: shall we ever arrive there, trundling along on dry land in that machine now swinging below the sea in the hold?

Why Dowsett? He thought of partners. All the personal life left behind. Where was Miffin in all this, he wondered? He hadn't seen him since Battle School. He probably never would: people came and went, all the time, in service life. Relationships never got very deep, despite the ordeals men went through together.

Around him, at their meal, in the crowded mess between

white-painted bulk-heads in the space pierced by deck columns were the others – Tomkins and Scotter and Bumpo. Men with no other common purpose, except to sail in this Armada, with the intention of using their machines against an enemy. As he felt the ship swaying in the restless sea, he realized how cut off he was from all lasting, and all emotional, ties: he had only a general relationship, with the Dowsetts of his regiment, with his squadron leader, and with the whole group of tank men, in their function in the Third British Assault division, directed at the Green Sector of Queen Beach, to the left of the Sword Sector of the Second British Army, between Ouistreham and Lion-sur-Mer. An odd one of 180,000: that was what he was, a spare officer in an armoured regiment in an assault division. Perhaps he had been a good deal else, too: but now the last residue of his personal life had been left back at the Gosport Hard yesterday.

So, he was obliged to give all his trust and allegiance for good or ill to this trained group of men, smoking and drinking their hot cocoa in denim overalls in the bare deck-spaces. Each man thus committed himself to be carried away, in this great undertaking, not knowing what the night or the morning would bring.

Now they heard footsteps growing more and more active on the decks, a stage by stage increase in the pulse of the engines, and the grumble of chains. They were for the real thing now, and its hazards; perhaps the flooding press of water through the plates if they hit a mine, or the sudden blast of fire and disintegration under bombing. More certainly, disembarkation into the teeth of howling missiles: there were no other alternatives. So, the loose group of men was drawn in fear and apprehension more tightly together. In the press of anxiety they strove to make their bonds of trust and loyalty stronger. Yet there was little personal identity left. Ashore, Paul, as a person, had always resented being cooped up with hulks of youthful energy like Dowsett – he was so inarticulate and aimless – such a bear. Nearly everything he said fell into any exchange between them as a large-limbed and healthy platitude. Yet here even Dowsett had to make some exchange, in the impersonal community of the launched assault.

'They must be right out in the open sea by now,' said Paul, mopping his plate for the last time. 'The first lot off.'

'Poor buggers. Expendable, eh?'

'Who isn't, on this trip, chum?'

'Ah, but there's still degrees. Why, man, you'd beef like hell, if we sent you to infantry.'

'You mean you last longer in tanks?'

'On land: no-one knows, in a job like this. But I'm glad to be on an LST.'

Paul shrugged cynically.

'Bigger target for subs.'

'But at least we'll have one good night's sleep. They're all stretched in the bloody bilges, mate, all under open sky, in those LCTS. Seasick as hell and all. In this liner we got *bunks*.'

'Plumbing and all – like last night!'

'The heads are overflowing again – that's Yankee plumbing that is – Liberty ships. They just join the bloody pipes like that.' Dowsett made a 'T' with his hands. 'The bumf jams in 'em, you see. We'll have to swim to bed again.'

'Of course, if the Rhinos are sunk, we'll be right up the creek.'

'On the bottom, you mean!'

Paul tried not to give way to nervous irony.

'Well, there's nothing we can do now,' he said, with weak bravado.

'Except say your bloody prayers, chum.'

'Shall you sleep, d'you think?'

'Sure: so'll you; won't you?'

'I suppose I might: I did last night. But it seems a rum thing to do, in the middle of all this.'

'You'd better get some kip while you can, mate: you won't get much over there, 'cept the permanent kind.'

They ate the remaining pieces of dry bread and one large remaining bluish potato between them, and then polished the large white plates. Sailors removed the plates to the galley, ambling with casual familiarity about the decks.

'Padre and the Quack are on board,' said Dowsett.

'Mooching round the decks, like unemployed ghouls.'

'Well, they can't start yet: old Doc, he went all round the ship, dishing out sea-sick pills. But the sky-pilot – what can he do? We've stowed his tin of paint, gravemarking, black, so all he can do is rehearse the bloody burial service. Plenty of work tomorrow.'

It was always this surface talk, whatever the occasion, however deep feelings were under the surface. Paul was tired of it. The badinage was becoming louder, as the tank officers' supper warmed their bodies, and they lit their cigarettes. He wanted to go away, and think about the Great Moment. For a while he hesitated, wondering whether it mightn't be better for him if he stayed to chatter, instead of trying to sleep. But he rose, having decided on the latter.

'I'm going to doss, I reckon.'

He could feel the ship turning towards the open sea. They were definitely under way.

'Don't be late for breakfast.'

Paul went up a companionway and took a glimpse over the rail. The wind was cold, and they were out in open water. In a flurry of rain and sea spray he saw a vague distant line of shore behind: the last of England. He was glad to leave the hiss of the waves, and go down into the warm depths of the ship, with its smell of oil, and the drumming pulse of the engines.

While those in the LCTs lay in the scuppers or had to improvise hammocks of tarpaulin in the open, the LSTs had sleeping quarters. Paul's sparse wire bunk was comfortable. It even had a thin hair mattress. There was an electric light and an air duct that buzzed slightly, blowing. He could feel the ship rocking on the swell. But it was a luxurious way to make a

D*

sea assault: just a cruise, really. Men's feet clanged up and down the bare companionways, and he could hear the noise of a soldier being sick already in a distant heads down the hollow gangway. But compared with those in the small craft they might almost be on a pleasure trip, under cover in the larger LST.

The young officer pondered the great weight of the tanks, weighing down the ship. Would they ever touch land again? Everything depended on the arrival of that flat pontoon deck of the Rhino ferry which the Navy was towing through the wild open sea somewhere. The Rhinos were written into the complex loading tables. They sounded too grotesque ever to materialize. Supposing they never turned up?

The Rhino ferry was only one problem, he reflected: there was the need for the success of the amphibious D.D. tanks in the leading wave, thirty-ton tanks virtually made into a boat for the run-in with huge canvas sides. These were to swim ashore from four miles out – in this sea. He knew the cold gale winds of yesterday must still be blowing in the sea-fog off Normandy. Then, those fantastic tanks invented by General Hobart of the 79th Armoured with great mechanical arms, bundles of fasces, or 'beehive' explosive charges on long mechanical arms, had to clear the first obstacles: suppose they never got ashore? Or met some unknown obstacle, *fougasses* or *panzerfausts*. What then? At this moment on the airfields the parachutists were climbing aboard, or perhaps were even air-borne: the wooden gliders were lying ready to be drawn into the air by their bomber-plane 'tugs'. He reflected how he had, at various times, thought of joining each of these outfits. But here he was: going to bed in a ship, as if he were on a passenger ferry, while all around on the water floated two whole armies – eight or nine divisions. He had heard the details at conferences: 20,000 vehicles; 3,000 guns; 1,500 tanks; 5,000 other armoured vehicles. Now it was all scattered over the open sea. Yet in the tight little cabin of the LST it all seemed as unreal as Christmas.

The whole escapade, in Paul's mind, as he cleaned his teeth

in the slopping 'heads', standing on a flange above the swilling water overflowing from the lavatories, seemed like a great ramshackle fairground, with all manner of side-shows afloat on fifty fathoms of uncertain water. It seemed unbelievable even after so many months of detailed planning the venture could possibly come off. When had anything like it ever come off? Certainly nothing since 1588, and then an Armada in the same waters had come to grief in a similar gale. At this moment he believed in 'Overlord' less than ever.

He stepped from rivetted flange to flange across the lavatory, in which the water bore a flotsam of cigarette ends and ribbons of Navy toilet paper. The overflow swirled and slopped now with the ship's movements and splashed noisily against the bulkheads.

Paul lay down on his bunk fully clothed, his cork life-jacket beside him, his harness ready with the loaded pistol. He had put on a clean shirt and string vest, for the clean corpse he was going to be if he was to be one. He knew he probably wouldn't change his clothes again for many days. Dowsett, who was to share the cabin, was still above, drinking whisky with the Scottish doctor from bottles the medical officer had stowed away in his half-tracked stores carrier. Paul hoped he'd be asleep by the time Dowsett lurched below decks. He pulled his blanket over his face in the top bunk and tried to doze off.

As he lay he could feel the ship's steady movement, and the engines' onward throb. He had dimmed the cabin light, and could now feel his heart beating quickly with tension. The outer life excluded, he came back to himself. Here I am, he thought, the end of training. This is what I asked for, after all. This is the last moment for thought: tomorrow would be a whirl of maps and briefing, explosions, action, alarums and excursions. He couldn't imagine what it would be like. In his mind's eye he recalled newsreels of men walking with bayonets in smoke, the Dunkirk beaches palled with black clouds, men's fraught faces as they clung to clattering machine-guns. Something like that. The regiment would wade through waves and beach debris and come together, the tanks assemble in French fields. But what happened after that? He could visualize the landing, the bright moment of touching down on the beach – but could not imagine what would come next. They all had an intense feeling for beaches and beaching. But he might be over there for months – he could see that. Yet what he would be doing he couldn't think. They had no clear picture of their function, beyond the beach and beachhead. He turned over and felt a lump in his trouser pocket. To make himself more comfortable he took out his compass and his phial of morphia, like a small tooth-paste tube with a hypodermic needle, and put these in his helmet hanging on its hook. Everything was provided in the modern world, Paul Grimmer thought, except peace.

As he sank to sleep he thought of the other young men of his generation, each young man, alone, like him, thoughtful and apprehensive in his place in the flotilla, on deck or below deck, his heart thumping. He was glad Dowsett wasn't here to keep him awake, talking in that superficial way, in his animal anxiety. It was so exhausting: Paul recalled their exchange at supper. Here was a great historic moment – the inception of 'Overlord'. Yet he and Dowsett had talked in platitudes as flat as those exchanged in any dentist's waiting room. Of course, even Dowsett had spoken of death: but with no real gravity. Dowsett as a person offered so little escape from isolation, so little real contact: one could be bitterly lonely among a crowd of Dowsetts. Yet he was a decent young man, too. But there was something dead about him. There were so many people like that in Army groups, with whom one was forced to share experiences, but who were so unrewarding, one simply found oneself just having to put up with them, because you were 'in it together'.

As he relaxed in his bunk Paul wished there were someone else there, someone sympathetic and sensitive, to share the experience in all its momentous excitement. As it was, Dowsett would come in, a little tight, and paddle into the overflow swirling down from the heads. His boots would stink all night in the cabin. Paul knew that. Then he would snore.

Now the young officer, as the ship swung him, dream-wished, falling asleep, that Lucy were suddenly with him, or his mother. He would conduct them on a tour of the historic battle, and explain it all to them, proudly.

He saw the face of Staff Sergeant MacAllcane at Blackmoor in those first winter weeks.

'I'll send you back to ye' mithers so she'll not recognees y'!'

The language had been almost incomprehensible. Those noises for commands! The training centres, in retrospect, seemed such kindergartens, such play-places, with their artificial enthusiasms. Battle-schools! The foolish lingo – *wordsacommarnd!*

'SCHO'!'

'Uup! toop! threep!'

Animal noises! What use would all that be tomorrow? The long preparation of men as beasts. As some Nazi leader had said, 'Marching kills thought'. Today the young man, educated, trained, effective: tomorrow the beast, or the corpse.

But the danger! He wouldn't want Lucy to share the danger. Nor his mother. They would hear the news tomorrow and wonder if he was there. A distant touch of the soft sheets of home, and then of Lucy's bed came to him in the dark slopping cabin, and he felt his closed eyes moisten. So young! He felt how young he was, then clenched his jaw under the blanket. His ridiculous collapse in the Glasgow phone box came back to him with distaste. But then he let himself feel the misery. 'Us' and 'we' and 'me': it was something a whole generation had to do. To give up, and yield to this. Dowsett and a hundred thousand others, a myriad young, were lying in this darkness, ready, their hearts beating with nervous anxiety, on the water, in airplanes, in gliders, concealing their anxiety with hard clowning chatter. Soon to tear into the sleeping Germans: he thought balefully of them, and their corrupted fanaticism. Under their advancing boots and the roar of Stukas and motor-cycles, the hollow-eyed subjects of Europe, the pinch-faced children, the ragged refugees.

The vast loneliness of the warring young men of the forties fell on his soul. In the warmth of his bed he found his sorrowing true identity. He loved his body, as he listened to his heart beat and felt his chest rise and fall in breath. The older men, generals and politicians, with insensitive perceptions and corrupt old beliefs, with their habitual indifference and duplicity, had let the maniac thing build up, ever since 1914. Violence and madness! He recalled a shot in a captured film, of Hitler's boots, dancing a jig at Berchtesgaden over the occupation of Czechoslovakia, and remembered the amazement and shock with which he had responded. The fiend! The madman! Yet so many had acquiesced in him.

Lieutenant Grimmer girded himself thus in his thoughts. But his convictions felt weak, as he sank further towards sleep, in the stir and sway of the boat. He felt in his flesh only a hope-less loneliness in common with the shiploads of young men sailing to the French coast and saw them dropping one by one under the guns into unknown and unmarked graves, under clouds of black smoke. Over there, the eyes they once knew in living companionship would never find them.

Even so, he fell asleep, twenty miles out from England, as the boat's engines stopped, to pause in Area 'Z', the assembly zone. When they throbbed again, at the signal 'half speed ahead', the LST was in the swept channel leading to Sword Beach.

D Day

PAUL WAS UP at four. The ship was pulsating as her screws drove her through a heavy wash of waves. The weather was still grey and the sea had a rough swell on it. Dowsett was snoring, still wearing his boots, wreathed in toilet paper. But someone had cleared the lavatories in the night. Boots clanked everywhere on the foetid plates of the deck. Paul went to the heads for a last warm shave.

Later he pushed his arms through his webbing and put on his steel helmet. He felt his pistol knocking against his thigh in its holster. It was loaded, and, though he knew how difficult it was to hit anything with it, its weight gave him confidence. He had slept well for six hours and felt taut and bright. His morbid night thoughts had gone, but his mouth was dry with fear. Surely now there would be action – bomber attacks, E boats? He went up to watch for skirmishes.

But on deck the overpowering sense of loneliness returned. Only the sea was alive and active, still full of surge from the gale, grey lines of wave running down the Channel. The ship drove briskly and confidently through the swell, the wake hissing, her whole steel frame throbbing to her onward progress. There were two LSTs well ahead and two well astern. But there was nothing else to be seen! There were these other ships, far afield, ahead and astern, but swallowed up in the sea, just a wisp of smoke here and there. Yesterday the packed flotilla: now, just after dawn, nothing but an empty grey rollicking sea. The whole fleet might be at the bottom. Yet he knew it was strung out fore and aft across the Channel, fifty miles of ships at fifty to the mile – other fingers and strings of ships making their way along, along swept channels, marked with buoys at intervals to port and starboard.

Paul caught one glimpse of fighters, four or five single-engined planes in formation, rapidly flying along the line of ships. He had expected the sky to be full. Where was everybody? Had something gone wrong? The ship ploughed on as if by itself, a heavy object dwarfed by the immensity of the sea. Was that a destroyer to the flank, under a wisp of smoke?

Suddenly Paul found a head beside him, in its dark grey-green pot of a steel helmet. A dark, middle-aged plump man. With his collarless shirt and unshaven red cheeks he was the comforting image of the English working-class Dad, a plump pug-faced Yorkshireman. It was Sergeant Whatmough of Paul's squadron. He saluted, informally, with a little hop, like a tame bear.

'Not very exciting like, is it, Sir?'

'You wait, Sergeant Whatmough.'

'Ye're oop early and keen, aren't ye?'

'I'd slept enough.'

'Ay. It were queer down theer. Foony to think as all the chaps is abooard going over theer.'

Whatmough nodded at the other three ships and the slight smokiness which now they could see marked the line of the long sea column.

'S'many of 'em'll never coom back. Nor'll oos, p'raps.'

'Too late to worry about that now.'

'Oh well, it's no matter, ye don't feel it fer yerself, like, do ye'? If ye' 'as ter go, ye' go. Only I was thinkin' of some of the young woons, like y'sel'.'

'What about you? You've got a family.'

'Ay. Ah've got that to think of.'

The older man was silent. They called him 'Daddy' Whatmough. The plump little man fumbled in his battledress knee pocket and brought out his pay book, from behind the plastic box containing his emergency rations, cubes of dried meat, oatmeal block, Horlicks tablets, and a compass. Paul looked out at the sea, silvering up from grey and brightening now. The

112

little group of Hurricanes had disappeared: but the horizon ahead was a little more definitely smoky. A high drift of thin black smoke! Was that it? Landfall? A sailor came out on deck and began to work at some hatches. A Bofors gun swung round in an armoured turret at the back: the teeth were bared.

Paul looked down at the sergeant's crumpled shiny photographs, black and white. A hatless and slightly bald Tom Whatmough in mufti knelt down beside a trim plump woman of about thirty-five, her hair neatly drawn to a bun. She had a genial attractive face, plain, maternal and careworn. Tom had his arm round a fair child of six, standing with her belly thrust forward in a Sunday frock all lace and pink sateen. The child was laughing and her hand was on Tom's ear. Then there was a boy, plain, with glasses, about ten, standing in knickers on the grass plot by a garden fence of railway sleepers – a backyard in Keighley. Above them hung the linen line. The boy had the expressionless face of adolescence, not laughing like the mother and little girl. Paul took them in with a pang, yet somehow couldn't feel deeply interested in them: it was a shadow of a past moment in a back-street in a Yorkshire town. Gone for ever, the laughter and the nonsense with the camera. He felt cold-hearted and repelled the surge of feeling. He looked back at the great grey dividing sea. Yet he said:

'No good wishing we were all in Keighley now, Tom.'

'Ah, it were bloody loverly at Keighley. Still, theer it is. My boy's just started at t' grammar school. Poor little boogers havin' to face all this, war and that. And yoong men like yoursel', Sir.'

'Too bad.'

He felt a touch on his shoulder, and the older man went below to organize his crew.

The touch broke Paul's obsession with his loneliness. Technical skills, a degree of quick thinking-power, capacities for 'leadership', of a kind – these had been given to the subalterns by their long training. At the OCTU sergeants from the ranks, hardened men, had failed to keep pace, to their profound disgust with themselves, and had been returned to their units. The young man toughened himself by cutting himself away from the personal life, becoming an efficient animal. But the family men? What was it like to come out of this, leaving one's wife and children? Paul frowned at the thought. Damn old Daddy, he thought, the silly old bugger's upset me.

Yet he cherished the man's warm-hearted touch. For in the field, he knew, even from exercises, the sergeants fathered the subalterns: in them was embodied the warmth of working-class life, and it sustained the British Army in the field. The classless, rather faceless young men like Dowsett who became subalterns were hot-headed, or inefficient, or coldly effective, or useless – they came and went, were promoted, killed or replaced. But the stability, order, and enterprise of the Army was with the sergeants, kind, hardened, versatile and careful older men, working-class fathers, mostly. It was they who sustained the patrols and found their way about the chaotic battlefield, supporting and standing by the subalterns, with their pistols and maps. They gave the fighting community a family strength. The bravery of the young officers was made possible by the devotion and reliability of the sergeants and corporals. The best sergeants were fathers to their young leaders. All this Paul felt he took in from the compassionate touch on his shoulder from old Tom Whatmough, at the rail of the onward-thrusting landing ship.

Paul went down below to check over his radio and kit, and to help Dowsett check the other four in the troop. A headset was missing until they found it in the swirling bilge. A despatch rider's motor-cycle fastened to the side of Dowsett's turret was in his way, so they heaved it across and lashed it to his corporal's tank. It took a long time to manoeuvre the heavy machine across three tank superstructures, all hung with spare bogies, spare sections of track, lifting gear and extra boxes of rations, the ship rolling. Everyone cursed Dowsett, but Paul could see the subaltern was only exerting himself and commanding activity to brace morale, deliberately. They had been stagnant too long, waiting for the gale to subside. Some drivers started their engines, but the air quickly grew stifling with diesel fumes and they had to forbid engine trials. So it was strangely quiet in the great cavern of the hold, lit by yellow electric lights. There was a blackout on all radio, so the wireless operators worked in frustrated dissociation: they could only warm up their sets, receive, listen, but not transmit.

Paul's squadron commander, 'Bumpo' – Major Bumpton of 'C' Squadron – held a briefing at 6 a.m. The sealed maps had been opened the day before, as soon as it had become known that 'Overlord' was under way. The atmosphere at such order groups was like that of those occasions on which you are presented with symbols of crucial change – with new names and new directions for living – like a birthday, Christmas morning, or a school examination. At the 'O' groups a boyish excitement buzzed in the nervous chaff and banter, helping to provide a defence against everyone's deep underlying fear.

Bumpo was a short little man with an ivory-coloured skin and a long sharp nose. He managed always to wear his black beret like a black puffball, too full of air and all standing upright. He read a long message from the Supreme Commander to the officers and N.C.O.s. They all gathered in the dark swaying hold, to stand braced against the ship's movement, to listen. Bumpo's county voice and solemn manner were those of a hunt meeting. He tended to grin and close his heavy eyelids at the close of each paragraph: yet he was undoubtedly in his most solemn mood. Brought to think about their predicament, they now felt penned in by the ship. They longed to leave the steel plates of the ship for land, and felt the insecurity of the ponderous vessel. Missiles might at any moment breach the hollow metal envelope of the ship: it suddenly seemed a large target, vulnerable and a trap. They wanted to get out of it, on to land, whatever happened.

Paul wondered how he would have phrased the commander's message, had he written it himself. He came to the conclusion that it was good: one could give assent. He found it strange that with his socialist adherences he could thrill to such a message, from a brass-hat.

You are soon to be engaged in a great undertaking – the invasion of Europe.

He felt the ship swinging under his feet. Seldom were the messages of high policy given such physical enactment to their terms.

Our purpose is to bring about, in company with our allies, and our comrades on other fronts, the total defeat of Germany. Only by such a complete victory can we free ourselves and our homelands from the fear and threat of the Nazi tyranny.

A further element of our mission is the liberation of the people of western Europe now suffering under German oppression.

It was enough. Paul gave assent. All doubt was gone – the kind of doubt bred in his months of Sandhurst, with sadistic parties in the mess-rooms under the villainous gaze of Empire builders in daguerreotypes. *Raubstaat England* was the title of a German propaganda book he had read, and much of it had been true – the massacre of Indians in times of trouble, the terrible cruelty in the past, in colonial plantations. His heart had sunk at some of the talk of senior officers about 'getting to Berlin before the Reds get there'. 'Oh, we ought to have a crack at *them*, too,' some of the County backwoodsmen of the fox-hunting yeomanry would say, winding their moustaches. They were ridiculous, if brave: the present message would make them uncomfortable. Paul could see one or two diehards now standing on one foot then the other – Horsey Parter the Adjutant for one – as the good political aims came over.

The inhabitants of Nazi-occupied Europe have suffered great privations, and you will find that many of them lack even the barest necessities ...

116

He had not thought enough of the people of Europe. From the sadness of his own loneliness and his concern for Whatmough and his family he turned to thinking of the French. What did the starving children of Europe look like? Would he, soon, see mobs of thin children greeting allied trains, begging, fighting over scraps, their faces dull, thin, shadowed and hollow, with none of the bloom of happy childhood? He could only summon a grey image of sad faces in subjection to his inward vision: yet this was enough.

Thus shall we lay the foundations for a lasting peace, without which our great effort will have been in vain.

Bumpo stopped. Then he read a message from the Colonel which said God Bless You at the end. Everyone stared into the bilges, embarrassed. And then the major became solemn for his own part, obviously with a great effort, and spoke of his 'splendid team'. Paul had a shock, because the words transcended the public school platitudes which he loathed so much. The emotions of men like Bumpo were sparse, taboo, and firmly suppressed under a surface politeness, and a kind of *Tatler* and Cavalry Club orthodoxy of cliché. Their efforts to be grave and serious in matters of feeling came as a shock if ever, as now, they transcended their limitations. At this moment they did: they achieved gravity. The apprehension of it gave him a stirred vibration in the mind, and a solemn, stunned, excitement. In the perspective of this new awareness his own individual harm or death seemed less important, even insignificant. With a beating heart, he willingly submerged his individuality in the group.

They went off to read the message to the men, and to show them the maps. This was the first time the tank crews knew the landing was to be in Normandy, near Caen. The regiment was to land to the east of the assault front with the Canadian Army on their right, and the Canal-de-Caen-à-la Mer on the left. They gazed unbelievingly at the mint purple and green maps which spelled out places soon to become too familiar: Queen Green Beach, Lion-sur-Mer, Périers-sur-le Dan, Douvres la Delivrande, Lebisey, Cambes.

Radio silence was broken now and the operators were calling across from ship to ship. H Hour had come! Messages were received from troops already on the shore! Some of the 13/18 Royal Hussars reported by wireless just after 7 a.m. that they had landed with engineer tanks to clear the beaches. Paul's brigade was in France.

Surely, then, something was going on above? Quickly, he checked that everything was in order below, and then clambered up the steel ladders to the deck. He wanted to go up to the daylight and fresh morning wind, away from the nervous sound of radio messages on crackling earphones in the fume-filled hold, and the babble of men calling across the dark cargo spaces of the hull. He gave one glance along the domes of the sixteen grey-green steel tanks in the dim lamp-lit hold, and went out to the deck rail.

And there he saw France. Here was land, in the hand of the enemy!

Away on the left were the blue hills of the Le Havre peninsula and the shadowy mass of the distant port. Away in front was a low stretch of coast, that smoked heavily for miles along the horizon's rim. The smoke was all colours and densities in the morning sun. 'Overlord' actual! Gradually Paul took in the hugeness of the fires over the low fringe of coast, great columns of smoke miles high mounting into the air, sluggish and strangely immobile in their immensity even in the brisk breeze. He stood up on a bollard to see. The coast was far away still, a white, green, and grey sliver at the sea's horizon – but as they moved steadily onwards out of the sea before them rose – the flotilla! The long coil of hollow little oblong boats, the long winding queue of the Armada – it was all here, crowded in a thick huddle offshore, like a packed boating lake! At first he noticed a ship here and a ship there, but then he saw they were just a confused mass – it was too much to take in the huge-ness of the fleet. Destroyers, cruisers, battleships, mine-sweepers, dark turrets and grey hulls galore, were scattered over the bright choppy sea, hulking over the crammed small assault craft. There was too much for any one pair of eyes to see, however actively they moved: yet all the secrets were re-vealed starkly, and he soon tired himself trying to take in everything. All over the ship men climbed the rails and rigging and strained to see the incredible sight, of slowly circulating, firing, burning, sinking, jammed, capsized, shifting or anchored ships. The larger ones lay strangely immobile, even looking commonplace. But then they would be enveloped suddenly in smoke. Among them the vigorous waves still drove, hissing and heaving: above them the silver fish-like balloons, here and there. The offshore was crammed, and the beaches belched bursts of smoke. Excited, taut, finding the sunlit waves brighter than anything he had ever seen before, Paul wanted to take in everything, drink it, experience it. The sun glittered on the shoreward waves, and there were all the ships, packed in the offing, all the accumulated flotsam of the invasion, a greatest ever press of marine traffic, black, grey, smoking, with points of pyrotechnic light glimmering and soaring. Along the whole coast for mile after mile savage clouds mounted into the clouds. Paul remembered distantly momentous phrases of the liturgy, of a cloud covering the whole earth, and of the moon passing away like wax.

Now as the LST rode in closer to shore he could follow the outbursts of flame. The squat grey mass of the largest battle-ship, the *Warspite*, flung swelling clouds of incandescence out of the long trunks of her fifteen-inch guns. The flames, as long as towers, unrolled into clouds of smoke as big as castles. A noise like an express train at full speed followed, as the projec-tile was thrust through the high air into France. One could see the missile, flying, at times; each shell weighed nearly a ton. Then on the shore, from time to time a red spark of flame would expand to yellow, then peter out, throwing a black or white mushroom into the summer air.

The scene was so full of incident and so incredible – and it was so unbelievable that he was there to see it – that Paul felt light-headed. Everyone rushed about looking for the best vantage point. They forgot every duty, and all sense of danger. It was like being at some fantastic circus, and the great shore and sea disasters seemed no more real than such images of war as one watches in a newsreel. They seemed outside themselves and outside the catastrophe.

A fighter fell burning from the grey cloud bank and slowly dropped twisting over and over, the other side of the River Orne. As he followed it with his eye a house on the shore blew up and obscured the falling plane with a rising cauliflower head of flame. War has come to us and to me, Paul thought: a grandstand view. He clambered on to the rail, holding a wire rope. Behind them the convoy was coming on and on through the swept lane: offshore the larger landing ships were moored ready, black and grey hulks, with large code names in white on their sides.

Then the LST turned, with a seething of wake, about two thousand yards out, and sailed along the shore to the west. The tank men, festooning the rigging and rails, reacted with murmurs, wondering why, turning their helmeted heads this way and that about the ship enquiringly. Queen Green Beach was ahead. The seaside villas of Lion-sur-Mer were just visible, at the edge of the sea, rising above the low streak of beach and dune where the smoke blew and billowed. They were set to land to the left of those. Why turn?

Paul soon knew.

There was an impact in the air, like a close stroke of lightning, that flung him about where he was, gazing from the rail. He swung for a moment on his rope, having lost his balance, and jumped down on to the deck. But not before he saw, beside the landing ship, a tall spectre rise from the water, like a monstrous Apollyon thrust greyly into the air. Water fell on Paul. It was thrilling, like a great *feu d'artifice*. A sailor blew a whistle and the seamen put on steel helmets. The sudden column was a salvo of 172 mm. shells from the Le Havre coastal batteries exploding astraddle the ship. The LST had turned westward, to present a less visible target. Ponderously now the *Warspite* swung broadside on to the east and threw flame and smoke out in regular gouts, firing back at the shore batteries.

Paul retreated into the entrance to a companionway, with a sudden anger and resentment in him. He had been shot at! With no warning, no opportunity for heroism, while just gazing at the wonderful spectacle of H Hour plus three! They had tried to kill him! They had tried to sink all their tanks – after all that work! A devilish trick! Inwardly he was full of bitter resentment, and a rising flood of hatred. All night they had seen neither enemy ship nor plane: there had been no mines. Now the war was in there on the coast and they itched to get ashore. But to be suddenly attacked by long-range guns, miles away, which one could not even see! It was unfair!

He was to learn that the true bitterness of war comes with the sudden stray shot, the flying fragment of one of your own shells, the falling anti-aircraft shell-case decapitating a man in the night, the self-inflicted wound. 'All's fair in war' – the phrase is playful. But now he knew what it meant. He now had his first taste of the impersonal treachery of machine warfare, as the shore battery shell spoke monstrously under the ship's side. The steel plates were even scarred already – not by old war wounds, but by shells of a few minutes ago. There was the smell of unfamiliar explosives in the air about the ship.

The long tedium of waiting was over. They were 'on the job' as they had all sworn they wanted to be. This was no exercise. The terms of the new mode were very different. A second salvo of tall grey shell bursts underlined the message like giant ghosts: a bracket – taller than the ship on each side, before it had gone far enough into safe water. Paul's shocked mind calculated that another salvo, if it hit the side, would settle them for good. Could he bear to think of the men striving at those guns in Le Havre, soon to be blown to pieces by the huge projectiles from the *Warspite*? In a few minutes, they were.

A terror now began to blow in Paul's mind with each pillar of white or black smoke from the beachhead. The small first taste of the madness of war is a taste of unexpectedly actually ripped flesh, of instantaneous surprise death. This Paul soon savoured now. The first small LCAs and LCTs, the small open boats like shoe-boxes, that they had seen under way at tea-time yesterday, were coming back out. One passed close to them, with great jagged holes driven through the superstructure, and old junk of shell-cases, ropes and tarpaulins thrown about in violence. All that neat stowing and organization wrecked! The sailors' faces were grey and singed with explosives, and they were now but limp sacks of men, from exhaustion and shock. The freshness of those on Paul's ship seemed like an insult to them. We next, Paul thought, gulping painfully – we shall soon look like those men. Day was gone: here was night.

And in the slushing mixture of oil and water in the hull lay what looked at first like sea-sick men, or perhaps old bundles of clothes. The mind leapt away, supposing in defence that they were dummies. But they were not. In the brown patches staining their yellow battledress their epitaph was written: they were bodies. The active-limbed men they had seen last night on the way out lay still this morning in the oily bilge of the battered LCA. One man, laid charitably under blankets on a wire stretcher, whose covers a dull-eyed sailor pulled to his chin, turned a ghostly face of pain to them as the ships passed. It seemed as if the questing eyes turned lifeless as they looked, for the body stirred with a grotesque spasm, and was then rigidly still. They had looked for the first time into the true

122

face of battle, and a grey melancholy horror began to spread over the watching tank men's souls.

The LSTs lay offshore until the early afternoon. The tank men sank now into a rhythm of group morale. They had all fallen into a depression at the first shock of encounter with that broken little ship and its cargo of dead, as it had passed close by, mingling wakes with theirs. The shock deepened as delay lengthened. The appalling backdrop of flame and black smoke, at first so exciting and vivid, frightened them now. They felt sitting targets for the bombing planes that must, surely, turn up sooner or later? Helpless, they did see one fast bomber run in over the beaches. At once three allied fighters were after it, and it could only drop its specks of bombs at random as it was chased away. But from on board the LST they heard the bombs, and felt their concussion. Next their attention was taken up by a group of American light bombers making precision attacks on targets in the rear, bunched close together. The troops watched the bunched planes among the angry bursts of black flak not in excitement, but in fear. They began to watch the sky at all points, for bombers directed at the larger ships. After each incident their apprehension grew, and the anxious activity of their eyes. One had to watch all the time: this was war's second lesson, that, in spite of oneself, one watched, as do thrushes and blackbirds on the domestic lawn, ceaselessly, for destructive predators, above and all around. There was a price to pay for the exhilaration of being present at D Day.

By now the shore batteries had been destroyed. Their ship turned into the shore, and anchored half-a-mile from the beach.

Never were such vivacious waves and bright glimpses of fine sun so welcome to the tank men in the dim hold, as the two great doors in the front of the ship opened, and they warmed up the tank engines. The hold became hazy with diesel fumes, and full of the thunder of the huge engines. At a signal the tank men began to move the great steel elephants one by one out over the lowered drawbridge where daylight burst in between the

123

bow doors. The breakers were rolling in fresh and the 'Rhino', pontoon ferry had actually appeared. Its glistening flat plate about as big as four tennis courts, bucketed, a small island in the sea, large enough for twenty tanks. It was a flat platform of pontoons bolted together, swimming just above the water's surface, with large outboard engines each side of it. When it lay under the ship's bows the heavy ramp between the fore doors went up and down over its deck. Sometimes the ramp crashed down on the wet metal plates, pressing the ferry into the sea, then rose sickeningly for the next pitch, leaving an impassable gap, over many fathoms of water. The drivers had to drop each tank forward while the drawbridge lay on the swilling pontoons between the bulky engine cases either side. The tank commander had to give his signals to a driver who was shut away below, using periscopes, in sea spray, as they emerged from the dark fuming belly of the ship. The tanks had to seize the brief moment when the drawbridge lay flat on one end of the Rhino ferry, and then roar across. The sea swirled and seethed, indifferent to the crammed activity on its surface, along the long wild Normandy coast.

Paul took over. He leapt gladly on to the slippery pontoon ferry. This was a challenge he could meet: something to do. Waiting in the ship, a sitting target on the sea, had been telling on his nerves. It was a relief to have to move one's limbs to a different movement on the heaving water.

Had he looked at the shore he would have been able to see that battle was still raging only half a mile away and tracer still flew across Queen Green Beach. But there was no time to look: the tanks plied on to their ferry, and he had the rhythm of the waves possessed. He judged their pitches, and by confident signals he was able to reassure the drivers. Off they came, one by one, the great steel elephants nodding out of the tall doorway in the ship's bows, leaning as if to plunge to the sands for ever, to race out rumbling at Paul's waving arms, on to the heaving pontoon platform all aspume and awash. Soon the big ferry motors in their sheet metal cases would roar, and the load drive away to the sands some eight hundred yards away, rolling and pitching. Then each tank would drive off, half submerged, into the beach breakers, and, snorting a great column of exhaust and spume, run on up the beach. Later the ferry would return to the next ship.

Around them in the water were rusted girders and occasionally other devices, rusty bombs, fused shells. Watching the ferries Paul could see the water break on these obstacles. Some craft must have been blown up on them: there was one lying askew and useless a few hundred yards along. But French *maquis* informers had warned the invading forces about these obstacles after much dangerous reconnaissance, and the attack had gone over them at half tide – though the gale had blown the sea level up higher than normal. At midday these obstacles were nearer the surface, but many had already been destroyed by engineers. Yet it seemed incredible that already other fresh-armed Sherman tanks were driving one by one safely through the surf and up the beach.

Dowsett came down and took Paul's hand in both of his.

'Come on. Our turn,' he said.

Paul took the handshake as a compliment on the work of unloading the tanks: he was thrilled – the obtuse Dowsett was not easily generous. But this was a matter of life or death, the quick sureness of delivery, and in the frenzy Dowsett was thankful and willing to show it. They scrambled off the slippery wet deck of the Rhino ferry and leapt on to the ship's ramp as it came pitching down.

Paul shut himself in the hull of the tank in his co-driver's seat, and called up regimental headquarters.

'Hello Sugar Zebra, hello Sugar Zebra. Grasshopper unloaded. We are the last: Sugar Zebra O.K. going into Queen Green on our Rhino. Over.'

'Sugar Zebra O.K. Best of luck. Don't drown it. Out.'

'Don't drown it' meant don't drive off into too deep water,

or swamp the air intakes by too fast driving. But the warning put drowning into Paul's mind. Even in training two men of the regiment had been drowned in landings. Much more chance now . . . I shall drown now if I am to drown. He moistened his dry lips and repressed a vision of green water roaring in to suffocate them. He felt the tank move and watched the driver beside him manipulate the levers, the sticks which controlled each track. Both were sweating. They could feel the ship's movement, pitching a little still. The unloading was left now to one of the Rhino ferry crew. The sailor hadn't the proper gestures for tanks. But Dowsett took over. Paul inwardly cursed Dowsett's clumsiness and his poor co-ordination. Paul heard him bark a little uncertainly over the intercom. The driver was too late, the tank tipped over and hung perilously for a second on the very edge of the drawbridge, thirty tons swaying on a wave's back. Then through his periscope Paul saw the sky move, the broken be-smoked shore, the beach, the sea, and, please, please God – yes, the ferry deck still there.

The tank crashed on the pontoons and its weight drove the end of the loaded ferry under the water. They lurched badly, but they were on, pulling forward among the other tanks. A howl of the great motors, and away through the waves. A long passage heaving with the sea. Would they get shelled now? Would this crazy ferry system work? They sat helpless. Paul could see nothing. A jar and a lurch, the headphones whining. The swaying water heaved under them. Suddenly the tank budged and heaved, then fell forward heavily again, into water this time.

'Driver advance.'

Green swirling water came over Paul's periscope. The huge steel vehicle rocked and stumbled. What was that grinding noise? Earth! Shingle! Sand!

With a roar of the engine and a sucking of air within the machine their tracks bit into the French beach.

Queen Green Beach was still under shellfire, confused, smoking and congested. But the landing had gone so directly forward there that the leading infantry regiments, the East Yorks and the South Lancashire Regiment, had been temporarily stunned by the anti-climax, when they found themselves so soon beyond the beaches. Instead of pushing on inland to the first rise of high ground, the Périers ridge, and to the relief of the airborne troops which had come down in the night to capture the Orne bridges, they had begun to dig in behind the beach roads. In the confined space of the restricted beachhead behind them congestion grew, as more and more troops landed.

On the beach were white windsocks to mark gathering points, and roadways were marked by white and green flags. Exits freed of mines were marked by large white tapes between the obstacles and derelict vehicles, twisted across the dark sand which was churned and blasted into turmoil, like the surface of the moon, by tank tracks and shell craters.

The flags and tapes, and the semaphore signals of beach officers were broken and erratic. The muddle and congestion made the landing very different from the neat practices in Scottish bays, or on the sands of Southern English beaches, of former months. The landing tanks squealed and thundered on, trying to follow crudely the broken signs, hidden in smoke, littered and disorderly. But the marks were there, all the same, recognizable, the ripped and winding lengths of tape, the flags, the arrows and the insignia of units, all of which they had been trained to recognize. Paul could see through his periscope a waste of confused track marks, sometimes running over lengths of twisted steel strip with punched holes in, laid over the clay patches. All the beach was ploughed and rutted with traffic. He could hear, even inside the tank, an incessant roar of falling shells, clattering tracks, and small arms fire. A chaos of broken things strewn on churned brown sand appeared in glimpses between clouds of smoke.

But it was not the chaos that made the essential difference, between this beach experience and all the rehearsals, as his vision swam in the green glass of the periscope.

The essential difference was in what lay under the fluttering windsocks, under the marker flags, here and there, in alien uncomfortable postures – impossible postures – the dead. He was on the beach only a few minutes: but all was at once changed. From the uncaring fallen forms in the ridged brown sand, and the holed litter of broken machines, came the first apprehension of that terrible waste that made 'Overlord' – made actual war – so different from all the dry and dummy runs of two years' training.

At first Paul had an unconscious expectation that the tension and discomfort would soon be over: soon, the lazier part of his soldier mind said, the exercise will be over, and the umpires will come forward, to tell us how we did – we'll get the score. On the beach ran and crouched men in steel helmets with white-lettered helmets, gesticulating and directing – these must be the umpires.

But then he saw through the periscope one of the 'umpires' running in an ungainly way, undignified, ridiculous in his wet khaki battledress, like Buster Keaton or the Keystone cops in an early comedy film, the animation jerky and grotesque, a bag of clothes with arms and legs comically and impossibly flailing. Others scuttled like animals in a bunch with the beach officer, and they dived into a large sand hole. They ran like abandoned creatures. Blast waves and smoke blinded his periscope, and then hammering blows rocked the thirty-ton tank which lurched and swayed under them. The blows were blunt and their violence ugly. Paul found resentment rising in him, as he had when the shore battery shells had nearly found their mark on his LST. Unfair! They were trying to kill him! Now they were shooting at the umpire! The men he had seen through the periscope had been breaking away and seeking refuge in shallow pits in the beach sand from a barrage of high explosive shells.

Dowsett had shut down, cursing and yelling to his driver.

'Driver speed up. Come on, for fuck's sake man, don't piss about in the surf.'

The tank lurched on up the soft sloping sand, over the holes where the last salvo had just fallen. They could smell the chemical gases mingled with the fresh sand smell and the stench of bnrning rubber, all drawn into the tank's rushing air intake. Paul, anxious for the beach officer, turned the periscope round to the flank, but could not see him. All was dark with smoke now, thick rolling smoke, which had burst out from the big explosions. As the tank swung into its exit he saw the hulks of ships along the surf-line, some burning, some still active with men and vehicles emerging. Then the smoke came down thicker, and with squeals and jerks of the tracks, they climbed towards the houses along the beach road.

Then the smoke cleared and he had a good view of the beach. Images came into sudden focus in the greenish oblong of glass. High up along the beach he saw a tank burning, and then, suddenly, under its dipped and useless gun, a row of dead beside it. The full dreadful sense of waste came flowing into his gorge, the first full flavour of machine warfare. There are moments, short moments, from which we never recover, and this few minutes up the beach was one of those for Paul, as it was for hundreds of thousands of men besides. The loss of one's virginity takes only a little time, and leaves one forever changed – if happily, for life and love. But this first minutes' baptism of fire changed Paul's sensibility for ever, for ever to be a little deadened. He tasted the full price of death, the abominableness of which human nature was capable, the immense destructivity of man, and the frail predicament by which in the midst of the apparent stability of life we are always in the instability of possible immediate obliteration. This is a truth with which we always live: war uncovers it mercilessly. The small mirror image of the voraciously burning tank with its luxuriously billowing black and red fire, and the row of baggy sack-like dead beneath it did this for him now.

After so many years of preoccupation with the care of an efficient machine a man comes to develop a pride and affection for the thing. Soldiers in an armoured regiment are proud of their fighting vehicles and deeply attached to them emotionally – cold, clumsy, uncomfortable mastodons as they are. The Paul Grimmers and Dowsetts had slept in them and under them, bivouacked with them in wild places, and driven them recklessly through scrub and forest. They had maintained them to a high pitch of efficiency, and had kept them clean and neatly stowed. They tended their tanks, so they might have confidence in them. The machines became substitutes for home, with their stowed cooking stoves and their bulkhead stores of food and water. The steel walls of the Shermans had protected them from shellfire and bullets in exercises when live ammunition was used, and they expected them to protect them in war, the American mastodon-mothers in whose bellies they lived. Each greenish steel dome with its armoured flanks was home for five men. Their tanks had private letters tucked behind the No. 19 set, as behind the clock on the mantelpiece at home; and in handy places here and there the tank men kept their round tins of cigarettes and their bars of motoring chocolate.

It seemed hideously wrong that the mastodon mother herself could be destroyed: and so the first sight of a burning tank dislodged a fundamental security in the trooper's soul. Tanks burn in a way that has its own grotesque poignancy. The flames are explosively fierce and yet are tightly contained in the hollow steel shell: so, the smoke rushes out with tumbling fury. The occupants, if they are not already torn to pieces by the penetrating armour-piercing shot, must be very quickly asphyxiated, then burned rapidly to cinders by the fierce flames of diesel oil and exploding cordite charges, raging through the hatches and the turret. From the turret black smoke alternating with intense flame thunders forth in a monstrous jet. But then from time to time the smoke is forced into huge expelled puffs by the exploding shells within. Each black puff, from the circular turret hatch becomes with grotesque perfection a rolling smoke ring. Such a smoke ring we associate with quiet reflective moments – old men showing their skill with a pipe in the chimney corner, to admiring children. The perfect black smoke ring shooting up from a burning tank suggested some grotesque devil's game in the thing, a derisory joke of the fiends, over dying men. A burning tank, because of this, looked like a monster, a dying dragon, vomiting up the life within it in black gouts, and blowing aloft ghostly rings which mounted, curling in on themselves, high into the air. Beneath these sad signals, a red and white glower would roll in the eyes of the dead monster, the hatch holes, through which the crew had entered, never to emerge again. For there within, where once was chattering comradeship, offers of chocolate and tea, gossip and chaff, where the men had sat with their headphones on and worked with maps or preparing meals, was a tempestuous fire, licking the red hot or blackened steel. Whenever he saw a tank burning, Paul felt impelled to gaze within, to see what had become of the life that had once climbed in so actively. Yet no-one dare do so, until the cindery mass was cold, because of the violence of the explosions from the shell racks – even though shouts could be heard from the interior, when the first terrible clang came from the strike of steel on steel.

This appalling sight Paul saw in the first minutes on the beach, at one instant, through his periscope. The meaning of it began to sink in, as the bewildering hours of his baptism of fire lengthened, generating in him his first taste of battle shock. It was not one of his regiment's machines – 'A' and 'B' squadrons had come in scot-free earlier from their LCTs, and were driving inland. The burning tank was a thirty-ton Sherman tank belonging to the engineers who had cleared the beaches earlier. It was a 'Crab' tank, with flails – long steel arms in front supporting a power-driven axle, on which hung chains. When the axle revolved the chains would beat the ground and explode anti-tank mines. It was dangerous work, as Paul knew. The Wehr-

131

macht knew about Crabs. Sometimes they would set a delayed fuse and attach the mine to a bomb, so arranged that this would explode under the tank, as soon as the beating chains struck a mine. He had learnt about such devilish contrivances, in the abstract, at courses on explosives. And he had passed over the phrase 'knocked out by anti-tank fire'. He had felt a little security in phrases such as 'covering fire' and 'defusing'.

But the first sight of the actuality had ripped the flimsy security from him. The massive steel turret of the Sherman was even dislocated from the hull by the force of the impact from an 88 mm. armour-piercing shot, travelling at some 3,000 miles an hour. The shot had churned round inside the tank, rending up the men inside into shamble-fragments like the pile of choppings that is thrown in a heap in the butcher's shop for the scavenger or the glue factory. Five men had been mixed for an instant with ripped cordite charges, the smashed wireless set, spare clothing, tins of food, belts of ammunition. And now in a refining fire the pulverised mass of flesh and artefacts blew its death-signals into the air through the turret hole.

Fascinated and sick, Paul heaved at his lightly sealed hatch, and thrust it open. Dowsett, who was back in the turret hatch, also tense and grim, barked at him:

'Paul, I shall want that hatch down to traverse.'

'Thought I'd watch down here for obstacles.'

'Righto.'

But Paul really wanted to confront the reality of the death and waste, in the open air. The green periscopic image was still too much like a newsreel, or a dream; there was nothing yet for Dowsett to shoot at. He must quell his reeling sickness. He must look.

He put his head out. The Sherman Crab was not the only knocked-out tank. There were others, monsters which had lumbered to carry large charges to the concrete pill-boxes, tilted on their sides and blackened with fire, boiling out smoke. Their bundles of fasces lay in place, or were spilled about the beach. Half-tracks, armoured cars, self-propelled guns and engineer tanks lay about the sand too, tipped over or blown open, burning, reddened and blackened by fire, smoking and blazing, their tyres or fuel tanks on fire. Other machines had simply stopped in their course, sunk in sand, their great metal tracks broken on mines. The surf drove up higher among them as the tide came in. But now he had his head out of his hull hatch and could see directly along the beach Paul was surprised at the rate things were moving. There were men and moving vehicles, congested and confused, but along the exits they poured steadily, in files and convoys, through the lanes marked with a jumble of tapes and flags, despite the broken machines and the dislocation. Here and there an outbreak of smoke, shouts and flung bodies marked a shell salvo: but this was a beachhead functioning briskly, with arms and men poured over the top ridge of the beach. The assault was well away from the water, the tripod-like beach defence obstacles, and the jumble of great wrecks. They were not to be stopped before they left the surf. Of course, they could still be driven back into the sea, by a determined attack. But they were definitely on shore, and moving. Even so, he couldn't think clearly what movement inland would be like. They had thought of beaches so much that to get off the beach in the first minutes seemed something of a flop.

Paul's tank reached the dunes and shingle-bank at the top of the beach, beyond the end of the row of some seaside houses, on the easterly outskirts of Lion-sur-Mer, a few small pink and white villas. The houses on the shore seemed to have been evacuated by the Wehrmacht: there were no French people about. The villas had been boarded up and were broken by shellfire, but still stood hopefully gazing out to sea as seaside villas do. They had caught a good deal of blast and some direct hits. As the troops in their drab khaki swarmed past them they looked forlorn, the boarded windows broken up here and there, the roofs, the walls holed. But yet many stood erect still, with four walls and a roof: some even with the telephone wires attached. Paul was surprised that everything wasn't flattened. He'd seen a demonstration of the intensity of the gun and rocket barrage: from the thunderous drumming it seemed that nothing could survive such an obliterating cannonade, the cliffs alive with packed flame and smoke, bursts as thick as bushes in a copse. To the left such a barrage had fallen: there smashed houses burned, and the roads behind the beach were almost impassable with craters. But as they pulled out to the west they moved into comparatively untouched seaside: many of the little villas were still more or less intact, their white walls and red roofs shining, despite an odd hole here and there. The village of Lion-sur-Mer itself farther along had escaped bombardment, as there had been no landing directly in front of it. In the gleams of sun it looked almost gay, with barrage balloons aloft beyond it, giving the place something of a regatta air. Paul studied the foreign look of the place with satisfaction, the pretty coloured shutters at each window, the curly insulators on the telephone posts, the blue and white street name plates, and the gimcrack French provincial finish of the newer houses. Certainly, this was not Littlehampton. As they climbed the track they reached their first road in enemy territory, a dusty torn strip behind the beach villas, with potholes in the asphalt, and stretches of loose aggregate.

Dowsett and Paul were so anxious to reach the clear road that the tank nearly ran over a line of dead before they noticed.

'Driver halt!'

A beach officer with shell-shattered nerves, a drawn grey face under his hat, his battledress filthy with water, oil and smoke, waved at Dowsett.

'Don't stop! Don't stop!'

But even Dowsett couldn't drive, yet, over the bodies of English infantrymen and pioneers. The driver awkwardly backed in the dunes, as the men directing the traffic in the exit waved them on, cursing.

'Poor sods have had their bloody invasion!'

As they went past Paul studied his first war dead at close hand. They were statuesque, holding their postures stiffly, and so not crouched in relation to the earth as live men would be: there is no relaxation in the dead. Most seemed whole: it seemed an outrage they could not get up and move on. There seemed nothing wrong with them: solid flesh in the thick cloth battle-dress. Most were khaki: two were grey-green enemy. But then Paul noticed the subtle difference in the colour of their faces from live faces – a greyish white or pale blue-green tinge. And then the sack-like, stiffening posture, the clenched fists. Perhaps a patch of black blood at the ears, a brown stain at the corners of the mouth. He's gone. The mind and compassionate impulses recoiled, as they never did from a wounded man. Hopeless! One was impelled to rush to a wounded casualty, to foster life. But a corpse one left alone. One could even drive over a corpse.

Yet Dowsett could not. And as they passed close by the row Paul could see what had made the difference between live and dead: the odd line of holes punched in the cloth of their dress: that was all. Sometimes edged with black, sometimes with brown, these small holes, round, or large and jagged, marked apart the statuesque thing that was no longer a man, marked it apart from the living soldier. The wounded man was different: his cloth was urgently cut away for a field dressing to be applied. Living but disabled, he was the pitiable infant of the field, treated the more like a baby the nearer he was to death.

But once life was extinct the heavy object, the dead meat of a man, became a nuisance, both materially and to the mind. Whether enemy or 'own troops', it must be hidden, dumped: must be driven over, even, in need. But Dowsett jibbed, and Paul was glad. After much slurring sideways in the heavy dune sand, among furious faces, grey with fear and fatigue, men shouting and waving, their Sherman tank tilted down on to the beach road behind the villas, and they nosed their way through the hawthorn hedges. They knew the lay of the fields behind Queen Green a little from the air photographs they had studied on the boat. The first objective was the Périers Ridge, already being violently contested. Dowsett made for an orchard at a prearranged map reference, half a mile inland from the beach. The mint maps were in use: Paul's tank was on foreign earth, moving inland, with live ammunition in the breeches of the guns, and the rich Normandy countryside gleaming behind the crosswires in the gunner's telescope.

The Norman countryside that first afternoon was beautiful in the sunshine. Paul was amazed by its rich greenness, shimmering in the warm uncertain light. In the orchards a few scattered just-formed apples, the blossom fragments still attached to some, lay in the rich green footgrowth. The thorn hedges were high and thick with white flowers in them here and there. In the fields the corn was tall and a rich blue-green. The grass was lush everywhere in the orchards, and the cultivated land seemed to smell more richly of dung than English fields. They smelt of the rich humus of corn growing in a countryside that relied on animal manure. As the heavy tanks bruised the earth, the rich smell of humus was sucked into the tanks' powerful air intakes. Even the dust on the white roads, thinly asphalted, seemed generous and rich, and the yellow buttercups and white umbelliferae were sturdy and fat among the thick growth of green grass. Paul's squadron assembled, and the tanks drew behind walls of weathered brick. They paused in the sunlight, the engines still, to await instructions. Waves of blossom scent and hay smell surged up from the warm orchards and cottage gardens. The sky showed patches of blue in the grey, and butterflies hovered: birds sang against the constant loud explosions, amid the fantastic chatter of the machine-guns, and the intermittent crashes of great detonations.

The light shone, and the fields around were patched with moving areas of grey, green, brown earth and gleaming shadows. Everywhere a rich green light rose into the glad summer day. Through the orchard boughs they could see glimpses of black and white cows, in Pissarro settings, under the hanging elms, beeches, poplars and apple trees, the foliage all *pointilliste* in the afternoon sunshine.

But then the smoke and the guns were fecund, too, fecund with abomination. As their vehicle drew in behind a pink orchard wall, Paul looked enquiringly round the rural scene, with his head still out of the co-driver's seat. All at once he learnt a new sound. Suddenly the air was thick as if with bees, but with red fires streaking across the orchard air. Unlike the Bren shots at Battle School, they seemed not individual sparks, but a continuous web of rods of light, drawn across the gay pastoral scene. The rods of fire battered up dust and flying stones from the road, chipped flying fragments from the pink wall and ripped clouds of leaf and twig from the apple trees. The landscape was torn apart before his eyes, fragments of the rustic scene ripped away parcel by parcel by the fire. The white and red rods of flame spoke at the same instant with an intense and painful noise.

WHACKumpWHACKWHACKWHACKumpumpump-WHACKumpWHACKump.

Fast and furious this voice, the 'whack' not a sound reproducable in words, but a clap on the eardrum from a violence in the air. The 'ump' was the noise of gas escaping from the gun itself, several hundred yards away. Strange and new among these sounds was the noise of the German Spandau machine gun, a fast rippling snarl, with the crack of bullets following one another in the air as thick as hail. The face and ears stung, resentfully, and the eardrums felt likely to burst. Paul felt all the hair on his face lift in protest and fear. Again, they were shooting at him, before he had 'begun' – and, indeed, as they were soon to know, the enemy troops were only a few hundred yards away, blazing at every movement, in combat with infantry.

E*   137

WHACKWHACKumpumpWHACKumpwheeezeefriiing-
WHACKump.

Paul closed down his steel flap. But this was worse, to be
impotent, hidden below, in a hail of fire. The small arms fire
continued as thick as hail in the air, not white but flame-red,
and driving horizontally. Dowsett moved his vehicle down
through a hedge into a lower field where he expected the regiment to foregather. Other tanks sidled about, uncertainly,
felling pieces of flint wall. At first there was confusion,
muddled voices calling on the air, lids closed down under the
crackling storm of shot, the engines roaring as the tanks
seemed to be moving blindly about, fearing to be overtaken by
enemy infantry. But then, as suddenly, the arc of fire moved
away, and there they all were, among familiar helmeted friends,
the regiment's tanks with familiar code numbers and insignia,
the troopers out at work unloading despatch-riders' motor-
cycles and other encumbrances which had been strapped to
them for the loading tables. The wave of light gunfire had
swung round towards the village. The air was not clean, as
after a storm, but troubled with columns of dust, and the stink
of tracer flame chemicals.

A command was given and all troops mounted, closed down
their hatches, and, at a signal, blew the explosive cords which
freed their waterproofing chimneys on the tank engine inlets
and exhausts. There was blue smoke, cracking reports in the
air, and then the troops emerged in their rimless steel hats, and
threw off the sheet-metal chutes, dumping them in hedges.
Now the olive-green elephants were free of their landing attach-
ments and in the broken Normandy orchard spread the familiar
spectacle of two squadrons of American-made tanks in the
hands of an English yeomanry regiment. Only barbed wire
strands with the word MINEN and skulls and crossbones on
tin plates in black and white showed that this countryside had
been occupied by the German Army. There were no mines –
the fences were mere bluffs: the area had been explored by

engineers, but after finding so much bluff the tanks had boldly gone over into the orchards and meadows, and found that no mines had been laid.

The discovery made the troops restive. Perhaps many more apparent defences were bluffs? Shouldn't they drive forward faster? What was to be done, now the beach was left behind? Paul heard over his radio link that the single raid-bomber they had seen from offshore had reduced the headquarters of the 9th Infantry Brigade to a shambles while its order conference or 'O' group had been assembled on the beach. The brigadier had been badly wounded and all his staff officers wounded or killed: so there was some confusion among the assembling troops. No clear orders about making progress inland came through yet. The Canadians to the west of the British Army were occupied with a strongly fortified radar station near Douvres-la-Delivrande. Inland, near Caen, the enemy were supposed to be planning a counter-attack by a Panzer division exactly between Paul Grimmer's regiment and the Canadian flank. Now, over the air, a request came from the Second Lincolnshire Infantry Regiment on the right, where fierce fighting was in progress. But still there was little initiative or movement. The tanks simply pulled outwards through hedges or behind walls, to point their guns, waiting. In the late afternoon sun a mood of dismay and inaction grew as the tank men waited. Bursts of shot swung now and then their way, red lights soaring in dotted lines overhead. Then one or two tanks were sent off, to try to help movement forward up the high ground in front, on the Périers ridge towards Hermanville-sur-Mer. Confused voices came over the air.

'Hallo Able one Hallo Able one. Enemy hornet is attacking my Able three.'

'Fire at the bastard,' an angry scream.

'Hallo Able two . . . Fire! Fire!'

Meanwhile a dull dogged voice here and there would be checking a net.

'Hallo Dog two, Hullo Dog two.'

'For Christ's sake get off the air, Dog two. There's a hornet attacking Able three . . . I want to keep through to Sunray. Where's Able three? Hallo Able three, Hallo Able three . . . report my signals. Over?'

But there was no reply from this. Nor was there ever to be. Sergeant Toynbee lay in the high corn with his legs shattered, while his turret companions, having scrambled free from the tank with their clothes on fire, ran for a stretcher under a hail of Spandau fire. The driver and co-driver were dead in their seats. The regiment had been blooded. The rest of the 'Able' crews destroyed the German self-propelled anti-tank gun which had drilled the hull of Able three, leaving the German crew riddled in a burning pyre.

Now gunfire was ranged from the hill into their orchard and down in the hull Paul felt it falling round them – shells thumping the summer fields like great doors slamming. Some of them rocked the tank. Paul grimaced at Jackson the driver, in the dark hull compartment, but the man was not looking at him. His face between the headphone pads was pale and his mouth twitched a little. In the dark interior they could only suffer and wait: the lack of something to do was telling on their nerves. They had begun, too, to learn that compelled lesson of war, that one must always listen. But as yet all the languages were foreign, and so every great sound was a menace. To listen for every predatory sound anew was too intolerable, and so their minds began to learn to distinguish, between machine-gun fire which was coming in your direction and that which was going for somebody else; between the ear-cracking noise of a warship's fifteen-inch shell scouring the sky overhead towards Caen steelworks, and the noise of a 105 mm. shell coming your way. Already, they had taken in that the nearer the missile is coming, the less you can do about it: you'd not hear a direct hit. If you could hear the whistle of a shell's trajectory, it must surely be past? Paul made some tired calculations about so many thousands of miles an hour: but he couldn't remember the speed of sound.

For a long time they sat listening to and feeling the exploding shells with dry mouths. Then Dowsett became restless and clambered down out of his turret to climb a gate and look out beyond the orchard through his binoculars at the ridge. The next salvo felled him and he lay in the high green corn now, gasping with pain and clutching his arms over his head, as if defending himself from being beaten about the ears.

Cursing Dowsett's recklessness, and his great-boned senselessness, Paul clambered out to see what had happened to him. As he got down on his feet Paul found his own legs were weak and beyond his control, and he could not stand up straight for reactive fear of the next salvo of shells: they had been in this corner long enough already to get the rhythm of the German gunners, now re-loading. Dowsett lay on his side, groaning, tangled in the shoulder-straps of his map-case. He was a heavy man, and large-limbed. A large tear in his battledress leg revealed a broad gash in his flesh, pulpy and glistening red, like fresh meat. There were splashes of blood all over him, and his previously healthy face had gone grey and pale. His leg, Paul thought, might be broken. Dowsett's eyes were closed, but he was conscious. His body had gone helpless a little with the pain and shock. In the air a bird sang, and Paul could hear Jack Symonds, Dowsett's wireless operator, reporting the casualty. Driver Jackson was climbing out of his hatch, but Paul waved him back to his seat. A furious crackle of small arms fire broke out to the west, and Paul sweated in the late sun for fear they would be overrun. Dowsett's wound was deep, but the bleeding was not heavy – no arteries seemed to be cut. Paul ripped open Dowsett's trouser leg and fixed a field dressing clumsily, tearing it open with his teeth, his hands shaking. He had to heave the man's other leg away and it was heavy like meat. Dowsett lay stiff and taut, groaning, bright beads of sweat on his upper lip. The large pale youth seemed suddenly pathetic, lying in the Normandy field in a patch of green corn bright with poppies, so far from home, broken, a casualty. The wireless operator came over running, his pistol flapping from his harness.

'Sir, Major Bumpton says flag . . .'

A sound as of a tube train's screaming brakes all squeezed up in a second was on them and with a buffeting of air a salvo fell all round. It was as if rough hands seized Paul and the trooper and flung them about. Paul was punched by air in the chest; the man was caught by the legs and rolled over. A frightened cry came from Dowsett. But no-one was hurt. The hands of the buffeted air had choked dust down their throats and ears, however, and their clothes were full of grit and smoke. When the dust cloud moved in the breeze they saw the shallow craters only a step from them. The bird sang on. Paul swore. Symonds spat and jabbered.

'. . . says flag him and Doctor will send a stretcher party. You're to take over the tank and move now up the ridge. I've got a map ref. Can we do anything, Sir?'

This kindly to Dowsett. The trooper gave the wounded officer his water bottle. They went to the hedge for a stick, and tied a yellow marking flag to it. This was erected beside Dowsett, who was recovering a little and taking some water. He looked up at Paul, and gave something between a grin and a wince.

'Back to Blighty already, sod it.'

'Lucky bugger,' said Paul. 'You'll be all right now. Shelling's stopped. Seems so. Let's hope so. Hullo, what the bloody hell . . .?'

It was about nine o'clock. A vast low hum came in from the sea, rising to a deep multiple growl. The light was waning into evening, and the sky was going cloudy. In from the sea, flying low, came a long column of black aircraft – four-engined bombers, Albemarles, Stirlings and Halifaxes, and Dakota twin-engined passenger planes. The procession seemed endless.

The Stirlings and Halifaxes were towing black gliders, Horsas and Hamilcars, clumsy looking long square boxes on wings. Paul recognized all the shapes from his Intelligence training. But he had never seen so many aeroplanes all at once. At first Paul felt encouragement, then, as the vastness of the black roaring convoy was obvious, astonishment, and then came an abandoned feeling of triumphant elation. The long steady line of black aeroplanes stretched far out to sea, to the horizon, five hundred planes and gliders in one great train. Even poor Dowsett propped himself up and cried, dustily,

'Christ! Christ!'

The tank men were bewildered, then elated, wildly. The crews clambered out of their tank, gasping, waving and dancing. The falling shells and machine-gun fire were forgotten as they clambered up vantage points. The air flotilla came over like a vast destructive cloud, on and on, relentless. Then, exactly overhead, the wooden gliders were released, and at the same time spread thousands of parachutes, most of them red, bearing ammunition. The sky was full of colour, flame and falling objects and it was impossible to know where to look. The black and white gliders nosed steeply down towards the fields by the bridges over the Orne, where, they knew, other sections of the 6th Air-landing Division had been dug in all day, having landed by parachute and glider in the night. The sky was filled over all with red, blue and green parasols, diving black gliders, and circling bombers.

For the weary troops of D Day the effect of the black gliders and the myriad coloured parachutes dropping behind the enemy's lines was to lift their morale to a high sense of triumph, as the light began to fail. The whole sky seemed claimed for 'Overlord', claimed by the largest glider force ever to take the air, and clinched by the spreading coloured blots that fell as thick as a fantastic snow.

The local fury on the ground dropped for a bewildering moment. But then, only a few hundred yards away the German flak guns and small arms turned upwards and the sky was alive with fountains of soaring fire. From the sky, to put the guns off their aim, Hurricane and Spitfire fighters detached themselves from their escort positions above the column, and dived first up and then swoopingly down like swallows to rake the German positions, their gun ports sparkling. It was wildly dramatic and beautiful, the black and white gliders turning and diving, through the coloured parachutes, slowly falling, into the fountain streams of bright tracer. They forgot all danger: Dowsett was acclaiming the spectacle as a child does a firework display, his wound forgotten. One tug plane was struck, and turned back out of line, and sank, engines on fire, towards the sea, with black trails of smoke behind it. From it puffed the white parachutes of the crew, one by one. The falling plane, enveloped in an orange glow, sank down out of sight beyond the beaches, now turning dark and ominous as the evening of D Day was coming on. The tug bombers turned and made for Caen. In a short while, silently, the land had absorbed the gliders and parachutes, and the roar and hum above now changed to crackling and detonation on land over towards the Orne. The bright hoses of flak rose still, from time to time, as single planes still marauded here and there.

Dowsett, Paul heard later, lay for a long time in the corn, before he was picked up. Paul took over the wounded officer's troop with its three tanks. Orders to move came, and they had to leave the prostrate figure, to join the squadron making its way forward quickly through two cleared villages, Hermanville and Colville. There, among the shattered grey and red buildings in the falling light were disordered and shattered French people, dazed but cheering. Strange it was to hear the rather ragged, tired noise of a few cheering human voices, among all the banging guns and clatter of war – as strange to hear as the blackbirds that had still gone on singing in the orchards in the day as though the guns were instruments of music. Some of the French had put pathetic paper tricolours on their houses already, pathetic scraps of jubilant colour. The Normandy villagers seemed mostly old men, grey-faced and shocked, others impassively smoking pipes. One or two old women appeared nervously at the doors, to wave briefly. Then they shrank back in uncertainty into the safer cover of the house. One old man in blue trousers and a beret was even digging potatoes in his holding. But most of the French inhabitants huddled away indoors, scared by the din and the great press of soldiers.

Then as they rounded a corner in Colville, the tanks squealing and roaring past some black barns at a road junction, Paul saw his first German in the dusk. He was in the turret now, and his tank was leading the troop. The road ahead was supposed to be clear of enemy, but no-one could be sure, in the confusion. As he cleared the bend Paul saw what seemed to be a cinema commissionaire, on a motor-cycle and sidecar: this was his first reaction to the strange grey uniform and the peaked cap. The silhouette of the enemy brought from him an automatic response, and he began a fire order, with a tremor in his stomach.

'Gunner traverse right . . .'

But then over the intercom came the voice of his co-driver: 'He's fookin' dead, Sir.'

The man was stiff, dead since the first hour. Even in the fading light Paul could see how his greatcoat was stitched with the now familiar dark holes from thigh to shoulder: but yet he still sat erect, as if motor-cycling into eternity. In the goggles and helmet the contorted dead white face was hideous, the eyes squinny in the goggles. In the falling gloam he seemed a grotesque statue to destruction: Paul felt his heart beating loudly, at the nightmarish aspect of the corpse rider. But he nodded with an ironic grimace at some infantry who grinned at him from a stable: they had seen his reaction, and had seen the turret move.

The regiment was drawing into a wood between Cazelle

and Cambes, churning about the fields around. The fields were like English fields in Suffolk, with tall elms, chestnuts and white poplars, and orchards among meadows, on the outskirts of the village itself. After their confused and indeterminate progress the little way inland, night began to come on. The regiment gathered and preparations were made for a night in which counter-attacks were expected. The crews slept under the tanks, except for those who were to patrol the laager: the squadrons were drawn within a rough perimeter, guns pointing outwards. There was a space of about a foot between the ground and the flat steel underplates of a Sherman. Sometimes tanks sank into soft soil, and so sleeping underneath them had been forbidden on exercises. Men had been squashed to death. But tonight it was a choice of evils. It seemed worth risking the settling of a thirty-ton tank into the earth to gain some protection, when the air was so full of missiles, if one could find some hard ground. In the first hour or so of dusk one trooper who slept out in a sleeping-bag on a meadow was brained by an anti-aircraft shell fragment: tomorrow they would leave his mutilated body behind under a groundsheet. Later the tank men learnt to sleep actually inside the tank, lying as best they could in the cramped interior, propped up against the gun shield, or racks of shells.

There was no pause in the violence and noise of battle all night. The bright hosings of flak rose continually into the darkness, hysterically, like crazy illuminations, far more spectacular than any firework display. Periods of shelling came on, from time to time, heavy here, sporadic there, the rounds landing and echoing in the fields and woods around them. Machine-guns thrilled or chattered, as patrols met in unclaimed territory. Flares popped in the sky and descended slowly on parachutes. The orchestra of bursting noise was punctuated by the sky-tearing reverberations of battleship guns: they fired monotonously on Caen all night, punctuating the night like Cyclopean clocks.

Paul lay awake for a long time in the darkness on the hard ground under his tank, watching the streamers of flak in the sky, jewel-like and beautiful, an angry sky-writing, from between the bogie wheels. Towards the sea bombs banged down, fires broke out and died from minute to minute. Here he was, at the end of D Day, still alive! He heard his crew snoring already – young men, boys some of them, like him. Some had gone already. Able three. He tried to recall their faces: faces somewhere under tarpaulins, or burnt for ever beyond recognition. As he relaxed under the steel plate above him, a great fatigue overwhelmed him, and he was driven deep into the nightmare halls of death. He wandered back over the battlefield to greet the corpses of Toynbee and his crew, to be with the wounded Dowsett now perhaps lying in the thick of the beachhead, where they expected bombing at night. He could no longer remember anyone's face nor could he imagine where any individual was. At times he was in deep oblivion, at other times acutely aware of dramatic glimpses of night fire, as huge detonations woke him, or fantastic necklaces of white flak rose into the sky in strings that swept the black June night. This, he mused, each time he lapsed back into sleep, was the greatest danger of war – not the personal danger, but the fact that in all its destructiveness it was beautiful, and even dramatically noble. The day that closed in these lights was as great a drama as his life would ever know, however much he now wished it a day he had never come to see.

The intense glitter of the strings of flak pricking the darkness seemed to fade from the sky, and Paul fell into his deepest sleep towards dawn. Yet he was still aware, when there were tremors in the earth on which he lay, from time to time, and when there were fiery glows from the beaches, glowering on the clouds. His nerves still tense and frayed, he awoke feeling he had been divided into two, the body that slept, and a ghostly self that strove to remain on watch, as if to forestall

147

attack on the prostrate self. In such sleep there was little refreshment. But Paul was surprised to find he could sleep on the battlefield at all.

When he awoke at last to the dawn, he felt as if half of him had been on watch all night: the pricking strings of flak resolved themselves into an itch in his sore eyes, into which filtered the poor grey light. In his fatigue, time began to fuse and confuse, as the painful noises never relented, guns slamming and growling incessantly in the weary ears. Battle never blows itself out. Gales blow themselves out; storms pass over. But in war the destructive energy can be fed interminably with fresh impetus, far beyond the limits of endurance of any individual. When one group became dead-beat, more men were brought in, fresh, with fresh ammunition. As exhausted men rested, the guns would open up on them again. Somewhere, always, a gun was going.

So the fresh natural stirring of a summer dawn was already a weary thing to Paul, as the light strengthened between the heavy steel and rubber bogie assemblies of his tank. Above his head the scratched steel plates were sweated with moisture. Crusted and sandy with exhaustion his eyes stared painfully at the colour returning to the wet grass and weeds in the hedgerow. He flexed his limbs in the sleeping bag, but they were like wooden things, twisted in his rucked clothes, and dull with stiffness and sleep on the hard earth. His body did not want to emerge from the warm blankets and expose itself to violence and hurt. But when a sentry thrust an arm under the tank and buffeted his shoulder, calling the crews out, Paul struggled out on all fours across the strong-smelling grassy earth, moist with cold dew. Lurching about numbly he bruised his head on the tank's hull as he cast around for his boots, and swore. The others, the wrapped and grunting figures of the crew, stirred too now in the dim morning.

At 4 a.m. the regiment was standing to, ready to move. Sentries and patrols had been out all night. The tanks were huddled in an orchard, and along a dark wood. In the queer crepuscule figures began to move, attending to equipment, snatching a face wash in cold water. They were forbidden to light fires, as these would draw enemy sights at once.

Paul stood up and scratched, and tried to straighten out and readjust his clothes. He walked down to the hedge to relieve himself. Dark figures were padding about the field in the shadows, and faces, blurred pallid ovals, spoke like disembodied visages in dreams. As he returned to his tank a thin shadow in blue denim strolled casually up and off-handedly seated itself on the track-guard of Paul's tank. As far as Paul could see the man was hatless with pale close-cut hair, uncannily long-limbed, and soft-footed. He seemed like a garage mechanic, come to service one of the vehicles: but he was dressed in a blue shirt and overall trousers, as if for athletics. He spoke easily, in good English, but with some alien notes, like a creature in a dream. Paul, still clouded with sleep, stared at him, was dumb with suspicion, but strangely disarmed.

'We the Maquis . . . we are so pleased to see you . . . Where are you going today?'

'God knows.'

Paul's throat was dry. He disliked talking before breakfast anyway, especially under such conditions. An angry irritation grew in his sleep-cramped mind, with this fellow's questions. Who the hell was he?

'What a lot of tanks you have here. My goodness.'

Paul grunted. There was an awkward pain in his thigh. He fumbled at it, and found his revolver holster was stuck upside down, caught in the lanyard. As he stooped he saw the feet of the strange man in overalls drop on the grass. He wore canvas running shoes. Paul knitted his brows, with an astonished suspicion that this was a spy, an enemy 'phantom' runner sent behind the lines, cunning and dangerous.

'Well, good luck. You are from North England?'

Paul looked up at the long nervous face, pale in the quarter-light. The smile, the expression of welcome, were fading, as the man made a last effort to draw Paul into conversation. He could see he had given himself away, by some slip of the tongue, and he had noticed Paul's reaction: his jaw had dropped. The man made a quaint gesture, a shrug of the head to one side. Paul realized he ought to kill him, at once, there and then, with his revolver. But in such familiar countryside, there on the tall fine grass, in a meadow, by a hawthorn hedge, in running shoes, hatless? At dawn? With no direct combatant provocation? What would the man do if he drew on him? Paul felt transfixed by indecision, ridiculously, like Hamlet. As he felt the hesitation, the kind of hesitation one sometimes has over killing a fly because it is alive, the figure vanished – simply vanished, loping quickly like a blue hare, among the vehicles. Paul felt angrily that the man had made a fool of him, then forgot him as deliberately as he could. He was dismayed by how easily one could be betrayed by conventional expectations – one simply didn't expect the enemy behind one's lines, except in violent fracas.

Yet the next moment, as he stumbled down to his next tank to rouse them, he was accosted by one of the regiment's own sentries, and challenged in a low voice, by a shapeless form in the shadow of the hedge.

'Halt. Who goes there?'

Paul's mind, angry and stupid in sleep still, supposed the query to be addressed to someone else. He even took another step. The man's voice came again, thick and trembling. Paul heard a click.

'Halt or I fire.'

'Hell,' Paul thought, with a sense of the Sten gun pointed at him being loaded and the sentry sleepy. 'What do I say?' he was irritated by what seemed to him troublesome waking dreams. After what seemed an age he managed to reply.

'It's me, Grimmer.'

Catching the officer's voice the trooper seemed to recognise it: Paul could hear him breathing thoughtfully. Both men stood still, the dawn breeze sweeping the hedge. Paul reflected with inward irony on the realities of identity behind the words in this uncertain darkness in which everything dissolved. He could no longer tell whether movements in the dark hedge were in the scrub or in his brain.

'Password . . . Sir?'

A hoarse embarrassed whisper. How unfledged they were! Paul couldn't remember the password. The sentry, uncertain, came closer. It was Corporal Smithers. He peered in Paul's face.

'Oh, it's you . . . Lieutenant Grimmer, sir.'

'Sorry. I'm not awake yet.'

'Browned off' – that was the password.

'Browned off!'

'Too bloody true . . . Sir,' said the Corporal, moving up the hedge, putting his hand up awkwardly to his rimless steel helmet, in salute.

Paul looked up at the night sky, just going pale with the dawn. A flare shot up over the beaches. A painful blow in the ears followed by a great squall in the sky came from another projectile from a battleship: with a great skirl and slam it landed. He felt his body begin to listen again, like a creature separate from him: his nerves and muscles were still teased by the long alertness of yesterday. To his relief, the wan daylight began to strengthen rapidly: the sun was coming up to the horizon. The uncanny mixture of shadows gave way to something more definite. He stretched and moved more briskly among the stirring troops, urging them to get quickly stowed.

His eyes were sore and sandy, and his limbs felt still strangled after sleeping in his clothes. But he was glad to be alive. He had never dared to hope that he would still be alive on D plus one. It was amazing to see the sun rise on it. He took his comb out of his tank overalls: it was broken – he must have rolled on it in the night. With the fragment of broken celluloid he pulled at his tangled hair and tugged out the knots. He had had his hair cut close for the Invasion, but even so it became matted in sleep. He tipped a handful of water out of a jerrycan and splashed his face, drying himself with a fragment of khaki-coloured towelling. Then he noticed some of the troopers were still wound in their canvas vehicle sheets under the tanks. Paul went round and stirred the bodies with his foot. The men gave domestic little groans as they came out of sleep. It seemed cruel to wake them. He knew they must feel as he did – dreading in the body that this might be their last day. His own driver and gunner seemed so young, even to Paul, lying there snug in their piece of tarpaulin. It was like waking children. How strange were the family intimacies of bed, shaving and washing, among the savage machines, in trampled foreign meadows!

Grumbling, the sleepy young men began to crawl out between the bogies, and lope into the early morning shadows to relieve themselves in the hedges, stretching. The noise of gunfire increased as the light strengthened, but so did the loud June birdsong with it. Yellow flashes and soaring lights still continually lit the pale sky over the beachhead and automatic cannon fire flew up in bright red strings as the grey gave way to 'first light'. The tank men were untried in battle, still dangerously relaxed and casual. They had yet to learn that this moment was the most terrible moment in war, the moment when the offensive was launched, the obliterating barrage was brought down, the aerial bombardment fell at the tail end of darkness, while the body and mind were at their lowest ebb. It would not be long before that savage time, 'first light', was established in their souls as a menace and a threat; then, the first glimmer of dawn would make them scuttle to their action stations. But this second day, they dragged themselves out unwillingly to greet the sunrise.

Paul climbed on his tank, whose greasy steel sides were slimy with dew. He heaved himself over the hard polished metal skull of its turret, and fetched out his plastic box of emergency rations from behind the radio set. Nothing better to eat had come ashore yet, though tinned food was expected that day, if all went well. He knew it was to be D + 33, July 9th, before the regiment expected to have cooked mess food, and even then no bread was to be available. In the first days they were to live as they could on their 'twenty-four-hour packs', though most crews had one or two tins of purloined food hidden here and there. So far, however, no-one had had the time, or had been able to relax sufficiently, to eat anything substantial. Paul realised that he had been through D Day on a handful of boiled sweets and a few Horlicks tablets. His stomach felt pinched, hollow and stony, and exhausted in its own way, by the pulsations and tensions of fear. He opened the plastic pack and fumbled at the contents: there was a block of de-hydrated meat like a compressed square of salty coconut matting flavoured with gravy. One would have to be very hungry to eat that. With this were four Oxo cubes. He was looking for the block of compressed oatmeal, about as big as a matchbox. This was delicious. His fingers found it, a little tufted and damp still where he had chewed it the night before. With the oatmeal were ten biscuits, thick, like sweet short-bread. There were tea cubes – tea, milk and sugar all mixed, dehydrated and pressed into blocks. These made a fusty, bitter brew, and one had to be in extremes of thirst to get it down. Then there were the Horlicks pills tasting of malt and dried milk, and two bars of chocolate. In the assembly areas before embarkation, when these rations had been given out, it seemed unthinkable that one would want to eat any of this tabloid food, so ersatz and clinical it looked, the tablets so dry and com-pressed that they hurt the gums. But early in this second morn-ing, as his fingers fumbled in the plastic box Paul became enor-mously hungry for the nourishing pellets.

He felt the dawn urge to wash, eat well, and go forth. He could smell the freshness of the grassy fields, and felt the invita-tion of the dew, in the mysterious darkness of the foreign rural place, with its small meadows among the elm and beech woods. He hallucinated bacon and eggs, hot rolls and coffee, actual emanations of them seeming to rise from the warm smell of his sleep-numb flesh within his battledress tunic. He had a soft longing for the comfort of home, for the familiar domestic voices. In this mood he took a swig of tired water from his enamelled tin bottle swathed in khaki serge, and gnawed greedily at the hard biscuits and the block of oatmeal. They hurt his mouth, but they were delicious: the oatmeal flavour seemed full and substantial in the dark chill of the Normandy morning. Around him the men were also busy gnawing, rubbing their faces with khaki towels and water: their eyes were dull and red.

After his tablet breakfast Paul became more relaxed. He recalled the unfortunate Dowsett and hoped he had been picked up and taken off back to England. As the first weak light came he felt a deep sadness grow on him, as if the ghosts of the many unknown thousands who died on D Day flitted past with those first rays. He felt an old warrior already, on his first morning. But only one day had gone! His inward weaker self recoiled at the thought of what was to come, in weeks and weeks of terrible fighting. But the foothold in Europe had to be maintained, he told himself. Whatever his own experience might be, it needed to be multiplied a million times, before it could be understood as the common experience of that generation swarming in that dawn on the doorstep of occupied Europe.

A high electrical whirr came from within the turret of his tank. There was a glow from the red light on the 19 set in the fighting compartment, where men stirred.

'Dog two. O.K. over.'

His operator was replying to a signal check, locking the dials to a new frequency, tightening up the netting screws with a penny. Frequencies and codes were changed each day: now, the headphones humming, they awaited the orders for the day. Paul licked his sticky fingers of the last of the oatmeal. The light was growing and so the co-driver had ventured to light a Primus inside the front hull of the tank to brew some of the sour tea cubes. A blue faint light shone under the half-closed steel hatch. The men were 'brewing up char'. They were developing a quick spontaneous capacity to make themselves as comfortable and easy as they could, under any conditions. Paul felt he ought to forbid the use of a Primus inside a tank, next to gallons of diesel oil, and hundredweights of cordite and high explosive. But the whole load might be blown sky high any minute by a stray shot – they were continually beyond normal consideration of safety out here – so what could it matter? It seemed as if a cup of tea might help save their lives by sharpening their faculties and freeing their mouths, dry with fear and apprehension.

Tactfully involving him in their offence against the regulations, the crew offered the first oblong aluminium mess-tin of acrid rehydrated tea to Paul, who sipped it gratefully as he gazed at the glory of the Normandy scene unfolding itself from the darkness. 'Homelite' battery-charging engines popped and whirred, giving off clouds of blue smoke. He thought there were more white poplars and sycamores here than in England. As the sun rose the scene took on its sparkling quality, of the bright flicker of a myriad green leaves, the countryside all radiant with moving points of light. The scene was becoming the rich Impressionist landscape once more – but now as the light returned he could see a sombre difference that had come on the scene – the cattle were all dead.

Yesterday a few cattle had moved about the landscape, black and white figures between the trees or moving behind the sparkling orchards. Where his squadron had drawn its tanks into its rough laager formation for the night there was a field with young calves. A stunted old peasant in thin blue trousers, grey jacket and cloth cap, his face wizened with fear, had come over to try to comfort his calves, making gestures of despair, and murmuring to the alarmed little animals. Now, as he stood sipping the hot tea, tasting of mess-tin, in the dawn light, Paul could see that the calves had all been killed during the night.

They lay in ungainly postures scattered over the field, their stiffening legs cocked up in the air. Near the house a tethered cow lay stupidly inverted, its legs and udder sticking rigidly upwards. In the next few weeks this strange sight of animal death touched the Englishmen deeply with its horror, a token of the monstrous denaturalisation of that lovely French June. Later the dead cows swelled, turned putrescent and stank, their bodies going bloated, then oozy and slimy with decay. Their corpses upset the soldiers more than those of their own dead. Paul felt a great surge of anger at the waste and meaninglessness of the death of the calves; he had not even heard the noise of the artillery that had killed them. Had the projectiles fallen a little his way, he would be lying so, stiff and inert: but he did not make this connection consciously and he only looked round anxiously in the advancing light hoping to see a calf that moved, for one of those peaceful black and white cattle to wander in the field, for the peasant to rescue or comfort, a living movement of beasts to gladden the scene. But they were all dead, in grotesque rigid postures.

In such ways the smashing of that beautiful Normandy countryside broke the capacity of the young man to identify himself with the gladness of natural creation, for ever. The sun shone, the grass shivered in a wild expanse of rich green, the full green foliage sparkled and danced. Even the rural houses, the farms and chateaux, with their pale grey stone and hospitable large courtyards, merged into a prospect full of that delight in the living countryside such as the great French painters had captured. But the rich red of weathered brick, the grey stone, the sparkling greens, the pale dust of the light soil – all that tender scene, showed itself remorselessly indifferent and apart. That Nature rejoiced with man showed itself a lie. 'The little hills rejoice on every side' – this was a lie. The waist-high daisies and the verges of poppy and cornflower lived on in the wind and sun, indifferent to the yells of the dying and wounded, the violence of explosions and the stiffening corpses among them. And the unoffending cattle were all destroyed where they stood in the fields around.

The sun was over the horizon now. To Paul's surprise he now saw infantrymen in the next plot to the tanks, dug into new slit trenches. He hadn't noticed them arrive. Each trench was an oblong pit just large enough for a man to crouch in. Under their hessian-beribboned hats the infantrymen were active over their heaps of earth in the morning freshness, cleaning rifles and rummaging in their packs of food and clothing. They worked among their heaps of gravelly spoil like a race of primitives, Stone Age dwellers. The whole orchard was crowded with these infantry. These would go forward soon, to make the front line and to win territory with their vulnerable bodies. Looking at them reflectively the tank men felt the luxury of their two inches of steel and weighed it against the tank men's special peril – the bulk of his machine at a distance and his special claim for attention from enemy anti-tank gunners and rocket teams. The sense of security of the tank men had evaporated on Queen Beach, where they had seen the first broken monsters. Even so, they were glad they were not infantry, having to dig themselves into the ground at every step, using their own muscles. The narrow slit trenches in the dark earth looked like graves. When the infantry left the security of their trenches there was nothing but cloth between them and the knife-edge fragments that whipped out in fans from exploding missiles.

Paul studied their faces under their yellow and green headgear, indistinct in the undergrowth in their drab costume. Even living, they resembled disturbingly the heavy sack-like corpses of the beach dunes. The wood, and the laager of tanks swarmed now with the drab shapeless animals that men are in war, shaving in cold water, digging, chewing, carrying arms, fumbling with grubby khaki towels or relieving themselves into the hedges and undergrowth. It was the moment before the cohesion of battle plans, when order would be restored. They bustled at toilet and packing, while the officers were in their order groups. Soon the crackling voices on the radios, crayonings on maps, orders spoken with quiet determination, would bring an aspect of system to these swarming night-stale herds.

The birds whistled loudly now, blackbirds and thrushes, as they do in English fields in summer. Larks were soaring in their striving way. A breeze of morning ran along in the poplars and elms and in the tall wheat, still green, as the sun threw a happy glory over the Norman countryside. Paul suddenly noticed a strange white and black shape on the ground behind the trees in the far distance – then another, then another. Aeroplanes? Then he saw that they were smashed fusilages – of the grounded gliders which had dived overhead last evening into enemy territory and now lay like huge broken magpies along the Orne, gaunt and queer. Intermittently the quick growl of fast Spandau machine-guns played away to the west: fighting which had never ceased to the flank had gone on all night and doubled its fury now in the growing light. Brens replied with their slow pulse: POCKPOCKPOCKPOCK. More intense became the noise of falling shells, like banging doors, slam after slam. Was it a counter attack? Already, after one night, these noises seemed accepted, familiar. Yet there would be new voices. There were other noises, new sounds, that Paul did not know.

He heard one now, as he watched the infantry. It was a soft *siffle*, high in the air, like a distant lark, or a small penny whistle, faint and elf-like, falling. But then, with a spiral pulsing flutter, it grew to a hissing whirr. Behind it he heard the soft sharp thuds, of the weapon, and was striving to remember where he had heard the noise before. Mortars! That was it! But hardly had the thought come before the first bombs were among them. He had never expected the violence to be so terrible. The mortar bombs landed with ferocious blasts, followed by a whine of fragments which cut into the trees, driving deep white scars into their trunks and filling the air with torn shreds of tree foliage whirled about in clouds of blue-black smoke. The concussion made his head ache and ring, but the sequence of bombs came on and on relentlessly, whistling and whispering down with their horrible fluttering shiver in the ears.

Men dived, the infantry into the earth, the tank men under their tanks or down the hatches, ripping their clothes as they became hooked on projections in the panic. Without ceremony or dignity the shapeless bodies flew and crowded into holes between tanks and earth, or lay trying to tear themselves into the ground.

The mortar bombardment lasted perhaps three minutes. But to Paul it seemed hours, as he simply lay with his face in the grass, a little way from his tank, pinned down. The wood heaved like a creature that bulged and rocked, as the mortar bombs exploded blackly in the trees. Paul watched at first transfixed in terror, but then pressed his head down into the grass as a bomb fell his side of the orchard, and fragments whirred over his head to clatter against the side of his tank. Dirt and fumes flew over him, the noise became a ringing pain in his head. The oatmeal taste became bitter with the taste of fear and death in his mouth. He clung with his nails to small pieces of earth, and twisted grass bents, tugging at them in expectation of losing a leg or half his body to one of the siffling streams of bombs. He prayed for it to cease: he willed himself away: he swore never to be caught out of a closed tank again: he lost every conviction, political, moral, human: he would have capitulated to any enemy, believed in any God he had been required to believe in – if only the reward were to be relieved from the terror of the falling spate of mortar bombs.

But then, suddenly, came a second wind of morale: the body, too much tortured by what it heard and felt, ceased any longer to react. He was beyond fear, beyond demoralization; his feelings had gone totally shocked and dead. He had withdrawn any tendency towards deep feelings from his regimental companions, long ago, before the invasion. Men exert a general comradeship in war, but deeper personal affections are largely closed off, like bulkheads sealed. They cannot be afforded.

But now Paul Grimmer cut off his feelings for himself: he no longer loved himself. He allowed his self to become expendable. He hated the Army for bringing him into this hell. He lost all trust in the regiment, in comradeship, in action against the enemy. He was utterly divided and alienated, bent only on survival. Now, he had discovered how to react to mortaring, by dividing himself from himself. He almost felt he was looking down on himself lying on the earth, while his intellect exercised fantastic tricks of detachment, seeking to survive. His mind felt it could survive, even if his body was hit.

As the mortar shells burst on, his mind concentrated intensely on automatically checking the bursts against the distant sharp thumps of their projection. Two failed to explode, his intellect calculated. He felt coldly triumphant, in his divided mind, over the fear that bathed his craven prostrate body in sweat. He planned with calculation that when he heard those faint sharp thumps of mortars in future, he would be closed down before he heard the horrible siffle of their falling. Mortar bombs take an age to complete their high-flying parabola: his mind felt this to be the clue to survival. And then to watch the faces of others. So, later when the engine was moaning, or the tank radio was loud, he would carefully watch the faces of the infantry. When they looked up, their faces turned drawn, and they hugged the bottom of the trench, then probably those swishing projectiles were in the air, and it was time to pull down the heavy turret lid.

So much can the human mind think in three minutes of time that no written work could encompass the voluminous thoughts and apprehensions of a man who takes that long to die. Paul died many times in that three minutes, and as many times preserved his balance by that strange intellectual dissociation, finding a way to go on living by a kind of magic, as each fierce stinging crack seemed to mean the end. After an age of it, still tugging at frail stems of grass and weeds, he suddenly saw that the early morning grass was full of rich beetles. He almost laughed with joy at the vision, under the bludgeoning bombardment. The insects crawled untroubled through the thick stems beneath his face, as the smoke and dust flew in the air. There were black beetles with rainbow colours in their backs, their shells engraved with ribs finer than the grooves on gramophone records, and beetles with mothlike patterns on them, wood-colours. There was one large green creature, shaped like a shield, jewelled like a brooch, catching gleams from the morning sun. With long delicate twig-like legs, it made its awkward way from small clod to small clod. Paul felt a great wave of empathy with the beetle, and pressed his face down to it. He saw it retract a step once as the ground shook with a heavy stinging blast from a mortar bomb. But, Paul wagered, if he gets to that clod six inches away, I shall survive this. If not, he, the green jewelled one, and I, will perish together. He clung hard, sweating and dry-mouthed, to his clump of grass, as the beetle slowly wavered its claw-like legs towards the clod. Halfway the creature met a difficult stone. Another whistling batch arched in the air far above. They fell rhythmically: bam . . . bam . . . bam. A bomb-tail whirred into the air like something to scare a bird. His beetle made it. The mortaring stopped.

It seemed nothing could withstand the deluge that had fallen into the whipped and blasted wood. Yet only one infantryman was wounded, mortally. His frightened shout was heard over the torrent of blast, and, white and limp, he was carried away on a brown stretcher as soon as the din stopped, which it did as abruptly as it had begun. The whole inferno raged, it seemed, simply to tear into the vitals of this one unhappy man, by whom, afterwards, squatted the tank regiment's Irish padre, offering what solace he could in his genial way, for all the last pain, and the final brokenness.

The sun shone brightly on the shattered wood and the fear-crouched men. One of the dead calves' bodies had been burst open, flinging a patch of blood and mess about the green meadow now pocked with brown pits. Orderlies struggled with the dying infantryman out of the wood.

They were stunned for a moment.

'Bleeders, bleeders,' shouted a trooper, white and trembling, angrily clearing and stowing kit.

Paul's driver shook the earth off his battledress. He lurched round where Paul had been lying.

'Mind that bit, Jackson.'

'What, Sir?'

The driver looked alarmed.

'Oh, nothing. There was a green beetle, where I was lying!' Jackson looked baffled. Then grinned.

'Are you all right, Sir?'

They laughed. Of course, Paul mused, I am not mad. Nor is he. We're sane! But how long, in this, can anyone be? Paul noticed he was trembling, and cold sweat caked under his battledress blouse. He had also severely lost some sense of wholeness in his identity. It was now as if one self would always be poised, ready to desert the other, in extreme situations. He felt inwardly split, demoralized and disloyal. He was too shaken and weary to dare to think about this, however, and clambered up the slippery tank with relief to help the gunner load a new machine-gun belt. From time to time he looked out.

He saw the Padre rise and cross himself, and walk away.

'That poor sod has had his lot.'

'Who'd be a bloody B.F.I.?'

'I shan't get caught out of the bloody turret again like that often, by Christ.'

It seemed incredible that anyone in the wood could have survived. Yet out of it came Major Bumpton, the squadron leader, fresh as a daisy, map-case in hand.

*

Paul stared at him as if he was a ghost. Had Bumpo really

162

been in that wood? If so, how could he have survived, to stroll
out like this with such coolness? He saluted his squadron leader.

'Good God, Sir, were you in there?'

'Having a stroll. Hun was a bit noisy, it's true.'

Bumpo sniffed and grimaced. He was a small bird-like man
with a large pointed nose. His eyes had genial puffy wrinkles
round them. His mouth was genial too, but a little crushed and
hard, too, like a beak. It was impossible to dislike him: he was
kind, energetic, brave and competent. Paul was envious of his
courage: Bumpo would never be confounded or prostrated.
But Paul felt the ability to be such a good soldier could surely
only go with a darkening of certain areas of human perception: you could only stand war so by splitting yourself into
fragments, or by being dead at the centre.

'Looks like we shall soon have a bit of a party. Can you get
Bright and Peters over?'

The little major was like a bright bird with his rimless tank
helmet, the steel shell sitting squarely on his head like half a
khaki egg, his map-case neatly lanyarded with its crayons in
place, his webbing clean and his brown boots polished. He sat
on a green jerrycan studying his notes, as if he were perched on
a shooting stick at the races. Then a thought struck him and he
went over to Paul's driver with his mouth open in a bird-like
smile, genial crowsfeet at the corners of his eyes.

'I say, Willis, I saw you come over on to the Rhino ferry
yesterday superbly, at a *very* rough moment. I thought it was
an awfully good performance.'

'Thank y', Sir.'

Paul admired this extrovert capacity: not to be prostrated by
one's own inward torment, but to train oneself in the habit of
outward encouragement, cheering others on – one here, one
there, remembering to say this to that person, and that to
another. Morale! As he made his way on foot towards the farm
buildings behind which Numbers Two and Three troops had
concealed themselves Paul realized how much he envied

163

Bumpo's 'well-bred' capacities to be cool under fire. In Bumpo were combined an almost inhuman indifference to danger with a meticulous genial care and kindness for his men. In the field he was admirable. He carried into the anarchy and chaos of war those qualities for transcending mere personal interests by a cold command over feelings learnt at public school.

Of course, thought Paul, it missed something, missed a quality of compassion. 'Good breeding' meant a kind of emasculation, too. Those peasants, there: what would Bumpo think of these? To him, Paul knew, they wouldn't count. He could see through the wood, briefly through a gap in the hedge, an old man in dusty blue overalls, and a youngish woman in dull blue peasant apron, working in the field. Whatever were they doing? Tears almost came when he saw. They were haymaking! Pathetically turning the crop among the craters, trying to prepare themselves for an uncertain future! His heart swelled with compassion for the old man, and the girl, his daughter he supposed, in their bewildered tenacity. But he feared for them. The girl wore ankle boots, and a blue cloth beret. If she came under fire! Paul felt waves of pity at such sights, and feared these would break him down as a soldier. He allowed them to touch his heart, which bled that human life should be reduced to such agony. As she looked up a moment from the little field into the wood, the woman gave the English tank men one furtive glance, her face dazed with the terror of the death and violence around her. Yesterday those few dazed French people had waved tricolours as the regiment had come through the broken village of Colville, happy to show their hidden flags again after four years. But such a storm of violence flew over the heads of the Norman inhabitants, that, though they were free, they were still in great danger. Their cattle were killed, their homes shattered; even so they applauded, standing clapping sadly in their doorways. Some died by ricochets, even as they dug their potatoes, by the chance whirling flight of fragments of hurled metal. Soon they would either be free, or would die: so the wretched French country people waited where the horror was hardest to bear, by their own hearths, and scratched at their earth, lifting roots and hay, waiting.

The terrible sadness of it all was vividly evoked in Paul by the woman's frightened face as she drew the swathes of bluish green hay grass over, working alongside the feeble old man. Such a sight was nothing to Bumpo. Yet one could rely on Bumpo in danger. Paul envied his indifference to danger: it seemed an incredible courage. But was it inhumane? Paul could not make up his mind. He was beginning to doubt the value of being brave in war at all: part of him already regarded courage, as did Falstaff, as stupid and pointless. The mortaring had already crazed the thin fabric of his youthful determined allegiance to the Army.

Peter Bright's allegiance was of a different order – cold, fanatical and single-minded courage. This pale young man, only nineteen, troop leader of number four troop, stocky and boyish, was already in battle-order, fed, shaved, mounted, with everything folded and stowed away, in the dark grey-green tanks behind the farm wall below the wood. He was in his element on a battle morning, straining at the leash. He jumped down with a clean and eager impetus as Paul reached the troop. To Paul he seemed a boy, though Bright was only two years younger than himself.

'Bumpo wants us for an 'O' group.'

'Righto!'

Bright set his square young jaw and looked 'set' in his bright blue eyes.

'We had a dusty packet of mortaring just now.'

'Did you say we had to get Peters?'

Damn him, thought Paul: by refusing to reply to my remark about the mortaring he's implying it's weak to speak about danger. Paul noticed two deep gouges running into the steel of Bright's own tank. So he's been blooded. Paul whistled: Bright took no notice. Paul felt a surge of irritation: to him such studied indifference seemed an affected pose. But yet he knew that Bright followed such an ideal of youthful gladiatorship that the rest of experience was pale to him. He noticed that the pale boy was restless for his reply: no time to waste.

'Yes – he's just at the other end of the wood.'

'I'll call him on the 'B' set: we have a link.'

So efficient! Paul watched the young subaltern give orders to one of his co-drivers, to call up Peters. He moved like the epitome of the Sandhurst-trained officer: everywhere at a quick step, his arms swinging, or at a loose double. His goggles, pistol, crayons, were all neatly ready for action. There was even a bulge in his breast pocket that spoke of a Mills bomb, primed and ready. It was all so tidy and, somehow, a manifestation of pious hate. Bright was the devoted soldier, utterly loyal, morale inlaid.

Paul had shared a room with him in Scotland, during training. Bright's effects were small: he had only a photograph of his mother over the bed, a stern-looking plain old woman with the same formidable chin as her son's. Even though she was only a photograph, she alarmed Paul. Bright had a Bible by his bed, and his soldier's equipment. If he ever read, he read his Bible, or a training manual. He was a short youth with even white teeth and intense blue eyes. He seemed to have had few of life's experiences. In so many ways he was callow and boyish – his body was that of a strong child, covered with pale hairs, clean, and full of wiry energy. He seemed entirely devoted to heroism, and to Christian murder. Paul was puzzled by him, as his companion seemed to have no political understanding, or, indeed, little interest in anything except fighting.

Paul stood by Bright's tank as he called up Peters from another. The tank's tracks were sunk into the leaf-mould, and the ruts of its progress had ripped up the saplings. Infantrymen were now crowding into the wood, cluttered green figures, loaded up and on the move. The wood was filling with a fresh group who were preparing mortars and mortar bombs in trailers: soon these would move out into the open sun to reply to the German fire. A plane flew over, and a crackling of loud machine-gun fire went up at it: someone was firing a turret-mounted machine-gun at it from Paul's troop. Shells began to land in the meadow beside the wood with familiar crashes. His heart throbbing, Paul wished Peters would hurry – he disliked being in the open, at conferences. Once in the tank, on the move, one knew where one was. The tank man felt at a disadvantage on his feet.

A hatch opened and a helmet came up, under it a trooper's broad grin.

' 'Ave ye seen where we copped it, Sir?'

'Bit close, wasn't it?'

In fact the hideous gouges in the steel made Paul feel sick and repelled, the marks of the intense hatred and violence directed against them, and the dreadful speed of the propelled missile. The steel was curled up round the troughs in small melted waves.

'Too fookin' close. 'E said – Lootenant Bright said – we'll stop here and have a look, like. So we looked and there was some bloody thing went WHACK-OOMP, like that 'ere, over'ead. So I said, "What's that?" and 'e said – Lootenant Bright said, "It's only strays." But it weren't, it were a bloody eighty-eight and next time a bloody great bough fell off a tree and nearly hit the coont – I mean nearly 'it the lootenant – on the beano.'

Paul laughed, despite himself.

'Then what does 'e do, Sir? 'E doesn't fook off like anywoon with sense. 'E goes and fooking well charges at the bloody thing, till Major Bumpton calls 'im back. That's 'ow we got them loomps out.'

'Well, you've been blooded.'

Instead of a cheerful grimace, the man's eyes became wide, and his voice hysterical:

'Too bloody troo. D'you know what 'e wants, Sir? 'E wants

to get 'is fookin' V.C. It's fookin' ooncomfortable. . . . 'E's too Bright 'e is.'

Paul moved away, followed by the man's frightened grin. There was nothing he could say, though he knew he shouldn't let a trooper talk like that about a fellow officer. But it was true, and he could see how the man's terror was expressing itself in this ironic clowning. He saw the eyes white with anxiety as the lid closed on the trooper behind him. How we all act a part, to escape our true feelings, Paul mused. He still felt the horror of the threat of molten metal.

Peters came running, a loose floppy young man with a dark cheerful face. He had just been given his second pip. Bright still had only one on his overalls. The three of them made their way clumsily back to Paul's tank, where Bumpo was waiting. They saluted.

'Now you young chaps must be quicker: you've taken ages to get here.'

'Sorry Bumpo,' murmured Peters. 'It was my fault. You caught me with my trousers down, literally.'

'You're lucky,' said Paul. 'I couldn't do that to save my life.'

'You feel damn vulnerable, I can tell you, with your arse hanging out like a full moon.'

Peters and Paul laughed. Peters was a genial handsome easy-going youth. Paul liked him. Even Bumpo smiled. But Bright didn't. To him such easy humour on the eve of battle was like acting the fool in church. Paul felt Bright's lips were still wet with bloodthirsty prayers: he was impatient to be on the move, and at the enemy's throat. Bumpo was amused, in his paternal way, with his subalterns – he regarded them rather like fractious spaniel puppies at a shoot. But even his smile was well-bred – automatic and brief. He withdrew geniality during his 'O' group. The other two troop leaders were waved up, Tompkins and Geal.

Bumpo showed them the map, and told them the story. The

168

casual Peters lit a Senior Service from a round tin of fifty. The Brigade in front had reached Caen the previous night, but had been too much stretched out to remain: the 21st Panzer Division who had been on exercises in the area had come up to support the German 716th Infantry Division. Our 185th Brigade in front had been therefore withdrawn slightly and brought back to consolidate their gains about ten miles inshore. The regiment and its infantry brigade were to take over a village called Cazelle. Paul peered over Bumpo's shoulder at the map. So – the haphazard violence bursting out sporadically round them, then, had some kind of shape, to someone. Paul imagined briefly the German officers, only three or four miles away, also at their early order groups.

'From there we shall attack the Hun in Cambes and the wood in front of it.'

'A' squadron would shoot into the village from the flank.

'C' squadron were to go in with the infantry.

'I want two of you to volunteer to lead your troops in support of the infantry.'

Bright volunteered at once, the request almost out of his mouth before Bumpo had finished. Paul saw him throw his chin out, until it looked as terrible as that of his big square mother, in the small photograph over his bed up in Forres. Paul supposed that photo must be now in his battledress pocket. One of the other troop leaders, Tompkins, was as prompt. Paul felt ashamed at first, not to be the first to volunteer – but then inwardly shrugged – there'd be plenty of occasion to show one's mettle. He was still resentful that the regiment had let him in for the mortar barrage: that was enough for one day. He stared at the broken trees along the wood and detested his predicament. That morning he could find no way of reconciling the sporting terms of the intentions and orders, and the hideous truths of steel breaking flesh.

The Major showed them a rough indication of where the allied line was, from the Orne to the base of the Cherbourg peninsula, in red crayon on his talc map cover. The little foothold the allies had gained on the mainland of France looked pathetically small: yet more troops were coming in behind them all the time, thick and fast, Bumpo assured them. Saluting briefly, the young officers doubled back to their tanks. They called up their crews and the loud, bellowing engines were started up all round. The elephant-like Shermans began to stir, squealing, their domes blundering out from under trees and camouflage foliage. There was a smell of fresh-pressed earth again. As Paul mounted his tank he felt a return of confidence in his unit and his Squadron Commander. Bumpo he knew had been forward at first light with the Colonel and the other squadron leaders, to scan the ground towards the enemy lines. They had been to the foremost infantry posts, in great danger, crawling in ditches to the foremost outposts. He felt ashamed to have been so critical of the man. He returned to a capacity to function with the automatism of his military training. The brisk voice of Bumpo came over the air now, clear and encouraging.

'Hello all stations Dog. Prepare to move in this order: Dog two, then four, then one, three and fi-yive. Follow green route. Move now. Out.'

The tanks began to move off. Paul was in command of Dog two, the first troop. The large village of Périers-sur-le-Dan was impassable because of bombing and shelling: they had to crawl round the fields and through minefields. They found that many of the small, black signs with skull and crossbones, or saying in black and white, 'Achtung Minen', had been hung round fields innocent of any such devices. But it took time to make sure. Men had to descend and work on foot with the squeaky head phones and scanning poles of electronic mine detectors. They had to sweep all the ground in front, as with a vacuum cleaner, the tanks nosing carefully behind them. Then the tanks bellowed forward, pressing the sweet-smelling grass. So the procession of the great grey-green machines was cum-

bersome in the early morning light, rucking up great troughs
behind them in the fertile earth, on the way to their first land
battle.

D + I to D + 3

SO, PAUL GRIMMER, a bewildered young man of twenty-one,
spent June 7th and 8th, 1944, crawling about green fields and
woods in Normandy with his squadron, among the thickening
herds of soldiers crammed into that slim stretch of Norman
countryside during those rough summer days. On their large-
scale maps, the area within which they moved measured less
than an inch square, lying between the villages of Cazelle,
Anisy and Cambes, with Beauville to the east. Towards Caen
were distant fortified villages – Cambes itself, Galmanche beyond, Epron, and the large wooded fortification at Lebisey.
The fields swept gently down, in rolling gentle slopes, from
the high ground south of Douvres la Delivrande, the Périers
Ridge. The fields were grey-green, the corn having just reached
its full height; the hedge-weeds and tall grasses were at their
most feathery, and the meadows were rich. In the uncertain
June weather the woods bulked thick and green, sometimes a
little blue with heat-haze, or soft with wind-blown foliage.
Above the woods here and there protruded a spire, and among
the trees were glimpses of bright red farms, grey roofs, or
orchard walls. So charming, the village names – so rustic:
Cresserons, Plumetot, Cazelle, Périers-sur-le Dan. Yet many
of them were packed with toughly constructed fortifications
in concrete and earth, from which protruded guns manned by
fanatical and hardened German troops. The soft rural landscape
held its fire, stirring slightly in the breeze, but then would
suddenly spit, rending the air, and spreading in the fields and

hedges the confusion of corpses, burning vehicles, and blackened relics of broken machines of war.

The battles in which young Grimmer became involved seemed to him tremendous, almost cosmic affairs. Yet, in the whole scale of things, as they came to be written up in the histories afterwards, they were but flank efforts, small spoilings and forays, unmentioned except in asides or footnotes. But to take in the whole aspect of the fantastic invasion, such episodes must be multiplied a thousand times – and even then one only glimpses a fragment of the huge and hideous suffering which such a large-scale campaign as 'Overlord' brings. The infantryman picking into the orchard soil with his short trench tool, the tank man pouring the pungent diesel into his filler pipe, the despatch rider coming up powdery with dust – these had little sense of the huge pattern in which they played their part – a pattern altering the whole face of the world, and of the century. Paul Grimmer worried more about what Bumpo would think of him, and whether he would survive this day, than of the whole conflict of intentions, as considered in Berlin and London, those tense days.

In the first stage of the attack on Cambes Wood, on D + 1, tanks of 'A' squadron of the East Northshire Regiment milled across some open ground in a valley to the flank of the wood, below Cazelle, probing. The defended villages seemed only a few fields apart. But as the situation in the beachhead hardened, the enemy's position became known a little more accurately. As yet, however, the landscape looked so tender and peaceful in the summer light that the tank men felt an impulse, when they found fresh-looking ground, to ride forward pressingly. Beyond the crowded turmoil of the rear areas they felt lost, nervously apprehensive of the sinister summer scene. As if sensing this, the German gunners held their fire.

As his troop of three tanks rode forward in the morning along the valley towards Cambes Wood Paul Grimmer thought he saw some enemy to his right – men in grey-green uniforms digging. The area was an unknown one, in the No Man's Land between them and the next Army. In apprehension, he paused behind a hillock and fired his turret machine-gun at the distant figures, who scrambled quickly into the grass of the orchard. For a second Paul braced himself for return of fire, the hair prickling on his face. But then came relief and astonished water stood in his eyes, as a man stood up and waved at him. Through his binoculars he could see a cursing face under a ribboned steel hat and a dancing gesticulating figure – in dark green battledress. He had found the flank of the Canadian Third Division! The Canadian infantry were digging in, on the right of the gentle valley, working at their trenches among the trunks of trees in an orchard. Beyond the orchard, smoke and a rain of bright tracer in the air suddenly denoted the fighting line. Through his glasses Paul could see vehicles moving forward towards Villons-les-Buissons. On the left were rolling fields of high green corn, towards Cambes hidden in the dark mass of a long wood. His three tanks left crushed wakes in the corn, like boats: they circled round and round in the morning sun, a little lost and confused. The tank commanders gazed at the distant stretch of green wood, of thick elm and oak, blue, green and dense, and seemingly innocent and peaceful. It was like any English scene, waiting for the sun to ripen the harvest.

Suddenly there was a clear sharp shock-wave in the air, a sound that stung his cheek. Paul looked at his sergeant across in one of the other tanks, who shrugged. No one knew what the sound meant.

'Hallo Peter Baker. Is that sniper fire?'

As if for answer the sound came again. This time there was a sudden explosion in a tree as it passed. The thick limb of an elm was smashed to fragments in the air, and a flurry of twigs, torn leaves and fragments of smashed wood was thrown all over Paul's tank. The tree had been shaken as if by a tremendous whirlwind as the shot passed. No rifle shot could do that:

173

they were under fire from an 88 mm. anti-tank gun. Dimly the perception came to Paul: this was no place to be swanning in confusion to no purpose. He ordered his troop back on the 'B' short wave set.

'Hallo all stations Dog one. Under fire from hornet. Return to laager area now. Keep hull down from wood at 016741. All stations Dog one, over.'

As the operators acknowledged in turn the tanks slewed and rattled back following a depression in the fields, returning towards Cazelle. Dust rose from them in clouds as they pulled up the hill facing Cambes Wood. Here they joined a group of headquarters tanks. Paul was anxious: the tanks seemed unable to escape exposure to the enemy on the ground facing out over the plain and into the wood. Some of the machines gathered together by a haystack, others preferred to work their way into orchards at the top of the hill where there were stone walls, or among the buildings of straggling farm steadings between Cazelle and Cambes. A fine dust flew into the air from the farm tracks and the fields where the tanks blundered squealing, like dazed elephants.

There now came a sun-laden quiet in the morning. Poppies and white daisies waved in the warm breeze: the place reminded Paul of scenes he had seen in a French film, *Les Otages*, the white tracks with no hedges, the cornfields level, stretching down towards the woods.

Peace seemed restored. Paul breathed more freely. He climbed down from his tank, and left the headphones hanging over the turret edge, to relieve himself against the haystack. He could feel the warmth coming off the sweet hay. Where he stood there were bright red poppies holding their fragile tissue flowers to the intermittent morning sun. Long stems held heavy, fluffy flowers of grass up to him. Next to his tank was Peters', and the other side a headquarters tank belonging to Eddy. Eddy was a headquarters major, and Paul wondered why he was down here. They all rather dreaded Eddy, a cold and

174

unbendable man, who was a Christian Scientist. If he was ever indisposed he believed he was being assailed by evil: so he punished himself remorselessly, by cold spiritual disapproval of himself, and icy prayer. Because of this sense of guilt he was as remorseless with anyone else who was sick or hurt. His moustache would bristle and his eyes would narrow as he refused a man a chit for the M.O. or compassionate leave. He was a middle-aged bachelor, reserved and bristly, with rigid habits and a paranoic egocentricity. Some called him a Good Old Stick by which they meant they hated and feared him. He walked as if he had a ram-rod inserted in the marrow of his backbone, and his demeanour was as stiff. He would sometimes be found praying in odd places and at odd times, his lips moving coldly under his moustache. Paul nodded at Eddy in his goggles. He wants to be where it's dangerous, I suppose, Paul thought, punishing himself. Well, I shall make myself scarce as soon as I've done my flies up.

Bumpton's voice came over the air, through Paul's headset.

'Er . . . Dog Sunray here . . . One and four: you're bunching too much. Spread out a bit. Dog one and Dog four, over.'

Paul did his buttons up hurriedly, and wiped his forehead clear of dust behind the stack. His driver started up.

As he did so an enormous bell sounded with a clangour that threw him off his feet. The loud gong-like noise was followed by a colossal roar, and from Peters' tank soared a monstrous column of white smoke that formed a huge ring in the air. Peters leapt, a huddled figure, from the side of his tank and crawled into the side of the stack, smoke wreathed round him, his hair alight. The tank, a moment ago the home and shelter of five men, now looked a terrible sight, with flames belching out of its front hatches and engine louvres, and a pillar of fire roaring out of the turret, colossal gouts of smoke billowing across the field in curled torrents. The 88 had struck home! Paul made impulsively towards the stricken vehicle, but then realized, as tremendous internal explosions thrust fierce gases from every aperture, that no-one within could have possibly survived. A rim of smoke and flame like a lace collar was squeezed in jets from where the turret joined the hull. The painted metal began to grow black as he looked, and eyes of white flame looked out at the holes where the armour-piercing shot had entered.

The men around were galvanized with rage. Choking voices came over the air. Peters, blackened and furious, leapt on to Paul's tank, and screamed fire orders to the gunners below. Tanks began to fire, the dust whipped up in clouds by the tossed tongues of cordite flame. Confusedly Paul looked round, still dizzy with the noise and now buffeted by the blasts that spoke from the guns of his own squadron. Then he saw the goggled Eddy waving at him: he climbed his turret. Eddy had a stutter. He shouted, his whiskers twitching in a red agitated face with goggles under the grey steel helmet.

'C-c-come and load. My loader's g-g-g-gone to . . .'

The man was convulsed for a moment.

'G . . . aitch -c-c-c-Q. C-c-come and load for m-m-me.'

It was like some dream of terror, and Paul knew it was his end. He knew that this must be the final irony, to be deprived of his own machine, to be cooped up in a tank with the frigid Eddy, to load his gun, while the self-persecuting bachelor, with his maddening and convulsed precision, stuttered fire orders. Eddy in barracks was bad enough, inspecting men on parade he was heartlessly thorough about detail. But Eddy in this situation Paul dismally supposed capable of anything. He'd drive into that wood in sheer futile cold-bloodedness, his whiskers bristling. Paul clambered up unwillingly and squeezed into the cramped fighting compartment. He swore under his breath and abandoned all hope of emerging again. He gave one last valedictory glance at the bright scene and the hellish column of fire and smoke alongside. The heavy steel canopy around him had lost all the old assurance of security. It was a prison and a tomb. Paul looked miserably around at the rough dark interior of the steel turret, and the packed ranges of gadgets, the telescope, the guard rail round the breech block, the red lamp in the radio. Eddy's gunner was grey with funk. Paul's mouth was dry: he twisted and turned in his seat, and hung on to his periscope, through which he could see nothing but the blue line of the wood, occasional bursts of flame, and the sky.

Eddy drove forward, boldly, in front of the burning tank. The tanks on that forward slope were spaced out like sitting ducks. Every rule from training, about the use of ground, was forgotten. The tank men had gone berserk with rage. The ferocious fire they were returning was ineffective. All they could do was to relieve their feelings by blasting high explosive at the highly fortified wood nearly a mile away. For, while it was within the range of German guns, it was well beyond the range of theirs.

'G-g-g-gunner, t-t-traverse right, steady, on. Up f-f-f-five ... H.E.'

'Fucking hell,' murmured the Gunner.

'F-f-f-f-fire!'

Eddy kept it up for twenty minutes. Paul heaved the heavy 75 mm. cartridges out of the racks, bruising and bleeding his knuckles. He slid each round into the gun, with a hysterical sense that away across in the wood a German gunner was sliding in the shot that was to tear him limb from limb. His hair stood on end and his limbs quivered in fearful anticipation, like those of a man condemned. His bowels were water with fear.

'God, Sir, we're next! God! God!'

The gunner breathed at him, his eyes large and white with terror in the dark interior lit only by a feeble electric bulb. But then Eddy's stammer glued him to his telescope sights again. Sometimes the recoiling gun seemed to blow back slightly, as it slid back in its cradle: their eyebrows felt singed, the gun too hot to touch, and around their feet rose a pile of hot empty brass cartridge cases. The fighting compartment was chokingly full of hot cordite smell and the exudations of frightened men's bodies.

Each time Eddy fired their ears were concussed by the wallop of the fast-burning cordite, the gun recoiled back to the rear of its mounting, and the whole tank rocked on its springs. At each round the breech opened with a clatter to drop the smoking case at their feet, under the painted gun cradle, releasing acrid fumes. Now they could hardly move, on their padded shelf-like seats. Paul could feel the sweat pouring down his back into his waist in rivulets. His brain teemed, and he could not loosen its harrowing anxiety. He loved his body, loved every ounce of it, and he started what he believed to be a final ritual of self-adoration, worshipping his toes, then each foot and instep, his heels and so on, through every limb, convinced that soon they would be cinders, like those of the men in Peters' tank, only a few yards away, already were.

Then, as so often in battle, the moment was gone, and the memory of it as quickly suppressed and forgotten. Later the tanks were ordered back, and a shaken and exhausted Paul dragged himself out of Eddy's tank, at the regimental laager. There he mounted his own tank again, the sweat of the cold fear of death drying on his limbs. He took over from Peters and was ordered to scout here and there carefully in the close country to the south-west of Cambes Wood, over towards the right flank. Were the Canadians in contact or not? Confusion had returned about troop dispositions. Battle was new to all the troops, and as the day's stress mounted there was more talk of an expected counter-attack.

Military historians now argue that the outcome of the European war was already decided, by the German indecision over committing their armour in Normandy. Nothing of this large pattern was visible to the men on the ground in the confusion of D + 1, as untried soldiers grew into veterans under

178

the ceaseless noise and treachery of battle experience. They only moved from bewildered moment's pause to catastrophe, from small triumph to inferno.

Radio links between infantry and tanks, and even between tanks and tanks, broke down, as tired or anxious men forgot to tighten the tuning screws, or to check their 'net', the short wavelength fix. Here and there troops were certain of the situation on their front, because they were engaged in a hail of fire and could see the enemy, partially glimpsed figures in grey, handling guns to shoot at them, or active groups forced into the open by infantry assault. Others, lost and bewildered, heard with alarm high-pitched, scared and excited voices on the air. Minute to minute their feelings wavered, as they felt abandoned, forgotten, sleepy, depressed, elated, or terrified.

'Hallo Able four. Moving now. Enemy hornet sighted at . . . Traverse left . . .'

'*Achtung! Fünf und fünfzig. Truppen und kanonen . . .*'

'I think we've got him. Hallo Able four. Hornet on left of wood disposed of. Other hornets ahead. Advise big Sunray. Over.'

'Able four, good. Press on.'

'*Achtung! Achtung!*'

'Hallo Able two hallo Able two. Tiger hornet . . .'

Even the noise of machine-gun fire came over the radios sometimes among the voices, and the microphone echo mingled with the sound of live bursts and ricochets that buzzed in the country air around.

Paul's troop was ordered out to the right, along a wood, to watch for a counter-attack from the flank. Hidden from Cambes by a hill, the fields here had been left in peace by the advancing troops. They were scarred only by the burnt-out black wrecks of two German tanks, their white turret paint crosses bubbled up by the intense heat of their burning. The metal, now cold, was bright red with the oxidisation of combustion. Round each the ground was scorched and blackened in a circle among the green. Paul was relieving two tanks from 'B' squadron which had been on watch against the wood, where infantrymen were digging. In the leading tank he was pleased to recognize the paternal plump figure of Sergeant Whatmough.

'All quiet so far, Sir, though I did see a Jerry digging over theer in that wood. With glasses, o' course. Me orders was not to shoot or I'd 'ave doon 'im in.'

'We've just to watch here – that's it, I gather, unless they attack.'

'Well, I moost be getting back to "B" squadron: best o' loock, Sir.'

By the end of the wood was a cottage, small, with orange-tawny tiles and white walls hidden in the trees, still inhabited. By the cottage was a hen-house, also still inhabited, in a depleted fashion. The infantrymen had bartered chickens for tins of pineapple from Whatmough's troopers, which they, in turn, would swap for chickens. Whatmough's co-driver had already passed over a strangled chicken to Paul's driver in exchange for half a loaf of bread the latter had hidden in his tank while on board the ship. In the teeth of death the troops quickly sought to make the best they could of whatever life was left to them. Here the wood and fields smelt fresh, and everything seemed peaceful. There was even a pigeon cooing, and the continuous Spandaus and artillery seemed distant, in another world.

'Any mortaring, Sergeant Whatmough?'

'Theer was soom in the next wood, so I've no doubt they'll get it heer before long, poor boogers.'

He nodded at the German tanks.

'Them's the woon's B squadron knocked out just after we come in. I 'ad a look at the bloaks inside 'em. They're all burnt oop, but I broak a bloak's finger off and it were still red inside, like. . . . Foony thing. . . . Room bloody goa, this 'ere is.'

Whatmough, with a genial wide-brown-eyed grin, yet a

little pop-eyed too with fright, saluted with a little hop of his teddy-bear legs, and climbed into his turret. As quietly as sixty tons of steel can, his two tanks reversed, scraped round in the squashed green corn, and trundled down the edge of the wood. But the wind caught dust from them and flung it through the wood. German observers saw it and sent over a heavy mortar barrage. Seeing the infantrymen wince and dive into their fox-holes, Paul pulled down his hatch. The wood was alive with bursting missiles and even from down in the tank turret Paul could hear now the sinister soft whistling of the high trajectory of the bombs. Paul watched anxiously, at first through his peri-scope, but then, feeling his field of vision inadequate, through a half-raised turret lid, to make sure the mortaring was to cover no foray. The infantrymen huddled in their slits. But at the bottom of a slit-trench here and there a chicken went on cook-ing, and now one was also on the boil on a Primus in the front compartment of Paul's own tank. The feathers, feet and guts were stowed away crammed in empty shell-cases. After a while the short bombardment stopped, and the tank lids could be opened.

Paul thought he was dreaming when the first odour of cooked chicken reached his nose, as he gazed through the wood to the distant line of trees across the fields, where the enemy lay. His troop sergeant, who was at the wood's farthest corner, could see German soldiers digging, and begged on the 'B' set troop net to be allowed to have a shoot at them.

'Ah, goo on, Sir,' he pleaded.

'Hallo Dog one Baker. Orders are to sit quiet. Don't fire. Out.'

But even Paul's cold military tone didn't suppress Sergeant Black.

'Joost *woon*, Sir,' came over the air, plaintively. Paul had to get down and run to the man's tank, to explain how necessary their discretion was. The mortaring had stopped, but the white slices on trees and the ripped and bruised leaves everywhere depressed his inward feelings and evoked bodily fear. The bright quiet noon, even here, was infected. Sergeant Black took in from the subaltern clambering up to his turret that all the available effort was going in on the left flank into Cambes Wood: behind them support was very thin on the ground, and there seemed to be something of a weak spot between them and the Canadians. If the Panzer troops chose to assault here they could drive straight through round behind the main attacks, and swarm into the beachhead. It was important for any organized movement to be detected quickly and dealt with, and for the armour not to reveal its strength until then. The young sergeant changed his facetious enthusiasm for a look of apprehension, as he took in how much depended on how carefully he continued to watch ahead, and to be ready. Together Paul and Sergeant Black went carefully with binoculars over their field of vision bush by bush. They were worried about a knoll half a mile beyond the wood, and what it might hide from view.

A whiff of acrid high explosive fumes still hung about the shattered trees, combined with the smell of hot nettle-beds, bruised summer foliage and boiling chicken. Birds sang sporadically and the sun came out and faded again period by period in the uncertain day. Stormy clouds drove unheeding over the turmoil below. The continuing sounds still came, of artillery and the low savage thrilling of Spandau machine-guns, on all sides of them. In the men's ears these were even beginning to fade into the background of their perception, just as birdsong fades beyond hearing, after the first rapturous loud outburst of spring. Their ears picked out now only the sound of the projectile that was coming their way, with defensive economy of effort. But the sound of enemy guns from the rear, where the outpost at Douvres still held out, provoked at times the deep anxiety caused to soldiers by a noise of battle in the rear.

Paul felt he must go over to some rising ground to the left, from which he could scan the copse. It would mean a walk of only a hundred yards, but some of this might be just in view of the enemy. Yet until he knew what he could see from the little copse over to the left Paul didn't feel he was performing his function as lookout adequately. He wished he had asked What-mough about the knoll.

'Cover me,' he told Black.

But, he reflected, they could only shoot after he had been shot at. He hated the idea, and his heart gave a leap. He hated being on his feet. If Black seized an opportunity to 'have a go' he would bring all Cain down.

'Don't for Christ's sake start anything.'

He walked out across the field, gingerly, his legs unwillingly taking his orders to move. He found that if he crouched low he was below the line of a straggling hedge: but they might have other observation points, and his heart sank at the thought of advancing there in the storm-flattened wheat among a rain of mortar bombs. He found himself straining with every capacity of ear, to hear the first soft siffle of the mortar bomb. At every shell-burst in the distance, falling like a door-slam, his whole frame would contract in tension, ready to throw itself to the ground. Battle nerves had taken over his system and he had to fight with his limbs to move along at all. He watched every feature of the landscape, the hedge, the beech copse, each ditch and hollow, with uneasy fear, and whenever he caught sight of the ruined German tanks down in the hollow behind, they seemed to be moving again: especially as now, from one, a thin column of unextinguished oilfire broke out again. He found himself involuntarily flinching and bobbing at any sound.

As he reached the copse he kept his hand on his pistol, watching for shapes in the undergrowth. And then, in sudden panic, he saw them – German helmets, and grey-green forms, pale faces. For a moment his whole body was galvanized as if for a last fight – and then in an instant he saw from the statuesque bagginess of their postures that they were dead.

Four corpses lay in the elder and nettle clumps, like men

side by side in bed. Their legs were in a rough trench, their helmets resting on their Mauser rifles. Their clean uniforms made them seem alive: but the faces and hands were dead, a dead greenish colour, with strange blotches of yellow and grey, as on butcher's meat. The eyes were not quite shut, but leered with a gristly shine, hideous and uncanny, while the lips were drawn back from teeth, false teeth, broken teeth and gold-wired teeth in the meaningless snarls of the dead. Their legs were sodden and crumpled by the dew during the nights they had lain there.

Paul hesitated. He had had some intelligence training and strove now to remember what to do. He was so new! He thought he should collect *soldbücher* and regimental tabs. But he recoiled from the feel of heaving over the damp baggy stiff corpses, and fumbling in their pockets. There seemed something indecent about it. He pondered the hidden cold dead manhood, and his own delight in his threatened body in Eddy's tank, an hour or so ago. He felt the dried sweat still on his thighs. He took another unwilling step towards the bodies.

'We've *doon* them, Sir.'

He leapt a centimetre or two into the air in an involuntary reflex action, and quailed all through his body, off his balance. There was a grinning face under a hawthorn bush, under a steel hat trimmed like some May Morris man's with garlands of green, the face blacked with cork. Another joined it: two infantrymen sunk in the weeds like two Green Men, with large white toothy smiles.

'And no fookin' watches either.'

'Any papers?'

'Officer took 'em.'

The two infantrymen manned a Bren machine-gun. Paul reflected that for all he had seen on his way they might have been fanatical *Panzer Jugend* with a Spandau.

'Christ, you made me jump.'

'Never mind, Sir. We saw yer coomin'. But we're not even

184

supposed to talk oop here, so we couldn't warn yer. We was anxious in case yer let off that bloody iron at oos.'

Paul looked down to see that his hand was still involuntarily clutched tightly round his pistol butt. From the copse no more could be seen than Sergeant Black could see from the wood's edge. But he was glad he had come: it helped to fill out one's sense of where everyone was. And where were they, an ironical voice within him asked, of the four stiff grey figures lying in the nettle-clumps?

Paul ran, bent double behind the hedge, to his tank, feeling a strange exuberance at moving so, on foot, only a few hundred yards from the enemy. The flattened and track-scarred corn flew under his feet like a green sea.

Back in the turret, breathless, he was handed a piece of stale bread with a leg of hot boiled chicken on it. It was the most delicious thing he had ever tasted in his life, as he dug his teeth in it, still panting from his run. Suddenly a carrier wave buzzed in his ears, and Major Bumpton's voice came over sharply.

'Hallo Dog One. Rally at map reference DOG-CHARLEY-LOVE-X-RAY-LOVE-DOG pronto. Move now. Dog One, over.'

'Dog one, O.K., Out.'

'Driver prepare to advance.'

There was a wail of despair below. The Primus had to be dismantled, and the billy-can of chicken soup would have to go. Pieces of chicken were hastily thrust into mess tins. The hatch opened, and the can of hot chicken liquor was flung into the wood.

'Fook warr for a bleedin' lark!', the driver shouted, cursing as he emptied the boiling pan. But they stowed what they could of the hot chicken in an ammunition box.

Paul was on the 'B' set. Black waved and began to turn. They crept as quietly away as tanks can, the tracks chocking dully; but again the wind threw huge spurts of dust over the wood. The last Paul saw as they left the wood was an infantryman, his face drawn with apprehension, squat lower in his slit trench. They expected more mortaring, because of the tanks' movement, and Paul felt the grief of bringing it on them. But, looking back, expecting the wood to burst again into the wild fury of a barrage, he saw only the breeze playing along the pointilliste bright scene, among the leaf masses of the elm and white poplar trees. It was still unspoilt by war, a rural farmed landscape of uncommon beauty, in changing lights. And as they carefully retraced their tracks he munched what remained of his chicken and stale bread, happy to be alive.

*

When they returned to the slope below Cazelle they found a nervous confusion among the headquarters tanks, drawn up in agitation below the village which the regiment had now taken over. The tanks were grouped untidily about the track just above where Peters' tank, still pouring out black oil- and rubber-smoke, burned beside the haystack. Behind them in the farm-buildings and an orchard other tracked vehicles, Bren carriers and armoured half-tracks, had drawn in under the trees. The men in the turrets everywhere were intent on their radio communications. It had been a weary afternoon, after a long crawl forward through mine fields, for the two squadrons to support the first infantry attack on Cambes Wood. German fighter planes had appeared, firing with cannons and machine-guns. The 2nd Royal Ulster Rifles, walking down into the wood supported by 'A' and 'B' squadron, had met unexpectedly heavy barrages of artillery and mortar fire.

The first attack on Cambes had failed, and a huge smoke-screen blowing across the countryside had been brought down to cover the retreat of the infantrymen. One whole company of Irishmen had been nearly all killed, the remainder being taken prisoner. By late afternoon now every man was tense and the air was full of broken messages. In these began to thrive a hysterical fear of 'Tiger' tanks. These vehicles had been developed on the Eastern front, the German Mark VI. They

186

weighed fifty-eight to seventy tons, and carried an 88 mm. gun which was effective at 2,000 yards. The armour piercing shells of Allied 17-pounder guns would bounce harmlessly off a 'Tiger' tank even at close range. The use of the words 'Tiger' and 'Panther' for their largest tanks was a subtle stroke of psychological warfare by the Wehrmacht. There were in fact only about thirty-six 'Tiger' tanks on the Normandy front, but the legend of their invulnerability was paralysing. In the drawn faces of the tank commanders on that weary afternoon came an apprehensive wildness in the eyes: it was their first taste of defeat. The word 'Tiger' came over the air, and was passed around crews in the interiors of fighting vehicles glumly. Back through the smoke came wandering broken infantrymen, wounded and bleeding, filthy with dirt and smoke, some supported hobbling between two comrades, staggering with weariness and despair. Their faces were beyond horror but had rather taken on the blankness of psychic withdrawal and were expressionless, like those of the dead. Yet the tanks on the ridge could do nothing, except listen to the broken messages on the air, nervously.

'Can Baker Two get help. Enemy hornet at . . .'

'*Wir wollen aufbrechen . . . nach Osten, sieben, sechs und fünfzehn. . . . Achtung, kanone.*'

'Charley Four, report my signals, Charley Four, over.'

But Charley Four, all the afternoon, had been called for in vain. The spirits of the unengaged tankmen sank, deeper, as their machines stood hopelessly on the ridge in the battle smoke by the still burning relic of Peters' tank. This ruin was still blowing great dismal smoke rings into the late afternoon air: now and then it wafted at them a sickening cloud of burning chemicals. Charley Four failed to answer. Already the dead and dying of the day seemed to be crying in the atmosphere, in the voices of the melancholy whine of tank radio sets, the sporadic small arms fire, and the whistle and buzz of strays from the battle down in the plain.

Then suddenly to the left came a rumble and clatter, in the smoke, from the direction of the fighting. A breeze brought a louder noise of Spandau drill and the Bren rattle and an outburst of the bark-like detonations of grenades contested each other. The noise of ricochets that whirled and howled over their heads from the Cambes engagement seemed suddenly to double. A devilish apprehension swirled in the murky smoke-screen. A form seemed to loom with the clatter, and then did loom. Perhaps this was the counter-attack! What was the Tiger's great form? The unfamiliar clatter of an alien machine? Hearts palpitated. Many voices tried to get on the air at once: the radios babbled, 'Hornet! . . . enemy Hornet!' As the smoke swirled the headquarters tanks anxiously swung their guns. Others backed away towards ridges and barns, heaved round behind walls. The smoke swirled and thickened: the form vanished. Paul, who had just arrived, drew his tanks behind an orchard outhouse. But the radios whipped up a mad chatter, out of hand, while a Headquarters officer's voice tried to calm them.

'Hello Baker three, wait for orders.'

'Baker four. Expect counter-attack supported by hornets.'

'Tiger sighted.'

Whoever it was used the emotive 'tiger' instead of the code 'hornet', the effect was to stampede, and tired men in terror sought with red and painful eyes the threatening shape in the smoke, the shape of the irresistible monster. The whole force of the opposing Panzers might be rolling up the hill at them that instant.

As soon as the lumbering tank's outlines became visible in the smoke as it crawled up the hill it was drilled by half a dozen guns. Their blast swept up a huge pillar of white dust that soared into the late afternoon air, now a golden haze with battle smoke.

Almost instantly the tank men recognized it as an English Churchill tank which had made a confused retreat from supporting the infantry in Cambes. There was a note of obscene despair on the radio.

'Cunts!'

And then silence, as the now familiar flames and hideous smoke-rings soared from the machine, their own brother weapon, destroyed by themselves. Between the tanks, from which stunned tank men looked out pale and harrowed with dismay under their goggles, walked the large sad figure of the regimental padre in his steel helmet, the genial Irish clergyman. Two of the Churchill's crew had scrambled out of the turret, exhausted, maimed things no longer men, riddled internally by a hundred fragments, their legs shattered. They lay in the smoke and died, only a few yards from the North Countrymen who had killed them in their panic, pointlessly. Above them in sheets of raging fire thundered the bursting ammunition of their heavy machine, the great wasted motor-driven fortress seething and boiling with white incandescence. They all watched transfixed and sickened. A column of black smoke billowed in ghastly wriggling spouts from the tank fire and rose high into the fog of phosphorous particles put down to screen the withdrawal. Beside the ragged figures knelt the homely Irishman, his tired compassionate face streaming with tears, trying to offer what solace he could as they died, half unconscious from huge morphia injections from the little toothpaste tubes with the hollow needles, on the bare earth of the field.

Paul was glad he had not fired, though he had been terribly frightened by the dark looming machine in the smoke. It seemed to him that the genial plump Padre had the most appalling task of all those undertaken on D + 1.

*

Bumpo sent Paul over to connect with the Canadians on the right flank, as nothing had been heard of them, and the flank felt exposed. It was a relief to the young man to be able to get away from the atmosphere of the fringes of the failing battle

189

at Cambes, and the tall swirling fire of the Churchill tank that mocked their panic. The No Man's Land to the west seemed so inviting, untouched and unblasted. Yet it might be that the enemy armour would decide to drive to the beaches through this very gap.

'Watch out for snipers in the village here, now, Grimmer!' said the major, chirping at him, as if Paul were his spaniel.

So Paul drove back through Villons les Buissons with the tanks, each with its turret machine-gun directed among the broken housetops, the commander watchful. Had there been any snipers Paul would have been dead by the far end of the village street, for the head of a tank commander between his turret flaps makes a perfect target. The habit of fighting a tank with one's head out, developed in desert warfare, was to prove fatal to many commanders in Normandy's closer country. There were snipers at the front who had taken a heavy toll of men on D Day. But in cleared villages like Villons les Buissons ghostly snipers, projections of men's fears, were commoner than real ones – sometimes taking the form of mythical fanatical women, the molls of German officers, who were supposed to linger in church towers and attics. Yet, to give grounds to the projected fantasies of fear, a German youth would actually hold out here and there, in a water-tower or spire until brought down out of it by being shot to pieces. At the beginning the raw soldier did not know what to believe, and his mind added its own breeding horrors to the real threats.

Villons les Buissons was beyond contest. If anyone was still in the ruins, they must be sitting in fear in the cellars. Not one building was undamaged, and some hung perilously, their walls weakened by shell holes. The church steeple was riddled by direct hits, and it would not be long before it fell. Broken green wires hung down in festoons into the rubble-strewn streets, and every building gaped with ripped roofs and shattered windows. The village could not absorb war and remain beautiful, as the countryside still could, for the first few days at least. Where there were unbroken trees in the streets their green freshness made the pocked detrition of the houses still more melancholy. Here and there the colour of a wall, or the form of the timber architraves of a house were beautiful, soft with the patina of long rural peace. But the bursting shells and ripping streams of small arms fire had made the village dirty, broken and unkempt: there was no-one to gather the scattered timber of roofs and shutters for firewood, or to shovel the scattered mess of broken wall and tile off the street. The blue street name plates with their quaint curly white letters and figures on blue plates spoke to a wreck. Ragged lace curtains flapped at burst windows, and shutters swung crazily. Everywhere was littered with pale dust and broken fragments. The village had died, except for a paper tricolour nailed insecurely over the mayor's house door. There was a dead smell everywhere of broken brickdust and damp plaster.

In the back of the village, however, beyond a kitchen garden, a new civilization had arrived, the orderly camp organization of an untried Canadian unit. Paul found himself with surprise following bright fresh-painted brigade signs to a meadow, leading him and his sergeant's tank to a dark green tent. Paul drew up to be scrutinised by two efficient-looking sentries. The tent was a square one with a pointed roof, poles and guy-lines such as is used by palm-readers at village fêtes in England. Outside the tent two Canadian officers were taking tea, at a table, with canvas chairs, with a real tea-pot, hot water jug, and *scones*. Paul gazed at the scones, agog. The Canadians were listening to a field telephone and filling in a map on the table. Paul could hardly believe it! Less than a mile away on his side the infantry were still cowering in their fox-holes, broken men were dying in the smoke. It was nearly nine o'clock in the evening of D + 1, in a tight and bloody beachhead. Yet here was tea with the Mounties!

191

'Hallo, hallo,' cried the Canadian officers. 'Come in. Have some tea! Mitchell – give these tank men some tea.'

Heads popped out of the hatches of Paul's tanks followed by hands with mess tins ready: the astonishing apparition of the tea tent had been observed through periscopes. Paul sat at the table, feeling too filthy to be at such a respectable occasion – rather like a tramp at a bun-fight. They had cups and plates! And batmen waiting! Paul's feelings shifted between happy relaxation and an especially taut fear; having escaped the irony of dying in Eddy's tank he knew now that he was to suffer the irony of being blasted out of existence, or bayoneted, at afternoon tea. The waning evening light made the moment feel like the endless summer tea-time on the country-house lawn of a polite novel. In his fatigue it seemed a hallucination. But he gobbled three scones hungrily, and drank three stimulating cups of delicious fresh Indian tea, with profound gratitude. He then sank in his canvas chair into a perplexed semi-slumber. A vicarage afternoon post-prandial sleepiness came over him. He was confused: it seemed like tea-time, yet the evening had nearly gone. Only with difficulty did he hear the easy Canadian voice explaining the disposition of the Canadian First Army, and bring himself sufficiently to the surface enough to copy the details in Chinagraph wax pencil on his map-case.

Perhaps he did doze off for a while. But then a thunderous series of explosions stirred him: the Germans were bombing the beachhead. Tracer and sparkling flak soared beyond the dark hills into the sky. It was dusk! A tank was helpless in the dark! The Cambes battle was still raging! Where was he? He rose unsteadily to his feet, shaking his head.

His men were out of their tanks, sitting on the ground with their backs to the tracks, dozing against the bogies – except for the wireless operators, who manned their sets sleepily. The Canadians had been talking on all the time, in easy, quiet voices. They seemed, with their strong tea, like Sirens luring the Englishmen into a soporific trance. Paul fought hard to come to the surface, but it seemed impolite to retire hastily from the agreeable conference. The Canadian officers rose and shook hands.

'Thank you *very* much. That was *very* pleasant.'

Paul reflected he had told them very little about the English dispositions. He realised that hardly anyone knew, since the retreat from Cambes Wood. Where would the regiment be? His heart failed. He did his best to bark an order.

'Troop mount.'

As the engines started he realized that it was going to be no easy task to find his way back to the laager – even if it had not been overrun – in the dusk. The tanks seemed to make such a noise in the fading light that he felt the whole German front line must be registering his progress. They had no headlights, nor dare he use a torch. The great roaring elephants had to bellow along in the boiling darkness.

Somehow they seemed to miss the village, and Paul began to follow a track, supposing it was that which led back to Cazelle and their chosen laager for the night. It was almost dark, and bushes and woods were already black. Strangely, thought Paul, they passed nobody. But he drove slowly on, now seeing in every bush a *panzerfaust* team, or hearing beyond the engine's roar a voice to challenge his passage in German. The bushes writhed in the heavy dark. But there was nothing, and the lack of all contact was becoming unnerving. He cursed the Canadians for their sleepy tea-party. He was so exhausted that he could no longer think clearly. Again, in his mouth rose the taste of an ironically purposeless death. Thank God he seemed to be approaching some kind of slow ridge.

'Ye're not fooking lost are ye', Sir?'

The alarmed wireless operator spoke as if to make sure Paul was still awake. The truth was, as it dawned on him, that he *was* lost, in No Man's Land, within half a mile of the enemy, by night. He might come on a German patrol any minute. Black's tank dutifully followed him.

Then he was saved, by the panic wreck of the afternoon. Suddenly the fire in the hull of the destroyed Churchill tank reached a further store of ammunition, in the front hull. A huge ball of fire puffed into the air, followed by smoke-ring after smoke-ring, marking in flame the terrible end of that crew's lives and work. The wreck was now about a thousand yards to his left and rear, and from the ridge they had reached Paul could now see the beachhead glowing with anti-aircraft fire and fires. He knew where he was, suddenly and alarmingly. He had been driving towards the enemy, and was even beyond the line of the wood where he had been in reconnaissance earlier in the day!

With the realization came a bloodcurdled apprehension, but speedy determination, too. Suddenly he saw the terrain in his mind as clearly as a map. The village would be there to the left: he could see the tilted spire – yes. And he could skirt it along the road which came to a fork where Peters' tank was knocked out. Yes, there it was, glowing red still. What a day! He called to Black on the 'B' set.

'Hello Dog one Baker. I can see where we are now. Follow me close. Dog one Baker, over.'

'Dog one Baker. O.K. Out.'

Even with faint and crackly reception, the man's fear came through.

Paul's engine roared, and he shot along the dusty track at some twenty miles an hour in the dark. At the orchard below the hamlet appeared dim alarmed faces from their slit trenches of the Canadian infantrymen at whom he had fired the day before. Fortunately they were not as trigger-happy as he had been, but only gazed stunned as two English tanks hurtled down the tracks blindly in the dusk, the commanders in the turret waving yellow flags with torches shone on them, the 'our troops' signal. Paul passed Peters' dead tank by the hay-stack, a yellow tongue licking from the black hulk still, the crimson ash of the interior glowing. Beyond, fire still bubbled from the burning Churchill, uttering flickering rays of light across the darkness from its hatches weirdly.

Paul's mouth was dusty and dry with fear, his body bathed in sweat. The track became mud and the road became familiar as he roared down it, and the tension eased. Then he suddenly realized he was going too close to Cambes Wood, broadside on, and swung off on to the fields to the left of it, through a hedge. As they crashed through hedge and ditch his helmet caught the turret edge and stunned him painfully.

Suddenly he felt a blow in the air, and called his driver to halt. They slowed down, puzzled by concussion after concussion in the air. His wits dull, Paul sensed danger and managed to reach out to undo the heavy catches of his turret-lids and pull them down. They had run into a heavy artillery barrage on a cross-roads. The shells were unlikely to damage them, shut down, but the tank rocked to the blows. Paul called into his microphone:

'Driver speed up!'

And into his 'B' set called quickly to Black:

'Hallo Dog one Baker. Close down. Under shellfire. . . . Keep going. Dog one Baker. Over.'

'Dog one Baker. O.K. Out.'

The tanks rocked blindly on. His periscope reversed, Paul saw the dark shape of the other tank pass the cross-roads behind him. There was a twilight glow from flak in the beachhead, and flashes from shelling. One shell seemed to strike the suspension of his sergeant's tank, but the great machine only rocked and came on at speed. Now he could see the seahorse, insignia of the 27th Armoured Brigade, in a blue shield, painted on his companion's machine. They were closer to home and the operator could get through on the 'A' set. The radio had gradually slipped off net during the day, and so long-distance communication had been too faint for speech. As they came closer the operator could get on net again. In any case Paul didn't want to talk to Bumpo until he knew where he was. But now Bumpo came through strong. It was a great relief.

'Hallo Dog one. Report my signals. Dog one, over.'

'Dog one. O.K. Over.'

'I say, Dog one. Where the hell have you been? Over.'

'Sorry Dog one. I've been having tea with maple leaves. I have the picture. Over.'

'Dog one . . . O.K. . . . Out.'

Bumpo wasn't sure what to say. But then the bird-like voice came up again.

'I say Dog one. If that's you at speed over there for God's sake slow down or you'll have all hell let loose at us. Out.'

Even Bumpo had an edge to his voice by now. They were all possessed by utter exhaustion. It was nearly midnight. A reaction set in from the initial excitement, and the night had brought on an oppressive fatigue. The Germans were still bombing the beaches, now brilliantly lit up with searchlights and flares, while tracer soared behind the trees and the Periers ridge behind them.

Paul slowed down, and found himself driving again among crowded troops, vehicles packed closely together, the ground riddled by trenches. It was a welcome contrast to the lonely terror of his hour lost in No Man's Land. The beachhead was a bizarre place – within a mile or two were the confused hordes of fresh new-landed troops, and in other places the weird emptinesses of unclaimed front, forlorn meadows and deserted cornfields crossed with fire. There were infantry everywhere near Cazelle now, and fresh troops gathering of a kind he had not seen before, mortarmen with trailers, gunners manhandling field guns, and half-track guns like tanks without a turret and open to the sky. The traffic was considerable, and Paul's two tanks filtered unsteadily through a confused jam of vehicles on rough ground, with no lights, in the flickering glow from the beaches. Then he found his own regiment, recognisable by the large code letters and figures painted on the vehicles,

196

packed into a field by a wood, all the tanks ranged in a 'Wellington square', their guns pointing outwards into the dusk. The forward side of the square was along a wood, with guns pointing into the trees. Beyond the road was close country, small fields and hedgerows, and the larger fields towards Cambes. But no-one quite knew now what the situation was between the regiment's night laager, and the scene of the afternoon's defeat.

Paul tracked round to the outside of the wood, where the ground was clear, in order to make his way round to a place in the far side of the square of tanks. He no longer cared that he was on the enemy side of the assembled forces: he was too tired to care where anything was. They had been up from 4 a.m.: it was now midnight, and he realized with amazement that it was only D plus one that was passing. He felt wild with relief and beyond caring for danger, to be back with the regiment. He stopped his tank in the wood, and dismounted to relieve himself. He needed to, badly, after the tea and his scare: but one's bodily functions atrophied strangely in battle, and he had never noticed the discomfort. There was quiet this side of the wood and he felt with contentment and some pain the warm flow from himself in the dark.

But the sleepy troops were at their nerves' edge still, as they prepared for the night: orders were being given for strong all-night guards. Orders had spoken of the likelihood of strong offensive patrols from Cambes. These orders had become embroidered with 'Tigers' and 'snipers'. Sleepy and jaded men held triggers of their gimcrack Sten guns and peered into the darkness. All day they had strained their ears and eyes – now the unwelcome darkness had come down over all, and their nerves sought to defend their tired bodies against surprise. The defeat had shaken them. They heard sounds that did not exist, and saw phantoms in the darkness which were no more than emanations from the weary blood-inflamed retina.

In the same wood, unknown to Paul, two senior officers were out observing the flank, his Colonel and the Second-in-

Command of Paul's regiment, looking out towards Cambes Wood. There were also sentries, looking for suspected German scouts who were supposed to be infiltrating. Paul was doing up his buttons with a sigh when someone somewhere fired a shot. It may have been a tired gunner cleaning a gun, having left one 'up the spout', by mistake perhaps. Or it may have been a genuine brush with enemy scouts. No-one knew any longer exactly what was afoot.

Immediately the whole mass of tanks on the wood side raked the wood with machine-gun fire. First two machine-guns fired, then six, then twelve. Once having blasted off, they kept going, as the exhausted gunners held on happily to the sprung grips of their remote-control triggers. The air was barred with red tracer, like lines on exercise-book paper in the air. Paul, knocked off his feet by the noise, stumbled for a moment aghast, and then became frightened and enraged, as he took in what was happening. Now the whole row of tanks pulsated at once, pumping ball and tracer up and down, then raking the wood from side to side. About thirty machine-guns were going, and the air hummed fantastically with the shock waves of parted air. A burst ripped the side of a tree opposite Paul and flung splinters of wood painfully into his face. His nerve broke and he yelled, fell and grovelled, beating on the ground to let him in. But he saw instead the red bullets smacking against the stones of the track just in front of his eyes. Fascinated, he saw them hitting the ground and bouncing off in all directions, in scarlet 'y's' and 'v's', angles which seared into his vision in the dark. It was like an incredible dream; untouched, he seemed to float among the flaming bars of light as the bullets swept by him.

Then, unable to believe that he was still alive, he ran to the shelter of his own tank. Red lines caged him in the air: the noise was deafening. He climbed the sloping front of the elephantine machine, slithering on the metal. A hail of bullets ripped up the front of the tank, marking the steel as he watched, shooting sparks, and smacking off at angles with terrible whines and buzzes. He was utterly beyond fear, now, wholly given over to death, and without hope. His body, shaking, awaited this last of the ironies – to be shot by his own side in panic. He wrenched at the flap of the turret: the gunner had closed it. For a moment he struggled with the crazed gunner, and then tore it open. An hysterical eye looked at him in the dark and then backed into the fighting compartment with a cry. Crumpled, in a last hope, the panting officer dropped in head first, and lay sobbing for breath against the cold steel of the turret floor until he could move. Then he grabbed a microphone, enraged.

'You fucking bleeding cunts. Cease fire.'

Then he recollected himself.

'Hallo all stations Dog. Stop firing.'

Another voice joined his.

'Hallo all stations, Dog, Zebra, How. *Cease fire.*'

The machine-guns ceased one after the other. One gunner went on pumping long after the others. About 10,000 rounds had been fired. Nobody had been hurt. The Colonel of the regiment and its second-in-command had had to lie in a ditch. Paul sat for ten minutes in his slippery sweat waiting for his heart to subside. Then he pulled himself together and they moved in.

But when he finally joined the Wellington Square of tanks and switched off Paul felt himself crack, to the depths of his fatigued tree of nerves. He came down from his tank and gave his map-case to Bumpo in the dissolution of a dream, explaining the Canadian positions in a thick unfamiliar voice. It was as if someone else now moved and spoke. There was nothing of Paul Grimmer left. Perhaps he had been shot to pieces after all? And all this was a dream in death? Automatically, in the close dark square of machines swarming with men, he arranged his guard. They were to call him at 3.30 a.m. But then he wandered in the enclosure looking up at the elms, a few windy stars, and the top of the wood, feeling his soul detached from his body, and an unearthly melancholy possess his being, from which he knew he would never recover. He was beyond cynicism, beyond hope, beyond ever feeling deeper fear or deeper abnegation of spirit. He was mad: he knew he was mad. Bumpton had told him, in his clipped efficient way, that they had had a bad day. Whatmough had been killed with all his crew in B squadron. Soon they would mount a yet larger attack on Cambes Wood, but at the moment they were in defeat. A row of dead lost men stood lifeless in the laager. More tomorrow would go stiff and holed, their eyes leering.

He didn't care about the battle. He cared about nothing except the horror of loss. As he staggered about the field he came across tanks with huge gouges in their sides from armour-piercing shot. Then he saw on his own tank the mark in the steel where a shell had burst, the thick metal all gouged with metal. He took in the taste of the violence that melted steel, everywhere pointed at the tender human breast. He felt the breaking bones of men, and the mountainous pain of their dying. The thick dark falling June night seemed drowned in foulness.

He went on his knees for Whatmough; he saw the old man's paternal face among the dark stars. A long way away beyond the guns and the corpse-laden sea he heard the bicycle tyres of a messenger taking a paper slip to the mother and children he had seen in the photograph on the boat. In phantasy he broke the charred fingers of old Whatmough's blackened corpse. The vision overwhelmed him: he sank to the ground. There was no more for him. He could not. . . . The thing was. . . . Nothing would. . . . He. . . . The.

A young sergeant found Paul on his hands and knees, weeping silently, shaking all over. Sergeant Fry was a tall, sprightly young man, much of a clown. He came from Whatmough's village, and knew him well. He liked Paul, and Paul responded, because he found in Fry the same warm qualities of the

200

humanity of Yorkshire working men. Fry took him by the arm, laying something down on the grass.

'What's oop, Sir?'

'Sorry. Be all right in a minute.'

He knew he would never be all right again.

Paul went dry and hard, struggling to be an officer.

'Oh, it's you, Fry.'

'Is it Tom, Sir?'

'I could have stood the rest of today without that.'

Fry took the young officer by the arm.

'Look 'ere, Sir. I knew him better nor you. I'm not letting meself think of it. I can do summat when I get home, for his, like. Meanwhile, well, Dad doesn't know no worse nor better. He was gone in a wink, I know. Have a drop of this with me: we liberated the booger this morning.'

'This' was a bottle of Veuve Cliquot. Fry deftly thumbed out the cork. It popped ridiculously into the cold night shaken by the endless thunder of guns and the smashing crumps of bombs. They both drank deeply from the foaming bottle. Paul reeled and belched, and then hooked a small loop of sense round a large star that stood out over the North Sea. A necklace of bright jewels went up: the night flak display was filling the night with its sinister beauty again. The subaltern and sergeant knelt like ancient warriors at a pledge.

They drank the bottle in a few minutes, like an anaesthetic. Then they parted and shook hands. No more was said. When Paul reached his tank, stumbling across the laager, he was offered a hot tin of kidney soup, holed, and warmed by a firework fuse down the middle which had been lit and burned out. Into his other hand someone shoved a cold sultana pudding in an opened tin with a fork stuck in it. He took them with silent thankfulness, and even as he sat perched on the commander's stool in the turret and finished the last fragment of sweet sponge, he fell into a deep and death-like sleep.

D + 2

GROUPS OF MARAUDING fighter-bombers now flew so frequently overhead that the Allied troops ceased to notice them. But they knew these buzzing Mosquitoes and Hurricanes were attacking the German armour forming up to assault.

For the East Northshire Yeomanry D + 2 was a day of waiting, while preparations were made for a set-piece attack on Cambes the following day. Some of the regiment's tanks went forward from Cazelle to the hill below Villons les Buissons to fire sporadically at the defended wood. Other squadrons spread themselves about, among the busy units of infantry and mortarmen in the fields, patrolling and awaiting a possible counter-attack.

A cold night merged into a dark dawn: stand-to was at 4.00 a.m. Paul had been awakened for a guard duty at 3.30 a.m., and had spent a dazed half-hour peering into the black hedges in the dark, fighting the cramp of tiredness as he held his tinny Sten gun, oppressed by a headache and still paralysed with fatigue. It seemed incredible that the light automatic, a simple welded collection of black steel tubing with its toffee tin of a magazine that rattled in the breech, would ever fire: though he knew it would, only too viciously. But it gave no comfort in the grasp, as did the heavy wooden stock of a rifle, or a Tommy gun. The primitive feeling remained, of needing to have something in one's clutches with which to club a man. But this was the war of the cheesewire, the flick-knife, the plastic grenade – and the gimcrack 'Spam' gun, as the troops called it.

Trying to feel confident behind the thing, Paul tried to stop his tired brain spinning phantasy. Thought leaped up in him, as though the intellect sought to live its last hour in ebullience.

But he knew that thought is a grave disadvantage when you are supposed to be watching for German steel helmets, or blackened faces in the dark. He had no sentry experience in war: really, he could not imagine what it was he was looking for. He couldn't challenge or shoot everything that moved, since bushes moved in the night wind, and as a star shell soared a whole hedgerow would suddenly advance like an army. He peered into the swimming darkness with his raw eyes, and hoped the thirty minutes away. He walked carefully along one side of the square of tanks, stopping at every three paces to listen. The world seemed to be dead except for the guns.

An angry beachhead din had continued all night. Stray shots cracked and buzzed over, burst of Spandau and Bren growled backwards and forwards in the copses at the front, and across the Orne. Patrols were out from both sides, and all forces were nervously alert. Four miles away on the beaches, as the June twilight grew to dawn, pale glares hung while the rapid-firing guns still threw strings of fire into the sky.

In the gun-orchestrated small hours Paul strove to remember what day it was. He could no longer work it out, and felt disorientated. It was still Thursday, June 8th, but he was aware only of a long expanse of hours, broken into light and darkness. Already, he couldn't recall how many nights there had been, or days either.

His half-conscious vigil was broken by cannon-fire from two German aircraft. Before there was any sound, bright lights shot across the fields where the tanks were, about thirty feet above them. Then came ripped thwacks in the ears, and a deep pumping noise from the copses and orchards behind, as the 20 mm. shells, about as big as pepper pots, exploded. The rods of red flame in the air cracked, and the hair on Paul's neck stood up, from the painful force with which the cannon-shells cleaved the atmosphere, and ripped it into sound waves. Behind the cannon-shells came the planes, their engines thrumming on a high foreign note, their lightless bellies just visible in the weakening darkness.

There was nothing anyone could do, but Paul was relieved. The cloaked impalpable hostility of the darkness had been eroding to the nerves. Here was action! Now men scrambled to the .300 Brownings mounted on the turrets and fired at the planes which were turning in for a second shoot. This time it seemed they would touch the trees, as they came from behind the just-visible tips. Their cannon began to sparkle, and the cracking roar of red tracer flying towards them was deafening: but it all flew high, and sailed away like lines of red happy birds into the sky behind. More and more machine-guns threw orange dots into the sky, excited men opened up with rifles, and a ponderous half-inch .500 machine-gun, about the use of which everyone was puzzled, had its first shoot in Normandy, from a special bracket which Paul had invented for it. It threw an unsteady stream of lights skywards, then jammed.

Much of the effort and display was a waste. The planes buzzed away to their bases. But because of their appearance the regiment was awake, and flexed. In a way Paul found himself almost grateful for the comparative sanity of the firing: the dissolving darkness that surged at the anxious mind seemed a greater threat. The light grew, and the troops on foot began to stir. The tank regiment had to move at 5 a.m.

Hastily they washed and bundled up their gear. There was no time to brew tea, but as a gesture at breakfast they stood round chewing oatmeal blocks and slices of luncheon meat, and drank stale water. Paul was sent with his troop into a meadow by an orchard, by a farmhouse at a cross roads near Cazelle. There they were to carry out elementary maintenance, tightening tracks and cleaning guns, ready to move in ten minutes. Most of the tanks had restocked with ammunition and diesel oil after they had come in to laager in the Wellington Square in the field the night before. But Paul's troop had been late, and had to collect their tall square tins of diesel fuel now.

The sides of these thin four-gallon tins flexed with a musical noise, the tin plate crumpling as they were handled, and the fuel gulped into the funnels. Shining brass shell cartridges with black or yellow shells fixed to the ends of the brass charge cases were handed up and lowered into the turret racks together with long bands of machine-gun ammunition, each a shining chain of reeded brass and copper like some fabulous breast ornament for a dead Pharaoh, with their serrations of clips and polished teeth points.

Paul sat in the turret and took the gun to pieces, to clean the breech and moving parts. The soothing mechanical activity reminded him of the comparative security of his training days, with its rote-learnt phrases, 'clean, dry, and slightly oiled'– and the filthy old gunnery jests. The troopers were exchanging such badinage inside the machine, as if they were back on Thetford Heath. Even in moments of rest, now, none of them said anything they meant, or anything real or genuine. They acted a comic part, rather hysterical. The feelings cowered low in the frightened and exhausted body. The harrowing fear was relieved by surface gossip, and a superficial obscenity:

'Don't talk fookin' daft.'

'I tell yer, it's the "*K*" pack that 'as the bloody fruit salad in it. *And* the steak and kidney pooddin'.'

'I wish they'd make a tin of fookin' Yorkshire.'

'Eh – Harry!'

'What?'

'Which pack has got tinned Bingley coont in it?'

'That dooff were lovely.'

'What dooff?'

'The woon in the "L" pack with plooms in it.'

They paused, trying to think of jokes, grinning.

'What pack's got coont in it?'

'Fookin' Barney let oon of them fookin' firework soups off without making 'ole in 't fookin' top.'

'What happened?'

'Blew oop and covered the booger with pearl barleh.'

They all laughed. Barney was the lanky and gentle signals officer with a sad droopy moustache.

' 'is fookin' tash was all 'ot and wet like a tart's bush and all full of bits of stew and barley.'

They made cawing noises, laughing and heaving in their seats. They knew Paul was listening, and went on talking loudly but obliquely, for his benefit, being wildly obscene, and relieving the tension of the night's descent into unconsciousness, where every man's infantile terror lurked.

A head put itself down a front hatch, from a perambulating trooper.

'Eh, Jack.'

'What?'

'Do you know what?'

'I don't know fook-all this morning. I'm wore out counting the noomber of bloody times we nearly got doon in yes'day.'

'What's today? Wens'day?'

'Fookin' isn't.'

'Fookin' is.'

'I was going to tell yer summat.'

'What?'

'Eddy's piping 'is bloody eye.'

'Eddy? Christ, what's he doon – lost 'is fookin' 'ymn-book?'

'Ees sorting out what's left of Toggs and Hartesty.'

'Poor boogers.'

'He were all right with t' socks and mess tins and that. But when 'e coom to the bits they'd writ 'ome like 'e started to pipe 'is fookin' eye.'

'Eh, I'm going to 'ave a look: I'd not fookin' miss that. Fancy that hard-hearted booger ever feelin' sorry for any poor coont.'

The co-driver was gone. Paul could see Major Eddy sitting against the hedge at the back of the orchard, sorting out the effects of the dead men. The rigid bachelor, lonely in his spirit, sat with a trooper's letter-form in his hand, his other hand over his eyes, and an uncontrollable stream of tears flowing down his face. The drawn moustached face looked wretched, pink, blotchy and awful in its collapse. Paul's heart went out to the man, for the breakdown of his taut self-control must have been so painful. Even the co-driver came back silent and chastened. They lapsed into a quieter mood, murmuring of the past.

'Hartesty, 'e married that red-haired bint that woonce went round with Sern't Fry.'

'Ah, yes, I remember: she coom to that first bloody dance we give at Bingley.'

'Fry were fookin' noots on 'er, broke is bloody 'eart it did when she chooked 'im oop.'

'Hartesty were loocky.'

' 'E's not fookin' loocky now, is 'e?'

' 'E weren't all that loocky before. She ad 'is kid, but there's anoother – an' 'e 'adn't been 'ome on leave to give 'er it.'

'Oon of them voluntary efforts, eh?'

'Veergin fookin' birth.'

'She weren't no fookin' veergin ever.'

'Moost 'ave been once.'

'She were takin' on wi' a Yank.'

'Spoongin' flash fat-arsed boogers.'

' 'As thee soofered too then, Jack?'

Jack began a long and complicated story about an American airman and how he caught him with his wife, arriving home on leave.

' 'E'll not fook around with no-one's fookin' missus again,' he kept saying.

' 'E were half fookin' dead when I'd done with 'im.'

'What about missus, Jack? What'd yer do to 'er?'

'It weren't 'er bloody fault.'

'Moost a been six of woon and half a doozen of t'other.'

'Oh no it fookin' weren't. She's only yoong and he was flashin' 'is wad at 'er. She didn't see what he were oop to.'

207

'Moost 'ave knowed when he slapped it in 'er 'and, Jack.'

'You shoot oop!'

'No fookin' woman doesn't know.'

'Well I gave her t' benefit of t' bloody doubt . . .'

There was a pause.

'Ow's Doris, Jim?'

'She were all right when *I* left 'er.'

'Bowleggéd you mean.'

'Couldn't fookin' walk, neither, I bet, Jack.'

'Nor could 'e, randy sod, neither: had to carry the coont to the station.'

'Fookin' roll on.'

They thought sorrowfully for a moment about their women at home.

'I tell yer what I'd like just now.'

'Never mind, Jack: leave it alone. You'll either get your chips, or a blighty woon. You'll have to wait 'is Majesty's fookin' pleasure now.'

'Fook it.'

'Shut oop, 'ere's fookin' officer.'

A fresh load of diesel arrived, and the men were detailed out to fetch one big squarish tin each. The driver held the funnel as the pale golden fuel swished into the tank. The tank filled with the acrid smell of diesel – the smell of the Esso world at war, of Krupp and Shell: how much were they to blame? At the political thought Paul sighed, and looked out at the smoking Norman countryside in the dawning sun. 'Open a second front now!' He was right in it! He checked that his wireless operator was vigilant and on net, and checked that his sergeant and corporal had one man responsible as constant look-out. Then he returned to his gun. He disliked having the gun out of action, and was feeling panic about having stripped it.

Paul had the gun in pieces, and was cleaning the breech block with cotton waste. When it was clean he put it on the roof of the turret, with the breech block handle, and a crank.

The springs, split pins and such vital parts as the firing pin he laid carefully on the ledge by the wireless set. Day-dreaming a little, he recalled the kind of letter Eddy had been reading when he broke down in grief for the dead man. The officers had to read and censor every man's letters. Paul had studied his first batch on board.

ENY APO England
Wed.

My dear darling wife,

Well, I am in France at last as I except you know with the Regiment. We come in on D Day and it has been pretty rough since I can tell you love. Still we are all in one piece so far and cheerful tho the food is terribel, biskits hard tack and that but we have some tins of soup that are good that you light up with a match and a good cup of char now and then.

Well my dear love I am looking forward to been in your arms again as Bert Lyon sings or is it Jaimy Russell I've forgotten and forgivan the bizness with the Yankee and I trust and pray you won't ever go off the rails again tho I understand being it's wartime and people get lonly belief you me I'm lonly enogh here sometimes tho the offices and chaps are good companions and we have some good ole talks even when the stuff is flyin. Goodnight my darling Beryl kiss the children for me your loving husband

Harold
Passed by
CENSOR
No
10534   P. Grimmer

Paul then realized that he hadn't written home himself. He took out a blue letter form and wrote in pencil on the flat surface of the tank in front of him. On the address side he wrote O.A.S. ('on active service'), looked at the letters with a mixture of pride and disquiet, and then his parents' address, evoking strongly to himself the quiet dullness of the suburban Norwich street. He could see his mother knitting automatically in the window with her horn-rimmed spectacles on, even the flash of the light on the lenses as she glanced up now and then to scrutinize a bicycle. The bicycle of the telegram boy was the messenger they dreaded. The flimsy blue letter-form was life: the telegram was the other message.

My dearest Mother and Father, (he wrote)
   Here in the Bridgehead we live in eternal noise, of our own guns, bombs, tanks and planes. The crops are heavy that we run over, and the fields are littered with dead cattle. We have unpleasant periods of waiting when all kinds of mortars and shells drop on us. Advancing is elating, but sitting still in this hot beachhead is a bit nerve-racking. We are all keen to get on and finish him off. I am rather keen to return to be a student when Nazism is broken. I get very browned off at times – and I am not really a soldier – only an intellectual fighting on political morals and beliefs. These waver a bit at times, although I haven't done badly so far. Send me some newspapers and magazines about second front if possible. Tell people to write to me.
                                              Love
                                         Paul

He stared at the pencilled letter, as a paper emanation from himself among all the bustling troops and machines. He licked and pressed down the edges of the thin blue form and sent the co-driver over to the post-box at HQ with his letter tied up in a bundle of others he had signed and stamped with his censor's stamp. He wondered if the flimsy packet would ever reach England. In the next tank the men were singing now, wistfully:

> *You are my sunshine,*
> *My only sunshine:*
> *You make me happ-ee*
> *When skies are grey . . .*

In a few minutes, into the orchard hard by their tanks had moved a body of four-inch mortar men: he heard a loud spoken command, and suddenly the air was violated again, this time with the painful cracks from the mortar barrels. The noise stung the eardrums painfully as shiny fat brown bomb after shiny fat brown bomb was dropped backwards down the large barrels, and shot up invisible in its velocity through the grey smoke of the fierce cracking discharge of propellant. The helmetted bombardiers moved briskly, ducking smartly in their familiar rhythmical routine among the cordite smoke: they stood their fat mortars on the large base plates and let the first few bombs drive the plates into the ground, swinging the bombs about like gnomes at work. Then they adjusted the sights again, and corrected them according to wireless messages from observers ahead. The bombs could be heard whistling away, and then, long after, blamming down in enemy territory, behind Cambes Wood.

Paul kept his head down inside his tank, to lessen the effect of the blast. His eardrums were a little numb, but the nervous reaction to noise was becoming worse. The mortar barrel noise was agony in the ears. At first the infantry and the tank men were encouraged by the sight of the mortar crews.

'Jerry is catching it,' said Paul's driver, with satisfaction.

But the satisfaction evaporated as soon as the barrage had been delivered. With disturbing alacrity the gnome-like mortar teams dismantled their weapons, loaded their equipment on trailers, and left precipitately, drawing these away on foot, doubling away back towards Cazelle down a track from behind the farmhouse. In ten minutes all that remained of them were strips of green and yellow tape from their bomb packages, and the torn cardboard tubes from which the bombs had come, littering the orchard and meadow.

'What's the fookin' hoory?' asked Paul's wireless operator.

'You'll see, mate,' said the co-driver: 'we'll get the shitty end of it, you'll see.'

'You mean the coonts coome and blow off 'ere, and then fook off before he coomes back at 'em? What about oos?'

'You'll catch your packet, choom. Put t' bloody lid down!'

'Bloodywell watch out!'

But no mortar fire was returned. Instead there was the sudden appearance of a plane. It was quite definitely an English fighter-bomber, a Hurricane. They looked at it calmly. About fifty feet above the orchard it dropped a bomb. Paul saw the bomb leave the machine and gasped: it looked like a 250-pounder. It slid through the air towards the waving foliage of the apple trees. He shouted and ducked, holding tightly to the gun carriage. There was no time to close the turret lid. The bomb whistled for its short descent, there was a thud, and then there was silence, long enough for Paul to wonder whether the thing had been defused, and merely jettisoned, or whether it was some kind of oil or phosphorous bomb to be used against tanks. When it exploded and rocked the orchard he was glad it was nothing worse. A huge spout of black earth darkened the orchard and filled the air. It became a dark cloud and then fell away, leaving brightness again. The blast stopped his breath: when he breathed in again it was to breathe in with a gasp a fine cloud of dark wet humus, while clods of earth, stones and dark dust poured on his head and into the turret. The tank was covered with a thin coating of earth, as if ready to be sown with grass seed. His clean gun was filthy, and every hole and crevice, human or machine, was full of sticky black dust.

'Oh, Christ!' said the gunner, who had been helping Paul, a London boy.

'Well, we're still here,' said Paul drily.

'Was there a bastard jerry flying that sod?'

The wireless operator plucked off his headset and asked Paul:

'Shall we report it or do they know, Sir?'

Paul looked over at HQ in the corner of the field. He saw an officer throw a sod of earth off the top of his tank at another, hitting him on the helmet. When the squadron leader turned round alarmed and angry, only to realize that the regimental second-in-command had thrown it he turned pink with annoyance and then roared with laughter himself. They were beginning to cultivate that clowning capacity, an irony which knows no mercy or hope underlying it, that protects the mind from disintegration in war. HQ knew, in its manic way.

But the infantrymen were digging hard: one of their men had been buried alive. He was under part of the huge rim of soft black soil. They dug quickly with their short pointed trench tools, flinging the soil behind them. Then they found a surface that heaved, and dug more carefully. A leg appeared, then buttocks; their faces were expressionless with expectancy. They were at the crisis of developing one or other of the two separate feelings for other men in battle, one the tender care for a wounded man: the other the suspension of all feeling for a corpse. Two men grabbed the leg, and one shovelled away at the neck. Suddenly the figure gave a colossal heave and withdrew itself, clawing at its head and face and shaking itself like a dog. It jumped and blew plugs of filth from its nose, and gasped through the earth-choked hole in its blackened face, shaking its head. Another infantryman dug out the man's helmet and rifle. The victim stood bent trying to scrape the muck from his eyes. Someone brought him a mess-tin full of water and he daubed at his eyes.

Then, once they were sure he was unharmed, they all relaxed into the luxury of laughter, slapping the victim on the back, and rocking backwards and forwards: it became reminiscent of digging father out of a castle of sand on the beach, a holiday joke. Paul could not hear what they said, but found himself with tears in his eyes and laughing quietly to himself.

It was a little like Lazarus returning from the grave: and yet obviously none of the infantrymen felt that to be alive, in their beachhead predicament, was to be worse than to be obliterated. The strong hold of life hope was on them all. Battle experience, instead of teaching the stern truth that war is so dangerous as to be unbearable, fostered instead a magical hallucination – because a few cheat seemingly impossible odds against survival. So the huge horror was swallowed by the greedy fantasy of each individual, who tried to see portents of his own survival in minutiae, or at least clung to the thinnest hopes of it, in every stick and straw. Only by this strange capacity of the human mind to defend itself against the truth before it, is war possible. Even the wounded and dying seemed outraged and surprised to find themselves, as individuals, singled out as casualties. One could hardly tell them then that by the remorseless logic of so much metal chasing flesh, somebody had to go. 'He's had his lot,' was how his unharmed comrades would put it. They pretended that there was a kind of lottery, by which only those whose 'names' were 'on' the projectiles would get hurt: the others would escape. Some got their 'chips' – as gamblers sometimes 'come up'.

Some groups of tanks were out that day, probing. But Paul's troop rested and cleaned their machines. Laboriously Paul cleaned the gun again, while the others brushed and scraped the earth out of the turret and forward compartment. There was much domesticity to tank routine: and the domesticity reinforced the tank man's false sense of security.

Then Bumpo appeared, calling Paul. The young man clambered down: he could see Bumpo's tireless, keen, rather watery eyes summing up his state of body and morale.

'I'm afraid I've a bit of a shock for you, Paul. You know you're, well, our spare officer, since you're trained in mines and that sort of thing. Well, look, Peters wants a crack because he lost his crew, and I've promised him a go with your troop at Cambes Wood. You're not the sort to mind, what?'

Though he felt it was a death sentence withdrawn, Paul's face dropped.

'The Colonel wants a very special job done. You're to take his carrier. He wants you to liaise with Infantry Brigade, over the artillery cover tomorrow, as they go forward.'

Paul's face fell further at the thought as a tank man of taking part in a full-scale battle, forward with the infantry, in a Bren gun carrier. The Bren carrier was a tracked vehicle with only quarter-inch steel sides, proof only against fragments and distant rifle fire. It had no top. The crew would be strangers, too, he reflected.

Paul was to man a wireless link between Headquarters and the infantry commander at the beginning of the assault, to call on the supporting tank troops, and to be ready to give word when the various gunfire barrages were to be lifted. They wanted to keep the barrage down until the latest possible moment: then lift it as the infantry went in. The first stage was to lift the heavy gun barrage. Then Paul would guide the regimental support by tanks. Fire from the latter was linked with that of some self-propelled howitzers commanded by a Marine Commando officer who had happened to turn up with no very clear instructions – so he had just joined in. Paul was to take his carrier a little forward of Regimental Headquarters, and then walk forward behind the infantry assault, with the infantry brigadier. He was to carry his microphone and head-set, attached to a long reel of wire leading back to his carrier, and connected with a No. 19 set. This contraption had been invented by the Signals Officer, for observation purposes.

The rest of the quiet day Paul spent in inward dismay as a tank man obliged to enter his first set piece battle tomorrow – virtually on his feet. Ah well, it was just bad luck – and he shrugged. In the evening he checked the carrier, and trans-ferred his bedding and effects to its open hulk. He then checked the radio link with Regimental Headquarters, and attended an 'O' group in the farmyard in the dusk with the Infantry Brigade Commander, a quiet, modest, soft-spoken, wiry small man, to whom he took an instant liking. The young brigadier was small in stature in his denim overalls and had soft brown eyes. He responded to everyone with sympathetic keen interest. In peace Paul thought perhaps he might be a grammar school headmaster – a good one. One trusted his humanity, his calm maturity. How dreadful for such a good man to be killed! Yet he probably would be, tomorrow. In tense apprehension the regiment laagered after dark, with instructions to move to form up at 3.30 a.m. on the Friday.

D+3

THE FOLLOWING AFTERNOON, just below the haystack and the burnt-out hulk of Peters' tank, Paul set off down a track at the side of the quiet figure of the infantry brigadier, surrounded like a king by his court of headquarter staff, most of them carrying radio sets, towards Cambes Wood, again. Paul was connected by a wire to his carrier, where the operator paid the cable out from a reel. He carried a headset that linked him to his Regimental Headquarters.

The second battle of Cambes had begun. But how different was the reality from the quiet aims as expressed at the conference in the farmyard, and delineated in red crayon on talc sheets over maps. Situation. Enemy. Own troops. Intention: we will. On the actual terrain was no such equation.

Behind the advancing infantry on the slopes down to the wood was the scattered pack of grey tanks, some tucked away behind buildings, and half-concealed by smoke-screens. Away below the great fields in front, their grey-green crops flattened, was Cambes Wood, which was now seething with explosions. From positions one to five miles behind, 5.5-inch guns and twenty-five pounders were drumming projectiles away. These hummed in waves over the assembly areas. The tanks on the ridge were firing more directly just over the heads of the infantry, splitting the air with the noisy cracks of fast flat trajectories. Above these the barrage shells travelled in loud waves, wooo, wooo, wooo, salvo after salvo, to crash in pulses into the wood. Other gunfire was drumming in from the left flank, and the air about Cambes was a chaos of flame and smoke. Pieces of tree and other debris could be seen flung in the air from time to time above the thick leafy mass. Blast waves swathed dust up from the fields and the skirts of the wood. The blast from shells whipped horizontally just above ground and could be seen from a distance, like swift and tangible under-linings to the crashing fall of each salvo.

Down the long slope towards the defended wood, three-quarters of a mile away, the infantry, well spread out, marched slowly into battle with their stubby bayonets fixed. Spread out haphazardly, dozens of men scattered over the fields in rough lines, walking down into the wood, which everyone had so gingerly avoided for two days, because it was death to approach it. It still was. The casualties were heavy. Under their mush-room-shaped dark green steel helmets that stirred from side to side as they walked the infantry seemed to be looking for some-thing – as if they were beating the territory for game, or a lost comrade. Each man carried his rifle with short bayonet gleam-ing, sloping across the front of his body. The Royal Ulster Rifles were to be followed by the King's Own Scottish Bor-derers and the Lincolns. They had these heraldic names and badges: but they were only soft-fleshed men, like one's father, or oneself.

Paul felt an inward gulp of protest at first. He wanted to shout 'Stop!' to the onward march of these steel-helmeted men, their orchard colleagues of the day before, walking up-right through the smoke, into the enemy's sights at point-blank range. They walked so slowly, looking occasionally right and left, as if they were on exercise on Salisbury Plain. But they were not. They were a few hundred yards from a fanatical Panzer division and experienced German infantry, dazed by the barrage, but battle-hardened and angered. The ground as they walked spattered up in small and large fountains of earth.

So, at once, men fell, as Paul had seen them do in newsreels, inert, or clawing the ground for a while afterwards, or rolling and squirming in the corn, until one ceased to watch them, but returned one's eyes to the scattered crowds still marching for-

217

ward. Paul's heart leapt as each man fell, and he wanted to say to the Brigadier, 'This is murder: this is terrible. I cannot watch men dying like this, in an open field. I cannot bear that I can do nothing about it. Let us do something.' But he could see that the sensitive man next him did not need these things said aloud: he was feeling them too, but accepted that nothing could be done. This was battle. The creatures cut down by steel along the field were 'his' men; and the Brigadier sighed, between the orders that he crisply gave into his radio sets, these strapped to the backs of his own headquarter soldier.

'Headquarter party. Advance.'

Smoke swirled round them. The Infantry Headquarters was going down the track, to see better, so as to decide with more accuracy at what point the barrage should be lifted. The closer the timing the better chance of helping the infantry, if the barrage were to keep the enemy's heads down, preventing them shooting with a clear aim. The little headquarter court was going down among the scattered men, where as they walked they could see some fall victims to the hail in the air.

'Your tanks can come down now.' The quiet Brigadier, the small dark man with brown eyes, said to Paul, with brisk sharpness.

'Hallo Roger Baker, Hallo Roger Baker. Able Zebra asks for hornet support. Roger Baker over.'

'Roger Baker O.K. Out.'

It was his Colonel's voice. Two troops of three tanks each, Peters' and Brights', detached themselves and roared down the slope, their tracks whistling, their guns firing as they rushed, under gyroscopic control. As they approached the wood their machine-guns opened up, barking sporadically over the sound of the battle. They looked elephantine but gallant too, like great metal horses as they threw up clouds of dust behind them, their engines roaring, their guns flaming. The infantry-men looked round at them, with obvious satisfaction. Blood was up. Paul could feel the thrill of war, the obscene stir of

218

blood to see the cavalry charge. There was a pause in the fountains of dust, even, and a lull in the fire from the wood.

'Stop the guns.'

'Hallo Roger Baker, Hallo Roger Baker. Stop Samson. Stop Samson. Over.'

'Roger Baker O.K. Out.'

A few seconds later the drumfire of guns and the whooing in the air stopped, except for one or two strays. The infantry were nearly in the wood. But now the enemy came to life. They knew how to wait for this moment, from long experience of similar savagery in Russia and Italy. The wood, a moment ago blanketed under bursting shells, now came alive with rifles, automatic weapons and larger guns, chattering and drilling. Where one infantryman dropped before now dropped four: Paul was appalled to see them. But some had dropped, under command, to seek cover and wait their chance.

The tanks had gone out of sight. The Infantry Headquarters walked down the road, like a party of hostages.

'Spread out,' said the calm young Brigadier. Paul stayed by the small man's side, his wire now vibrating as it drew out from the revolving drum in the Bren carrier a hundred yards away. The noise of the battle had quietened to a stutter and chatter of small arms. Strays whirred over them: then larger luminous shots: anti-tank guns were firing. Down in the valley by the wood there was a thunderous clang and a roar: a smoke ring soared between Paul and the wood. A tank had gone. Paul did not know whether it was one of his, now commanded by Peters, or one of Bright's. In fact the explosion marked Bright's death, from whose tank the shot ricocheted with an angry snarl over the head of the Headquarter party, and then over the turrets of the tanks above, like the soul of a man rent in agony.

Paul, one aide, two operators, and the Brigadier now walked on still down the track, Paul trailing his wire. The Colonel's voice called.

'Hallo Roger Baker, Hallo Roger Baker – ah – has your Sunray any further orders? Roger Baker. Over.'

The Brigadier was talking rapidly into his own set. The men on the left were pinned down, but the tanks could not help from where they were. In any case tank support was difficult now they had reached the stage of in-fighting. Far below his men were already using the bayonet, and men were dismembering and disembowelling one another face to face. Paul took his chance and asked if there was anything. . . . Noise drowned him. Just below them a line of infantry were dropping to evade a volley of machine-gun fire.

The small wiry man was wild-eyed, but calm. He shouted in Paul's ear.

'No, look, we must get on, closer. Tell your colonel to tell Fox Charley to expedite. Then there's nothing more I want from you. Thanks.'

He smiled, a grey and bitter wince. Paul saluted. He meant it.

When shells are not coming your way, they can be heard to whoo or whine. Those coming at you arrive with a short shriek and burst before you can hear in time to take action. As the Brigadier smiled a salvo arrived, bursting all round them. Paul felt as if he were inside the sound of their bursting. The Brigadier and he were flung off their feet by the blast, which seemed to play round them for an age, tugging at their clothes. The two operators and the aide were flat. But all five were unwounded. They sat up dazed in the holes.

Another salvo arrived, toppling them over like sacks. The blast was irresistible: Paul could see the holes in the ground round them, shallow saucers in the earth. They were stung with stones and choked with dust. The Brigadier looked cockeyed, for his helmet had been knocked sideways by a flying stone. They looked at one another like passengers in a train that has left the lines, and is tossing about before plunging into an abyss.

A third salvo flung Paul over again, and for a moment

he lost his microphone. He could no longer think what he was doing there, half-way down the field, where these quick screaming blasts arrived. The Brigadier crouched stunned in a crater: then decided. He stood up and walked down the hill saying, quietly,

'Come on.'

The Headquarter party walked on between two dead Royal Ulster Riflemen not looking at them, and the Brigadier called up his Colonels on his walkie-talkie pack radio as he walked along. Paul admired the calm man who walked in that strange field among the bursting shells, towards the cracking of small arms fire at close quarters. Paul wanted to go and shake his hand and say goodbye. But his own legs were wobbly with fear, and all their strength was drained away, as he tried to regain his feet among the small shell craters. His gullet was taut with fear at the buffeting, and his mind counted, involuntarily, the time between salvoes. Another salvo arrived with a howling slam: Paul this time was thumped hard in the back by blast, and thrown harshly against the ground: the explosion seemed very near: it seemed incredible that he had survived. He was alone, and dazed, unable to decide what to do, unable to recollect his function. He sat stupidly on the edge of a shallow crater, trying to control his twitching legs and collect his wits. But he could not control them, because his nerves were counting the time between salvoes, beyond his volition.

Then he remembered the Brigadier's words. He called, choking into his microphone.

'Hallo Roger Baker. Hallo Roger Baker. Report my signals. Roger Baker. Over.'

There was no reply. Somehow the wire must have parted. The only reply was another screaming slam and hail of stones from the gravelly path. Yet he had survived the falling of nearly thirty 88 mm. shells, within a radius of a few square yards. He took one astonished look at the pattern of shell craters and then tore back up the hill along the track as fast as

221

his legs could carry him, tripping over the wire he dragged behind him. The fear broke in him as he ran, and every whining shell overhead was coming at him. His back and knees were moist, cold and hot with sweat.

The carrier crew were dogged with fear as he ran through the dusty air and smoke, leapt in, cut away the trailing wire, and ordered them to reverse. In his haste the driver recklessly pulled at the sticks, and the tracks ground so fiercely that one of the steel caterpillar bands nearly wrenched itself away. Paul grabbed the lever and thrust it away. The engine revved hysterically and when the man let in the clutch Paul fell sprawling over the wireless set, catching his knuckles on a steel plate. The pain was excruciating. He groaned aloud, gripping his damaged hand. Yet it was nothing. Nothing! Nothing, he reflected, to what he expected to feel at the next salvo. What was the summit of pain? How did one measure the agonies before them and around them? The fields around and the air were drenched with huge human agonies.

Sucking his knuckles he reconnected his head set to the radio and passed on the Brigadier's message. At once a second wave of infantry came forward from the houses and walls behind, and made their way down the slopes. The air all round hummed and cracked with projectiles flying into the wood, and out of it, at the troops and tanks on the slope.

It was impossible to watch men in the familiar khaki of battledress falling into the tangled corn, and remain at the top of the slope with no weapon, and no function, helplessly. Paul motored in his carrier about Regimental Headquarters. But no-one waved or called him up: they were busy registering targets at the wood's extremes, or intent on radio network. Above them buzzed strays and odd crackling bursts of machine-gun or rifle fire.

Down in the fields men could be seen still falling. Paul was functionless. He paused for thought. Then he drove down, back into the flattened corn. Stretcher parties would be out later: he was looking for bad cases to bring out. They did not have far to look. In tall green wheat lay silent men, their faces dull and expressionless with pain, crouched, defeated and bewildered. The first man was a large infantryman whose upper left leg was burst open by a shell splinter. The greenish battledress was split and the dark red flesh rose in the space, like the pulpy flesh of a burst fig. What struck Paul was the great beauty of the flesh, ripped open and glistening scarlet in the summer light, like fruit or flower. The man was helpless in his pain and shock, and the wound was too huge for a field dressing. Together they heaved him on to the front of the Bren carrier, where there was something of a flat surface, and tied him with straps to hooks on the plates. Another man with a shattered arm, his battledress blouse soaked with dark blood, his face ashen, climbed painfully and unsteadily into the carrier, and they set off. Blood splashed on the metal. The man with the shattered arm kept saying as if to himself, in a hushed growl, 'Will I be all right? Will I be all right?' The driver crept slowly, despite the whipping angry noises in the air, sounds that were beyond the bounds of tolerance and drove them into panic. No-one spoke, except Paul in his anxious but urgent low orders to the driver: but low exhalations came from the man with the leg-wound in his pain. They slowed down at another figure, but sped up when they saw his colour and the way the contents of his bowels stained his tattered battledress. The carrier crew worked with devotion, and Paul felt the satisfaction of relieving a particle of that horror, of the men walking and falling, vulnerable flesh, in the long fields on the slope.

Above, towards the top of the ridge, stretchers appeared, and medical orderlies. Against farm walls were the field dressing stations, with stretchers, bandages, surgical instruments laid out. The infantrymen had set off past these stations. Paul had seen men trying not to look at the bright rows of gleaming steel instruments, tourniquets and white bandages as they walked out to battle. These spoke of the ghastly prevision in

223

war, that 'casualties are to be expected'. Paul had seen the field dressing stations laid out, on the landing ship, in rear areas, and now among the dust of the open fields, a confession of the brokenness to be expected, as the sound men walked down into the machine-created hell of a battlefield. It seemed hideous to have to prepare beforehand for wounds and agony, as it did for the Padre to have to learn and practise his Field Burial Service, as he had done on the boat, coming over. It seemed unbearable to have to walk past those silvery and snowy tokens of inevitable disruption and pain. But now hobbling men, solitary in the great field spaces, or in twos or threes, supporting one another, came back crippled, to the dressing station they had passed.

They brought back about a dozen men from the fields before Cambes Wood. The last three came out with the dusk. One man, smashed and blood-spattered, lay biting the ropes of tangled corn, fumbling at it like a baby and moaning hoarsely in his agony. Paul could barely recognise the low muttered word, 'mother!' As they reached him he became unconscious but still writhed, like a dying insect. The squirming creature they dragged on to the carrier seemed so little like a man any longer.

Most of the tanks now withdrew, leaving the fields littered with dead infantrymen in all the unexpected postures of death, and the broken wood and village beyond in the hands of Englishmen. In the chaos burned two of the regiment's tanks: the driver had taken charge of one and drove it towards the sea until it suddenly burst into flames. Then he dragged out his wounded mates, those that still had life in them. The machine burned on. In it burned the mangled corpse of the fair-haired determined boy Peter Bright, who had shared a bedroom with Paul in Forres.

The Battle of Cambes Wood resulted in an allied victory.

D + 4 to D + 14

D DAY AND THE days immediately following became to those in the beachhead an interminable war-fogged period without division. Paul lost all sense of time, and the only permanency seemed the two aspects of creation that were indifferent to one another – the ceaseless orchestration of the guns on the one hand, and on the other the darkness and light, the birdsong, and the pale small faces of the wild flowers as one's eyes opened and saw them between the tank bogies. Every dawn some hedgerows and swathes were starred with large wild daisies, the first living things to open and appear in the light – just as there were always some men's faces, in ditches and holes under the hedges in the battered and track-scarred countryside. But the weariness and the deathliness increased: the countryside now stank, of dead cattle and dead men, of burning tanks and stores, of stale cordite fume, of phosphorous and other chemical stenches of human hatred. At the front line at Cambes, where officers had to go forward for observation, life was a nightmare of stench, broken trees, recurrent mortar and shell-fire, noisome and dangerous. Night and day, sound and unsound, the live and dead, merged into one long terrible dream, the broken woods and meadows crossed by the clarion sounds and lights of projectiles, and made beautiful intermittently by sunlight and shower.

But, later, days became days again, as habit reasserted itself, and the horrors became absorbed, as though the body shrugged and said to itself, 'life is always going to be like this now: the only means to survive is to adapt, to become used to it.' So, sitting like condemned angels in eternal hell, the soldiers enjoyed even the great destructive dramas of battle, even as a relief from the nauseous continuity of petty destruction that came to them hour by hour.

There were perquisites too: one day, the regiment had drawn back a little towards the beachhead for a rest, and Paul's troop found a store of food in an earth-covered bunker. In the damp darkness were bottles of Vichy water and tins of pork and bean stew, labelled RESERVÉ POUR LE WEHRMACHT. To these they added hard brown French bread and unsalted French butter, purchased from a family in the ruins of a farm. The meal was ambrosial, after the tablets, the biscuits, the stereo-typed 'Compo' food from emergency rations and the repetitive packs of tins. They all had internal disorders from the 'Compo' food by now, and the biscuits hurt their mouths. After a lunch of the oily pork stew they all shaved in the Vichy water. It was refreshingly astringent to the jaded skin of their faces. It was almost as good as a visit to Paris, somehow orgiastic, and liberating.

As Paul and his crews stood drinking bottles of Vichy water a close-packed group of American light bombers came in to bomb Caen, a cluster of small-winged machines with two engines. It was as if a spectacle had been arranged: they felt as if they were at the races up on the Périers Downs. They watched through fieldglasses the black knots of flak bursting round the planes, feeling some sympathy with fellow com-batants, but yet with something of that stony discompassion, by which the soldier in the field makes strong his heart.

One of the twin-engined planes was hit, and began to burn. It turned out of formation, and then began to decline towards the beachhead, obviously out of control. They followed it with glasses as it spun out behind it a long black line of smoke, counting the parachutes of the crew as they baled out: one, two, three, four. The men floated down slowly under the fragile white canopies, thousands of feet above the battlefield. A thunderous crumping came now from the area where the bombs fell, shaking the ground, even, from six miles away. A pall of smoke rose, and was blown over slowly by the wind to merge, at the top, with the permanent pall over burning Caen, that rose up taller than a thundercloud, into the atmosphere.

But the plane still declined towards them: and now they realized that no-one was in it. Yet its bombs must be still on board. Trailing black smoke, and one wing burning fiercely, it dived towards them, its engines now audible as an approaching roar. They watched at first fascinated, then apprehensive, and then, suddenly, in a panic. There was a mile to go, half a mile, a few hundred yards, and the plane was flying directly at them: it seemed unbelievable that it would fall on them. Such a thing could not happen. Yet it obviously must; and yet their legs refused to move. In any case, faced with such a situation, where was one to run to? They were on a hill with their tanks, with a ridge between them and the sea, on an open down dotted with juniper scrub. Fragments of the plane and its splashed fuel would spread in crashing over a large area: to get into one's tank might be to trap oneself. So they stood thunderstruck, their minds working, to seek a way of escape. The windows of the plane could be seen now, and its bomb-doors. Its engines screamed and it was coming straight at them. Men swore and cried out, falling at last to earth.

But then, in a ghostly fashion, the plane soared, banked and turned. Perhaps an automatic pilot was set. Or perhaps a live pilot in the machine, wounded and doomed, was struggling to avert his death? It roared over them, the small lettering on hatches in its belly legible. The plane climbed away, and the troops jumped to their feet, swearing with relief. Paul, still paralysed, relaxed and wiped his forehead.

'Too fucking close,' said his gunner.

'It's not bloodywell down yet,' said the driver, his eyes white and wild.

The plane turned, and dived again. It must obviously be on automatic pilot: a live pilot would have tried to ditch the machine in the sea. The machine, bright and silvery in the morning sun, ran in again on exactly the same path.

'This is our fucking lot!' groaned the driver, on his knees, still holding a Vichy water bottle.

But as their hearts sank and they grovelled the plane pulled up, banked and soared again, showing its belly to them like a great shark, its engines roaring. They could hear the petrol flames now. It was uncanny, and terrible. By now thousands of other men in the beachhead must be watching this dreadful automatic cat-and-mouse game, of tens of tons of aluminium and two tons of high explosives, controlled as it were by some malevolent gremlin.

A third time the plane came roaring down, but this time the fire had eaten one wing away, and it banked away to port, lay for a time on its side in the sky, and then crashed out of sight behind the ridge. A fountain of flame and smoke shot up into the sky over the beachhead with a roar, and the engines stopped. The strangest thing was the way the engines stopped at speed, in the great roar.

The crew looked at one another: they were ashen-faced and their hands were all white as hands become after swimming in a cold sea. Some were trembling visibly. But Paul stood still, stock-still, unable for a time to move hand or foot, and when he did move his legs they felt as though they had gone to sleep. They all felt suddenly terribly tired and drawn, as they did after every great drama, at each one of which it seemed that heaven and earth had no greater horror to offer them. Yet they went on drinking Vichy water, automatically, at once, from the bottles in their hands.

By now they knew something of a similar automatic threat from the air was being felt back in England, since Germany had launched the flying bombs, the pilotless V1. But they had no interest in running half-a-mile to the ridge, to see what damage this crash had done. None of them would put himself out any more, to see more destruction and more twisted metal and corpses. Let it lie! A disinterested indifference was sinking into every soul, in self-protection. So they sat stupidly in their small patch of sunlit grass drinking the fizzy water and brewing up tea, smoking and waiting. The cold sweat on their limbs and in their hair gradually dried, and the incident of the falling bomber passed into the limbo of packed memories of the first few days in Normandy. They were all dreadfully different, from the men they were when they sailed. They were now men who had aged, men who had had more than the most hideous experiences of a whole normal lifetime crammed into a few days, so that there was no further capacity for alarm, surprise, joy or pity. Timon's 'Destruction fang mankind!' was the phrase which hung in Paul's mind, over the dusty shambles among which they performed their mechanical routine of the day.

The Regiment moved up again, back to the area of Cazelle. On the way Paul stopped to investigate the contents of a knocked-out German half-track gun. Everywhere the Germans had dug pits for these self-propelled guns, constructed so that the hull would be below ground level. Water lay in the bottom of the pit, with nettle-covered sides, from which the half-track had climbed, only to be overrun by infantry, presumably, since it had not burned out. Inside was a mess of filthy kit, old shells lying about, the rust showing through their yellowish paint, and the marks of bullet strikes on the grey armour plating rusting, too. The German machines looked so second-hand, compared with the English tanks: most of them had seen rough service in Russia or had been repaired and brought back from campaigns in Italy or Egypt. There were German instructions painted here and there, and in the coarse bolted turret there was a black telescopic sight and other registering equipment of great precision and fine engineering, the threads exquisitely turned.

Among a pile of discarded bags, small empty tins and rags Paul saw an exercise book. The cover was worn and covered with oil smudges. In this book were tables of figures.

The tables read thus, roughly scrawled:

Villons les Buissons Geschützstand B.

	236517 ×	256	062
	237618 ×	261	075
	239620	271	095
Cazelle G.-e.C.	258613	2558	08̸2̸76
	250745	273	115
Plumetot G.-e.D.			
	Cresserons	262	11̸0̸̸3

Paul puzzled the scrawls for a while, and then noticed the corrections. Yes! ... The figures represented gun-settings, in each gun emplacement, registering on crossroads, chateaux, churches and other houses in the area! The thoroughness impressed him: but left him with a thought. The day before he had been up to a conference at Regimental Headquarters. They had settled into a grey stone house on a crossroads, with a signpost on the other side of the road, saying 'Caen 6 km. Anisy 2 km. Carpiquet 7 km.', in white on blue. Many of the farmhouses had high stone and brick gateways. This farmhouse had such a gate, in a fence of iron railings which was overgrown with lilac, now at the end of its blossoming, and turning brown at the tips of the blue petals, sun-singed. The house was empty-looking, but was untouched by war. In the gateway a heavy wooden door stood open.

The house had been a German headquarters in the village of Matthieu, by Cazelle. The house had an air of isolation, of lifelessness, unlike the farms around: it was as if it wanted to spew its contents out.

Telephone lines led into the courtyard, where crouched to the wall sat two grey Sherman tanks and a small amphibious tracked vehicle called a Weasel. Electric voices cracked out of earphones hanging over the old apple trees and over the wall of a glasshouse. Tired men sat over code pads, listening to the voices and occasionally replying, a dynamo whirring for their transmission. An uncertain summer sunlight lit the court. Four pigs, cut up and cleaned, hung on hooks in an outhouse on the other side of the courtyard: there were butchers in the regiment, and the peasants had been willing to sell. Among the activity of Headquarters they hung in the cool shade of the outhouse, a clean sweet image of death.

All over the courtyard lay German stores, boxes of neat little hand grenades, incendiary bottles with puzzling instructions on them, coils of wire, little blocks of explosive looking like cheeses, black and yellow flat Teller-mines with handles, like goods in a hardware shop.

Headquarters had just moved in yesterday: the Colonel liked to be near a house. Upstairs there was a gilt mirror on the landing, and everywhere comfortable chairs. The Headquarters officers had a mess, with a table with a tray of drink on it. There was an established feeling, as at the Canadian tea-party.

But Paul had walked into the kitchen quarters with Tom, the technical adjutant who had just arrived. Tom, an actor in civilian life, tended to seek to make everything dramatic: in the kitchen doorway he made a striking 'entrance', holding Paul's shoulder:

'Look, Paul, old boy, I'm frightfully anxious not to make a thing of this. Only the Colonel's chosen this place and ordered us all in. Now it may seem silly ... but, well, you've been on a mines and booby traps course, and well – I wonder – could there be anything of that sort I mean, I thought I'd ask you on the doorstep here, old man. You don't mind, do you?'

Paul had striven to remember his training: but obviously had the house been booby-trapped the lot would have been sky-high by now with Headquarters officers lumbering up and down stairs for half a day. In any case the German staff had obviously left in too much of a hurry. Yet there was a possibility, he supposed: and Tom, as Paul knew, always had to be satisfied about details. He remembered staying with Tom in a London Services Club and noticed with amazement the time the Captain took to fold his clothes, clean his teeth, wash himself and get to bed. It had been an astonishing performance to watch, the long gamut of attention to minutiae. Tom was marvellous with engines: to cross him over detail would leave him distressed and angry. Besides, he was senior to Paul.

So Paul went through a rigmarole of search, examining the door, the electric light switches, looking round the floor for trip-wires and other connections. There was a bell wire, but worn and frayed: booby trap wires would be new. Then Paul edged a penknife round the doors of a cupboard, in the cracks. At last he pulled the grey cupboard doors open.

Immediately a pile of paper, diaries, photographs, magazines of Mauser pistol ammunition, and boxes of small cakes of blue *ersatz* soap fell on the floor with a crash, giving out a musty foreign smell. Tom jumped, and Paul laughed. They picked up the papers which were training notes, and some of the photographs. There were hundreds of these, all of the same scarred face, in various poses. The German Commandant must have been disgustingly vain: the heavy plump face with its large eyebrows and its scar lacked any indication of humour or irony. The photographs, scattered all over the kitchen floor, looked like a hundred petty Napoleons. Tom and Paul deliberately kicked them about, looking for what else there was. One was of a stout German woman in black Civil Defence uniform with boots and braided hair. They looked at her with stupefaction.

'Bloody old Aryan cow, what?' said Tom.

But there were no booby traps.

'Then the Colonel will start up a bit of a mess in here, old boy, I expect,' said Tom.

'You know,' said Paul: 'I always learnt we should keep clear of crossroads, didn't you?'

'Well, yes. I suppose we did,' Tom replied thoughtfully. 'Still, the old man knows best, what?'

But after Paul had found the registering notes in the half-track gun, he was certain. Every crossroad and house in the area was registered: a German ex-headquarters would certainly be due for attention. It was only a matter of time before the enemy artillery worked their way through the codes. He would go to the Colonel himself today.

As he reached the grey stone house he thought he saw his premonition confirmed. It was a brighter day and the elm-copses and groups of red farm houses in the landscape stood out against the scene, still green and bright at large. He could see Anisy, the next village, standing on a crossroads. Suddenly Anisy went up: not with the low cracking blasts of mortar, but with the high bursts of a heavy artillery concentration, that flung smoke and pale dust high in the air. He gazed astonished at the intensity of the small bombardment across the fields. The whole village was swallowed in smoke. There was no time to be lost: Cazelle might be the next on the list.

He went in the house leaving his tank at the back of the orchard. There was Parter, the stout adjutant, impressive in full battle rig. Paul saluted.

'Can I see the Colonel, please, Sir?'

'In conference, I'm afraid.'

'I've found a list of artillery registrations on these crossroads. I think perhaps this isn't a good spot. Do you think I could tell the Colonel that?'

'Shouldn't if I were you, old man . . .'

Then, seeing Paul's face fall, he added:

'Well, look – I'll tell him when he comes out. O.K.?'

'Have you seen the map?'

On the wall there was a map of the whole beachhead, covered with celluloid sheet, on which, in red wax pencil, was shown the progress of the American finger driving across the Cher-bourg Peninsula. The German dispositions were given in blue. Red for own troops: blue for enemy. In the beachhead everyone thirsted for elbow-room: Paul looked at the extend-ing lines hungrily – it was good to see progress. It was noon, and quiet in the summer sun. Voices came from the conference in the next room. Then the door opened and the majors were breaking away.

By now a distant shell would evoke a lift of the eyebrow and a slight feeling of tension: this had remained with Paul as he came in. But a shell meant for you was always a clarion trumpet, an arrival of ferocious sound, screaming peremptorily that *this is it*.

To the quiet of the house came this sound now, in horrible force. A howl of steel terror descended the scale in a split second, and then it was as if some hand of great power came tearing into the walls with a great cracking noise. Bricks scurried and hurtled from wall to wall. There was a smash and tinkle of glass, a thump of timber. The guns were directed exactly on to the house, which swayed and groaned overhead, dust spurting from the walls and floors. The air became choking with fine dry dust.

Parter came rushing through.

'Cellar?' shouted Paul.

'Full up!' cried Parter and rushed out the back.

In fact there was no-one in the cellar. But Paul took the phrase as an order, and stood dazed against the wall of the lobby outside the kitchen.

He could see into the yard where flurries of steel and slate fragments were tearing into the bushes and across the grass as if driven by the gusts of a gale, the tremendous sucking and hurling of the blast. Bushes and trees waved as if in a great wind, at every crashing salvo. A man's shrapnel-riddled body lay collapsed grotesquely against his tank. The air in the yard was criss-crossed with visible blast waves and hurling pieces of steel. Across the yard in the dark outhouse the pig carcasses swung about violently on their hooks as if they had come to life again. The air was filled with dust and the noise was unbearable in the ears. There was no gap between salvoes: the shells burst as rapidly as the thudding of huge potatoes being

234

tipped out of a box, but each thud was catastrophic. Suddenly there was shouting in the orchard as a sequence of shells burst there. A crackling petrol fire blazed up, and ammunition began to explode in it: two half-tracked vehicles, one belonging to the doctor, had gone up, the crew of one truck shouting as they died with it, two men.

Paul hugged the wall of the passage which rocked with the house. He could feel the blast of the shells and pieces of brick and timber occasionally tear at his clothes. His whole body was bathed in cold sweat and trembled in its own terrified animal life. His mouth was like dry wood and constricted, his mind again disconnected from his body in bewildered stupe-faction. His mind could not think why he should not be in the cellar. Suddenly he went to the door, like an imbecile in an automaton gait, to look for any wounded he could help. Two dust-covered figures, like stone statues, clung to the wall by the door. He pulled them in, and once moved they rushed for the cellar entrance, and blundered down. But Paul stayed puzzled, trying to interpret the shouting, appalled by the flying bricks that shot through the floor of rooms above as the house creaked and writhed under the ferocious explosions.

A great shock came, the floor bulged, half the ceiling fell, and Paul suddenly felt a deep prick in the top of his right shoulder, followed by a wet cool sensation under it. In his concussed state he thought perhaps some water tank had been punctured, and some water flung over his back.

Then the shelling stopped, all at once. The uproar continued with tense pitched voices. The fire and exploding ammunition roared and crackled in the orchard. The trees were torn to pieces, their limbs hung shattered and fallen. Most of their leaves were stripped: those that remained seemed dead and grey. A fine dust covered everything, and smoke soared over the house at Matthieu as it had over Anisy half an hour before. Cables were flung and twisted everywhere, and there was a dripping noise of water and petrol.

235

From one collapsed figure in the yard, a heap of bundled clothes with many rents in it, came a snuffling burble. The man, with his brain showing through a small wound in his skull, was still alive. He was lifted on to a smashed door and carted out: a Red Cross truck was waiting ready, and two more were winding up from the rear Headquarters across the fields. The other helplessly collapsed figure was roughly dragged away and hidden. Behind in the bushy garden among the chicken houses a naked man stood bewildered, drying himself on a khaki towel. He had been taking a bath in an old zinc bath tub left out for cattle, in the apple orchard. The bath had been holed, but he was untouched.

The roof of the house was pocked with large holes and the walls shattered. Through a huge hole in the wall Paul could see the gilt mirror at the top of the stairs, still whole, but coated with dust. The tray of bottles had disappeared. The flames behind were now taller than the house, with a tree-shaped column of black oil smoke standing over all.

A sergeant and a corporal had been killed, ten other ranks wounded, some seriously. Two majors were wounded, one dying later of wounds. A captain was wounded in the buttocks, and two men badly burnt, one in extinguishing the other who was covered with burning petrol. The casualties were speedily loaded into ambulances and driven away. Only the burbling man with his brain showing remained, now, inert on a stretcher.

Paul helped with some clearing and picking up in a stunned daze. Then he suddenly remembered the pricking in his shoulder. He looked over his shoulder, backing up to a shaving mirror still hanging in the porch outside the back door. There was a huge tear in his battledress, and within it the rich red pulp, like fig flesh, which he had seen in so many casualties those first days. He could hardly believe the shoulder was his: but now he felt the pain.

He went up to Tom and turned his back to him.

'I say, Tom, have I been hit?'

'My dear old boy!'

Tom moved quicker than Paul had ever seen him. Almost brutally efficient he took a pocket knife and cut off Paul's sleeve, then cut away the right side of his battledress, ripping away the shirt under it. Different entirely from the attitude of one combatant officer to another, he adopted that attitude of the fit man to the wounded – of sympathy and tenderness, mingled with fear and apprehension. Both were straining ears for the whine of more shells as Tom roughly bound a field dressing to Paul's shoulder. Paul could feel Tom's hands trembling.

'Let me put you in an ambulance, old boy.'

The last ambulance was just going. Paul sat in the back, while on the red stretcher on the floor lay the burbling figure, cut in so many places that no-one thought it worth starting on him, with the small field dressings. Yet he was going to take a long time to die, so tenacious is life in the body, in the young body.

The ambulance jolted away down the country road, jolting badly, the summer sun coming warm through the windows whenever the vehicle turned to let the beams in. It was strange riding in a 'soft' vehicle, as if in a bus on a country lane. At every jolt the burbling man gave a choking snuffle and a low gargling groan. Paul tried not to look at the square inch of whitish brain showing and the terrible dark rents in the body. The man's mouth seemed already to be taking on the hideous snarl of death, blood and spit bubbles seething between his clenched teeth.

As they reached the rear clearing station Paul saw the doctor grimace as they slid the broken figure out of the ambulance. It gave a great choking sigh as they drew out the stretcher, like a child going to sleep. Paul noticed that they did not take him into the tents.

He jumped out of the ambulance, trying to be helpful and cheerful. But as he landed his knees gave way, and he stumbled.

The tired orderly looked at him, with the compassionate eye of one who is wearied with the sight of suffering, and gave the faintest of softenings to the face, that one could yet not call a smile.

'Take it easy: come and lie down, Sir.'

Paul protested: but yet he was glad to lie down. He argued that he was of no consequence: a day or two and he would be back in the squadron. But the orderly taking his name looked gravely at him and shook his head.

In white tents marked with large red crosses in long lines lay rows and rows of men, some able to talk, some groaning, others lying dazed, in pain, or drugged. There was, hanging in the fresh seaside air, the hospital smell of spirituous disinfectant. And all around were other medical tents, no doubt for operations, stores, and catering. It was rather like a garden fête or gymkhana to look at, or another vicarage tea-party. Above rode fleecy clouds, and blue patches shone.

He dozed and woke as in a dream to hear shells falling nearby. He looked up astonished. A woman in brownish battledress was attending the next man. She left him and came to Paul, offering him a plastic mug of water. She was a plump dark pretty woman: he hadn't seen a woman since the peasant girl in the orchard, flittingly. He suspected she was another dream. Her eyes entered his emotions. They were brown and dark in the late afternoon light, and he gazed stupidly, not answering her question.

Another salvo of shells fell, only some half a mile away.

They were shelling women! These women put themselves in danger! A wave of anger came over him that he, young man, was forced to be inactive when women were still on their feet, where shells fell. Then, as he realized he was stupidly impeding the brave young woman's work by not answering her, he burst into furious rage with himself, his eyes filled with water, and he answered her with feeble humiliation, giving his name, rank, regiment and name of next of kin.

The girl pinned a red disc on his blanket and moved on. Paul gazed at her adoringly, and admired the courage of her, with her plump young limbs in the khaki slacks stooping over men in that tent, in the teeth of war.

'What's this mean, I wonder?' he asked his neighbour, of the red disc. His mouth felt sluggish and swollen.

'It means you've got a Blighty one, mate,' said the officer beside him, from under his blankets.

'Oh Hell,' said Paul. He hadn't done anything yet. He wished to get quickly back to England, get well, and be back. He would be back in a week or so, just in time for the breakout.

But the sheer effort of contemplating the organization necessary to get him out of Normandy, and back again, and the long series of arrangements to complete this circuit, so taxed his tired mind that he sank into a deep sleep of resignation, deeper than any sleep he had dared to take while at the front.

And from then on it seemed he only woke for periods from this long sleep. He woke that evening, to join a long straggle of casualties led by women in battledress down to the beach and up the ramp into the cavernous hold of an LST which had been converted into a hospital ship. He felt, parting at the drawbridge, that it was appalling that he should go back to England leaving among the shell fire the frail girl with fair hair and freckles who escorted him. All his fatigued and frayed emotion expressed itself in a gesture towards her as they parted, a wave of deep gratitude.

Then he went to sleep again on a steel net bunk, for a whole day and night, woken only for dressings and bowls of soup now and then with bread broken in it, and glasses of water, handed him by nurses in white. There was a gale – a serious gale that wrecked the Mulberry Harbours and held up Allied progress dangerously – but Paul Grimmer knew nothing of this, except that the ship rolled badly, hurting his arm. He simply slept, and slept. At last the ship ground its anchor away, shuddered and shuddered with its screws, and they began the long night crossing, heaving across the Channel. Other men who, as well as being in pain, were seasick, groaned and howled in the night. Paul slept and in a vivid phantasy lived each battle over and over again, the lights of shells and tracer streaming before his eyes.

Then he woke again, a bright English light streaming in through the great open doors in the bows of the ship. A medical colonel stood over him, with an orderly. He bent down and felt Paul's head and took his wrist for the pulse. Then he smelt Paul's dressing – a strange act, Paul felt, in his half-awake state, to be smelt by a Colonel with a purple hat band. But the man drew back with alarm on his face, and snapped a command. He had smelt the odour of gangrene. Paul tried to rise to his feet. Outside the doors was an English pub. But the Colonel gestured him down.

'Stretcher case. Haslar hospital. Pin an emergency card on this officer, please.'

Paul disembarked on his back, carried on a stretcher up exactly the same hard down which they had reversed into their LST some eighteen days before. He even recognized one of the bystanders from his stretcher, outside the same public house.

*

The bees circulated over the warm aubretia in the garden of the semi-detached house marked by a tall stench-pipe. A lad in a navy blue uniform with a belt and pouch cycled down the street on a red bicycle, whistling. At No. 4 he stopped, and his whistling ceased. Mrs Agnes Grimmer lowered her glittering steel knitting needles with a ridiculous prescience that the sock she was knitting might never be needed, as she saw the telegraph boy stop at the gate leaving his bicycle. She tucked her brown hair back, her brown eyes clouded, as he came up the short concrete path to knock. Behind her in the parlour her husband Frank rose awkwardly from his *Daily Express*, and went to the door with an expression of angry resignation, his large-limbed figure moving unwillingly, pathetically, like a large sad boy. He came back into the room with a flimsy yellow envelope marked PRIORITY. For a moment neither dared open it. The wife took it off him and stood for a moment staring at it, the tears welling. With a pallor in his bony face, the man said, 'Here, give us it, Agnes: I'd better open it. Boy might need us.'

Clinging tightly inside to the hope of continuing life, Frank struggled to focus on the swimming printed tape, his weak left eye transfixed and pale blue, unwilling.

PRIORITY CA MR FRANK GRIMMER 4 SMITH-SON AVENUE NORWICH
YOUR SON LIEUT P GRIMMER ADMITTED TO THIS HOSPITAL ON 22/6/44 WAS PLACED ON THE SERIOUSLY ILL LIST SUFFERING FROM WOUNDS SYMPATH IS EXPRESSED IN YOUR ANXIETY FURTHER REPORT WILL BE TELEGRAPHED = RM HOSPITAL HASLAR GOSPORT + Gt 4 22/6/44 + +

*

The throbbing pain became the soughing of sonorous voices and the echo of metallic clatter, down the long corridors. He drank a yellow fluid to soothe him for his anaesthetic. Glistening white underground tunnels. Lights and faces swelling as if in a dream. The bright operating theatre. Haslar Naval Hospital. 'Is everything prepared?' Boom, um, aired. Voices, counting hissed away into a night which lasted for an age. Out of a grey soft swirl the next day's daylight came. Paul Grimmer found himself being sick, in a bowl by the pillow of the first comfortable bed he had been in for a month. He couldn't enjoy the bed, because he couldn't find a way of lying. If he lay on his right side he was lying on his wound: if he lay the other way the blankets dragged on the bandages. The only way was to lie on his back, a little to his left. But he felt too vulnerable face upwards, and woke in sweats in the night feeling the vibration of shell-bursts and seeing tracer scours where none were. A girl by his bedside held his hand. How nice of you, Mary. Was it Mary? Who was Mary? The distant cousin faded and in her place were flowers.

*

'SYMPATH IS EXPRESSED'. The keys clicked also for the next of kin of the boy with the broken brain in the ambulance and for the wives of the men burnt to death in the explosion behind the house at Matthieu. The envelopes were delivered. Their houses were silent.

*

A purple label.

GOVERNMENT ABSOLUTE PRIORITY
PLEASE TO INFORM YOU THAT YOUR SON
LT PAUL GRIMMER 285396 HAS THIS DAY
BEEN REMOVED FROM THE SERIOUS CASE
LIST STOP IT IS HOPE THIS PROGRESS WILL
BE MAINTAINED=MOIC RNH + 4285396 PT/T
OHMS

*

In the hospital train the compartments were all gutted, and the inside walls of the coaches were painted cream, and fitted with racks for stretchers. As the train pulled out of St. Pancras an air-raid siren wailed in waves of howling sad diminished thirds. In the stillness, broken only by the men's snores and occasional muffled groans Paul Grimmer heard a strange noise, like the deep rapid banging of a huge oil drum, but sharply intermittent, too, like the exhaust of a monster motor-cycle. It stopped. There was a long silence, in which the feverish officer actually began to doze. Suddenly there was a great swoosh, and the roar of a huge charge of high explosive detonated among buildings. The train rocked from the blast waves, but, after some halts and starts, drew on. *Vergeltungswaffen* 1.

*

At Greenwood Park Hospital, Leeds, a mentally deficient patient blabbering his lips with a finger, under a sooty yew tree on the lawn.

'Blubberblebberblooberblebberblubber.'

The noise continued all day. The creature stared expressionless under heavy brows, palpitating his lips with a wet finger. The mental patients had all been packed into the main building, leaving a new wing for an emergency war hospital. In this South wing fifty officers who were supposed to be sound in mind suffered over again the insane terrors of the Normandy battlefields, and waited to become sound again in limb.

*

The clean beds under the gay sunny windows were all full, two lines of figures, some roped up in strange postures, broken men, swathed in great dressings, smelling of foetid broken flesh, and garbed in baggy hospital pyjamas of rough grey cotton. They slept most of the time, at first, in a drugged state of loss of sense of night and day, and from sheer exhaustion. Sometimes one or other would give a terrible cry, or a groan, fall on the floor, or crouch under the bed. The cleaners' vacuum cleaners and floor polishers produced the weirdest mêlée, for whenever they were switched on, the high-pitched whines, evoking the sound of the flight of shells, brought the dreaming men to reflex activity. They threw themselves on the ground, or under the beds, shivering.

*

Everything was very new, the beds, lockers and trolleys: so were the nurses. They were attractive young girls of eighteen or thereabouts, crackling and bosomy in their white starched uniforms; but they knew very little about nursing, having been only emergency trained. They were even dangerous, having an innocent indifference to the exact number of minims for an injection and to the air-bubbles that lurked in their hypodermic needles. The sick men had to rouse enough energy to stop the girls killing them out of sheer ignorance.

The girls giggled, but the men had been too near pain and death to find the insecurity of inexperienced girls attractive, or amusing. So the giggles turned to bad temper. It filled the men with fear and alienation that the girls were coy about the urine bottles and bed pans. And the girls' shame about their inefficiency was in conflict with the irritability of battle-weary men.

*

Dear Paul,

I'm sorry to hear you've been wounded. I hope it isn't bad. So you got to the 'second front'!

We are moving to London this autumn. Gabriel is to work in the B.B.C.

It was good to hear from you. We were sorry to hear you were wounded.

Yours,
Lucy

*

Opposite Paul lay an infantryman with multiple wounds in his back. His huge plaster really now smelt very bad: it was time it came off. The officer had only survived the terrible wounds because he had been given huge quantities of penicillin, tens of millions of units pumped into his bloodstream. He howled with pain daily as the nurses gave him these heroic doses with an enormous hypodermic in his buttocks. On his card they listed the millions of units with staggering rows of noughts. Then the time came for his dressing and plaster, a mass of dried blood and pus, green in places, to be removed.

But the girl nurses refused, absolutely, to face it.

So Paul took over with scissors and shears. He took the infantryman into the bathroom and worked on him, a little awkwardly, because his own arm still hurt and constricted him. The great plaster covered all the man's shoulder, and much of his back. It was all *pourriture*, nauseating: Paul grimly reflected that it was exactly what the troops obscenely called 'scab and matter pie'. But it was the decay of recovery, not of death. By

244

controlling his breathing Paul managed not to vomit, and clenching his teeth he strove to clip and carve carefully down the stiff mass of bandage, plaster and dried exudations. At times the man winced: and sometimes shuddered as he felt his body born again, cramped and weak, out of the binding dressing.

But eventually the filthy thing lay on the floor, and the marvel was revealed of the white healed flesh, the creature come whole again by itself. Creased, discoloured, seamed, and scarred, still messy with filth here and there: but vital, sweet and good.

Then Paul bathed the man and washed the surface of his mended skin. It was like bathing a child, and he felt a deep joy in the attention to another creature. The man's chest was robust and strong, but smooth with being in bed, softened and gentle in its muscular forms, full of animal energy and glow. The man gave great grunts of pleasure, puffing out his cheeks with pain as he moved the released shoulder, and uttering great 'ah!'s of satisfaction as he eased himself in the hot water: it was the first bath he had had for six weeks. The man even had, Paul noticed, a slight erection: even such intimacy, no more than normal affectionate care, evoked emanations of bodily love, even between man and man. Paul regained through the experience a sense of the strange wonder of shared bodily life between creatures, that he had forgotten. The man's body with its recuperative power, and its joy in the pleasures of release, warmth and cleanliness, seemed to him a marvellous thing like some great wild flower, in its own tissue-growing life. He thought weakly of how he wanted such flesh intimacy with a woman. But he was angry too, at the giggling coyness and inhumanity of the young emergency-trained nurses.

*

A soft voice was lisping metallically through the loudspeaker:
'*This war will only be won, if we keep Chrithst at our sides, guiding uth, and telling uth in our hearts what ith right. We should feel he ith with uth at home where we wait, perhaps, quietly and dutifully,*

for a loved one to return. Or even in battle, we must learn to feel the Mathster at our elbow . . .'

'Oh Christ, man: can't you turn that bloody drivel off?'

An infantry officer with a shattered shoulder blade and broken rib cage heaved up his trunk bound in heavy plaster angrily in the bed.

Benson, a BBC war correspondent in the next bed, turned pink. He was a ginger-haired plump man, a great favourite of the nurses, being famous.

'*I* don't think it's drivel!'

'Well, listen,' gasped the infantryman, 'I used to believe in God in His goodness, rot it. I don't expect the Almighty to come anywhere near me after what I've done out there. I certainly don't expect Him to help me fire a bloody gun into a chap's guts. And if Jesus Christ visits *my* home perhaps He can tell my wife what to do with the Air Force bloke she's carrying on with.'

The man was in pain and a little hysterical. He was forced to lie back, with an expulsion of breath. But he said from the position of lying exhausted on his back,

'But . . . I can tell you . . . Benny . . . if you don't stop putting on those bloody snivelling parsons at the crack of fucking dawn I'll get up, feeble as I am, old boy, and *do* your wireless set into . . . into bloody bits, old boy.'

Having delivered this the officer lay back gasping. Benson of the BBC, red with rage, crossly turned his set off and sulked like a child. The others groaned, as they wanted to hear the eight o'clock news. The break-through was under way at Caen: their own work was being completed.

*

Paul Grimmer developed a serum rash, which brought out huge blisters all over his body, and severe pains in his joints, so that he could hardly move. Because of his deep wound he had been innoculated against tetanus with a vaccine made from the plasma of horse's blood. His body turned out to have an allergy to the horse. When the rash came in the night the irritation was intolerable, and it was impossible to bear bed-clothes on his body. He would leap in a frenzy from bed, strip off his coverings, and run naked up and down the ward, berserk with fiery irritation, blistering skin and pain. The nurses had orders to give him injections of pituitrin every twenty minutes: adrenalin had ceased to be effective. But they funked the engagement with the naked, crazed young officer. Besides, one or two of the night nurses, especially one dark girl, preferred to sit half in bed with a favourite patient, kissing and caressing him, while the others swore at her for it, mutter-ing under their blankets, night after night.

*

At first the wounded men jabbered compulsively about their battle experiences. Each in turn explained how he came by his wound. But then they suddenly stopped talking about these things altogether. They denied them. Of course, they followed the wireless reports of the progress of the fighting in Normandy, but no longer referred to their own experiences, which were beginning to be repressed. Why recall all that pain?

And there was something worse than pain: there was the penalty of being brought to realize each his insignificance in the great events, and the meaninglessness of their own acts, terrible or futile as these may have been. They learned, lying there recounting their days in Normandy, that nothing they could claim as a deliberate act had done anything that had helped move the battle fronts one inch farther forward or backward. They could not escape a sense of the futility of individual action, in such a great historical turmoil of machine war. Half of them had been wounded by their own side, by strays, or by the impersonal accidents of bombardment from a distance. Others could say they had been shot at, but whether by routine 'fixed' barrages or by being singled out for indi-vidual attention, none could say – except for one man wounded in the neck by a sniper. Most had fired into German positions,

247

or had shot at distant figures, as Paul had. But only a few had ever actually killed men face to face with their own weapons – these included the shattered infantrymen. But even then, it had often been in self-defence, in panic, or in confusion.

The virgin soldier entered battle expecting to make decisions, act, shoot men dead, and act effectively according to the order groups, for 'own troops' against 'enemy'. But, they had discovered, it was never like that. Black and white were restored in newspapers, communiqués, citations, official histories, afterwards – in the grammar books of war. In the field there was always chaos, confusion, squalor; and each man was lost in the impersonal hell, where metal chased flesh, in one great mêlée. No individual made effective decisions, but reacted for the most part blindly to stimuli, and fought wild. One's greatest enemy was chance, and the complex and elusive laws governing odds, where metal was flying fast and bodies of flesh were among it. The guns babble and thump, men shout and yell, smoke drifts between, there are lights, howls, explosions. Perhaps a band of men are in fox-holes where other men were before. Others are broken and dead. Out of this chaos the reassuring grammar of war is written. But the experience itself is always hellish confusion, and submission to a bestial surrender of individual choice, to less-than-human action, as a pack of savage organisms, far more savage than any animal could be. The individual knows he might as well have never been there, for all the difference it made, that he was, and that he suffered. The price of submerging the individual life in the bloody fracas seemed on reflection too terrible: yet, in the face of the organized and maniac hatred of Nazism, it had had to be. They could see that. But on reflection, they found it intolerable, trying to reconcile the suffering, with the aims of war, and so they went dumb on the truth of war, and took refuge in weak-minded occupations, reading trivial detective stories, and flirting with the foolish young nurses.

*

'You'll be leaving soon,' she said. She minced rather at him, Paul thought, with mannerisms she had learnt from the films. But she was young and delicious with freckles on her small *retroussé* nose, her big brown eyes, and the black nurse's stockings. The inside of her dark blue cloak showed a brilliant red as it swung open. But her childishness made him uneasy, and he felt weak: she couldn't have been much more than sixteen.

'Look, the others are watching,' she said, dimpling.

It was a little like courting a pupil in a girls' school, Paul thought. Weak with convalescence he tried to remember what one said to a woman. It came out rather schoolboyish in his feebleness.

'I want to take you away to have some incredible adventure,' he said.

'What sort?'

'Well, we could stay in a hotel together,' said Paul, lamely and directly.

'You soldiers,' said the girl, wriggling a little, and waving to her nurse colleagues. They stood by a wall of the morgue by a holly hedge, in the acid damp darkness of shrubs blackened by the sooty industrial atmosphere.

'But it would be lovely.'

Paul found everything he said came out weak, gross, obvious and pathetic. He had only a faint hope that something kind and good would come out of it. Yet he knew, even in his desperation, that it wouldn't: he was feebly gesturing at relationship, in terms of his silliest dreams – and yet actual tender memories. So he looked baffled at the slight girl's figure, with stiff crackling white uniform over her breasts, standing against the mossy wall of the grim little outbuilding and its dank ivy cladding.

He drew her into the shade and kissed her. She liked being kissed, and enjoyed his lips, holding him close to her starchy uniform with her small hands. But she enjoyed the kissing too consciously, as if she were living a magazine story. When Paul looked into her big eyes, he was aware of a cinematic pose in himself. Then he asked her, thickly:

'Beryl, will you come and stay with me at the Metropole?'

'When?'

'This week-end.'

She looked at him boldly, and was obviously inwardly wondering what answer a woman should give, on the lines of magazine advice. Poor girl, he thought, she can't have left school long: what am I trying to do? But, the voice also snarled, she can take care of herself. I'm only asking. Yet he was miserable and angry with himself for his weakness. But her pretty young nurse's legs in the black stockings inflamed him.

She affected an indifferent sophistication. But he could see her pupils dilated with panic.

'All right. . . . What time?'

He fixed the time and place. But he was puzzled by her flatness, her apparent acquiescence and by the mechanical way the conversation had gone. It hadn't seemed quite right. Back in bed in the ward, however, his weak dreams overtook him, and he became unsteadily excited, at the prospect of a night of love with the beautiful young creature.

*

Of course, she never turned up. No doubt she went off to consult the back numbers of *Woman* on 'Those romantic young officers.' Or perhaps she asked one of the older nurses and was put wise to soldiers who go lightheaded in convalescence. Paul sensed the eyes of the other girls on him, smirking rather, some of them, and he felt uncomfortably that he was making himself ridiculous, a baby-snatcher.

Paul waited for an hour, feeling weak and untidy, at the door of the largest hotel in Leeds, all brown varnish, and full of stuffy self-importance. He had even gone so far as to book a room for Lieutenant and Mrs Grimmer.

He stood outside at first, pacing up and down, trying not to keep in step with the uniformed commissionaire. He had simply absconded from the hospital for the night, without telling anyone. All the officer patients now took nights off from time to time. Paul wore his old field battledress, cleaned, but with the tear in the shoulder still, where the shell splinter had entered his body. A nurse had repaired the split seam, where Tom had ripped it, and sewn on a new sleeve. But the big hole had defeated her. The tear made him look and feel untidy, in the dark drizzle of the Leeds evening. Through the hole the wind's chill touched his wound, its tissues only just healed, raw and new, through the light dressing.

People passed by, giving him only a glance sometimes; a soldier, now and then, a lazy salute. Paul responded with his left arm: his right was still stiff. One middle-aged motherly woman passing by saw the tear in his shoulder, and then, as she walked on, looked back compassionately to see if he wore a hospital shirt and tie, red and white, then looked enquiringly into his face. But Paul wanted to make no claim, no impact. He felt childish, and only wanted, weak and drained, to find his own feet. He wanted to be back with his regiment: but, though he had written several times to the War Office, they seemed to have lost his records.

After an hour, damp and depressed he went into the hotel to have a gin, drooping and bedraggled among the press of smart customers. A large gleaming major from a supplies depot in Macclesfield was airing his views on how to finish the war.

'I think we ought to go in and finish Jerry off, throw absolutely everything in.'

'What you and all?' his companion guffawed, a neat businessman, with a carefully pressed new worsted suit.

Laughing, the large major stepped back heavily on Paul's foot. Paul exhaled a surprised breath, grunted sheepishly and fled, leaving the man apologizing absently over his shoulder, casual. Inwardly he was in a fury: the English Midlands seemed to go on in such a stupidly unchanged, unmoved way, even after the great drama of Normandy. How would he ever bear the aimless dullness of civvy street? The people seemed to him senseless and moronic.

He looked round outside with one last despairing glance for Nurse Bravington: once, with a quivering thrill in his belly, he thought he saw her standing there in her long dark blue cloak: but it was a man selling newspapers in an old gas cape. The blacked-out streets were forbidding: yet dark taxis drew up full of women in furs and jewels, and businessmen with polished heads. Away in France the same drizzle was falling on the exhausted and vulnerable infantry who were making England safe for private enterprise, the wretched bundles of weary men sleeping like children by their sticks of rifles, in their lumbering tanks. Paul felt a bitter contempt for the vulgar guffaws of the people in the bars, and the deep-piled ease of the luxurious life in the hotel. Deferential servants held the doors open for the opulent revellers. Paul wanted to rant aloud at them, about conditions at the front. But he knew it was useless. There were so many different lives that could be led. Conscience led to one: cultivated suppression of conscience to another. Obviously, many of those in the hotel were black-market racketeers and those who grew fat on Army contracts. But why was the destructive activity better? What were the rewards? How did one judge?

A single gin in him became a fire: he had not taken drink since his wound, though he had taken up smoking again. He took out a packet of Woodbines now and lit one. In the smutty drizzle he took a tram out to Greenwood, and walked down suburban backstreets to the hospital. He was glad to be back in the bright warm ward, in bed again, out of the clinging damp. He clung gloomily to the pillow, like a sick infant.

*

The lunatic under the tree continued to bleb away at his lips. For him, happily, no war existed: there were no shortages, no fear, no pain, no nights in nervous torment, no broken rela-

252

tionships, voyages, or terrors. There was only the sun, the tree's cool shade in July and August, then the falling autumn leaves, the bustling wind of the Equinox, and the happy sound, 'Blibberblubberblooberblebberblubber.'

1945

A BELGIAN CROWD, lawless, happy, and determined stormed the troop train. From Ghent to Antwerp Paul Grimmer had two fat nuns in voluminous black habits on his lap. They had been bowled into the train by a great press of country people, some carrying bundles, others with squawking chickens in basketwork crates. No-one could move in the compartments or corridors. At junctions crowds of grey lean children, with faces like dwarfed old men, fought for scraps of sandwich and butt ends of cigarettes.

Paul had been back in hospital. In the weakness of convalescence he caught dysentery in an epidemic. So he did not cross the North Sea until Boxing Day, 1944. As Paul reached Antwerp on December 31st, Von Rundstedt started his winter offensive, the last kick of the dying Reich. He spent the night in a dismal transit camp. Next day he rode into bitter winter weather in the open back of a lorry, rocking over bad *pavé* and along endless hedgeless roads, hundreds of miles east, in heavy snow.

*

262 *Forward Delivery Squadron*
R.A.C.   B.E.A.
January 6th, 1945

Dear Mother and Father,
   Nearer and nearer the Front. Here we are about thirty miles from it, but here, where we are billeted in a clean little Belgian village, there is a quiet winter calm about everything. I am in a farmer's

*house, with an enormous white bed, and a good deal of comfort. I'm
writing in the kitchen of a café which is kept by a tailor and his wife.
He sits crosslegged on the table by the window sewing a black coat:
she's ironing on the table where I write. There is a splendidly ornamental poêle with polished rails and ornamental feet, covered with
smoothing irons and tall filtre coffee pots. They're very kind, and
grateful to us, in Belgium. But they're terrified about the present
battle.*

*Yesterday, on the frozen road, we stopped at a café which had been
a centre of the resistance. They showed us with pride some photographs of engines they had derailed (comic they looked), and of
comrades shot for sabotage (not so). They say the government takes
no notice of the Résistance as a political force – they are lax in their
treatment of traitors and blackshirts, and over the Black Market and
rationing. They had a terrible time under the German occupation:
and now things do not improve as rapidly as they had hoped because
of the government forced on Belgium by what they call the 'Black-
mail'. 'Les riches sont toujours libres', they say: but for the ordinary
people there is no coal, soap, no meat. They only get half a hundred-
weight of coal a month, if there is any transport. Which is why I'm
in the kitchen – there's no fire in the café itself.*

More later,
Paul

P.S. Send me some real coffee.

*

By three-ton lorry he climbed, into the pine-covered hills of
the Ardennes in deep snow, in the dark frosty weather. In an
isolated village they passed peasants cutting up a pig. Its head
was cut off and planted ridiculously upright, staring heaven-
wards on the snow on top of a wall. The corpse was being
scrubbed and blanched in great wooden tubs, over fires. In the
snow the scene could have been a painting by Breughel.
Children were throwing pieces of hot gut and bloody tissue at
one another. The snow all round was bright red with blood
splashes.

The lorry ground up steeper inclines, icy and treacherous.
After a while they began to hear the guns of battle. At last they
found the tanks, slithering on thick ice, on a wooded slope. It

was bitter weather, in many degrees of frost. Headquarters was in a village called Hotton in shell-broken houses. Suddenly there was Tom again, and other old faces, under steel helmets, and in the hatches of tanks.

'My dear old boy! Welcome back. I say, you must have caught a packet to be away so long.'

'Nice to see you again. I had dysentery.'

'Sleeping with some black totty, I suppose?'

'It was lease-lend dried egg in a Cypriot café, as a matter of fact – at Cambridge!'

'You can put your stuff in here, old chap, and sleep here tonight. Only keep your pistol by you. The little grey men are very pressing, and you never know who'll turn up. It's too fucking cold for this caper, but bloody old Rundstedt has got his rag out.'

Paul was too tired to take in more of his surroundings. Outside squealed the grey elephantine tanks again, and the radios whined and crackled. As he fell asleep on his camp bed in the draughty downstairs farmhouse room, he heard gunfire again, large shells falling near, and felt strangely at home.

*

His last night in Brussels turned damp and sad. Here and there from one café or other, all of them more or less empty, Paul could hear a piano accordion. One was actually playing a nostalgic tune he knew from an old film, *Sous les toits de Paris*. But the streets were wet and the lights dim: one could be very lonely in such a big city on a week's leave, much more lonely than with the regiment. Paul had wandered the cold streets on the last day of his leave, seeking a touch of sympathy, of human kindness, with a hunger that March had evoked.

At about ten o'clock he felt tired, and turned into a bar with coloured lamps over the door and ordered himself a carafe of wine. An English airman was incoherently importuning one of the women of the café, while she waited for him to pass out.

'Si'dahn . . . look . . . si'dahn. '*Sayez vose.*'

255

But the girl was holding him up. He clutched at her large black beads and broke them. They rolled all over the floor.

'*Mon dieu!*' she exclaimed. '*Quel brute!*'

Paul smiled. One of the other girls, and a workman in a cap with a glazed black peak, went down on their hands and knees and searched among the puddles of *grenadine* and splashed *apéritif*. Paul knelt down too, under the brown varnished bentwood chair legs. As he crawled near her Paul caught a fascinating mixture of smells, Pernod, garlic and sweat, from the woman whose beads they were hunting. She was dressed in a shiny black frock. Her face was puffy and pale. The airman by now lay on his back on the drink-splashed floor, and was half singing, half wheedling.

'I wanna bit o' tennerness, thass all I wan'.'

He put his forage cap on his chest and folded his arms over it. Paul saw in him the image of his own callow inward needs, and he drank his wine quickly. He must get out of here: the collapsing man was becoming too infantile and ridiculous.

The girl had all her beads now and sat threading them thoughtfully in the corner. Because of this she looked deft and domestic. She dragged her hair straight, patting it with her fingers, looking in the wall mirror. Paul found himself studying her with a sense of hopelessness. The café woman reminded him of that whole area of life and relationship which, while he was away at war, was becoming increasingly remote and which he felt he was being increasingly disabled for, not least by the expectations, aroused by 'leave', of a 'good time'. All a soldier could do on leave was to 'look for a woman'. And here was the kind of sad creature who had learnt to put up with a succession of hungry soldiers, like the man on the floor. What good did it do anyone? Yet she seemed generous. He thought of her life under the Occupation: had she had her beads broken by drunken Wehrmacht soldiers last year? Well, wasn't starving worse? Did she have to sink to satisfying their bodily hunger, their grunting needs, to earn a little extra for bread, cigarettes and coffee? Saddened, he drank off the rest of his carafe of wine and went out, stepping over the airman who was now snoring loudly. The girl looked up and he smiled. She met his smile with a wry grimace of her scarlet mouth. In that flash of recognition Paul and the girl suddenly revealed to each other a human sympathy, of the sadness of human needs, and the broken days of war that frustrated them, in one brief ironic gesture.

Outside, Paul sighed. But what was one to do? He had tried to forget his loneliness by searching the bookshops, and going to the galleries. He had spent seven days' leave in the Belgian capital, having come over from the Rhineland where his regiment had moved after the bitter campaign in the Ardennes. He was staying in the Salvation Army Allied Club in relaxation and comfort with its soft beds, hot baths and good plain meals. But because he lacked companionship, the very comfort of the Club and the relaxation had created a torment. With no woman of his own in the world, and in the reaction from long tension and anxiety on the Rhine, he struggled inwardly with the hallucinations of desire and was tormented by the cruel recklessness of a soldier's lust. Even such a moment's exchange of smiles with such a café girl aroused anguish in his unhappy and hungry flesh.

The struggle had been made worse by an act of kindness. In the train he had fallen into conversation with a charming blonde girl. At first he had wildly yearned for her, to be his companion for leave. But she turned out to be married, and they met her husband at the Pelicon Restaurant, where they had given him a splendid meal. They had been gay, all together, and argued vivaciously about art, and Russia, and the war. Then they went to a recital. A sensitive man 'cellist played, mostly solo pieces, without accompaniment. It was a subtle and stirring occasion. Paul was deeply stirred by the meal, the wine, and especially by the dark sweet sounds of the instrument. By its thrumming whole areas of unfamiliar feeling were opened in him again. He had so hoped that on this furlough

I   257

he could make touch with some of his real interests, and the delightful couple had given him this touch with them, so beautifully. They did all they could for him, and asked him back to their flat, where they gave him wine, and cheese and salad. Then they talked well into the night about music and literature, in England and in Belgium. Paul felt in touch once more with the university world, with books, and all the unexercised interests of mind and sensibility of old.

But the very comfort of their soft sofa, and even the very warmth of the personal exchange, made envy rise in him: he found himself wanting to oust the charming young husband – a doctor in a Brussels Hospital – and lie with his wife. The desire shocked him, hurt him with its brazen and oafish ingratitude. The blonde woman was so vivacious and her teeth so white as she laughed, while her breasts stirred, that Paul became unable to speak. He gazed at the bright green jewel against her white neck, which she stroked with clean pale fingers. They sat round a small polished table. It was the closest Paul had been to a woman for months: he was shoulder to shoulder with her and could smell her sweet flesh. Such a strange creature, woman, with shining fair hair and the pretty ears! He held the seat of his chair to stop himself from impulsively stroking her hair or kissing her cheek: he could hardly restrain the impulse. His abdomen seethed, where the creativity of his manhood lurked, desperate with loneliness and the long months under threat of pain or destruction. But then, as it came to be midnight and time for bed he left them waving, managing to seem grateful. But inwardly he was maddened with envy, because the husband was going to bed with his wife. He hated himself for being such a crude boor of a soldier. You're a helot, he told himself.

So he walked the Brussels streets alone, for the next few days. Now he was due to go back to the front the following day. The Rhine crossing was imminent. The regiment was training for it at Dilsen, a small dismal village in Holland. After midnight it began to drizzle, intermittently. The cafés were closing. There was to be no woman for him this leave. He thought wrily of the lies he would have to tell, back in dismal Dilsen.

'Shagged, I suppose?' Tom would ask.

'Half dead, mate,' he'd reply.

And he would have to look knowing, as if he held back revelations. Whereas in fact he probably would have gone to bed miserably sober in the Salvation Army Services Club. Salvation! The vile loneliness, the emptiness of this damned muddy and dangerous life, month after month! He recalled the dismal weeks of convalescence, and how he had made such a fool of himself with the nurse, and how she had turned him down. But she had been a child – no more than sixteen, surely? He drew up the collar of his British warm and thrust his hands gloomily into his coat pockets. He would look for an all-night café. Surely there would be one? He hadn't had enough drink. He walked through the student quarter, where the cheaper cafés were, near the Beaux-Arts. The March night was full of airborne promise: the sky cleared in patches through which the stars twinkled merrily.

It was in the Rue de Naples. She was carrying a jug of milk. Obviously she had slipped out of her flat, and had thrown her coat over her shoulders. She had slippers on only. She was casting about no inviting looks, and the way she parted from the woman who had served her at the door of the *bistro* was so quiet and reserved that it was obvious she was not one of the *poules* who haunted the cafés.

The jug of milk made her deliciously domestic to Paul, whose timidity and embarrassment left him. Surprisingly, it was not that he felt that here was his last chance of a woman, but that there was something strangely dramatic about the way they met, in the empty street, in a March breeze at midnight. Paul could tell by her manner that she was alone, and by her glance that she was as lonely as he was. A gust blew down the street and her coat slipped. He went over to her with

I*   259

a natural ease and pulled the coat back round her shoulders. She had loose brown hair and a white blouse. His belly gave a thrill. Her teeth were white and gleaming like the young doctor's wife as she laughed. She was about twenty-five. They looked at one another with that direct understanding that can come between a man and a woman, unmistakable when it comes, even in mere starlight. He knew at once as soon as she spoke so easily to him that a good moment in life had come again.

'*Merci, Monsieur l'officier.*'

'*Est – ce que je peux vous aider?*'

Paul's French was clumsy: the gesture even clumsier. Ah well, here we go, he thought, the brush-off. Front tomorrow. She had a husky voice.

'*Vous êtes si jeune . . .*'

'*Pardon?*'

'*Vous êtes en permission?*'

'*Jusqu'à demain.*'

'*Demain?*'

'*Puis, en retour à les* . . . er': he couldn't remember the word . . . '*chars*'.

'*Les chars? Ah, un regiment blindé!*' She paused. '*Et vous êtes seul toute la permission?*'

Paul gave her a wry grimace, and laughed. Her face looked at him concernedly, her eyes wide in the faint light.

Paul shrugged.

'*Oui. Tout seul.*'

'*Quel dommage!*'

Paul stood unbelieving in his good fortune: the girl laughed so warmly, close to his face, alluring him.

She looked up at the sky and held her hand out.

'*Il pleut un peu.*'

She must wonder what sort of a man I am, thought Paul, standing here numbstruck like a fool. He felt his English reserve coming over him.

'I . . . er . . .'

The girl caught his arm, laughing into her shoulder.

'*Venez.*'

It seemed too bold, almost coarse, and Paul almost resisted. But, what the hell, he told himself, accept that Latin kindness: women want men, men want women. They have this capacity for spontaneous warm-heartedness. She sees I'm stone-lonely. They've only just been released from worse than hell, and they're overflowing with gratitude; let the overflow warm you where you need to come to life again. But it seemed so much like a dream, and he dreaded even the tender stirrings that began painfully in his body.

They climbed some steps hand in hand. She pushed open the door of her flat which she had left on the latch, and went up some more steps within. There was a glass-panelled door, and then he found himself in an apartment. There were two small rooms, one single bedroom, a sitting-room, and a very tiny kitchenette, really only big enough for one to work in. There was a bathroom with a lavatory, and a *bidet*, in another small space, though not much smaller than the living rooms.

It was obviously not a street girl's apartment: she was a young business woman or secretary, Paul supposed. The rooms were well-furnished in the style of the Belgian middle-class, with glossy veneers, frosted glass and machine-embroidered covers. There was a desk with family pictures in metal and wooden frames. Between the little living room and the bedroom there was a curtain. The wallpaper was oatmeal-coloured and the general effect nondescript and dreary. But the apartment was cosy, and glowed with an electric fire in the wall. Underfoot were warm rugs, and newspapers and books lay around.

'*Comment vous appelez-vous?*'

'*Paul. Et vous?*'

'*Lili. Lili Dubois. Vous voulez de la soupe? Ou peut-être une omelette?*'

She laid a table for them and poured out two glasses of wine, then rapidly made an omelet, cracking the eggs with sharp vivacity, and whisking energetically. Paul removed his officer's flat hat. Perhaps, he thought, she's just going to feed me. But then he remembered her eyes in the dark. She wants me to be properly fed before I make love to her! What forethought! His loins stirred with painful heat. It was such a long time since he had known a woman's generosity, in passion. He sat in a dream.

'*Vous êtes très gentille,*' he said.

'*Vous êtes un soldat allié. C'est très simple – un peu de reconnaissance. Tu n'es qu'un gosse, pour te battre contre les Allemands. Mon dieu! Quel age as – tu?*'

'*Vingt-deux.*'

'*Hélas! Et moi, j'en ai vingt trois!*'

'*Voilà – nous sommes passés tous les deux. À la reconnaissance!*'

He relaxed under the influence of the wine. He emptied his glass. Lili gestured at the bottle.

'*Mon dieu,*' said Paul, the wine loosening his tongue to fluency, if not accuracy. '*Comme je me sentais seul. Mais, l'amitié, ça n'est presque possible pendant les sept jours d'une permission.*'

'*Donc, il faut être gentille.*'

'*Un espèce de devoir?*'

'*Non, gamin, quand j'ai envie d'être gentille, je le suis.*'

She pushed her face into his, and kissed his nose. Her eyes were grey with orange flecks. She dished out the omelet, lacey with brown markings, but still runny in the centre – perfect! But Paul could hardly eat. His throat was clenched with desire. The woman's kindness spread in his young veins like love: how seldom did one meet it! He just managed to swallow the last forkful of omelet, when Lili sprang to him and kissed him full on the mouth and stroked his nape. He pressed her breasts to him, and felt them soft against his chest, still strapped in his leather Sam Browne. Then they both let go, and quickly began to undress. Lili put out all the lights except a small lamp by the bed. He took his shiny leather gear off like a harness.

Lili got into bed naked, while Paul finished undressing. He felt with a strange tired delight once more the strange awkwardness of a man in lust, the awkward flesh rising and swinging from his body. He was suddenly ashamed.

'*Tu es si gentille. Je me sens . . . si . . . farouche – un fauve!*'

He went to her. She laid a hand on his body and then looked seriously at him.

'*Attention . . . vous n'avez pas . . . quelque chose?*'

Paul felt a fool. He knew at once what she meant. He never carried one. He had given up carrying preparations for chances of loving, half in despair, half in rejection. He could certainly never bring himself to carry the Army Issue 'Early Treatment' packets against syphilis – with their grotesque and unlovely instructions, 'urinate in gushes' and so forth. For a moment everything went cold, and sad. He stood, rather dismal, his potency fading and his body relaxing.

Then Lili had a thought. She was obviously not prepared for chance either. Two amateurs they were, he mused, happily glad that it was so.

'*Peut-être . . .*'

She rummaged in a bottom drawer. Paul revelled in the comedy of it, the implications were all so comic. He laughed quietly, '*Comme c'est drole!*' He watched the girl's white buttocks moving and her breasts swinging as she turned over the clothes.

'*Aha!*'

'*Dieu merci!*'

Lili laughed and lay in the bed, the sheets and coverlets turned back.

Paul embraced her lovingly, with great and tender gratitude in his heart. The weary tension of days in fear and danger, in the deep snows of the Ardennes, and the bleak marshes of the Rhineland fell from him, and he swooned to be released to the warmth of female generosity. He felt amazement and awe as he touched her soft warm breasts with his hard soldier's hands.

At last he entered her with a cry, and recognised again, as from distant memory, the warm cleaving satisfaction that a woman can give, in love in the flesh, with all its soft heat and scents of love. He was gentle and kind to her, and they lay embraced in transport through the night. In his mind, he felt blissfully relaxed by the clasp of another body all that night, and felt solutions coming to the questions which that winter had dogged his hopes for the end of the war – 'What for?' 'What does one survive *for*?' She brought the answer home to him – the strange generous girl on whose pillow he lay. That one night's warmth more than compensated for all that he had suffered since the last time he lay happily thus with a woman's body, generously given, two years ago, with Lucy. The Belgian girl's *amitié* restored his faith in human nature, and his hope, by the renewed experience of what joy could be. She, cooing happily to him in pidgin English, stroking his back and nape, murmuring,

'Boy soldier . . . my boy soldier lover.'

He kissed her again and again in a passion of gratitude.

They lay enwrapped until dawn, always more or less awake, and then Lili got up and made coffee. The girl was full of sweetness for him, but they both knew the parting must come before the sun was high. She perhaps had a lover – a potential husband – in a prison camp, or maybe at the Front. He had to go back to the Rhine. There could be no future: there was only the momentary gift of love-kindness.

The intimacy of the petty domestic things reinforced his rediscovery, of a possible future to believe in – washing himself in her *bidet*, shaving in her mirror. That was what he could look forward to – something like that, only lasting, domestic joy, in peace, after the war. How marvellous it would be! Fortunate, he thought, with a mundane reflection, that I hung on to my briefcase, in case of theft in the Club. In it were his towels, soap, razors and pyjamas – and some coffee he could give Lili.

'*Mon dieu! Je n'ai pas mis mon pyjama!*'

Lili, who was cooking him a poached egg this time, went off into peals of laughter.

'*Voilà!*'

Paul produced his pound of best coffee beans. Lili's face grew serious, on the verge of anger and tears.

'*Non – il n'y a rien . . . à payer.*'

Her face was full of anger and a kind of hauteur.

'*Je ne suis pas . . . c'est seulement pour vous, soldat, que je . . .*'

Paul protested in a way he had seen French people do, murmuring *non, non, non, non!*

'*Celui-ci, c'est de rien pour moi – ça coute rien chez nous. C'est un petit cadeau, pour l'amitié!*'

He disarmed her at last, and she relaxed. In Brussels still a pound of even imitation coffee cost a good deal. Real coffee beans like this were unobtainable. He grinned at the label, 'Lamberts. Norwich': he wondered what his mother would think if she had known where her parcel ended up.

And Paul hid a 500 franc note in the coffee. He had eaten and drunk that much. Why should she give materially when she had given him so much of her generosity?

'*C'est un cadeau, seulement. Je ne veux pas remporter tout ça iusqu'au front encore. Absolument pas!*'

He came close to her. She was half-dressed, doing up her blouse. She was suddenly sad, over all the violence and death of war, the broken relationship, the evanescence of such moments. He felt a great flood of tenderness, and a deep sense of absolute loss, as he held her soft breasts to him. Suddenly tears fell hotly from him and he wiped the salty liquid from his cheeks.

'*Adieu, Lili. Jamais . . .*' He broke down and moaned the rest, no idea how to phrase it. '*Jamais je ne vous . . . oublierai pas.*'

It was true: she knew it. Her mouth, soft with physical love, murmured her reply, tremblingly:

'*Jamais.*'

It was, it had been, that March night, and could not be denied. How much she had done for him! Everything! He dressed and went down, recovered from his tears. But then he returned to her door, and made her come down, to kiss good-bye again. He must go. He fought with himself until he was round the corner, but gave one glance back, to see her pale and weeping in the window, her forehead against the pane.

She should not care. Yet it was death not to let one's feelings flow so, whatever the cost in pain.

Amitié!

The empty streets were beginning to fill with cars.

Strange – that he would never see her again!

He was in agony all the way to the Salvation Army Allied Services Club, where he mounted the stairs under the blue and red banner proclaiming blood and fire.

*

Rain fell over the flat land, washing the debris of the wind-swept trees into the ditches. The Maas swirled and eddied through the Biesbosch. Sentries watched the brown dykes fill; water edged down their necks, fell all day long out of the muzzles of their rifles, slung upside down against their sodden greatcoats. April clouds, like thin grey sponges, washed over the dismal Dutch villages. From the outposts guarding the river-line all the sentries could hear was the rattle of soaked trees and the paddle of cattle in the mud. Sometimes a damp intermittent voice on the telephone would ask for a report, a cigarette would sizzle, go out, and be relit.

There were five groups of grounded tank men, each an NCO and six, along that part of the bank. The rain washed as if with cold tears the lines in their faces, lines deepened by des-peration, from the days when they had been caught in the nets of tracer, or had run the gauntlet of flame and drilling shot. The Dutch rain flushed from their eyes the images of blossom-ing red wounds of fallen men; washed from the roots of their hair the sweat of hate and fear. Across in Germany the war was

266

ending. Here in Nord Brabant the machine-guns were rusting half-heartedly in the marshes. The campaign mud dropped quietly off the reddening tracks of their tanks in the village. The Rhine had been crossed: the last chase was on, to Berlin. But the East Northshires were left in the sodden 'hinge' of the Biesbosch Fens.

Here, they were in a backwater of the land battle, as insignificant as the dark creeks in the Land Van Altena on the opposite bank of the river. In this wet swampy peace they began to think of themselves for the first time in unsoldierly ways, as persons, as men. They had not dared to do this for the past year. Each had preferred to be no more than a digit in the daily 'strength return'. If one stuck to that, the fear and uncertainty could be held at a minimum. To become human meant to suffer, in one's feelings: to be a digit had minimized the pain, casualties had to be 'accepted.' Now in the five huts, cottages and lean-tos in the shelter of the flood-bank, each man saw in the other six something that seemed to have been panned out by that week's rain. Till then it had been too dangerous to know somebody well who might at any time be in agony, or be destroyed, suddenly and terribly, at your side.

Now they would never go into action again, not in Europe: and they knew from intelligence reports that Japan had begun to sue for peace. Each hand that held a cigarette had suddenly become newly alive and precious. They saw each other as fresh as the washed roofs and pastureland near the road behind them. They shared their families seriously now in the space of a slit trench. If each other's wives were unfaithful or pregnant, their children ill, or their houses bombed, they earnestly discussed the problem together – daring now to speak of the future. For some of them 'civvy-street' seemed at times hardly worth going back to: but the others tried to find possible points of fresh growth for them. They were full of hope and feelings: yet stunned with the newness of release.

A labourer took his horse and cart along the dyke-wall on

the enemy side of the river. Nobody fired. The plodding tracks the horse was making in the road, bent under its load, were the tracks they had seen everywhere of the movement of people across and among them in Europe. They had watched the Normandy peasants saving their cattle; seen the infantry walking into the barrage; watched helplessly the father in Houffalize dragging his bleeding children from under the guns; had been overwhelmed by the wanderings of crowds of liberated, the aimless, and the hordes of captured prisoners, trekking over the rutted roads and burst-open cropland of open country everywhere.

Beyond the moving figures of horse and peasant were the enemy, some of them cut off, trying to keep their ammunition dry, defeat closing in on them, penetrating like the rain. These saw and knew nothing but the flat quiet fens, over the sights of their silent wet machine-guns, their fast, snarling voices dumb. They waited: but no messages came, because their Headquarters were in chaos.

The tank men did not see, that morning, across from where the main dyke joined the river, three men waiting in the reeds, crawl, drop into the brown sluggish stream. Two men and an old man fought and turned, caught in the circles of swollen water, choking, drifted, sank, struck out again. As the current carried them their mouths spewed: a black head disappeared, was hauled up. A circle of water caught them, flung them against the rubbish of a destroyed bridge, their hands bled in the noisy sluices under the girders. They dragged one another arm over arm towards one bank, the Maas pulling at them until they could thrust themselves on to the end of the shore.

Ten minutes later the water and blood dripped from their tunics and snaked dirtily across the floor of a cottage room among the untidy grey beds of Number Four Post. The Yorkshire soldiers studied their light transparent blue and ochre faces, deep pits in them under ten days' hair and mud. The old man's beard moved, his filthy hands fought against his shuddering, wrung the edge of his muddy German tunic. One of the sentries held his gun the right way up and pushed over the safety catch. The corporal found and opened a sodden *soldbuch*. Lieutenant Paul Grimmer was sent for, to look at the prisoners: he came down in an armoured scout car with four heavy wheels, sloshing through the muddy tracks. He got down from the slippery steel sides of the car. The corporal saluted wetly in his gas cape and dripping helmet.

'Where are these chaps?'

The corporal solemnly jerked his head. 'By the stove, Sir.'

The mud caked on their steaming trousers; the blood on their bruised hands blackened. A faint stir of movement ran along their limbs as the heat from the red hot stove forced its way in. Gradually they lifted stiff arms and felt their hair and beards, their calves, as though they were feeling them for the first time. The soldiers gave them mess-tins of tea. One young man with a torn filthy grey green tunic spilt his tea quickly out of the mess tin, half over himself, half into his mouth. Then he parted his aching and swollen lips and muttered to the other two, lifting his hand on to the old man's shoulder. They took off their boots with pain, emptied the water into the ashcan, so that it hissed and stank on the hot metal. The others stood round while Paul studied the *soldbücher*. Then they all stood solemnly waiting for an interpreter, for whom Paul had signalled by radio. Paul and the soldiers felt they were watching in the three the deep-scarring sorrows of themselves and Europe. Nobody spoke. The old man fumbled with his cigarette-end, watched the water smoke out of the sides of his trouser legs.

An interpreter came by motor-cycle and one of the young men told him their story in German from a narrative brokenly gathered in Russian from the other two. Number Four Post heard it as it was taken down. 'Three deserters 261 Free Mongolian Division. They say they were captured by the Germans near Kharkov, held in a concentration camp in Poland for one year. Then moved to an open camp near Warsaw, were given arms and uniforms, and told they were in the German Army. They were used against partisans in Russia. Say they took part in revolts in Holland and Texel Island. They say they have lived for two weeks in the marshes on a loaf of bread, intending to desert. They know nothing of German troop dispositions, but they believe the Biesboch occupied by units of enforced foreign troops who know nothing of events and do not know that they are cut off, nor that the war is nearly ended.' The interpreter then said in German, 'The War is almost ended, the Red Army is in Berlin.' The young man repeated it in Russian. The old man bent his head to the fire, pulled at his hair. Inside a crust of mud the eye of the other turned a different hue, as though a membrane had burst or he had come up from some oppressed depths to the surface. But there was not much other change in any of them, unless it were a wave of the hand in some long-forgotten direction of greeting or triumph.

The Englishmen felt that they were confronted by the damned when they themselves were ending their time in Purgatory. A wave of great pity possessed them, such as they had seldom been able to allow in their cautious hearts since D Day.

Paul Grimmer gave the corporal orders for the transfer of the captives to a unit concerned with Displaced Persons. A lorry would be sent. The corporal saluted in the rain once more.

From his scout car Paul watched the sentries walk out in twos. Two of them were discussing thoughtfully under a groundsheet how the Russian deserters could get home. Home! The distances from the Biesboch Marshes to Kharkov or Mongolia seemed cosmic. They had no idea where Mongolia was. They were debating sadly how far away were Yorkshire and the home fireside: there was much sentry go, entraining and soldiering to do yet. But to get 'home' – to Mongolia! It was too much for the mind to encompass. And himself? Paul thought. Before them all stretched a long brown dyke into which fell a host of raindrops steadily.

*

One wet night a few weeks later, Paul Grimmer had gone to bed in his billet in the Dutch town of Dongen, when suddenly there was a coarse unfamiliar parping noise, and an unrecognisable shuffling below, in the mess-room. He came down in his pyjamas to find the village band, in flat patent leather hats and black uniforms coming in through the mess-room window – first two trumpets, then a silver euphonium who stuck in the window and couldn't unwind himself, then a trombone, then a bassoon. They were red-faced, plump and very ugly Dutchmen: and they were hopelessly drunk. Half the band inside played with deafening loudness; the other half outside tried to keep in time, in the wet blackness. The drum walloped outside: it was too big to go through. Through the open window flew fat brown May bugs which dashed at the lamp, buzzed in a bristly way, dozens of them, and then fell on the floor to be squashed by the band's boots, or slid into their instruments' horns. At last all the band were yanked in, and walked heavily round and round the small room of the villa, trampling on a squashed mess of beetle, parping brisk martial music, boozily out of time and out of tune. They played 'Tipperary' and 'Jingle Bells'. They staggered: but they would not stop.

Paul poured himself a glass of rather flat champagne from a bottle he found open on the sideboard. Other officers, partially clad came down. Outside the whole village gathered in the streets. The Colonel brought a telegram. Hostilities had ceased.

*

Paul found a possible dark grey worsted suit at the Demob Centre. He surrendered his pay book. There were several forms to fill in and an orderly measured him with a tape. After that he joined the other officers busy in lines of cubicles between hardboard screens where hung rows of suits, and pigeon-holes of smaller garments. There he collected, in a large cardboard

271

box, two cotton shirts, two pairs of socks, one suit, one hat, one pair of shoes, and a gabardine raincoat. The officers were in a giddy delirium, but rather sheepish, too. Here was their dream realized at last; but there was a plunge to be taken at the end of it all, on the steps leading out into the street, in York.

'That's a good 'un,' said the suit orderly. 'Fits all right and all. Some of 'em . . .'

He made a thumbs down gesture, and shook his head.

'Bloody disgrace, mate. Shoddy. Never mind, you're all right. Next please.'

Paul bridled a little, at the mateyness. Yes, that was it. He wanted to say to the orderly ' "Sir" to you'. But then he caught sight in a long mirror of a tall brown-faced young man wearing a brown porkpie hat indoors, and very new cheap factory shoes. He seemed featureless, a thin shadow in a nondescript pin-head mottle black suit, with meanly cut lapels, and a white shirt with faint stripes. The shadow wore no tie. To his dismay he took in that this was himself, the himself of the future. Of course, no-one would call such a shadow 'Sir': the orderlies knew that none of those passing through their hands was going to stay in the Army a minute longer than necessary – certainly not to attend an orderly office session to put a soldier on a charge for insolence. They weren't really very insolent: but they were matey. And this was the first touch of the cold plunge, into the grey dullness of that Street where they had all longed for so long to be. Paul sighed.

'You better 'ave a tie,' said an orderly.

There were rows of terrible factory patterns, porridgy or criss-cross, in dull colours, brown and grey.

'Haven't you any *plain* ties?' Paul asked, trying to summon a last shred of authority and self-respect.

The orderly grinned.

'Nothing fancy, chum!'

'But these *are* all fancy. That's what I don't want. I want one that isn't.'

It seemed ridiculous to fuss over a free tie. Who had ordered hundreds of thousands of demob ties? How fantastic! The orderly shrugged. Then he actually turned away; grinning deliberately, to attend to someone else. He even winked at the other officer. Paul inwardly fumed, and blushed with anger. He looked malevolently at the awful ties. 'Who's in charge of this unit?' – the words came to mind, and the tone of voice which he had learnt to instil submission in the Army. But the phrase remained unspoken. What was the use? That kind of organization was behind him now, for ever: he hoped. Or so he had hoped: but hope's fulfilment is often so ironically different from what one had expected. So, Paul took the least offensive tie from the hanging rows, a dull speckled brown thing in glossy mercerized cotton. He was trying to think what some of his mess-mates would look like, with the bizarre ladders and zags of black and green, or maroon and grey, round their throats.

Most of the others were still out by the shores of the Kieler-haven. A fortnight ago Paul had been reading the *Daily Telegraph* in the lounge of a café they had taken over as a mess, opposite the sunken hulk of a huge brothel ship in the Estuary at Laboe. Suddenly he had spilled his coffee all over his lap, so electric a start had he given, to read that university students could be demobilized at once under a Class 'B' release scheme. He read the paragraph over and over again, and went off at once to his room, with a burning face and a galloping heart.

In two weeks he was in a train, having said his goodbyes to everyone – rather curtly, for they did not hide their anger and jealousy. Even the older men had to stay in for months as yet. But Paul was relentless: serve them right for their damned contempt of culture and learning. Yet he was sorry for those with families, and especially for Tom, since his theatre career, interrupted in middle age, would be terribly hard enough to take up as it was, and every week he was losing ground to younger men. There was even a moistness in Tom's eyes, and

273

he alone of the other officers came out to the waiting fifteen-hundredweight truck.

'See you in Town, old chap,' said Tom: 'You know, you'll never guess how bloody lucky you are.'

And he turned quickly away, overcome by chagrin and unhappiness.

'Cheero,' called Paul – but it stuck in his throat. So long their hearts had been set on release. But when it came it evoked much bitterness. So, a little downcast, Paul sat in the train across Germany and the Netherlands, to the ferry boat at the Hook of Holland. He sat withdrawn, in a state of silent shock, unable to believe his good fortune. The wheels tapped away a drowsy rhythm, 'Going to be out, going to be out.' At every junction and station yard the crowds of grey-faced, thin and dwarfed children stood in lines, holding out their hands for sweets, crusts, cigarettes and money, pitifully. When a package of stale sandwiches was flung among them they plunged at it like animals, among the sleepers of the oily and puddled track. Paul watched them gloomily aware of the mountainous problems of Europe, staggering to her feet. War solved nothing, except gross negative matters: the greater human concerns had lain in limbo, until the end of the savagery. Now they came to the surface. The hungry eyes of the lean grey children followed him in his inward vision, over the North Sea, in the oily darkness surrounding the ship, in the drizzle.

And now he stuffed his extra shirt, his flat hat and service dress, his new raincoat, his badges, odd pullovers, and his Sam Browne belt, in the cardboard 'demob' box, with green issue string.

'Ow, gonna keep it on are you?' said the matey orderly. 'Takin' the plunge straight away, eh? Some of 'em – cor! It does 'urt and all – you can see it. Cor!'

He was rather like Miffin, Paul thought: the devotee of 'belonging' to an Army ethos to which all else was lesser. With an assumed look of self-possession, and a final signature, he walked out, rather loftily, holding his awkward box of manilla-coloured cardboard.

He could feel the pavement through the thin shoes, and the suit was rather cold in the chill October air. He shivered. Then a soldier passed him, without saluting, of course. Then two office workers, noticeably smarter than he was. Then another soldier, who took no notice of him at all. As he went on he noticed that people no longer looked at him, or only looked with indifference. He walked on a little and looked at himself in a shop window. He hardly recognised the reflection at first. Whoever was that? Who was this unknown civilian man, in such very ordinary factory clothes?

The horror of being nobody stretched before him like a chasm. The pavement felt as though it would open: yet, at the same time, through the thin soles, it felt all too solid.

For a moment of terror he wanted to go back – to claim his lieutenancy, his functions, his number, his rank, his qualifications, pay, board and mess. He'd go anywhere, to be someone again. The long hoped for change might be a new birth – but into insignificance! Who was he now? He was no-one, out here, in a Northern city. He was no-one *anywhere*. He had no obligations. No-one saluted him. Men had saluted him in the street for two years, until he had ceased to notice it. He had always assumed he didn't care about such forms. But he did now. It was a marked loss. There was no organization to back him up in authority, or in dealings with others. No woman would respond to him in the role of a young officer bearing the insignia of units with a bloody history. He was nothing, nobody. How awful!

He wanted to go back. But instead, he crept away, resignedly, with the foolish cardboard box of jumbled clothes, and oddments of sentimental value – like the cloth shield with a sea-horse on it, from his battledress. The junk of detached insignia and belts rattled in the box, which he carried by its green string. Demobilization was like some amateur conjuror's trick:

275

only, in the end, a flop, with no applause, leaving nothing but a sense of futility in the dull November air.

Being such a shadow without identity gradually began to feel like an illness. Later that day a pale and glum young man in the same brown pork-pie hat and dull grey suit was reflected in the mirror of the lounge bar of the Bath Hotel, in Bene't Street, Cambridge. The long cardboard box, a little battered with the train ride, perched on a stool beside him, like his only companion in life. Paul sipped a half of bitter beer, sullenly. Two undergraduates, boys straight from school, cheeped in loud voices behind him.

'But wouldn't it be utterly devastating? I've simply no inclination . . .'

'I'm trying to encourage someone to appropriate a niche . . .'

'Someone? You must introduce me to this admirable character . . .'

'Well, it's me father actually . . . an advertising agency.'

'Oh, how *wholesomely* realistic!'

'You're sure you're not being *revoltingly* ironic?'

'Ironic – my dear fellow! The remuneration . . . surely makes irony *dumb?*'

They giggled: such a *bon mot!* Then whispered; the subject of money in the English middle class being indecent.

'Two or three thousand I believe, quite early on . . .'

'I'm *prostrate* at your niche, my dear. I must appropriate one of my own. What about old Turnip?'

'Oh, how you never forget you were Turnip's fag. Something *gorgeous* in the City, isn't he?'

They giggled. Oh, Christ, Paul thought: two years of this. How shall I stand it? The rows of bottles on the shelves and the ample bosom of the plumpest barmaid he had ever seen seemed to his miserable eyes the only answer.

'What's yours, Violet?' he asked her, with affected vulgarity.

'Tiny to you dear. A gin, love.'

'And me.'

Paul threw down two half-crowns on the mahogany counter. 'Is this the peak of this place's bloody night-life?'

Tiny wound a plump bangled arm down from the gin dispenser and dipped her breasts towards Paul, with a nice open-eyed pout, as she planted the glasses on the counter.

'I'm most of it, dear. . . . Skin off yours. There's not much for hungry boys with the box.'

'With the what?'

Tiny began to heave, and choked on her gin.

'Bee! Box!' she struggled, pointing to his demob luggage. 'Mind you, they've often got both. You have to watch it.'

'Watch your Bs and Ps, Tiny!'

Tiny heaved so much she developed hiccups, somewhere deep down under the amplitude, and had to be thumped and squeezed. In a ridiculous way, Paul began to feel at home.

*

Streamers of blue cigarette smoke snaked out of the open window of the crowded little sitting-room. Paul had digs overlooking the Fellows' Garden of Pembroke, at the back of Tennis Court Terrace, a little paved cul-de-sac behind the Natural Sciences laboratories. As he listened to the discussion he watched the rain rilling down the roof in the evening light. A pattern of shoots of water ran down the tiles like fish scaling. Down in the street a landlady's broom swept away a mush of leaves and water noisily. The smoke floated in ribbons and then suddenly shot up out of the half-open window: his room would stink of Weights all night, he thought. But George was making his point well:

'Emotions may be completely illogical and to the politician they may in the arts be irrational and misleading. But we simply have to accept this dark, ungovernable side of man's nature. . . .'

George had been in the Death or Glory Regiment, another tank outfit, the 17/18th Hussars, in Italy. He had once been in

Paul's student work scheme in those faraway days of 1942. But now Paul was a little envious of the man. He seemed to have solved so many of his 'demob' problems so quickly – most of them by finding Brenda. So, while Paul was pleased they should all be in his room that rainy November day, he was glum with envy, too. The group of undergraduates were discussing society and literature, about twenty men and women. George, the big historian, not long after his 'B' release, had quickly formed a relationship with a girl called Brenda Howes, a shy girl with long dark hair and big freckles. There she sat, opposite Paul, with her large brown eyes and dark colouring. She wore wide skirts and pullovers: her hands were long and delicate. Paul once found a poem on a chair in George's room at Corpus. He only read the first line,

My girl is white . . .

Then he put it down in a fit of uncommon discretion, and with a strangely envious pang. He wondered if George had slept with her. He dared say the poem would have told him. Perhaps George meant white all over? But he was restrained from reading the badly typed lines by anger rather than tact. Why should a great galumphing shaggy man like George, naive as he was, find a girl so quickly? Paul found himself fascinated by the brown-eyed creature, with her big forehead and her upturned nose. How did people meet one another and become intimate? He'd forgotten.

Because he was so puzzled, to try to remember how it was done, Paul found himself unconsciously intruding on the couple and their privacy, at tea-times, with the toast crumbs gathering all over their books and files of lecture-notes, in George's room. Then he found himself so much wanting tender affection like theirs that he began to identify, and found his desire for Brenda aroused. So he withdrew from their company. He found that easy enough, though he missed the teas of toast and honey. He missed George too, and George missed him, and the way Paul used to act the fool and make him laugh his breathless grimace of a laugh, by mimicking the troopers, and the up-county type of officer.

'Who's *Bismarck*, Tom?'

Paul imitated a country-gentleman Colonel.

'A German statesman, Colonel.'

'Fellow came to my regiment one day called Bismarck. Couldn't be the same chap, could it, huh? . . . What?'

But today, suddenly, in the middle of this meeting in his rooms, Paul noticed that Brenda, with the frills of her petticoat boldly showing, was quite definitely alluring him, inviting him, not George at all. There was no doubt. And as he listened to the callow political arguments, he became irritated and impetuous – prompted to unleash all the old Army modes of behaviour, and get the girl for himself. She was making her invitation: seize the chance! He winced at the way his crude self put it; the old voices urged it. She'd be lovely! Old impulses writhed within him, and old barrack-room voices. 'Cor!' they said, within, obscenely, 'Cor, Christ, you amateur!' He wanted to 'start work' on Brenda, in the old habitual manner of the eight-day leave. He'd show her a thing or two! He could hear the old voices in himself, with loathing: but there was no denying they voiced a need.

Yet he knew, as he studied her face, that she was no more than a grammar school girl, in her experience. She had no notion of the latent soldier's greed on which her brown eyes played in the light of Paul's gas-fire. She was simply using him, to tease George: playing with fire. Cruelly, Paul's soldier self saw a chance. Yet his better self could visualize her dismay, if she did, and then realized what she had done. You can't do such things, he said to himself. Yet he was at a loss to know now what he should do, at all.

George was uneasy. A long-legged shaggy man with curly pale hair, his great chest was covered by a loose oatmeal pullover, rather grubby. He had holes in the soles of his shoes. He sat in the opposite corner from Brenda, and showed his inward anger by deliberately not looking at the girl. He chain-smoked all through the meeting, his knees crossed and his insteps tucked behind his calves, his forehead knotted in assumed intentness. Paul felt the intensity of hostility between the lovers. Lord, she was playing him up.

He sighed and turned the gas-fire down, uncomfortable. He would be glad when they all went. The talk was petering to an end. Brenda uncrossed her legs and smoothed her skirt, then recrossed them. Paul caught a glimpse of her naked thigh among the frothy lace; he caught his breath.

She was neat and feminine, her delicate hands twisted now in her long brown hair, glossy in the lamplight, and with the colour from the sighing gas-fire flues, incandescent reds and white, playing in her big brown eyes. She wore a pinafore frock of red corduroy, with the lace frills peeping out from under it. Paul found she was poising her face at him, softening the hollows under her prominent cheekbones, narrowing her eyes at him with their big lashes.

He realized dismally that he had no idea how to deal with the situation. He had learnt certain useful tricks of self-control during his time in the Army, but only by suppressing such feelings as now threatened to leap out. There had been sections of experience which one had had to cut away and stifle, in service life. Threads of relationship had had to be picked up rather clumsily on periods of seven days' leave three times a year. Now he had to open up dead and unexercised areas of feeling, and do so in circumstances in which there was continuity and to which one had to be responsible. This was Civvy Street: and you were in it for good! So now, when he sat with the mixed group of men and women, and allowed his feelings to range as he was doing now over Brenda, he felt as if he were sitting on a flimsy cardboard box, like that damned ridiculous demob box, from which something grotesque seemed to be struggling to get out. Only by the tightest hold of his fingers on the lid was he able to hold it down. If he took the string off this demob box – what would fly out? Would it matter? The inclination arrived now to leap off the box altogether and let come what would, perhaps even tomorrow, if Brenda was willing. What *would* it matter? The signal was of the kind he would have seized at once on a seven days' leave: men need women, women need men. There was the chance in it of getting a woman to bed, he could see. Yet, in the new conditions, the new reality of civilian life, to seize this seemed anarchic; it would only lead to frustration and suffering, he knew. So he clung to his fragile box, the green string still untied, feeling as if a corner of some rude and ridiculous tail of a demob shirt was sticking out. He felt he wanted to apologise that the government had given it him – it was not his own choice.

The rain was still beating down in the November night outside. He looked round the darkening room in the fire's glow. This softer life, the domestic interior with the woman in the chair beside you, was far more alarming than battle.

It was an upstairs room in an L-shaped house at the bottom of the little terrace of grey brick houses. The windows overlooked a builder's yard and beyond it the bare trees and the mess of fallen leaves in the rather shabby formal college garden. One open window looked up the little paved cul-de-sac, with its green gas lamps just coming on, shining on the wet flagstones. A door led into Paul's bedroom, cold and sparse, with ewer and jug, on a marble washstand. The furniture in the parlour was solid and Victorian in style, four dark mahogany dining chairs with moulded legs and green plush seats around a mahogany table, two ungainly upholstered armchairs and a dumpy sofa, all covered with dark green fluffy material. There was an oriental style carpet, going threadbare in places among its blue and red lozenges, and bookcases in heavy 'Jacobean' varnish. On the wall was a large faded Medici Society reproduction of Botticelli's *Birth of Venus* which a friend had lent Paul for his rooms. The perfect sea-fresh goddess failed to inspire the homely little room. She was irreconcilable with the frayed

281

bobbles along the bottom edges of the putty-coloured curtains. Yet Paul's eye strayed now and then to the surf-blown cloak of the naked figure, and soared up the flutes of the shell from which she was flowering. In her billowing veils he caught a faint, if tonelessly reproduced, echo of the beauty of the Italian artist's concept of love, even against that nondescript speckled wallpaper.

Suddenly, the naked figure and the image of the girl who had just been sitting in front of his gas-fire evoked a memory of Lucy and himself naked before the fire in Newnham, three years before. The blue gas-flames illuminated her translucent ghostly body. Tears came into his eyes, and an old taut barrier in his abdomen walls seemed to break. Brenda suddenly saw him looking at her, saw the tears, and was at once uncomfortable, and yet fascinated.

The argument in the room stopped. Some students left. Only snatches of phrases and jokes uttered by a few of the company were left behind, utterances from those who had for the moment been prepared to expose their opinions and feelings, willing to be proved wrong, or to be taken up and argued with. Not many were: so, the endless debates left the whole self in the flesh a little dry and limp.

Brenda did not go off with George, but went alone. She turned in the lane to wave back at Paul in the window. As he emptied the ashtrays the smoke cleared and the gaslight in the street sent up a green shimmer among the leafless twigs. He would, he supposed aloud, always be glad to meet again most of those who had just left. But when he turned round George had gone: he heard him lumbering down the stairs. But George made no attempt to catch up with Brenda, he saw. George hadn't even said goodbye to him – he was usually so polite. What a state he must be in! Perhaps George had seen her poising at him? He sat and waited until he calculated Brenda should have reached home.

Paul knew as soon as he stood by the telephone in the dark

hall of his lodgings, however, that he was lost. Beyond this point he had no clue; here was a line of country which he had forgotten how to reccey and mark out. In a month he had perhaps got to know twenty people closely in Civvy Street, but for reasons which were not personal, and most of them only superficially. He had no capacities yet for dealing with the inward life, in any real circumstances, and he was fearful of this state. To take up the telephone for the reason in hand seemed indecent because he could not say to himself or to anyone else, 'I am doing this, or that,' and make it sound convincing. He knew that if he rang Brenda it was as if he were saying, 'I want you to forget George and let me make love to you.' What did one say? He seemed to have nothing to guide him, only an inward confusion.

As he looked through the telephone book he became conscious of people passing him in the hallway of his lodging. To his angry wretchedness he felt himself blushing, at the fear that they were aware that he was telephoning a girl, and thus demonstrating his grossest needs.

With an angry sigh, he tossed back his dark hair, grown longer now than he'd ever dare let it grow in the Army. Why not? Why not with Brenda? He knew if he came to be alone with her he might quite possibly abandon his self-respect and offend her, by impulsively making love to her, in the depersonalized soldier's way. But why not? If she didn't want to go on, she needn't. With a surge of aggressive feeling in his throat he lifted the telephone, dialled, and in strained lighthearted terms asked Brenda to meet him by the river next afternoon, 'to' he dropped pathetically into the mouthpiece, 'walk off the intellect of this afternoon.'

'Yes,' she said, laughing gaily. 'Wasn't it dreadful! Rattle is such a monster.'

'And George being so pompous.'

'Oh, don't speak to me about it.'

'I . . . ah.'

'What?'

'Nothing. Are you sure it will be all right . . .'

'What?'

'For you to go out with me?'

'Oh, God, you're not going to rape me on Grantchester Meadows, are you?'

'Of course not.' Paul blushed and paused. She'd think that a damnfool thing to say. To reply so, as if she'd meant it, let slip that it was just his impulse to see how far he could get that he feared in himself. There was a long pause, Paul weakly said, 'Goodbye. Three o'clock then.' Now, he thought, I've done it.

She dressed up for him in a gay striped frock, the red and white stripes running down a fine woollen fabric under her camelhair coat which was open. Her long hair blew free, enticing. They climbed over a fence, dropping down on the mud track between the fields. His anxiety detected a threat in the air. There it was! A watery anvil of cloud rose to thin fans of ice, bright in the sun, but intensely black beneath. It was a distant thunderstorm. He began to make a mental plan to avoid it. Enemy. Own troops. Intention. . . . We will.

They walked in the thin yellow light of late autumn as it slanted low across the ploughed fields. Shadows started up behind the clods of earth and moved with their feet among the grey and white pebbles along a footpath. Brenda knew a quiet walk, she said. In the sunlight the wind eddied, stirring the twigs in the hedge and rattling the leaf-piles. The light drained from the weak sky into the darkness of the plough and the dark autumn colours of earth soothed him and relieved some of his discomfort. He dared to look at her more closely: she was sweet and gay, but not wildly attractive to him. Her freckled face was rather a little pug-like in profile. She was nice. But he couldn't see himself kissing her. This was a good start. He gathered a surprising amount of confidence from the thought. He had been almost sweating with fear of being alone with a woman. But now conversation developed with ease between them, though it still flowed at a discreet intellectual level, as if they had brought the previous evening's dry discussion with them into the fields.

Any direct warmth of words was as scrupulously avoided as he avoided her hand as they crossed the fences. It struck him now that taking hold of the telephone the evening before had been much more significant and bold. He even took no advantages when she began to mimic George – 'the earth . . . the great maternal breeding regenerative monster'. He felt with relief that she was using him not generally against George, but just to get away for a period from George's impetuosity. She was so little more than a schoolgirl, afraid of the insistent pressure of intimacy, of George's desperate need for it, the ex-serviceman's need for love.

Thinking of this, between them, Paul found he could bear the thought, and even enjoy it. He began to enjoy the company of a woman, as herself, for the first time for many years. He walked along happily, thinking to himself – Lord, I'm just enjoying a woman's *company*. I've stopped thinking about how I can get her into bed. Yet he did allow himself to think of what it could be like, to sleep with her, as he glanced at her pretty face in the afternoon sun, just from time to time. A painful eroticism stirred in him. But yet he felt a greater happiness in rejecting the impulse as impossible. There was no relationship there! He was merely projecting his own needs, over the poor girl! Release her! He felt terribly lonely, and yet relieved by the thought, that he was learning. But he found himself suffering a good deal, all the same.

Then she laughed and the reflection of yellow light in the brown eyes opened reservoirs in his feelings and released a fresh pleasure in him flowing like water. His delight at her as a woman flowed over the fields into the new furrows swinging between curved lines of corn shoots, as generously as the sun gilded heaps of dark dung from the steadings ranked over the plough. He relished a freshly awakened affection, for a woman as a companion, as a different kind of creature. Every natural image in which he delighted was the token of the progress of a constructive mood in him from which something marvellous was going to come, he felt. The pink reeds dipping in the wind could be understood, and a movement of air among the haystacks signified a new and thrusting life to the joint step of their shoes on the pebble patches in the light mud. He could feel a threat, a battle fear (where was the thunderstorm?) seeking to panic him, as he still always did, out in the open. The coarse soldier in him was also in fearful memory about haystacks. But he didn't tell Brenda. He didn't want the excuse of the experience of the horror of battle as excuse for brutality in personal relationship, or even for being bloodyminded, he urged himself glumly. The solutions now were fearful – but soft, and kind.

Yet something in him remained hysterical, and urged him to 'work on her', in that old way, anxiously, with a nervous patter, crudely seeking what a woman could give, as a salve.

Mind you it looked innocent enough all right but that haystack signified a great deal because the bastard suddenly disappeared in bloody smoke and there was a noise like a bloody steam-hammer and Peters' tank crew were going up in a bloody column of white flame. I was out to have a pee behind and it was the first time I felt about the landscape like that. Jesus Christ, Peters' tank was puffing out bloody smoke rings and gouts of black billows like a thunderstorm gone bloody mad and through the flaming haze every bloody bushy topped tree was leaping about in every form of bloody significance – we can see you, they said, your bloody turn next. Then all bloody bedlam let loose with bloody cordite flash singeing the hair on your face so you could smell it and everyone deaf as bloody posts. I was in a hell of a state in the laager that night till they gave me half a litre of Cliquot and I passed out wide to the bloody world.

He used to think that such things in the back of one's mind could be an excuse for anything. It had, of course, been the excuse for much of what had been done. He remembered his

286

driver's conversation, as he was taken on his last trip to the station at Hamburg, in the fifteen-hundredweight truck.

We was sent up the back areas for a rest and Bert and I had a quick wash-down and nipped off to Ostend for a night. Tom had given us some addresses which I wasn't too keen on as I had never been to a bloody knock-shop before but Bert said we were in a hurry and if we wanted to get the dirty water off our chests before we went on again we couldn't fuck about picking and choosing and making any sort of serious job of it. Christ, you have to have some sort of tale to tell the other randy sods what never get a forty-eight when you got back. So we went straight in at this here place called La Phare and stoked up with a few cognacs. There was a bloody tart there who didn't look too bad but she was with a merchant navy bloke. But, you see – jammy! – after a little while after the coloured lights went out and some flak started up around and I was pleased when this chap said he had to go back to his ship now, poor sod. Well, I slipped this tart five hundred francs and a bloody tin of M & V and off we went upstairs. She smelt a bit of armpits and garlic but Christ she was good at her job all right: want to see a picture? Doc said we was silly buggers not to go to the PAC and it got us a bit worried but it passed off all right as it happened and when we got the next movement order we hadn't time to be worried. Fucking roll on!

How far from this, to walking with this Girton girl on Grantchester Meadows! Inwardly, a relic of his soldier self snarled contemptuously at his new delicacy.

He suddenly recalled himself from his reverie. Brenda was pointing to a white dead tree gesturing there as they circled round it along the by-road. Its bone-like limbs carried their eyes up to the grey-blue of the patches of autumn sky and signalled a pattern from its extended branches. Its life had grown there, in that place, in that shape, lovely and subtly spread. Two rooks fell blackly glistening from it, glided into the November air with a succession of caws. The tree had no memory, but yet its form stood there for what it had been, to mark what had happened to it since it had begun to grow, limbs fixed to tell that what happened to the vegetable creature over the years had come about this way and that. It was the

287

structural residue of a life. To them it was a symbol, of the need to accept what one was, one's roots, one's place, one's finite existence. They saw their own lives, reaching out towards the shifting air, in this dead wood with the bark breaking off from it. It had been what it was, and, living, had sought to fulfil itself in its growth, until, in the end, it left this sculpture construction of its life and being.

There was no escaping what the dead tree meant, and they both saw it.

So, they began to talk joyfully and ebulliently, without falsity and strain. They became themselves, and accepted the truth, that there was no relationship between them, while her hopes lay elsewhere than with Paul. For a few minutes, as they walked back through neat Grantchester, that notorious literary village with its self-conscious arcadian atmosphere, Paul, to his surprise, found he could dwell inwardly on the long savage episodes of war, for the first time since hospital, without distress or panic. He allowed himself to talk to Brenda about them, but without self-pity or exaggeration. He described them as aspects of the reality of man's destructiveness, with which they had to live. The feelings they shared ran deep now, and Paul looked gratefully into her brown eyes without fear.

He told her how it still seemed strange to be among trees without the need to listen for the soft whistling of mortar shells, or to strain for the puff of a rifle or a gun sending a crack of stinging blast past his head. He told her how in France the sparkling fields and orchards had been ghastly with dusty burnt-out hulks of tanks, and with the grotesque swollen bodies of dead calves and cows. He told her how suddenly you would find a stiff cheesey heap of corpses, in sodden blue-grey uniforms, with the dead lips drawn back from the teeth, in the ditch or a wood. It still seemed strange to him that out in the meadows the quietness of shady corners did not shelter the dumb horror of quick rough graves. The young woman listened, her eyes clouded, and her mouth fell open a little, then closed, and her lips softened. But, Paul realized with delight, she was not thinking of him at all: she was suffering for George! She was in love! He looked enthralled at the beauty of it in her face! She was realizing what George had been through. He'd obviously told her nothing: now she knew the source of some of the man's anxieties, her man's impetuous needs for love and peace, the ex-soldier's anguish at deprivation, which his battle trauma had aroused. Paul could see her polarity had swung fully round again to her man: she yearned to be with him. And in himself he found a surge of joy, even in his own pain, to have been able to give her back to the man she loved.

The clouds weaved over the sun, the tree and the meadows darkened; but Paul no longer felt a threat. The storm was obviously not coming their way. His balance was restored. He could have kissed her among the haystacks, but he was glad he didn't. It might have happened an hour ago: now it was impossible – it could even destroy a new found happiness. The crisis was over. Deep bonds of feeling had broken, but in no way had he offended the girl with whom they flowed. They had met as man and woman, independent, and respecting one another. He had done George a deal of good, he hoped. But he had done himself more.

Behind the lattice of a wood a line of puffed white drew, lifted, and was snatched away by the wind. As it was drawn out of sight the sound of the train rumbled lightly in the air, steadying now with moisture. It would rain before they got back. Tired, they became less interested in one another, talked less. Inwardly he was both glad and envious about what he had found out about her relationship with George. So they had been to bed together! He was cut by a pang of envy. Yet he found he didn't mind as much as he had feared. He had found the reality of his own needs, which were for whole relationship, not the mere gross and brief satisfaction of the soldier's hunger.

Paul sighed, and Brenda gave him a glance of sympathy and understanding kindness.

'You'll find someone,' she said.

'I'll find someone,' he echoed, sadly.

The damp meadows spread before them glumly in the early darkness. They talked less, and only occasionally could Paul summon the energy to utter.

He was grateful to Brenda, but there was an energy he could not afford to waste on her now. He would now never break open his demob box of fugitive winged impulses, with all their dangers, with her. He'd keep the string on it, for a time. His legs and tongue were weary only, at the thought of the distance home.

Brenda gave him the welcome chance of postponing any further explicitness, by inviting him to a party in her flat at the week-end. He decided that by refusing he was making his first personal decision in civilian life, and was glad it had been forced upon him in the way it was.